THE FIRE CHILD

Also by S. K. Tremayne

The Ice Twins

THE FIRE CHILD

S. K. TREMAYNE

HarperCollins*Publishers*

HarperCollins*Publishers*
1 London Bridge Street
London
SE1 9GF

www.harpercollins.co.uk

Published by HarperCollins*Publishers* 2016
1

A catalogue record for this book
is available from the British Library

ISBN: 978-0-00-810583-9

Set in Sabon by Palimpsest Book Production Limited, Falkirk, Stirlingshire

Photographs 1-3, 5-8, 11, 13-16, 18-19 © S. K. Tremayne
Photographs 4, 9, 10, 17 © The Royal Cornwall Museum
Photograph 12 courtesy of the Cornish Studies Library, Redruth
(Photograph reference no. Corn02273)

Find out more about HarperCollins and the environment at
www.harpercollins.co.uk/green

Author's Note

Morvellan Mine is an invention. It is, however, clearly based on the spectacular and historic mines scattered along the rugged cliffs of West Penwith, Cornwall. The tin and copper mines of Botallack, Geevor and the Levant were particular inspirations.

Tin has been extracted from Cornwall for maybe four thousand years. At the age of ten my maternal grandmother Annie Jory worked as a 'bal maiden' – a girl employed to crush rocks with a hammer – in the rich mines of St Agnes, North Cornwall.

This book is, therefore, written in memory of my Cornish ancestors: farmers, fishermen, smugglers and miners.

For Danielle

Acknowledgements

I would like to thank, as ever, Eugenie Furniss, Jane Johnson, Sarah Hodgson, Kate Elton and Anne O'Brien for their wise advice and many editorial insights. My thanks also to Sophie Hannah.

The photos in the book, of historic Cornish mining scenes, were taken by the Cornish photographer, John Charles Burrow (1852–1914). The images date from the 1890s, when Burrow was commissioned by the owners of four of Cornwall's deepest mines, Dolcoath, East Pool, Cook's Kitchen and Blue Hills, to capture scenes of life underground.

The original photographs are now kept at the Royal Cornwall Museum, Truro, England.

178 Days Before Christmas

Morning

The tunnels go under the sea. It's a thought I can't easily dismiss. The tunnels go under the sea. For a mile, or more.

I'm standing in the Old Dining Room, where the windows of my enormous new home face north: towards the Atlantic, and the cliffs of Penwith, and a silhouetted blackness. This dark twinned shape is Morvellan Mine: the Shaft House, and the Engine House.

Even on a cloudless June day, like today, the ruins of Morvellan look obscurely sad, or oddly reproachful. It's like they are trying to tell me something, yet they cannot and will not. They are eloquently muted. The rough-house Atlantic makes all the noise, the booming waves riding the tides above the tunnels.

'Rachel?'

I turn. My new husband stands in the doorway. His shirt is blinding white, his suit is immaculate, nearly as dark as his hair, and the weekend's stubble has gone.

'Been looking for you everywhere, darling.'

'Sorry. I've been wandering. Exploring. Your amazing house!'

'Our house, darling. Ours.'

He smiles, comes close, and we kiss. It's a morning kiss, a going-to-work-kiss, not meant to lead anywhere – but it still thrills me, still gives me that that scary and delicious feeling: that someone can have such power over me, a power I am somehow keen to accept.

David takes my hand, 'So. Your first weekend in Carnhallow . . .'

'Mmm.'

'So *tell* me – I want to know you're all right! I know it must be challenging – the remoteness, all the work that needs doing. I'll understand if you have misgivings.'

I lift his hand, and kiss it. 'Misgivings? Don't be daft. I love it. I love you and I love the house. I love it all, love the challenge, love Jamie, love the way we're hidden away, love it love it love it.' I look into his green-grey eyes, and I do not blink. 'David, I've never been happier. Never in all my life. I feel like I have found the place I was meant to be, and the man I was meant to be with.'

I sound totally gushing. What happened to the feisty feminist Rachel Daly I used to be? Where has she gone? My friends would probably tut at me. Six months ago *I* would have tutted at me: at the girl who gave up her freedom and her job and her supposedly exciting London life to be the bride of an older, richer, taller widower. One of my best friends, Jessica, laughed with sly delight when I told her my sudden plans. *My God, darling, you're marrying a cliché!*

That hurt for a second. But I soon realized it didn't matter what my friends think, because they are still there, back in London, sardined into Tube trains, filing into dreary offices, barely making the mortgage every month. Clinging on to London life like mountaineers halfway up a rockface.

And I am not holding on for dear life any more. I'm far away, with my new husband and his son and his mother, down here at the very end of England, in far West Cornwall, a place where England, as I am discovering, becomes something stranger and stonier, a land of dreaming hard granite that glistens after rain, a land where rivers run through woods like deep secrets, where terrible cliffs conceal shyly exquisite coves, a land where moorland valleys cradle wonderful houses. Like Carnhallow.

I even love the name of this house. Carnhallow.

My daydreaming head rests on David's shoulder. Like we are halfway to dancing.

But his mobile rings, breaking the spell. Lifting it from his pocket he checks the screen, then kisses me again – his two fingers up-tilting my chin – and he walks away to take the call.

I might once, I guess, have found this gesture patronizing. Now it makes me want sex. But I always want sex with David. I wanted sex the moment my friend Oliver said, *Come and meet someone, I think you'll get on,* at that art gallery, and I turned around and there he was, ten years older than me, ten inches taller than me.

I wanted David on our first date, three days later, I wanted him when he bought me the very first drink, I wanted him when he then told a perfectly judged, obviously flirtatious joke, I wanted him when we talked about the rainy March weather and he sipped his champagne and said, 'Ah but where Sergeant March is skirmishing, Captain April will headquarter, and General June will follow with his mistresses,' and I wanted something more than sex when he told me about his

3

house and its history and he showed me the photo of his beautiful boy.

That was one of the moments I *fell*: when I realized how different David was to any man I had met before, and how different he is to me. Just a girl from the council flats of south-east London. A girl who escaped reality by reading. A girl who dislikes chiller cabinets in supermarkets because they remind her of the times when Mum couldn't afford to pay for heating.

And then, David.

We were in a Soho bar. We were drunk. Nearly kissing. He showed me the photo of that enchanting boy again. I don't know why, but I knew, immediately. I wanted a child like that. Those singular blue eyes, the dark hair from his handsome dad.

I asked David to tell me more: more about his house, about little Jamie, the family history.

He smiled.

'There's a wood surrounding Carnhallow House, it's called Ladies Wood. It runs right up Carnhallow Valley, to the moors.'

'OK. A wood. I love woods.'

'The trees in Ladies Wood are predominantly rowans, with some ash, hazel and oak. We know that these same rowan woods date back at least to the Norman Conquest, because they are marked on Anglo Saxon charters, and continuously therefrom. That means the rowan trees have been here for a thousand years. In Carnhallow Valley.'

'I still don't get it.'

'Do you know what my surname means? What "Kerthen" means, in Cornish?'

I shook my head, trying not to be distracted by his smile, the champagne, the photos of the boy, the house, the idea of it all.

4

'This might amaze you, David, but I didn't do Cornish at school.'

He chuckled. 'Kerthen means rowan tree. Which means the Kerthens have lived in Carnhallow for a thousand years, amongst the rowans from which we took our name. Shall we have some more champagne?'

He leaned close to pour; and as he did, he kissed me full on the lips for the first time. We got in a taxi ten minutes later. That's all it took. Just that.

The memories fall away: I am back in the present, as David finishes his call, and frowns.

'OK, sorry, but I really do have to go. Can't miss the one o'clock flight – they're panicking.'

'Nice to be indispensable.'

'I don't think you could ever call corporate lawyers indispensable. Viola players are more important.' He smiles. 'But corporate law is ludicrously overpaid. So what are you going to do today?'

'Carry on exploring, I guess. Before I touch anything, I need to know the basics. I mean, I don't even know how many bedrooms there are.'

'Eighteen,' he says. Then adds with a frown: 'I think.'

'David! Listen to you. Eeek. How can you not know how many bedrooms you have?'

'We'll try them all in time. I promise.' Shirt cuff pulled, he checks his silver watch. 'If you want to do some real research, Nina's books are in the Yellow Drawing Room. The ones she was using, for her restorations.'

The name stings a little, though I hide it.

Nina Kerthen, née Valéry. David's first wife. I don't know much about her: I've seen a couple of photos, I know she was beautiful, Parisienne, young, posh, blonde. I know that she died in an accident at Morvellan Mine, eighteen months ago. I know that her husband

5

and in particular her son – my brand-new, eight-year-old stepson Jamie – must still be grieving, even if they try not to show it.

And I know, very very clearly, that one of my jobs here in Carnhallow is to rescue things: to be the best stepmother in the world to this sad and lovely little boy.

'I'll have a look,' I say brightly. 'At the books. Maybe get some ideas. Go and catch your plane.'

He turns for a final kiss, I step back.

'No – go! Kiss me again we'll end up in the fourteenth bedroom, and then it will be six o'clock.'

I'm not lying. David's laugh is dark and sexy.

'I'll Skype you tonight, and see you Friday.'

With that, he departs. I hear doors slam down long hallways, then the growl of his Mercedes. Then comes the silence: the special summery silence of Carnhallow, soundtracked by the whisper of the distant sea.

Picking up my phone, I open my notebook app.

Continuing Nina's restoration of this huge house is not going to be easy. I do have some artistic talent to help: I have a degree in photography from Goldsmiths College. A degree which turned out to be utterly pointless, as I basically graduated the same afternoon that photography collapsed as a paying career, and so I ended up *teaching* photography to kids who would never themselves become photographers.

This was, I suppose, another reason I was happy to give up London life: the meaninglessness was getting to me. I wasn't even taking photos any more. Just taking buses through the rain to my cramped and shared Shoreditch flat. Which I couldn't actually afford.

But now that I have no real job, I can, ironically, apply these artistic gifts. Such as they are.

Armed with my phone I begin my explorations: trying

to get a proper mental map of Carnhallow. I've been here one week, but we've spent most of that week in the bedroom, the kitchen, or on the beaches, enjoying the blissful summer weather. Much of my stuff from London is still in boxes. There's even a suitcase left to unpack from our honeymoon: our gloriously hedonistic, sensuously expensive trip to Venice, where David bought me his favourite martini, in Harry's Bar, by St Mark's Square: the gin in a shot glass, chilled nearly to ice 'and faintly poisoned with vermouth', as David put it. I love the way David puts things.

But that is already the past, and this is my future. Carnhallow.

Striking south like an Antarctic explorer, I head down the New Hall, examining furniture and décor, taking notes as I go. The walls here are linenfold panelling, I think, decorated with engravings of the many Cornish tin and copper mines once owned by the Kerthens: the adits and tunnels of Botallack, and Morvellan, the shafts and streamworks of Wheal Chance and Wheal Rose. Elsewhere there are ancient photos of the mines in their heyday: wistful pictures of frozen labour, forgotten industry, men in waistcoats pushing wheelbarrows, chimneys smoking by the sea.

The New Hall ends at a grand double door. I know what lies beyond: the Yellow Drawing Room. Pushing the door and stepping through, I gaze around with a kind of helpless longing.

Because this room, already restored, with its leaded windows overlooking the dreaming flowery green of the south lawns, is probably the most beautiful room of all, and therefore one of the most daunting.

I need to make the rest of Carnhallow as impressive as this. It won't be easy; Nina had excellent taste. Yet

7

the beauty of the Yellow Drawing Room shows the potential of Carnhallow. If I can match what Nina did here, Carnhallow will be startlingly lovely. And mine.

The idea is so dazzling it makes me giddy. And happy.

I have some notes in my phone about the Yellow Drawing Room. They don't do much, however, but show my ignorance. I've noted a 'blue pig on the table', '18th-century funerary urns?' and 'Mameluke knives'. Also 'David's father's pack of cards', 'they played chouette', and 'tortoiseshell inlay in brass'.

What do I do with all this? How do I even begin? I've already had a quick skim through Nina's books: books full of wise but puzzling advice on Georgian furniture and Victorian silver, books full of words that enchant, and confuse – hamstone quoining, aurora wallpaper, antique epergnes.

Everything sounds so exotic and obscure, and impossibly luxe. I grew up in a crowded little council flat. The most expensive thing we owned was an oversized TV, probably stolen. Now I am about to spend thousands on 'Stuart silver fingerbowls', and 'fill them with rosewater'. Apparently.

My daydreaming – half anxious, half rapturous – leads me to the corner of the Drawing Room, and a small, polished wooden sidetable. Cassie the Thai housekeeper has set a silver vase here, replete with lilies and roses. Yet the vase doesn't look right. So maybe I can begin here. With this. Just this. One step, then another.

Putting my phone down, I adjust the vase – centring the vessel carefully on the sidetable. Yet it's still not correct. Perhaps it should be on the left, off centre? A good photographer never puts her subject smack-bang in the middle.

For ten minutes I try to find the best position for this

vase. I imagine Nina Kerthen, behind me, shaking her head in polite dismay. And now the self-doubt returns. I am sure that Nina Kerthen would have got this right. She would have done it impeccably. With her blonde hair harping across her slanted, clever blue eyes, as she squinted, and concentrated.

Abandoning my job, I gaze down, sighing. The varnished yew wood of the table reflects my face in its darkness. A crack runs the length of the table, breaking the image in two. Which is appropriate.

People tell me I am attractive, and yet I never truly *feel* beautiful: not with my red hair and my peppering of freckles, and that white Celtic skin that never takes a tan. Instead I feel flawed, or broken. Cracked. And when I look very hard at myself I can't see any beauty at all: only the deepening lines by my eyes, far too many for my age – only thirty.

A delicious breeze stirs me. It comes from the open window, carrying the scents of Carnhallow's flower gardens, and it dispels my silliness, and reminds me of my prize. *No.* I am not broken, and this is enough self-doubt. I am Rachel Daly, and I have overcome greater challenges than sourcing the correct wallpaper, or working out what a tazza is.

The seventy-eight bedrooms can wait, likewise the West Wing. I need some fresh air. Pocketing my phone, I go to the East Door, push it open to the serenity of the sun, so gorgeous on my upturned face. And then the south lawns. The wondrous gardens.

The gardens at Carnhallow were the one thing, I am told, that David's father Richard Kerthen kept going, even as he gambled away the last of the Kerthen fortune, en route to a heart attack. And Nina apparently never did much with the gardens. Therefore, out here, I can enjoy a purer possession: I can wholeheartedly admire the freshly cut green grass shaded by Cornish elms, the flowerbeds crowded with summer colours. And I can straightaway love, as my own, the deep and beautiful woods: guarding and encircling Carnhallow as if the house is a jewel-box hidden in a coil of thorns.

'Hello.'

A little startled, I turn. It's Juliet Kerthen: David's mother. She lives, alone and defiant, in her own self-contained apartment converted from a corner of the otherwise crumbling and unrestored West Wing. Juliet has the first signs of Alzheimer's, but is, as David phrases it, 'in a state of noble denial'.

'Lovely day,' she says.

'Gorgeous, isn't it? Yes.'

I've met Juliet a couple of times. I like her a lot: she has a vivid spirit. I do not know if she likes me. I have been too timid to go further, to really make friends, to knock on her front door with blackberry-and-apple pie. Because Juliet Kerthen may be old and fragile, but she is also daunting. The suitably blue-eyed, properly cheek-boned daughter of Lord Carlyon. Another ancient Cornish family. She makes me feel every inch the working-class girl from Plumstead. She'd probably find my pie a bit vulgar.

Yet she is perfectly friendly. The fault is mine.

Juliet shields her eyes from the glare of the sun with a visoring hand. 'David always says that life is a perfect English summer day. Beautiful, precisely because it is so rare and transient.'

'Yes, that sounds like David.'

'So how are you settling yourself in, dear?'

'Fine. Really, really well!'

'Yes?' Her narrowed eyes examine me, but in a

companionable way. I assess her in return. She is dressed like an elderly person, yet very neatly. A frock that must be thirty years old, a maroon and cashmere cardigan, then sensible, expensive shoes, probably hand-made for her in Truro forty years ago, and now, I guess, polished by Cassie, who looks in every day to make sure the old lady is alive.

'You don't find it too imposing?'

'God no, well, yes, a bit but . . . '

Juliet indulges me with a kind smile. 'Don't let it get to you. I remember when Richard first brought me home to Carnhallow. It was quite the ordeal. That last bit of the drive. Those ghastly little moorland roads from St Ives. I think Richard was rather proud of the remoteness. Added to the mythic quality. Would you like a cup of tea? I have excellent pu'er-cha. I get bored with drinking it alone. Or there is gin. I am in two minds.'

'Yes. Tea would be brilliant. Thanks.'

I follow her around the West Wing, heading for the north side of the house. The sun is restless and silvery on the distant sea. The clifftop mines are coming into view. I am chattering away about the house, trying to reassure Juliet, and maybe myself, that I am entirely optimistic.

'What amazes me is how hidden it is. Carnhallow, I mean. Tucked away in this sweet little valley, a total suntrap. But you're only a couple of miles from the moors, from all that *bleakness*.'

She turns, and nods. 'Indeed. Although the other side of the house is so completely different. It's actually rather clever. Richard always said it proved that the legend was true.'

I frown. 'Sorry?'

'Because the other side of Carnhallow looks north, to the mines, on the cliffs.'

11

I shake my head, puzzled.

She asks, 'David hasn't told you the legend?'

'No. I don't think so. I mean, uhm, he told me lots of stories. The rowans. The evil Jago Kerthen . . .' I don't want to say: *Maybe we got so drunk on champagne on the first date and then we had such dizzying sex, I forgot half of what he told me* – which is totally possible.

Juliet turns towards the darkened shapes of the mines. 'Well, this is the legend. The Kerthens, it is said, must have possessed a wicked gift, a sixth sense, or some kind of clairvoyance: because they kept hitting lodes of tin and copper, when other speculators went bust. There is a Cornish name for those with the gift: *tus-tanyow*. It means the people of fire, people with the light.' She smiles, blithely. 'You'll hear locals telling the story in the Tinners – that's a lovely pub, in Zennor. You must try it, but avoid the starry gazy pie. Anyway, Richard used to rather drone on about it, about the legend. Because the Kerthens built their house right here, on the bones of the old monastery, facing Morvellan, yet that was centuries before they discovered the *tin* at Morvellan. So if you are suggestible it rather implies that the legend is true. As if the Kerthens *knew* they were going to find tin. I know, let's go and have some pu'er-cha *and* gin, perhaps they go together.'

She walks briskly around the north-west corner of Carnhallow. I follow, eager for the friendship, and the distraction. Because her story disquiets me in a way I can't exactly explain.

It is, after all, just a silly little story about the historic family that made so much money, by sending those boys down those ancient mines. Where the tunnels run deep under the sea.

162 Days Before Christmas

Morning

David is drawing me. We're sitting in the high summer sun on the south lawns, a jug of freshly squeezed peach-and-lemon juice on a silver tray set down on the scented grass. I'm wearing a wicker hat, at an angle. Carnhallow House – *my* great and beautiful house – is glowing in the sunlight. I have certainly never felt posher. I have possibly never felt happier.

'Don't move,' he says. 'Hold for a second, darling. Doing your pretty upturned nose. Noses are tricky. It's all about the shading.'

He looks my way with a concentrated gaze then returns to the drawing paper, his pencil moving swiftly, shading and hatching. He is a very good artist, probably a much better artist – as I am realizing – than me. More naturally talented. I can draw a little but not as skilfully as this, and certainly not as fast.

Discovering David's artistic side has been one of the unexpected pleasures of this summer. I've known all along he was interested in the arts: after all, I first met

13

him at a private view in a Shoreditch gallery. And when we were in Venice he was able to show me all his favourite Venetian artworks: not just the obvious Titians, and Canelettos, but the Brancusis in the Guggenheim, the baroque ceiling of San Pantalon, or a ninth-century Madonna in Torcello, with its watchful eyes of haunted yet eternal love. A mother's never-ending love. It was so lovely and sad it made me want to cry.

Yet I didn't properly realize that he was good at *making* art until I moved here to Carnhallow. I've seen some of David's youthful work on the Drawing Room wall, and in his study: semi-abstract paintings of Penwith's carns and moors and beaches. They are so good I thought, at first, that they were expensive professional pieces, bought at a Penzance auction house by Nina. Part of her pains-taking restoration, her dedication to this house.

'There,' he says. 'Nose done. Now the mouth. Mouths are easy. Two seconds.' He leans back and looks at the drawing. 'Hah. Aced it.'

He sips some peach-and-lemon contentedly. The sun is warm on my bare and tanning shoulders. Birds are singing in Ladies Wood. I wouldn't be surprised if they went into close harmony. This is it. The perfect moment of good luck. The man, the love, the sun, the beautiful house in a beautiful garden in a beautiful corner of England. I have an urge to say something nice, to repay the world.

'You know you're really good.'

'Sorry, darling?'

He is sketching again. Deep in masculine concentra-tion. I like the way he focuses. Frowning, but not angry. Man At Work. 'Drawing. I know I've told you this before – but you're seriously talented.'

'Meh,' he says, like a teenager, but smiling like an

adult, his hand moving briskly across the page. 'Perhaps.'

'You never wanted to do it for a living?'

'No. Yes. No.'

'Sorry?'

'For a moment, after Cambridge, I considered it. I would have liked to try my hand, once. But I had no choice: I had to work, to make lots and lots of boring money.'

'Because your dad burned up all the fortune?'

'He even sold the family silver, Rachel. To pay those imbecilic gambling debts. Sold it like some junkie fencing the TV. I had to buy it back – the Kerthen silver. And they made me pay a premium.' David sighs, takes another taste of juice. The sun sparkles on the glass tilted in his hand. He savours the freshness and flavour and looks past me, at the sun-laced woods.

'Of course, we were running out of money anyway: it wasn't all my father's fault. Carnhallow was absurdly expensive to run, but the family kept trying. Though most of the mines were making losses by 1870.'

'Why?'

He picks up the pencil, taps it between his sharp white teeth. Thinking about the picture, answering me distractedly. 'I really must do you nude. I'm embarrassingly good at nipples. It's quite a gift.'

'David!' I laugh. 'I want to know. Want to understand things. Why did they make losses?'

He continues sketching. 'Because Cornish mining is hard. There's more tin and copper lying under Cornwall than has ever been mined, in all the four thousand years of Cornish mining history, yet it's basically impossible to extract. And certainly unprofitable.'

'Because of the cliffs, and the sea?'

'Exactly. You've seen Morvellan. That was our most

15

profitable mine, in the eighteenth and nineteenth centuries, but it's so dangerous and inaccessible.'

'Go on.'

'There's a reason Morvellan has that strange architecture – the two houses. Most Cornish mineshafts were exposed to the air, only the pumps were protected, behind stone – because machinery was deemed more important than men, perhaps. But on the cliffs, above Zawn Hanna, the Kerthens had a problem: because of the proximity of the sea, and consequent storms, we had to protect the top of the shaft in its own house, right next to the Engine House.' He stares at me and past me, as if he is looking at the mines themselves. 'Creating, by accident, that poignant, diagonal symmetry.' His pencil twirls slowly in his fingers. 'Now compare that to the open-cast mines of Australia, or Malaysia. The tin is right there, at the surface. They can simply dig it out of the ground with a plastic spade. And that's why Cornish mining died. Four thousand years of mining, gone in a couple of generations.'

His cheerfulness has clouded over. I can sense his darkening thoughts, tending to Nina, who drowned at Morvellan. It was probably my fault, letting the conversation stray in this direction. Down the valley. Towards the mineheads on the cliffs. I must make amends. 'You really want to do me nude?'

His smile returns. 'Oh yes. Oh, very much, yes.' He laughs and peels his finished drawing from the volume, and slants his handsome head, assessing his own work. 'Hmm. Not bad. Still didn't get the nose right. I really am better at nipples. OK' – he tilts a wrist to check the time – 'I promised I'd take Jamie to school—'

'At the weekend?'

'Soccer match, remember? He's very excited. Can you pick him up later? I'm seeing Alex in Falmouth.'

16

'Of course I will. Love to.'

'See you for dinner. You're a great sitter.'

He kisses me softly before striding away, around the house, heading for his car, calling out for Jamie. Like we are already a family. Safe and happy. This feeling warms me like the summer weather.

I remain sitting here in the sun, eyes half-closed, mind half-asleep. The sense of sweet purposelessness is delicious. I have things to do, but nothing particular to do right now. Voices murmur in the house, and on the drive. The car door slams in the heat. The motor-noise dwindles as it heads through those dense woods, up the valley to the moors. Birdsong replaces it.

Then I realize I haven't looked at David's drawing of me. Curious, maybe a little wary – I dislike being drawn, the same way I dislike being photographed: I only do it to indulge David – I lean across and pick up the sheet of paper.

It is predictably excellent. In fifteen minutes of sketching he has captured me, from the slight sadness in my eyes that never goes away, to the sincere if uncertain smile. He sees me true. And yet I am pretty in this picture, too: the shadow of the hat flatters. And there in the picture is my love for him, vivid in the happy shyness of my gaze.

He sees the love, which pleases me.

There is only one flaw. It is the nose. My nose is, I am told, cute, retroussé, upturned. But he hasn't sketched *my* nose at all. This nose is sharper, aquiline, more beautiful: this bone structure is from someone else's face, someone else he drew a thousand times, so that it became habitual. And I know who. I've seen the photos, and the drawings.

He's made me look like Nina.

17

Afternoon

The drawing lies on the grass, fallen from my hand. I am awake, and surprised that I slept. I must have drifted off in the indulgent warmth of the sun. Gazing about me, I see nothing has changed. Shadows have lengthened. The day is still fine, the sun still bright.

I sleep a lot in Carnhallow, and I sleep well. It is like I am catching up, after twenty-five years of alarm clocks. I sometimes feel so leisured that my latent guilt kicks in, along with a hint of loneliness.

I haven't got any proper friends down here yet, so these last solitary weeks when I haven't been in the house I've been using the hours to drive and hike the wild Penwith landscape. I love photographing the silent mine stacks, the salt-bitten fishing villages and the dark and plunging coves where, on all but the calmest days, the waves throw themselves psychotically at the cliffs. Though my favourite place so far is Zawn Hanna, the cove at the end of our own valley. Morvellan Mine stands above it, but I ignore its black shapes and instead gaze out at the sea.

18

When occasional summer rain has sent me indoors I've tried completing my mental map of Carnhallow. I've finally counted the seventy-eight bedrooms and it turns out that there are, in fact, eighteen, depending on how you categorize the tiny, sad, echoing box rooms on the top floor, which were probably servants' quarters, though they have an odd echo of the monastic cells which must once, I presume, have stood on this ground, in this lush little valley.

Some days, standing alone in the dust of this top floor, when the sea-wind is combing through the rowans, it feels like I can hear the words of those monks, caught on the breeze: *Ave Maria, gratia plena: Dominus tecum . . .*

At other times I linger in the Drawing Room, my favourite part of Carnhallow, along with the kitchen and the gardens. I've checked out most of the books, from Nina's volumes on antique silverware and Meissen porcelain to David's many monographs on mainly modern artists: Klee, Bacon, Jackson Pollock. David has a particular liking for abstract expressionists.

Last weekend I saw him sit and stare at the solid black and red blobs of a Mark Rothko painting for an hour, then he closed the book, looked at me, and said, 'We're all astronauts, really, aren't we; interstellar astronauts, travelling so far into the blackness we can never return.' Then he got up and offered me Plymouth gin in a Georgian tumbler.

But my biggest personal discovery has not been porcelain or paintings but a small dog-eared volume of photographs, hidden between two big fat books on Van Dyck and Michelangelo. When I first opened this battered little booklet it revealed startling monochrome images of historic Kerthen mines and the miners within them.

The photos must, I reckon, be nineteenth century. I look at them almost every day. What amazes me about them is that the miners worked practically without light: all they had was the faint flicker of the tiny candles stuck in their felt hats. Which means that the moment the camera's magnesium flash exploded was the only time in their lives when the miners properly saw where they worked, where they had spent every waking hour, digging and hewing and drilling. One precious fraction of brightness. Then back to lifelong darkness.

The thought of those miners, who once toiled their lives away in the rocks right underneath me, stirs me into action. Get to work, Rachel Daly.

The drawing is folded and set on the tray, which is warm from the sun. I carry the tray with the lemon-scented glasses into the coolness of the house, the airiness of the kitchen. Then I open my app. There are only two significant places left to explore: I've left them to last because they are the ones that give me the most concern. They are the worst of Carnhallow's challenges.

The first is the basement and the cellars.

David showed me this bewildering labyrinth the day we arrived, and I have not revisited. Because the basement is a depressing place: a network of dismal corridors, grimed with dust, where rusted bells dangle below coiled springs, never to be heard again.

There are many stairs down to the basement. I take the first set, outside the kitchen. Flicking on unreliable lights at the top of the steps, I pick my way down the creaking wooden stairs, and look around.

Ancient signs hang from peeling doors: Brushing Room, Butler's Pantry, Footman's Room, receding into shadows and grey. At the end of the dingy corridor ahead of me I can make out the tall, arched stone threshold of the wine cellar. David and Cassie visit the cellars a lot: it is the one part of Carnhallow's vast basement that gets used. Apparently there are lancet windows in the cellar, blinded and bricked, showing the monastic origin of Carnhallow, one thousand years ago. One day I will sit myself down in that cellar and blow dust off old French labels, teach myself about wine the way I am slowly teaching myself about everything else, but today I need to get an overall grasp.

Turning down an opposite corridor I find more signs: Bake House, Cleaning Room, Dairy. The piles of debris littering and sometimes obstructing the corridors are stupefying. An antique sewing machine. Half of a vintage motorcycle, taken to pieces then left here. Broken clay pipes from maybe two hundred years before. A mouldy Victorian wardrobe. Some kind of light fitting, made possibly from swan feathers. An enormous wheel from a horse-carriage. It is like the Kerthens, as they slowly died out, or dispersed, or decayed, couldn't bear to part with anything, as it painfully symbolized their decline. So it all got hidden away down here. Entombed.

Phone in hand, I pause. The air is motionless and cold. Two huge antique fridges lurk, for no obvious reason, in a corner. I have a sudden image of being imprisoned within one of them. Hammering on the door, trapped in its reeking smallness, stuck down a basement corridor that no one will ever use. Dying over days in a cuboid coffin.

A shudder runs through me. Moving on, turning left, I find an even older doorway. The stonework of the doorjamb looks medieval, and the painted wooden sign hanging from a nail says STILL.

Still?

Still what? Still here? Be still? Please be still? The sign agitates.

STILL.

Repressing my anxieties, I push the door. The hinges are stiff with rust: I have to lay my shoulder on the door and shunt hard, and at last the door springs open, with a bang. Like I have broken something. I sense the house glaring at me with disapproval.

It is very dark in this room. There is no apparent switch and the only light comes from the corridor behind me. My eyes slowly adjust to the gloom. In the middle of this small room is a battered wooden table. It could be hundreds of years old, or it could have just had a hard time. Various bottles, greyed with dust, sit on shelves. Some have tiny labels on them, hung on exquisite metal chains, like little necklaces for tiny slave girls. Going close I see the handwritten names, scratchily penned – quilled – with ancient ink.

Feverfew. Wormwood. Comfrey. Mullein.

Still.

STILL.

I think I understand it now, maybe. This is a place for distilling. Making herbal remedies, tinctures. A still room.

Turning to go, I see something totally unexpected. Three or four large cardboard boxes in the corner of the room, partly concealed by a case of ancient glassware. The boxes have the name *Nina* vigorously scrawled on them.

So this is her stuff? The dead woman, the dead mother, the dead wife. Clothes, or books, maybe. Not ready to be thrown out.

Now I feel really improper, like a trespasser. I've done nothing wrong, I am the new wife, a keeper of Carnhallow, and David wants me to explore so that I can restore this maze of dust: but the act of almost-breaking-in to this room, and happening upon these sad boxes, makes me blush.

Trying not to run, I retrace my steps, and I climb the stairs with a definite sense of relief. Taking deep breaths. Then a glance at my watch reminds me. I have to collect Jamie, soon, which means I have enough time for my final task.

There is one more interior space I want to see: the entirely untouched West Wing. And at its heart, the Old Hall. David has told me it is impressive.

But I've not once set foot inside this space yet. Only seen the gaunt exterior. Taking the corridor beyond the grand stairs, I cross from east to west, and from now to then.

This must be it. A large but unpainted and very heavy wooden door. The handle is a twisted, cast-iron ring. It takes an effort to turn, but then the door swings smoothly open. I step, for the first time, into the Old Hall.

The tall arched windows are Gothic, and leaded. Obviously from the monastery. The vaulted stone chamber is cold; it is also totally uncarpeted and unfurnished. David says that centuries ago they used to pay the miners in this hall. I can see them now. The humble men, stoically queuing, summoned by their surnames. The mine captains looking on with crossed and burly arms.

The room is imposing, but also oppressive. I shiver like a child in here. I think the atmosphere must be something to do with the size of the room. Here in the frigid empty heart of the house, I realize the scale of Carnhallow. Vast and engulfing. This is where I truly comprehend that I am in a house with space for fifty people. For three dozen servants, and a large extended family.

23

Today, just four people live here. And one, David, will be spending most of his time in London.

Three o'clock. Time to pick up my stepson. Heading outside, jumping in the Mini, I gun the engine – then slowly navigate the narrow drive, up through the sunlit woodlands. It's a difficult road, but lovely, too. Inspiring. One day maybe my kids will play here. They will grow up in the magnificence of Carnhallow – surrounded by space and beauty, beaches and trees. They will see blue-bells in spring, and pick mushrooms in October. And there will be dogs. Happy, galloping dogs, fetching mossy sticks: in the glades of Ladies Wood.

At last I hit the main road – and I drive west, threading between the green and stony moors to my left and the rioting ocean on the right. This mazy B road takes in most of the little ex-mining villages in West Penwith.

Botallack, Geevor, Pendeen. Morvah.

After Morvah, the road splits: I take the left turn, heading over the barrens of higher moorland to Jamie's school in Sennen, a private prep school.

Two left turns, another mile of moor and the land-scape has subtly changed. Down here on the southern coast sunlight dapples calmer seas. When I park the car near the school gates and swing the door open the air is slightly but noticeably softer.

Jamie Kerthen is already here, waiting. He walks towards me. He is in his school uniform, despite it being a Saturday. This is because Sennen is a pretty formal school that demands uniforms whenever the kids are on the grounds. I like that. I want that for my kids, as well. Formality and discipline. More things I didn't have.

I climb out of the car, smiling at my stepson. I have to resist the urge to run and hug him, close and tight.

It's too soon for this. But my protective feelings are real. I want to protect him for ever.

Jamie half-smiles in response – but then he stops and stands there, rooted to the pavement, and gives me a long, strange, concentrated stare. As if he cannot work out who I am or why I am here. Even though we have now been living together for weeks.

I try not to be unnerved. His behaviour is peculiar – but I know he is still grieving for his mother.

To make it worse, another mother is coming out now, guiding her son, passing us on the pavement. I don't know who she is. I don't know anyone in Cornwall. But my isolation won't be helped if people think I am weird, that I don't fit in. So I give her a wide smile and say, all too loudly, 'Hello, I'm Rachel! I'm Jamie's stepmother!'

The woman looks my way, then at Jamie. Who still stands there, motionless, his eyes fixed on mine.

'Um, yes . . . hello.' She blushes faintly. She has a round, pretty face and a posh, clear voice and she looks embarrassed by this strange, loud woman and her wary stepson. And why not? 'I'm sure we'll meet again. But – ah – really must be going,' she says.

The woman hurries away with her boy, then looks back at me, a puzzled frown on her face. She probably feels sorry for this frightened boy with this idiot for a stepmother. So I turn my fixed smile on to my own stepson.

'Hey, Jamie! Everything OK? How was the football?'

Can he stand there in rooted silence for much longer? I cannot bear it. The weirdness is prolonged for several painful seconds. Then he relents. 'Two nil. We won.'

'Great, well, great, that's fantastic!'

25

'Rollo scored a penalty and then a header.'

'That's totally *brilliant*! You can tell me more on the drive home. Do you want to get in?'

He nods. 'OK.'

Chucking his sports bag in the back seat, he slides in, clunks his safety belt in its socket, then as I start the car, he plucks up a book from his bag and starts reading. Ignoring me again.

I change gear, taking a tight corner, trying to focus on these tiny roads, but I am nagged by worries. Now I think about it, this isn't the first time Jamie has acted oddly, as if suspicious of me, in the last few weeks: but it is the most noticeable occasion.

Why is he changing? When I met my stepson in London he was nothing but laughter and chatter: the initial day we met we got on brilliantly. That day was, in fact, the first day I felt real love for his father. The way man and boy interacted, their love and under-standing, their joking and mutual respect, united in grief yet not showing it – this moved and impressed me. It was so unlike me and my dad. And again I wanted some of this paternal affection for my own child. I wanted the father of my children to be exactly like David. I wanted it to *be* David.

The sex and desire and friendship were already in place – David had already charmed me – but it was Jamie who crystallized these feelings into love for his father.

And yet, ever since I actually moved in to Carnhallow, Jamie has, I now realize, become more withdrawn. Distant, or watchful. As if he is assessing me. As if he kind of senses that there's something awry. Something wrong with me.

My stepson is quietly looking my way in the mirror,

26

right now. His eyes are large, and the palest violet-blue. He really is a very beautiful boy: exceptionally striking.

Does this make me shallow – that Jamie Kerthen's beauty makes it easier for me to love him? If so, there's not much I can do; I can't help it. A beautiful child is a powerful thing, not easily resisted. And I also know that his boyish beauty disguises serious grief, which makes me feel the force of love, even more. I will never replace his lost mother, but surely I can assuage his loneliness.

A lock of black hair has fallen across his white forehead. If he were my son, I'd stroke it back in to place. At last he talks.

'When is Daddy going away again?'

I answer, in a rush. 'Monday morning, as usual, day after tomorrow. But he'll only be gone a few days. He's flying back into Newquay at the end of the week. Not so long, not long at all.'

'Oh, OK. Thank you, Rachel.' He sighs, passionately. 'I wish Daddy came home longer. I wish he didn't go away so much.'

'I know Jamie. I feel the same.'

I yearn to say something more constructive, but our new life is what it is: David commutes to and from London every Monday morning and Friday evening. He does it by plane, in and out of Newquay airport. When he gets home he burns his silver Mercedes along the A30, then crawls along the last, winding moorland miles, to Carnhallow.

It is a gruelling schedule, but weekly, long-distance commuting is the only way David can sustain his lucrative career in London law and retain a family life at Carnhallow, which he is utterly determined to do. Because the Kerthens have lived in Carnhallow for a thousand years.

27

Jamie is silent. It takes us twenty-five muted minutes to drive the tortuous miles. At last we arrive at sunlit Carnhallow and my stepson drags himself from the Mini, tugging his sports bag. Again I feel the need to talk. Keep trying. Eventually the bond will form. So I babble as I rummage for my keys, *Maybe you could tell me about your football match, my team was Millwall – that's where I grew up, they were never very good* – Then I hesitate. Jamie is frowning.

'What's the matter, Jamie?'

'Nothing,' he says. 'Nothing.'

The key slots, I push the great door open. But Jamie is staring at me in that same bewildered, disbelieving way. As if I am an eerie figure from a picture book, come inexplicably to life.

'Actually, there is something.'

'What, Jamie?'

'I had a really weird dream last night.'

I nod, and try another smile.

'You did?'

'Yes. It was about you. You were . . . '

He tails off. But I mustn't let this go. Dreams are important, especially childhood dreams. They are subconscious anxieties surfacing. I remember the dreams I had as a child. Dreams of escape, dreams of desperate flight from danger.

'Jamie. What was it, what was in the dream?'

He shifts his stance, uncomfortably. Like someone caught lying.

But this clearly isn't a lie.

'It was horrible. The dream. You were in the dream, and, and,' he hesitates, then shakes his head, looking down at the flagstones of the doorway. 'And there was all blood on your hands. Blood. And a hare. There was hare, an animal, and blood, and it was all over you. All of it. Blood. Blood all over there. Shaking and choking.'

He looks up again. His face is tensed with emotion. But it isn't tears. It looks more like anger, even hatred. I don't know what to say. And I don't have a chance to say it. Without another word he disappears, into the house. And I am left here standing in the great doorway of Carnhallow. Totally perplexed.

I can hear the brutal sea in the distance, kicking at the rocks beneath Morvellan, slowly knocking down the cliffs and the mines. Like an atrocity that will never stop.

149 Days Before Christmas

Lunchtime

'Verdejo, sir?'

David Kerthen nodded at the waiter. Why not drink? It was Friday lunchtime, and he was already en route home, for once ending work early, instead of at ten in the evening. So today he could drink. By the time the plane landed at Newquay he would have sobered up. There was barely any chance of being caught by the police on the A30 anyway. The Cornish police could often be spectacularly inept.

The drink might, also, allow him to forget. Last night, for the third night in a row, he'd dreamt of Carnhallow. This time he'd dreamt of Nina wandering the rooms, alone, and naked.

She used to do that a lot: walk naked about the house. She found it erotic, as he found it erotic: the contrast of her pale skin with the monastic stone or the Azeri rugs.

Sipping his Verdejo, David remembered the night they came back from their honeymoon. She'd stripped and they'd danced: she was naked and he was in his suit and the champagne was ferociously cold. They'd rolled back the carpets in the New Hall to make the dancing easier, he had put an arm around her slender waist, one hand clasped in another. And then she'd slipped from that grasp, running away from him, shadowed and arousing, disappearing into the darker corridors, a blur of youthful nudity.

The memories killed him. Their early happiness had been overgenerous. The sex was always too compulsive. It still gave him bad dreams, charged with a tragic desire or a child-like neediness, followed by regret.

He checked his watch: 1.30. Oliver was late. Their table was half empty, yet the dark, plutocratic Japanese restaurant was conspicuously full.

Unbuttoning his suit jacket, David looked around, taking the mood of Mayfair, checking the oil of London. The wealth of modern London was gamey: the city was marbled with success. You could smell the opulence, and it wasn't always nice. But it was heady, and it was necessary. Because David was a beneficiary of London's commercial triumph. As a fashionable QC he got a regular table at Nobu, a sleek office in the serene Georgian streets of Marylebone and, best of all, a half-million-pound salary, with which he could restore Carnhallow.

But they certainly made him work for it. The hours were grim. How long could he keep it up? Ten years? Fifteen?

Right now he needed more alcohol. So he sipped the Verdejo, alone.

David didn't like being alone at lunch. It reminded him of the days after Nina's fall. The dismal, solitary meals in the old Dining Room, with his mother self-exiled to her granny flat, refusing to talk. David winced internally as he recalled the eagerness with which he had returned to work after the funeral. Leaving his mother and the housekeeper to look after Jamie in the week. He had, in effect, run away. Because he simply couldn't face the way all the different emotions had combined into a symphony of remorse. London had been his escape.

Draining the wine glass, David gestured for a refill. As he did, he noticed Oliver, striding to the table.

'Sorry,' he said. 'I had a meeting that dragged. At least we are fashionably late?'

'Yep, a week after they lost their Michelin star.'

Oliver smiled, pulled out a seat. 'It doesn't, ah, seem to have affected business much.'

'Have a glass, you look as if you need it.'

'I do, I do. Sss! Why did I join the civil service? I thought I would be serving the country, but it turns out I am serving a cabal of halfwits. *Politicians*. Can we have the black cod?'

The waiter was attending, fingers poised over tablet.

David knew the menu by heart. 'Inaniwa pasta with lobster, bluefin tuna tataki. And that cabbage thing, with miso.'

The waiter nodded.

Oliver said, 'We really have been friends for too long. You know exactly what I want. Like a bloody wife.' He raised a glass, ceremonially.

David was happy to join in, to toast their friendship. Oliver was the only friend he still kept from Westminster School, and he treasured the sheer *longevity* of their relationship. They'd been so close for so long they now shared a form of private language. Like one of those obscure languages spoken by two people in New Guinea. If one of them died, an entire tongue would be lost, with all its secret histories, its metaphors and memories.

The third member of their trio was already dead. Edmund. Another lawyer. Gay. The three of them had formed a gang at school. A trio of conspirators.

So here they were, twenty-three years later, sharing their ancient schoolyard jokes. And talking about Rachel.

'It's just that,' Oliver sat back, his round face slightly flushed from the toil of eating a three-hundred-pound lunch. 'Well, I didn't expect it to get so far, so fast.'

'But you got us together.'

'Well, I know I introduced you, yes. And I also knew that you'd like her.'

'And how did you know that?'

'She's smart. She's petite. She's very ornamental.' Oliver dabbed his lips with a napkin. 'I think God designed her for you.'

'So why the surprise?'

Oliver shrugged. 'I rather presumed that you would do your normal thing.'

'Which is?'

'Sleep with her, get a little bored, move on to the next.'

David sighed. 'Christ. You make me sound terrible. Am I really that bad?'

'You're not evil, just annoyingly successful with women. I'm jealous, that's all.'

'Well, stop. I only do it on medical advice. They say multiple partners reduce rates of prostate cancer.'

Oliver laughed, and ate the last morsel of poussin yasai zuke. He shook his head. 'But, ah, Rachel Daly

34

turned out to be *different*. Of all the women you've bedded. *Rachel Daly*. And you married her within a month.'

David sat back, swirling his Verdejo. 'Eight weeks, actually. But it was a bit quick.'

'Putting it mildly.'

'But I really *did* fall for her, Oliver. Is that so implausible? And she got on so well with Jamie. It felt entirely right.' David scanned his friend's face for a hidden meaning. 'Are you implying it was too soon – after Nina?'

'No,' Oliver shook his head, emphatically, maybe awkwardly. 'No no no. Of course not. It's more that Rachel is so, well, different to your usual girlfriends.'

'You mean she's working class.'

'No, I mean she's underclass. You do know where she came from?'

'The rookeries of Plumstead. The favelas of Tooting Bec. What does it matter?'

'It doesn't, not really. It's more that it's such a *leap*. She's so very different to Nina. I mean she looks similar, that elfin face, that gamine quality you always go for, but in every other way—'

'But that's the point.' David leaned forward. 'That's one of the reasons I fell in love with Rachel, so quickly. She's *different*.' He was talking slightly too loudly now, his talk fuelled by wine. But he didn't care. 'All those nice girls from Notting Hill, from Paris and Manhattan – Rachel is superbly different to all that. She's had experiences I can't imagine. She has opinions I never hear, she has ideas I could never expect, she is also a *survivor*, she's been through serious shit, yet come out of it intact, intelligent, funny.' He paused. 'And, yes, she is sexy.'

The table was silenced. David wanted to say: *She's almost as sexy as Nina, she's the only woman I've met who might actually one day compare to Nina*, but he didn't. Because he didn't want to think about Nina. Instead he ordered two Tokays.

Oliver smiled affably. 'I suppose you and Rachel have also got things in common.'

'You mean both our fathers were bastards, and we're both clearly and ridiculously impulsive.'

'No, I was thinking that – you're both a little fucked up.'

'Ah.' David laughed. 'Yes. Possibly the case. But damaged girls are better in bed.'

'Sweet.'

'Though the same surely applies to men. Maybe that's why I was good at womanizing. I've got issues.' David looked across the restaurant at a young family. At a laughing child, happy with his parents. His words came as a reflex. 'God, I miss Jamie.'

Oliver offered a sympathetic smile. David summoned the waiter, and asked for the bill. Their wine glasses glittered subtly in the low restaurant light.

Oliver sat back. 'Is it worse, missing kids? Worse than missing girlfriends, or partners? I wouldn't know.'

David shook his head. 'Trust me. It's worse. And the worst of it is, there's nothing you can do. Even when you do have a nice time with your kids, it makes you regret how you should have done more of the same in the past. Having a kid is like an industrial revolution of the emotions. Suddenly you can mass produce worry, and guilt.'

'Well, at least you'll see him tonight.'

David brightened. 'I will. It's the weekend. Thank God.'

36

The lunch over, they wandered out into a bright, soft afternoon, into London at its most benign: the plane trees of Piccadilly caging the city sunlight in softening green. Shaking hands, and slapping backs, Oliver walked off to St James and David headed the other way, tipsily grabbing a cab to his office in Marylebone, picking up his weekend case, and then taking the same taxi, for Heathrow.

But as the traffic stalled through Hammersmith, the good buzz of the booze began to ebb. The bad thoughts came back, the wearying yet unavoidable anxieties.

Jamie. His beloved son.

It wasn't just that he missed Jamie: it was the fact that the boy was behaving strangely, again. Not as badly as the first terrible months after Nina's funeral, but there was definitely something amiss. And it was seriously dismaying. David had hoped that bringing Rachel to Carnhallow would mark a new chapter in their lives, would definitively draw an emotional line under it all, let them move into the brighter light of the future, but that hadn't happened. Jamie was, if anything, regressing. The latest of his letters, to his mother – which David had found in his son's room just last week – was particularly disturbing.

A quiet panic made David loosen his tie, as if he was being physically choked in the back of the taxi. If only he could tell someone he might at least feel unburdened. But he couldn't tell anyone, not his new wife, not his oldest friends, not even Oliver – as the lunch had proved. Edmund was the only one who'd known it all. And now Edmund was gone, and David was alone. David was the only one who knew the truth.

Except, perhaps, for Jamie himself.

And there again was the source of David's ongoing

torment. How much did his son know? What had she told him? What had the boy seen, or heard?

David looked out at the endless traffic. It had now come to a complete stop. Like blood frozen in the veins.

136 Days Before Christmas

The August sun is bright, the distant sea like beaten tin. David is taking me walking, on the final day of his summer break. This Sunday hike will lead us, David says, away from all the tourists, high up on to the peak of the Penwith moors.

David is in jeans, jumper, boots. He turns and grasps my hand to help me over a granite stile. Then we walk on. He is telling me some of the history of Carnhallow, Penwith, West Cornwall.

'Nanjulian, that means the valley of hazels. Zawn Hanna means the murmuring cove, but you know that. Carn Lesys is the carn of light—'

'Gorgeous. Carn of light!'

'Maen Dower, that's stone near the water. Porthnanven, port of the high valley.'

'And Carnhallow means rocks on a moor. Right?'

He smiles, his sharp white teeth framed by a holiday tan and dark stubble. When he goes a few days without shaving, David can look decidedly piratical. He only needs a thick gold earring and a cutlass. 'Rachel Kerthen. You've been at the library!'

41

'Can't help it. Love reading! And don't you want me to know all this stuff?'

'Of course. Of course. But I like telling you things, too. It makes me feel useful when I come home. And if you know everything' – he shrugs, happily – 'what will I have left to say?'

'Oh, I'm sure you'll never run out of *things to say.*'

He laughs.

I go on, 'I also looked up Morvellan: that means milling sea, right?'

A nod. 'Or villainous sea. Possibly.'

'But "Mor" is definitely sea, right? The same root as in Morvah.'

'Yes. Mor-vah. Sea grave. It's from all the people that died, in shipwrecks.'

I can barely hear his answer: I have to run, slightly, to keep up with him as we stride between the heather and furze. David forgets he is so much taller than me, and therefore walks much faster than I do. His idea of a stiff hike is more like my idea of a jog.

Now he pauses, to let me catch up; then we stride on, breathing deeply. The moorland air is scented with coconut from the sunwarmed gorse. To me it's the smell of Bounty bars, the coconut-and-chocolate sweets I rarely got as a kid.

'Actually, that name always creeps me out,' I say. 'Morvah.'

'Yes. And the landscape doesn't help – all those brooding rocks, next to the wildness of the waves. There's a famous line from a travel book which describes that bit of road: 'the landscape reaches a crescendo of evil at Morvah'. Very apt. Hold on, another stile. Give me your hand.'

Together we jump the warm stone stile, and continue

down the dried-out mud of the footpath. We've barely had rain in the two weeks of David's summer holiday. It's been an almost flawless fortnight of sunshine. And David has been equally perfect – loving, charming, generous: taking me to local pubs, buying me wine in the Lamorna Wink, and fresh crab sandwiches in riverside Restronguet. Introducing me to his rich, yacht-owning friends in St Mawes and Falmouth, introducing me to the hidden caves of Kynance Cove, where we made love like teenagers, with sand in our hair, and little seashells on my tingling skin, and then his dark, muscled arms, turning me over.

It's been lovely. And for this reason I've stayed silent about my doubts. I haven't mentioned Jamie's odd behaviour, the staring, the silence, that odd dream about blood on my hands, and a hare. I haven't wanted to fracture our summery happiness with some vague misgivings. The dream, I have decided, must have derived from Jamie's traumas, his grief. The silences are the confusion of a child getting used to a new stepmother, such a painful transition. I want to share this pain, and so dilute it.

Besides, all three of us have had a happy time this last fortnight. David's continued presence has apparently calmed Jamie down. I have brilliant memories of David, Jamie and myself, these past two weeks, walking the coastal paths at Minack, watching the seabirds playing with the waves, or lying in the warm clifftop grass, sharing picnic sandwiches, admiring sea-pinks on the way home.

Today, however, it's me and David. Jamie's friend Rollo has a birthday party. Cassie is picking him up later. I've got precious time alone with my husband, before he goes back to work. Before the perfect summer ends.

We are still talking about language. I want to know more. 'So did you ever try to learn Cornish?'

'God, no,' he says, striding along the stony path. 'A dead language. What's the point? If Cornishness survives as a culture it won't be because they revive the language, it'll be the people. Always the people.' He gestures at the weathered scenery, the eroded boulders, the stunted trees. 'You know these little paths were made by the miners? They would walk for hours over the moors, through the woods and heather.' He is facing away from me now, talking into the cooling breeze. 'Imagine that life: stumbling through the dark, walking to the mineshafts, across the cliffs. Then climbing down hundreds of fathoms, for an hour – then crawling for a mile under the sea, and digging the tin from the rocks all day.' He shakes his head, like he is doubting it himself. 'And all the time they could hear the ocean boulders rolling above them in the storms; and sometimes the seas would break through, pouring into the tunnels—' He stares wildly, at the sky. 'And then they would try to run, but the sea usually claimed them. Dragged them back, sucked them in. Hundreds of men, over hundreds of years. And all the time my people, the Kerthens, we sat in Carnhallow. Eating capons.'

I gaze his way. Not sure what to say. He goes on:

'And you want to know something else?'

'Uhm. Yes?'

'According to my mother, on really quiet summer evenings, when the stamps were silent, and the family was in the Yellow Drawing Room, sipping their claret, they could hear the picks of the miners half a mile beneath them. Working the tin that paid for the wine.'

His face is shadowed by a passing cloud. I have that

44

urge to heal him, as I want to heal his son. And perhaps I can try. Coming close, I stroke his face and kiss him, gently. He looks at me, and shrugs, as if to say: *What can I do?*

The answer, of course, is nothing.

Clasping hands, we stride uphill, nearing the highest point of the moors. Here is another ruined mine, with noble arches, like a Norman church.

Regaining my breath after the climb, I lean a hand on the fine brickwork of the Engine House. The view is magnificent. I can see much of West Cornwall: the dark vivid green of the woods surrounding Penzance, the grey road snaking to Marazion, and the dreaming mysteries of the Lizard. And of course the vast metallic dazzle of the sea around St Michael's Mount. The tide is in.

'Ding Dong mine,' David says, slapping the sparkling granite wall. 'Reputedly the oldest in Cornwall. It was said to have been worked by the Romans, and before them the Phoenicians. Or maybe the fairies. Shall we sit down, out of the wind? I've brought strawberries.'

'Why thank you, Mr D'Urberville.'

He chuckles. We sit down together on a rug from David's rucksack. We are in the lee of the high moorland breeze, protected by the Engine House at our backs. The sun casts vivid warmth on my face.

A couple of hikers in lurid blue windcheaters are navigating a valley below. Otherwise we are alone. David gives me a strawberry from a plastic punnet.

I snuggle closer to my husband. Here is a lovely moment. Us, alone, together: in the sun.

He says, abruptly, 'Don't worry about Jamie.'

My heartbeat quickens. If there was ever a time to

mention it, to speak out, this is it. But I don't want to hurt or upset David. I'm not sure I have anything important to say, so I shall say nothing direct.

'Jamie is still grieving, isn't he? That's why he is kind of distant sometimes?'

David sighs. 'Of course.'

My husband slings a protective arm around my neck. 'It's not even been two years . . . And it was horrific as well as confusing. So he can be absent, or distracted, but he's getting better. He's been good these last two weeks. Please don't worry about it. He will come to love you, and accept you.'

'I don't worry.'

David up-tilts my chin with a hand, as if he is going to kiss my lips; instead he kisses my forehead.

'Are you sure, Rachel?'

'Sure I'm sure! He's a lovely boy. Angelic. Fell for him the moment I first saw him.' I smile and kiss David on his lips. 'In fact, it was when I met him that I began to really fall for you.'

'Not when you saw pictures of Carnhallow, then?'

'Oh. Listen. Funny man. Idiot.'

We fall companionably silent. David sucks a strawberry, and tosses the green stalk into the grass.

'When I was a boy we used to come up here, my cousins and I, during the summer holidays. When my father was away in London.' He pauses, then adds, 'I think that was the happiest time of my childhood.'

I squeeze his hand, listening.

'Endless summers. That's what I remember, endless summer days. We'd go down to Penberth, beach-combing, looking for driftwood, old masts, crab-pots, Korean pickle packets. Anything.' He hugs me as he talks. 'The sea has a unique colour, at Penberth. Kind

46

of a transparent emerald. I think it's the pale yellow of the sand, seen through the blueness, the unpolluted waters. And there would be these amazing sunsets. Tingeing the hills and rocks with gold, filling the valleys with this purple glow. And I'd look at the shadows of me and my cousins, on the beach, the shadows getting longer and longer – going on for ever, until they were lost in the warmth, and the haze, and the midsummer dark. And then we knew it was time to go back to Carnhallow, for supper, heading home for cold meats and hot drop scones. Or strawberries and clotted cream in the kitchen. With the windows thrown open to the stars. And I was blissfully happy, because I knew my father was away in London.'

I am surprised, and touched. David is a lawyer, he can be very eloquent, but he seldom talks like this.

'Were you really that lonely, the rest of the time?'

'In the holidays, no. But the rest of the time? Yes. Before I toughened up.'

'Why? How?'

'They sent me to boarding school, Rachel, at eight years old. And there was no reason to send me away, Mummy wasn't working. It was simply his choice. He had one son, one child – and he sent me away.'

'Why?'

'That's the worst of it, I don't really fucking know. Because he was jealous of the bond between my mother and me? Because he was bored with having me around? Mummy wanted me to stay, and there are plenty of good day schools in Cornwall. Perhaps he did it to hurt her. A pure act of sadism. And now he's dead. So I will never know.' He hesitates, but not for long. 'I sometimes think the best thing a parent can do is live long enough for the children to grow up, so the kids are old enough to ask their parents, *How the fuck could you get it so wrong?*'

Another strawberry. Another stalk, hurled into the grass. The sun is dipping its chin in the west, turning rags of cloud to purpled gold. Some of those clouds look ominous, anvil-shaped: a summer storm, perhaps. Storms come so fast in West Cornwall, summer idylls to brutal squalls in bare minutes.

'On clear days you can see the Scilly Isles from here,' David says. 'I must take you there one day. They're beautiful, the light is marvellous. The Islands of the Blest. The pagan afterworld.'

'I'd love that.'

He eats half of the last strawberry, then turns, and gives it to me, lifting it to my mouth. A strawberry taken from his hand. I eat the strawberry, taste its lurid sweetness. Then he says, 'One day, perhaps, you could tell me about *your* childhood?'

I try not to flinch at this.

He goes on, 'I know you've told me a bit of it. You've told me about your father, the way he treated your mother, but you haven't told me much more.' He looks at me, unblinking, perhaps seeing the anxiety in my expression. 'Sorry. Talking about my past – it made me think of yours. You don't have to tell me *anything*, darling, if you don't want.'

I look at him, also unblinking. And I feel a huge desire to yield, and confess. Yet I am blocked, as always. Can't tell, mustn't tell. If I do tell everything, he might shun me. Won't he?

David strokes my face. 'Sorry, sweetheart. I shouldn't have asked.'

'No.' I stand up, brushing grass from myself. 'Don't

be sorry. You should want to know, you're my husband. And one day I will tell you.'

I want this to be true. I so want this to be true. I want to tell him everything, from my tainted entrance into university to the dissolving of my family. *I will tell everything.*

One day. But not today, I don't think. Not here and now.

Does David detect my sadness? Apparently not. Brisk and confident, he gets to his feet, and tilts his head to the west. To those darkening clouds, busily turning blue to black. 'Come on, we'd better get going, before the rains kick in. I told Alex I'd have a quick drink with him at the Gurnard's, last chance before I go back to work. You can drop me off.'

Afternoon

I do as I am told.

We climb in the car and I drive through the stiffening wind, and then the sharpening rain, to the clifftop pub, the Gurnard's Head, where David leaps out of the car, and shouts through the weather: Don't worry, I'll get a taxi. Then he runs, sheltering under his rucksack, into the pub. Off to see Alex Lockwood. A banker, I think. He's certainly another one of those wealthy friends of David's, those tall guys who smile politely at me in yachty bars, like I am a quaint but passing curiosity, after which they turn and talk to David.

Pulling away from the pub, I accelerate down the road – hoping I can get to the house before the lightning starts. Because this is definitely a big, late summer storm, racing in from the Atlantic.

By the time I reach the final miles to Carnhallow the rain is so heavy it is defeating the wipers. A proper cloud-burst. I have to slow to five, four, three miles per hour.

I could be overtaken by a cow.

At last I make the gate to the Kerthen estate and the long treacherous lane down Carnhallow Valley, through the rowans and the oaks. I dislike this winding track during the day and it is seriously dark now: storm clouds making night from day. I've got the headlights on, to help me through the murk, but the car is skidding, accelerating on the wet and fractured concrete, it's almost out of control.

What's this?

Something runs out into my lights. It is a blur through the rainy windscreen, a grey smear of movement – then a swerve of my wheel, and a queasy thump.

Jerking the car to a stop, the wind is salty and loud as I open the door, as I run up the track, heedless of the rain, to see what I hit.

A rabbit is lying in the grass, lit by my headlamps. The pulsing body is shattered, there are red gashes in its flanks, showing muscles, and too much blood. Way too much blood.

Worst is the head. The skull is half-crushed, yet one living eye is bright in its socket, staring regretfully, as I cradle the broken form. A milky tear trickles down, and the animal shudders and then, as I crouch here on the grass, it dies in my arms.

Filled with self-reproach, I gently drop the body to the ground, where it lolls, lifeless. Then I look at my hands.

They are covered in blood.

And then I look at the animal. I take a long frightening look at its sleek, distinctive, velvety ears. It's not a rabbit. It's a hare.

110 Days Before Christmas

Lunchtime

I'm lying to my husband.

'I told you, I'm going shopping. We need some food.'

His sceptical voice fills the car, disembodied. Calling me from London. 'Shopping in St Just? St Just in Penwith?'

'Why not?'

He laughs. 'Darling. You know what they say, the scagulls in St Just fly upside down because there's nothing worth crapping on.'

I chuckle, briefly. I'm still lying, though. I'm not telling him why I'm shopping, not yet. Not until I know.

'What's the weather like down there?'

I gaze through my windscreen as the car rolls along the coastal road. The stunted church tower of St Just is a grey silhouette on a grey horizon. 'Looks like it's going to rain. Bit chilly, too.'

He sighs. 'Yes, the summer's pretty much over. But it was good, wasn't it?' His pause is earnest. Hopeful.

53

'Everything is OK now, everything is getting better, with Jamie, you're feeling better.'

'Yes,' I say, and again I lie, and this lie is probably more important. I am certainly not feeling better: I am still thinking of the hare I killed. I haven't mentioned it, to anyone. As soon as the accident happened, I cleaned the car and quickly disposed of the body, I wiped the blood from my hands, and then I tried to wipe the event from my mind. My first reaction had been to call David, tell him, share the story. But a minute's thought told me that, no matter how trivially disturbing, it was probably better to stay silent. The moment I broached the subject, even as a passing and frivolous remark – oh your son said *this* and then it really happened, how *funny*, it could appear, to David, that I actually believe his son can foresee events, is clairvoyant, is a Kerthen from the legend. My remarks could make me sound mad. And I must not sound mad. Because I am not mad.

I don't believe that Jamie has any power. The accident was an uncanny coincidence: animals die on the narrow, rural, zigzagging Penwith roads all the time – badgers, foxes, pheasants, and hares. I've seen dead hares before, they always make me sad; hares somehow seem much more precious than rabbits. Wilder, more poetic, I love the fact they live in Penwith. But they do get killed with regularity, as people speed round those granite-walled corners. My encounter on that rainy lane through Ladies Wood was, consequently, Jamie's anxieties conflating with a simple accident. Yet it still faintly haunts me. Perhaps it was the way the body lolled in my hands. Like a dead baby.

'Rachel?'

'Yes, sorry. Driving.'

'Are you OK, darling?'

'I'm fine. Gotta find a parking space. I'd better go.'

He says goodbye and says *let's Skype later* and then he drops the call. I scan the streets for a place to slot my car. It doesn't take long. It's never that hard to park here. Remote, regularly battered by the weather, the 'last town in England', one of the last places in Cornwall to speak Cornish, St Just-in-Penwith on the best of days has an empty and melancholy feel: bereft of its mines and miners but not their memories. But it is also the nearest town with the shop I need, the nearest to Carnhallow, and I need this shop right now.

Pushing the car door open I sense the inevitable dampness in the air. It is threatening to mizzle: that specific form of fine Cornish rain which is half-mist, half-drizzle. Like a spa treatment, but cold.

The pharmacy is down the fore street, at the corner of which is the medieval church; the central square is eighteenth-century shopfronts and big Victorian pubs – which retain hints of that wealthier mining past, the days of count-house dinners and hot rum punch, the days when adventurers and stockholders would celebrate the boom days of another copper lode, when giddy mine-captains would bring their sweethearts into the saloon to drink their gin-and-treacle.

Crossing the road, feeling the odd sensation that I am being watched, I press the door. It opens with an old-fashioned chime.

The girl at the counter gives me a look. She's young. Very pale.

Slowly I make my way around the scented pharmacy. The girl is still looking at me, but hers is a warm, friendly glance. I realize with a sense of surprise that she's almost my age: I spend so much time alone, or with David, I sometimes forget that I am also young. Only thirty.

The beautiful tattoo of a mandala on her neck implies she might be arty, or musical, the kind of friend I would usually make, without a worry, in Shoreditch. Maybe she's working here to support a creative career; either way she looks fun and alternative. I'd like to go up to her and crack a joke and have a laugh – make a friend. It's what I would have done in London.

But I'm still struggling to make real friends here, and I'm not sure why. Over the last weeks and months Cornwall, or Carnhallow, or the Kerthens, have somehow muted me. Or maybe it's Jamie; the boy absorbs my emotions, even if we barely communicate.

The shelves do not have what I want. I am going to have to brave a conversation. With a glitch of anxiety in my throat, I approach the counter.

'Do you have any um, um, pregnancy testing kits?'

The girl gazes at me. Perhaps she can tell how important this is from the crack in my voice. Pregnancy is my escape from worry and the growing sense of point-lessness: I will become a new mother, meet other new mothers. I will have a proper role and a real job and something extraordinary to give to David and Jamie. I will forget my anxieties. And I will make my husband happy: I know David is very keen for me to fall pregnant.

I am five days late, as I realized this morning, staring in confusion and tingling hopefulness at the calendar.

The girl is frowning.

'There aren't any kits on the shelves?'

'Not that I can see.'

'Well, uhm. Not sure we have any left. I'll go check.'

She disappears. Gazing around, I see a poster for

some kiddie medicine on the wall. The poster shows a mother with an angelic little baby, superhumanly cute and flawless. The mother has a smile as radiant as the faithful on Judgement Day. *For unto us a child is born.*

'Here,' says the shop girl. 'Had a bunch at the back, must have forgot to put them out on the shelves. Sorry!'

I snap from my daydream. 'Thank you. Brilliant. Can I take two?'

The girl smiles. Two to make sure you are definitely pregnant. Grabbing my kits, I scoot out into the drizzle and wind. Shoppers in drab hoodies turn my way, as if they have all been there a while, waiting for me. *Look at her. Skulking around.*

Am I pregnant? It is what I've wanted, needed, desired, for so long, to make things whole. My heart sings at the idea. A daughter, a son, I don't mind. And a sibling for Jamie. This will repair the world. *I bring you glad tidings.*

The tension is too much. I can't even wait to drive home. I'm going to find out this very second. Climbing out of the car again I head for one of those rather handsome old pubs, the Commercial Hotel.

The pub is, inevitably, almost empty. Just one young guy at the end of the varnished wooden bar, staring at a pint of Guinness. He briefly leers at me, then stares at his beer again.

Into the Ladies. I take out the kit, squat on the loo. I pee.

And then comes the wait. I am actually trying not to pray. I mustn't get my hopes up. But oh, my hopes. My brilliant hopes.

Count the time, count the time, I must number the moments until I can call my husband and sing out the wonderful news, the news that changes everything, the news that will make us truly happy, properly a family.

I shut my eyes, tick off the final seconds, and look down. One line means not pregnant, two lines means pregnant. I need two lines. Give me two blue lines.

I look at the stick.

One line.

The sadness bites hard. Why did I get my hopes up so high? It was silly. We've only been trying for a few short months. The chances are fairly low.

Should I even bother with the second kit? I've got my answer. One line. Not pregnant. Get on with things . . .

And yet. Who knows?

I wait, counting the stupid seconds. I look at the stick.

One line. Crossing out my dreams.

Chucking the kits vigorously in the bin, I pause as I exit the toilet, then go to the mirror and give myself a hard, instructive stare. Looking at my white freckled face, my red hair, at Rachel Daly. I must shape up, snap out of self-pity – and count myself lucky. I have a rich, sexy husband, I have a beautiful stepson, I am living in a magnificent house which I truly adore.

And yet it is a house I don't want to go back to – not yet. Not with all its vastness and silence. Not when I am in this pensive mood. Trying not to think about the hare. That uncanny coincidence. The blood on my hands. Again.

Wandering into the bar, I check the array of drinks: local beers, Doom Bar, St Austell Breweries. But I don't like beer. Instead I ask the yawning bargirl for a rum and coke. Why not? After all, I am not pregnant.

'Here you go, my lover.'

I take the drink and sit at a table. The young man

is still looking intently at his Guinness, like it is a lap dancer.

Reaching into my handbag, I find my book. It's a thickish volume about tin mining, sourced from David's library. David's rhapsodies on the old mining life have got me interested. This is another way for me to understand my new family. The mine-owning Kerthens.

The book is old and has that annoyingly dense Victorian typography, very difficult to read, but it is full of curious, moving, even sinister vignettes of mining life.

The author toured the West Cornish mines in the 1840s, near the peak of production, and saw the wealth and the energy and the horror. He talks of the suffering and mutilation: the many cripples he met in the villages, men with permanently blackened faces from explosions; men missing fingers or hands or arms from shooting rocks with gunpowder; blinded and broken men being led around the humble Cornish villages by boys, eking out a pitiful living by selling tea, door to door.

In some places, he says, one miner in five died violently. Sometimes they died at each other's hands: from drunken brawling. The boozy violence of the 'wild men of the stannaries' was legendary. In the mid nineteenth century it was said that, in West Cornwall, wherever three houses met together, two would be alehouses.

Yet the author also saw a vivid beauty: how boats would sail up the night-time coast then anchor to gaze in astonishment at the sight of Pendeen and Botallack and Morvellan blazing away on the cliffs without cease, the rising and falling beams of the fire whims, the winding drums of the horse engines, the cries of the landers, the glare from boiler house doors, the crashing of the stamps. And the lights glowing in the windows of the great three-storeyed engine houses, halfway up the cliffs. And then, most magnificent of all, the mighty fires of the smelting houses lit by fountains of molten metal, springing up fifteen feet into the air, then splashing back into the basin, like majestic geysers of quicksilver.

And now, incredibly, it is all *gone*. After four thousand years. The men no longer work half-naked in the terrible heat at the end of undersea tunnels; they no longer climb a mile down ropes, like monkeys, deep into the reek of sulphur; and boys of eight are no longer sent down the pit to produce half the world's tin and copper and many millions in profit. All that is left is those ruins by the sea, those ruins on the moors, and in the woods. Scorrier, South Crofty, Wheal Rose, Treskerby, Hallenbeagle, Wheal Busy, Wheal Seymour, Creegbrawse, Hallamanning, Poldise, Ding Dong, Godolphin, and Providence.

Gone.

I look up from the book, hoping to see a face, swap just a smile with the bargirl. But now I realize the pub is deserted. The drinker has gone, even the bargirl has disappeared. I am totally alone. It's like no one else exists.

Afternoon

The house is quiet when I get back. The house is always quiet. The great front door opens and I am greeted by perfect stillness, the scent of beeswax, and the long and lofty New Hall.

Something brushes between my legs and makes me start. It's Genevieve. Nina's slender grey cat. Winding between my ankles.

When Nina died David gave her to Juliet to look after in her granny flat, because David doesn't like cats. But sometimes she leaves Juliet's apartment and stalks the house.

Bending down, I tickle the cat behind the ear, feeling the bone of her skull. Her fur is the colour of wintry sea mist.

'Hey, Genevieve. Go catch a mouse, we need the help.'

The cat purrs and gives me a sly, green-eyed glance. Then abruptly Genevieve stalks away, towards the Old Hall.

The silence returns.

Where is everyone?

Juliet is presumably in her flat. But where is Jamie? Heading right, I make for the kitchen, where I find rare human life. It's Cassie, busy unloading the dishwasher, listening to K-Pop on her iPod. Cassie is young, amiable, Thai, thirty-two. She's been with the family ten years. She and I don't interact very much. Partly because her English is still hazy, and partly because I don't know how to act with her – I don't know how to deal with 'servants'. I am of the serving classes. I feel awkward. Better to leave her to it.

But I feel like I need interaction right now.

Cassie is oblivious to me. She has her earphones in as she works and she is cheerfully humming along.

Stepping forward, I touch her gently on the shoulder. 'Cassie.'

At once she flinches, startled, nearly dropping the mug in her hands. 'Oh,' she says, ripping the earphones out. 'I am sorry, Miss Rachel.'

'No, please, it was my fault. I made you jump.'

Her smile is soft, and sincere. I smile in return.

'I was wondering. Do you fancy a cup of tea?'

She looks at me in a friendly, puzzled way. 'Tea. You want me make you cup of tea?'

'No. I thought . . . ' I am shrugging. 'Well, I thought you and I could chat and, er, y'know. Have a cuppa and a conversation. Girl to girl. Get to know each other a bit better. This house is so big! You can get pretty lost.'

'Cup . . . pa?' Her puzzlement is plain now and tinged with concern. 'There is problem, you must tell me?'

'No, I—'

'I collect Jamie OK. He is in the Drawing Room. But – is a problem? I have done something—'

'No, no no. It's nothing. I just, I just, I thought we might . . .'

This is hopeless. Perhaps I should tell her the truth. Sit her down with the teapot and spill it all out. Confess it all. Confess that I am finding it difficult to find my role. That David's friends are nice but they're his friends, older, richer, different. That Juliet is lovely but she is frail and reclusive and I can't keep intruding on her. That there is generally no one else to talk to, no adult in my days – I have to wait for David to come home to have interesting conversations face to face, or ring up Jessica in London and beg for scraps of gossip about my old life. I could tell Cassie the facts. Tell her that the isolation is starting to gnaw.

But I can't say any of this: she would find it bizarre. So instead I give her a big fat smile and say, 'Well, that's great, Cassie. Everything is totally good. I wanted to make sure you're OK, that's all.'

'Oh yes!' She laughs, lifting up her earphones. 'I am fine, I happy, I OK, I have a new song, I love Awoo, you know? Lim Kim!' She laughs again, and then she warbles a couple of lines, '*Mamaligosha, Mamaligotcha . . . alway Mamaligosha!* Help me work. Miss Nina she used to say I sing too much, but I think she make a joke me. Miss Nina was very funny.'

Her earphones are replaced, she smiles again, but her smile is a little sad now, and maybe sharper at the edges. As if I am something of a disappointment after Nina, though she is far too nice to say this.

Again, the awkwardness returns. Cassie is waiting for me to go, so she can finish her chores. I return her fading smile, and then – defeated – I leave the kitchen.

There isn't much else for me to do. The house looks at me in derision. *Why don't you do some restoring?*

Buy a carpet. Make yourself useful. I stand like a frightened interloper in the hall. I must go and see Jamie, check on my stepson.

I find him soon enough, in the Yellow Drawing Room, sitting on the sofa. He does not respond as I open the door, does not move a millimetre. He is still in his school uniform, and he is intently reading a book. It looks serious for his age. A lock of dark hair falls across his forehead, a single dark feather on snow. The beauty of the boy is saddening, sometimes. I'm not sure why.

'Hello, how was school?'

At first he barely moves, then he turns my way, and frowns for a second, as if he has heard something rather puzzling about me, but hasn't entirely worked it out. Yet.

'Jamie?'

The frown persists, but he responds. 'It was OK. Thank you.'

Then he goes back to the book, ignoring me completely. I open my mouth to say something but realize I have nothing to say to my stepchild, either. I am flailing here. I don't know how to reach out, to find common ground, to form the vital bond: with anyone. I don't know how to talk to Cassie and I don't know what to say to Jamie. I might as well talk to myself.

Lingering by the bookshelves, I strain to think of a subject that might engage my stepson, but before I do, Jamie speaks.

'Why?'

But he isn't speaking to me. He is staring at the large painting on the wall opposite the sofa. It is a huge abstract, a column of horizontal slabs, of hazy, throbbing colour, blue over black over green.

I don't especially like this painting; it's the only one

of Nina's purchases of which I disapprove. The colours are beautiful and I've no doubt the painting cost thousands – but the colours are evidently meant to represent the coast, here, at Morvellan: the green fields, the blue sky, the black mine houses between. It has a dominant and foreboding quality. One day I will move it. This is my home now.

Jamie is still staring, rigidly, at the painting. Then again he says, to himself, as if I am not in the room, 'Why?'

I step closer. 'Jamie, why what?'

He doesn't turn my way. He keeps talking into nothing. 'Why? Why did you do that?'

Is he lost in some deep daydream? Something like sleepwalking? He looks perfectly conscious. Alert even. But intently focused on something I cannot perceive.

'Ah. Ah. Why. There will be lights in the Old Hall,' he says. Then he nods as if someone or something has answered his question, and then he looks at me – not directly at me, but slightly to my right – and he smiles: a flash of surprised happiness. He smiles as if there is someone nice standing *next* to me, and then he goes back to his book. Reflexively, I snap my head right, to find the person who makes Jamie smile.

I am staring at the wall. At empty space.

Of course there's no one there. It's only me and him. So why did I turn my head?

Part of me, abruptly, wants to flee. To run away. To get in my car and drive as fast as possible to London. But this is ridiculous. I am merely spooked. The hare, and now this. It is unbalancing. I'm not going to be scared by an eight-year-old boy, a soulful stepson with traumas. If I leave the Drawing Room now I will be admitting defeat.

I must stay. And if we cannot talk we can at least sit in companionable silence. That would be something. I can read in here, as he is reading. Let stepson and stepmother read together.

Crossing to the bookcase on the further side of the Drawing Room, I check the shelves. Jamie turns the pages of his book, his back to me. I can hear him flick the pages, quickly quickly.

There is a section here of Nina's books that I have not read: tall, authoritative books on historical furniture, silverware, embroideries.

I pull out one book, *The Care and Repair of Antique Furniture*, flick through it and replace it, not sure what information I am seeking. Then I try another: *Regency Interiors: a Guidebook*. Finally, I choose a third: *The Victoria and Albert Catalogue of English Woodwork, Volume IV*. But when I pull the book from the shelf, something very different comes with it, flapping to the floor.

A magazine.

It looks like a gossip magazine. Why would it be kept here? Amongst Nina's books?

Jamie is still deep in his reading. His capacity for quiet concentration impresses me. He gets it from his father.

Sitting down in one of Nina's beautifully reupholstered armchairs, I scan the cover of the magazine and my question is answered. The magazine is dated from eight years ago, and right there, at the very top, is a small box. With a photo of a glamorous couple. David and Nina.

My heartbeat quickens. I read the caption.

Nina Kerthen, eldest daughter of French banker, Sacha Valéry, proudly shows her new baby, with her husband, Cornish landowner, David Kerthen.

66

We take a look inside their historic home.

Briskly I flick through the pages. Find the relevant section.

The article's prose is silly celebrity journalese, venerating David and Nina for simply being rich and good-looking, aristocratic and lucky. The world 'elegant' is employed in almost every paragraph. It is froth and nonsense.

So why did Nina keep it? She was highly intelligent: she wouldn't usually read this stuff. My guess is that she kept it for the photos, which are good. The magazine got a proper professional to do the job. There are some night-time exteriors of Carnhallow, showing the house glowing in the dark nocturnal woods like a golden reliquary in a shadowy crypt.

The photos of David and Nina are also impressive. And one, in particular, compels. I pause as I look at it, biting my own hair, thinking, reflecting.

This photo shows Nina, in a summer dress, sitting in a satin armchair, in this very room – the Yellow Drawing Room – with angled knees pressed together. And in this one singular picture she is holding baby Jamie. This is the only photo where we see their son, despite the promise of the magazine cover.

At her side, David stands tall, slim, and dark, in a charcoal black suit, with a protective arm poised around his wife's bare, suntanned shoulder.

The photo is mysteriously perfect. I feel a sudden and powerful twinge of jealousy. Nina's shoulder is so beautiful and flawless. She is so immaculate, yet decorously sensuous. Suppressing my envy, I scrutinize the rest of the image. The baby is, for some reason, barely visible. You can only just tell that it is Jamie, lying in his

67

mother's suntanned arms. But you can very clearly see a tiny fist, reaching from white swaddling.

If my heartbeat was quickened before, now it beats faster still. Because I am getting the sense I am staring at a clue, maybe even a distressing or important clue. But a clue to what? Why should there be a clue at all? I have to fight down my bewilderment. Regain my rationality. There is *no* mystery, there is *no* reason for me to be frightened or jealous. Everything is explained. Jamie is getting better, albeit slowly. We had a good summer. I will get pregnant. I will make friends. We will be happy. The dead hare was a coincidence.

'What's that you're reading?'

Jamie is standing beside me. I didn't hear him move.

'Oh,' I say, with a flash of startled embarrassment, quickly shoving the magazine between two books. 'Only a magazine. Nothing important. Have you finished with your book? Do you want something to eat?'

He looks unhappy. Did he see the magazine in my hands? See his mother? It was daft and wrong of me to read it in here, in front of him, the grieving child. I won't do that again.

'Tell you what, I'll warm up some of that lasagne, from yesterday, remember? You said you liked it.'

He shrugs. I babble on, eager to make the most of this conversation, however staccato. I can make us all a family.

'Then we can talk, talk properly. How about a holiday next year? Would you like that? We've had such a nice summer here, but maybe next year we could go abroad, somewhere like France?'

Now I pause.

Jamie is frowning intensely.

'What's wrong, Jamie?'

He stands there, black and white in his school uniform, looking at me, and I can see the deep emotion in his eyes, showing sadness, or worse.

And then he says, 'Actually, Rachel, you should know something.'

'What?'

'I already went to France with Mummy. When I was small.'

'Oh.' Rising from the armchair, I chide myself, but I'm not sure why; there is no way I could have known about their holidays. 'Well, it doesn't have to be France, we could try Spain, or Portugal maybe, or—'

He shakes his head, interrupting. 'I think she has been staying there. In France. But now she is coming back.'

'Sorry?'

'Mummy! I can hear her.'

He is obviously troubled: the terrible grief is resurfacing again. I respond, as softly as possible, trying to find the right words, 'Jamie, don't be silly. Your mummy is not coming back. Because, well, you *know* where she is. She passed away. We've all seen the grave, haven't we? In Zennor.'

The boy looks at me long, and hard, his large eyes wet. He looks outright scared. I want to embrace him. Calm him.

Jamie shakes his head, raising his voice. 'But she *isn't*. She's not *there*. She's not in the *coffin*. Don't you know that?'

A darkness opens.

'But, Jamie—'

'They never did. They never found the body.' His voice trembles. 'She isn't in that grave. They never found her. Nobody has ever found my mummy. Ask Daddy. Ask him. She isn't buried in Zennor.'

Before I can reply, he runs out of the room. I hear his footsteps down the hall, then the same light boyish steps, running up the Grand Staircase. To his bedroom, presumably. And I am left here alone, in the beautiful Yellow Drawing Room. Alone with the intolerable idea that Jamie has placed in my mind.

Pacing across the room I find my laptop, lying on the walnut sidetable. Wrenching it open, I hesitate, take a deep breath, and then urgently type into the search engine: 'death Nina Kerthen'.

I've never done this before: because there seemed no need. David told me Nina was dead. He described the tragic accident: *Nina fell down the shaft at Morvellan.* It was awful. I even went to see her grave in Zennor churchyard, with its poignant epitaph: *This is the light of the mind.*

My curiosity ended there. I didn't want to know anything more, it was all too sad. I wanted a brand-new life with my brand-new husband, unblemished by the past.

My fingers tremble as I scroll the page and click on a couple of likely websites. Local news reports. Neatly cached.

No body has been found.
Divers are still searching, but nothing has been discovered.
The body was never found.

Slamming the laptop shut, I stare through the lead diamonds of Carnhallow's windows: into the green-grey autumn evening, the black trees of Ladies Wood. Gazing deep into the gloom.

Jamie is right. They never found the body.

Yet there is a grave in Zennor. Complete with epitaph.

70

109 Days Before Christmas

Morning

It must be the most beautiful supermarket view in Britain. The new Sainsbury's, looking out over Mount's Bay. To my right is the crowded and steepled town of Penzance, the marina bobbing with boats and activity. On my left is the softly curving coast, disappearing towards the Lizard. And directly in front of me is the tidal island of St Michael's Mount, surrounded by vast and shining sands, topped by its medieval castle, comical yet romantic.

There is a coffee shop on the first floor, overlooking the bay. When I come here I always order a skinny cappuccino, and then I step past the dentured pensioners nibbling their pastries and sit outside at the metal tables even when it is cold, as it is today. Cold but sunny, with clouds gathering far to the west, like a rumour.

My coffee sits on the table, neglected this morning, because I have my mobile phone pressed to my ear. David is on the other end. Listening to me, patiently. I am trying very hard not to raise my voice. Trying not

71

to alert the pensioners. *Ooh, look at her, that's the woman who married David Kerthen . . .*

'So, again, why didn't you tell me? About the body?'

'We've been over this already.'

'I know. But think of me as an idiot. I need to hear it several times to understand. Tell me again in small words, David. Why?' I know this is difficult for him. But it is surely more difficult for me.

He answers. 'As I said, because it's not the sort of thing you chat about on a romantic date, is it? Oh, my wife is dead but the body is trapped in a mine, shall we have another drink?'

'Hmm.'

Maybe he has a point, yet I still feel *angry*. Or perhaps unnerved. Now it is in my head I can't get rid of the mental image. The gruesome idea of a body, preserved in icy minewater. Mouth and eyes open, suspended in lightless clarity, and staring into the silence of the drowned corridors, under the rocks of Morvellan.

David is very silent. I can sense his restrained impatience, along with his eagerness to calm me. He is a husband, but he also has a busy job, and he wants to get back to work. But I have more questions.

'Were you worried that I might not move here? Into Carnhallow, if I knew they never found her?'

A pause. 'No. Not really.'

'*Not really*?'

'Well, perhaps. Maybe there was a *slight* reluctance. It's not something I like to dwell on. I want to forget all that, I want us to be *us*. I love you, Rachel, and I hope and believe you are in love with me. I didn't want the tragedies of the past to have any bearing on our future.'

For the first time this morning I feel a twinge of

sympathy for him. Possibly I am overdoing it. After all, he lost a wife, and he has a grieving son. And what would I have done in his situation?

'I do kind of understand,' I say. 'And I love you, David. You know that, you surely know that. But—'

'Look, hold on, I'm sorry, darling – I have to take this call.'

The moment I am coming to terms with all this, the agitation returns. David has put me on hold. For the second time this morning.

I tried calling him last night after I discovered the truth about Nina, but his secretary patiently told me he was in some endless, mega-important meeting, until 10 p.m. Then he simply turned his phone off without responding to my many messages. He does that sometimes when he is tired. And normally I don't mind: his job is hard, if well rewarded, and the hours are insane.

Last night, I *minded*. I was shaking with fury as I kept reaching voicemail. *Answer. The. Phone.* This morning he finally picked up. And he has been dealing with me ever since, like a store manager with a furious customer.

As I wait for him to come back on line, I gaze at that view. It seems less appealing today.

My husband returns. 'Hi, sorry, that damn guy from Standard Chartered, they've got some crisis, he wouldn't let me go.'

'Great, so glad you've got more important people to talk to. More important things than this.'

His sigh is heartfelt. 'Darling, what can I say? I totally messed up, I know I messed up. But I did it for the best reasons—'

'Serious?'

'Truly. I've never deliberately deceived anyone.'

73

I want to believe him, I want to understand. This is the man I love. Yet now there are secrets.

He continues, his voice smooth, 'To be perfectly honest, I also presumed you might know much of it already. Nina's death was in the papers.'

'But I don't read the bloody papers! Novels, yes. Papers never.'

I am nearly shouting. I must stop. I can see a pensioner with a cinnamon whirl on her plate, looking at me through the glass walls. Nodding, as if she knows what's going on.

'Rachel?'

I lower my voice. 'People my age don't read news-papers, David. You must get that, no? And I had no idea who you were till I met you at that gallery. You might be a famous Cornish family. But, I'm from Plumstead. Sarf London. And I read Snapchat. Or Twitter.'

'OK.' He sounds genuinely mortified. 'Again, I'm truly sorry. If you want to know the brutal details, it's prob-ably all online now, you can still find it.'

I let him hang on, for a second. Then, 'I know. I printed everything out, last night. The pages are in my bag, right here.'

A pause. 'You did? So why are you cross-examining me, like this?'

'Because I wanted to hear your explanation first. Give you a chance. Hear your evidence.'

He allows himself a small, mournful laugh. 'Well, now you've heard my evidence, Justice Daly. May I please step down from the witness box?'

David is trying to charm me. Some part of me wants to be charmed. I reckon I am prepared to let him go, after he has answered one last important question. 'Why is there a grave, David? If there is no body, why a grave?'

His answer is calm, and his voice is sad. 'Because we had to give Jamie some closure. He was so bitterly confused, Rachel, he still is sometimes, as we know. His mother hadn't just died, her body had *disappeared,* been spirited away. He was bewildered. Kept asking where she'd gone, when Mummy was coming back. We had to have a funeral anyway, so why not have a grave? A place for her son to come and mourn.'

'But,' I feel prurient, yet I have to know. 'What's *in* the grave?'

'The coat. The last thing she wore, that coat with her blood, from the mine. Read the report, from the inquest. And also a few of her favourite things. Books. Jewellery. You know.'

He has fairly and candidly answered my questions. I sit back. Half relieved, half creeped out. A body. Under the house, in the tunnels that stretch under the sea. But how many bodies are already down there, how many drowned miners? Why should another be any different?

'Look, David, I know I've been pretty hard on you, it's like, well – it was a shock. That's all.'

'I understand entirely,' he says. 'I only wish you hadn't found out this way. How is Jamie, anyway?'

'He's all right, I think, he calmed down after that outburst. He seemed fine this morning. Quiet, but fine. I drove him to football practice. Cassie's picking him up.'

'He is getting used to you, Rachel. He is. But, as I say, he's still confused. Look, I have to go. We can speak later.'

We say our goodbyes, and I slip the phone in my pocket.

A sea wind from Marazion, laced with the tang of salt, ruffles the printed pages as I take them out of my

75

bag and set them on the table. There is a lot of information: I googled and printed for an hour.

Nina Kerthen's death was, as David said, definitely a news story. It even got as far as some national papers for a day or two. And it filled the local press for weeks. And yet, it seems, there wasn't that much to it.

It is believed Nina Kerthen had been drinking on the night in question. There is no suspicion of foul play.

Foul play. The antiquated phrase, from the *Falmouth Packet*, conjures ghoulish, fairytale images of a dark man in a long cloak. A Venetian assassin, grasping a beautiful woman, and throwing her in the canal. I see a pale face staring up through the watery grey. Veiled with darkening liquid, then gone.

More pages flutter in the wind. Even the southerly breezes are fanged with freshening cold, today. Distracted for a moment, I gaze out.

There is a lone man walking the flooding sands out past Long Rock. Walking aimlessly, in circles, apparently lost. Or looking for something that he will surely never find. Abruptly he turns and stares my way, as if he senses he is being watched. A strange panic fills me, a quick and sharpened fear.

I calm my anxieties. Hints of my past. Turning back to the pages, I read on. I need to know all this detail, nail it down in my mind.

The initial idea of a murder was journalistically appealing. At the time of her death the newspapers spiced their reports with the delicious possibility of homicide.

The questions were never asked outright, but clearly they hung in the air: the captions are unwritten but the meaning is implicit. *Take a look at this. Isn't David Kerthen a bit too handsome, a bit too rich, a man you want to hate? A potential killer of his beautiful wife?*

When all this was ruled out, early on, the national papers gave up, while the local journalists turned, with a rather forlorn optimism, to speculations of suicide. Who would go to a mineshaft in the dark? Why take the silly risk, on a cold christmas evening?

Unfortunately for the local press, the coroner was prosaic in his verdict.

I sip my cold coffee as I scan the coroner's summation for the third time.

It was a clear moonlit night: December twenty-eighth. Nina was seen by Juliet Kerthen, David's mother, walking down the valley and along the cliffs, in the vicinity of the mine stacks, as she sometimes used to do, to clear her head. She had been drinking that night, with the family.

Her actions were not unusual: the area around the mine houses was a fine place to take in the spectacular view: of the brutish sea, raging at the rocky cliffs below. Especially on a bright moonlit night.

But when Nina did not return, the alarm was raised. At first it was presumed she had merely got lost, down a path, in the dark. As her absence lengthened, speculation grew more negative. Perhaps she had fallen down one of the cliffs. Bosigran, maybe. Or Zawn Hanna. No one imagined she had actually fallen down Jerusalem Shaft: she knew the dangers well enough. But then, amidst the confusion, Juliet spoke up, and made the suggestion. *Search Morvellan.* That was the last place she was seen, after all: walking near the mineheads.

And it had been raining heavily in the preceding days.

77

And the mine houses were unroofed. And she was wearing heeled shoes.

The little search party – David and Cassie – made for the Shaft House, where the door was found ajar. David turned his torch-beam down the shaft. The watered pit revealed no body, but it did offer up one significant and melancholy piece of evidence. Nina's raincoat, floating in the water. Nina had been wearing that coat. She had surely, horrifically, fallen down the pit, then thrown off the coat as she struggled to save herself. But she had nonetheless succumbed. A person would swiftly freeze in those icy waters, then sink beneath them.

The raincoat was initial and crucial evidence. Two days after the accident, divers retrieved traces of blood and splintered fingernails from the brickwork of the shaft, above the black water. They also found strands of broken hair. The DNA was matched with Nina Kerthen: it was her blood, these were her broken fingernails, this was her hair. Here was the evidence of her desperate attempts to climb out of the mine, of her doomed and failing struggle to get out of the watered shaft. Evidence that could not be faked or planted.

Taken with the eyewitness evidence from Juliet Kerthen it seemed conclusive. The coroner delivered his verdict of accidental death. Nina Kerthen was drunk, her judgement was marred, and she therefore drowned, after falling down the Jerusalem Shaft of Morvellan Mine. Her body had sunk in the freezing water and would probably never be retrieved: lost as it was in the unnumbered tunnels and adits of the undersea mine, shifted by unknowable tides and currents. Trapped beneath Carnhallow and Morvellan, for ever.

I shiver, profoundly. The wind off the bay is cutting

up, and venomed with hints of rain. I need to do my tasks, and get back to the house. Binning my empty cup, I go downstairs and do my shopping and the shopping is done in seventeen minutes. It is one advantage of my frugality, born of my impoverished upbringing. A relic of Rachel Daly, from south-east London. I rarely get distracted in supermarkets.

Spinning the car on to the main road, I take a last look at St Michael's Mount, where a shaft of September sun is shining on the subtropical garden of the St Levans, a family five hundred years *younger* than the Kerthens.

Then the clouds open, and the sun shines on us all. And I realize what I need to do. I believe David's answers, but Jamie still needs help. My own stepson unnerves me, and that has to be explained: I need to read him, to decipher him, to understand. Maybe David doesn't need to know any more. But I do.

102 Days Before Christmas

Afternoon

It's taken me a week to pluck up the courage to come
in here. David's study. Where I will maybe learn more
about Jamie. My husband has come and gone from
London, the days have come and gone, palpably shortening now, I've done the school runs and talked to the
gardener and read my books on marquetry, carpentry,
and masonry, and I have hesitated maybe twelve times
in front of this imposing door.

The house is deserted. Jamie is still at school; Cassie
has gone shopping. Juliet is with friends for the day, in
St Ives. I have an hour at least. So now I must do it. I
know I am, arguably, going behind David's back, but
the grief in this house is too intense for me to keep
asking questions, directly. That way is too painful for
everyone. So I must be more subtle. Discreet.

A fine but angled autumn sun makes a rich amber
patch of light on the polished floorboards. These boards
creak as I step forward, and open the door.

I've only been in this spacious, cedar-scented room

three or four times before, and always in David's presence. Now I gaze about, in faint but definite awe. There are several ancient portraits on the wood-panelled walls. Clumsy, vernacular portraits of patriarchal Kerthens: portraits of rich men who could only commission very provincial painters.

I know the biggest and darkest of these portraits shows Jago Kerthen, the man who sank the Jerusalem Shaft in the 1720s. He had a reputation, David says, for severity, if not brutality. Damning men to death down risky pits, urging them on through day and night, his troops of willing Cornishmen with their tallow candles glued on to their little hats. Jago Kerthen's pale blue eyes glint with avarice in the gold-framed portrait: however clumsy the artist, he caught that look well enough. Yet it was Jago Kerthen's appalling greed that turned the Kerthen thousands into millions in the early eighteenth century.

David has positioned the portrait so that it stares out of the tall sash window, down the last of Carnhallow Valley to the just-visible blackness of Morvellan Mine. And then onwards, to the shimmering wastes of the sea. The greedy and violent Jago Kerthen is staring at the very same mine he sank into the granite.

I've no doubt this positioning is deliberate.

The rest of the room is also very David. A couple of fine abstract paintings, possibly even a Mondrian. The floor is softened by some of those Azeri rugs David likes, apparently superior to Turkish or Persian rugs. As I look down, I can hear him airily explaining, as is his wont, 'Oh, them, yes, the rugs, I bought them in Baku.'

Dominating the room is a large desk, solidly built, and clearly old. I walk closer, swallowing my sense of impropriety, the sense that I shouldn't be here. Prying.

A brand new Apple laptop, firmly closed, sits right next to military memorabilia, from all the Kerthens who went to England's wars: there are medals with faded sashes, from the Crimean and Peninsular wars, and beside them a rusty old revolver with mud still visible in its metalwork – probably, I'm guessing, from the First World War. Then a long, gleaming sword with a gilded hilt. Looking close, I see that it is engraved *Harry St John Tresillian Kerthen, Paardeburg, 1900.*

On the other side of this big desk there are three photos. Paired together is a tilted photo of me and David – and one of Nina and David. Both photos taken at our respective weddings. I try not to compare them: the swaying beauty of her wedding dress compared to my humble summer frock, the sense of grandeur in Nina's glamorous nuptials compared to my modest London party. I resist the urge to slap the photo of Nina face down on the desktop.

The third silver-framed photo is of Jamie, aged four or five, laughing unselfconsciously in the sunlit kitchen here at Carnhallow. It is a poignant, lovely image: Jamie is looking at his beloved mother, almost off-camera, who has apparently made him laugh. He looks piercingly happy, in a way I have never witnessed. I have never seen this laughing, happy boy, the untroubled son before his mother's death.

The sense of loss throbs, in this study, like a reopened wound at the heart of Carnhallow. And I feel like *I* am the shard in the flesh. Renewing the hurt.

And yet I am doing this for the best reason: helping Jamie. So I will carry on. Crossing the room, I examine the bookshelves. I know, from being here before, that one of these shelves is dedicated to Jamie: it holds everything from his school reports to his football rosettes. The last time I was in here with David I saw him take out Jamie's medical records.

I run my hand along the shelf. A school photo. Some exercise books. Vaccination records. Blood type, A. Birth certificate, 3 March. Gold star for English, Year 2. I pause at an untitled folder, then pull it out, and open it up.

There's not much in here. A few loose pages with some childish writing. Yet, as I read on, I am choked with unexpected emotion as I realize that I am holding Jamie's letters to his dead mother.

Dear mummy
I am riting this because the therappist in the hospittal says it is good if I rite to you now you are dead. I miss you mummy. You were funny wen you put sand on yor nose in France when we went on holliday. Every day I think of you after you fel down
~~Since you~~
Lots of things hapend some of them were very sad and daddy went away a lot ~~like~~ and he says he misses you to. I have a new pencil case now mummy.
After you fel in the water granny ~~tolld said~~ sayed you were on a very long holiday and I askd somewere like France and she says Yes. But daddy sayed you are not comeing back and granny sed a ly and you were dead and not comeing back.
I have a lift the flap book
~~After you~~
Today we lernt about dinosaurs ubdcefalus had a bony club on its tail for swinging at enemys.
Today we did litteracy here are my Sentences
can you hear me singing?
Did you ever see me kicking?

84

I am jumping.
I am starting to jump
I am lifting.
I'm shifting a table.
I'm crying.
I am flying in the air.

The man in the hospittal says I must talk to you mummy in my letters but sometimes it makes me ~~verry~~ sad and I remember the hollidays. Do you remember them mummy?

My best day with you and daddy was wen we went to France. Me and daddy went up a lighthouse then we went to the Shops with you and we got some mashmalows and delicous hot choclit. When we got back we toasted them on the fire. then I was going to have dinner but instead We went on a boat to go to another house to stay in. I was so amazed. Evryone was happy.

~~After you died~~

Mummy it rained a lot since Cristmas now you are not here. I got some wellys. Then I splashed puddles with daddy then we made lasanya and watched that film you liked again. Daddy cryed a little bit it is the onley time I have seen daddy cry he doesnt cry and he told me it was because I was alone like him. and he said sorry to me and mummy loved me I musnnt dout this ~~and~~

~~Why did you say that about Cristmas~~

Why did you

Anyway now I must go granny says we are having macarrony and cheese for tea. I hope you have a dog in heaven as you mite be lonely to

I love you mummy. I want you to come back

85

*but you cant come back because you are dead
daddy says. I miss you every day are you in the
ground so deep no one can get you even with a
bulldozer*

Jamie

The letter trembles in my hand. It has dark spots on
it. I think they may be dried tears.

There are two more letters. Shorter. The writing is
better in these; this is Jamie a little older, I think. I have
to lean close to look at the words – then I realize the
room has grown very dim. A glance at the window
shows me that rainclouds have raced across the sky, in
that startling Cornish way, turning day into darkness.
The impatient fingernails of rain tap the windowpane.
I reach across and switch on David's angular brass desk
lamp, then read on.

Dear Mummy

*Daddy said I must stop riting to you cos it
makes me upset. He said this in case you got angry
and I was worried you wud came back as a ghost
wich wud be very scarry.*

Ghost

*I dont want to stop riting to you because I can
imagin you in my head when I rite. You used to
kiss me on the nose to make things better ~~France~~*

*Mummy I remember it was Cristmas and
evryone was drinking their drinks and geting
louder and louder. Im sorry and daddy said it was
your fault and I ran out I cant rite it down I am
sorry you died I am sorry if*

86

Saturd

Here are the sentences we did yesterday
I'm liking my book exceptionally
I am not going swimming today it is too boring
I'm hoping I will see my mummy once more
I'm taking a toy robot to school
I'm guessing you haven't got a dog
Daddy is shaving
Mummy is waving

Mummy some nites I dream of you floting in the water. Someone at school said that bodys come back will you come back? They say that if you drowned in the sea then your body would be washed up on rocks like a starfish why weren't you washed up at Morvelan like a starfish?
~~Bleeding~~
~~THEY CUT YOUR FINGERTIP OFF~~
~~BLOOD IN THE~~
Fizzy drinks are bad for you and I remember at Critsmas I gave you a fizzy drink and I thought it was my falt you were dead and they buryd your coat but I don't think this any more.
I listen to the sea it sounds like a big man breathing, a big scarry man and mummy in the darkness and the blackness. I have fritening dreams about you with no fingers to Im sorry. you are smiling

Jamie xxxXXXxxx

One more letter to go. One more is enough. This final letter looks to be the most recent, the handwriting is significantly improved. I can see my name in the first paragraph, this letter must have been written after I entered his life.

Leaning closer to David's desk lamp, I take up the notepaper, and read.

Dear Mummy
Daddy's new wife is here now and her name is Rachel Daly but she is now a Kerthen like you and me and Daddy. Are you angry with her for taking ~~yor~~ your place? Don't be she is nice she teaches me photography but she is not my mummy YOU are my mummy.

Sometimes I do not like to look at the mine where you fell down Mummy I know you are alive and alright now but the mines friten me. They look like monsters. Rachel is sad sometimes she laughs a lot but then she looks unhappy.

I remember when you were sad a lot before the ~~accident~~ fall. When Daddy and then you said what you said I wont tell anyone?

Today at school Miss Anderson showed us pictures of heaven but I do not think I believe in heaven any more because I used to think you lived in heaven with grandad. But now you arent in heaven you are in the house at night so how does that work? Did you swim in the mine and climb out?

Yesterday we had swimming. I can do front crawl and back crawl but I can't do butterfly. It is very hard. You swam a long way in France when you went on and on and Daddy was laughing and saying you were swimming to England because you want to get away from us.

88

~~Wish you ha~~
~~I loved you just as much as daddy, I am sorry~~
I learned a story about penguins. There are penguins in Antartica that spend all the winter looking after the baby penguins. It is very cold so cold your eyes turn into ice and then you have to wear gogles. The penguins looking after the little penguins are daddy penguins. The wind blows and blows and blows and the daddy penguins keep the baby penguin warm with there fluffy feathers. Then after ages they see the mummy penguins. they thought the mummy penguins were dead but then they see the mummy penguins come back through the wind and the snow and they are happy. The mummy penguins always come back.

We are going to go to a castle this weekend and have a picnic with Daddy and Rachel. But it may be raining so we may stay in but I think it will be sunny. Today it is hot and we went swimming me and Daddy and Rachel at zawn hana and Mummy you were there in my head and then I saw you in the house.

I miss you lots and lots like wisky shots thats what Daddy says and I am going to go to sleep now. Bye bye

Jamie xxx

Carefully, I slip the letters back into the folder, and replace the folder on the shelf. Cassie will surely be back soon with Jamie, and Juliet too. I do not want to be caught in here, even though it is my own house. And I do not want anyone to suspect I was snooping.

Making my way around the study, I straighten anything

I might have disturbed. Then I pause at the window and follow Jago Kerthen's gaze down the darkened, rain-streaked valley to the mines and the cliffs and the sea.

What do these letters tell me? They tell me that Jamie is deeply confused, on a level I had not suspected. They tell me that I am possibly not helping, even though he seems to like me, or tolerate me, at the same time. They tell me that his grief is pure and ceaseless, that he is suffering deeply; they tell me it is my duty to help this poor boy in any way I can.

They also tell me one final thing. There were arguments that night Nina died. Arguments that were bad enough for Jamie to remember them.

Yet there were no arguments mentioned in the inquest.

What do I do with this information? Approach David? That would mean revealing that I have been sleuthing around his study. Sifting through his private papers.

My thoughts are brought to a stop by a piercing scream.

Evening

I turn off the desk lamp and run to the door, the anxiety tight and fierce in my chest.

'Please, someone!' Juliet yells. 'Someone come!'

The corridor outside the study is empty. It runs down to the New Hall. Then I see a figure emerging at the end – Jamie. In his school uniform. They all came back to Carnhallow and I didn't even notice? I was so absorbed in his letters.

'Rachel! It's the Old Hall,' cries Jamie, looking my way. 'Granny, I heard her, heard her shouting.' His face is pale, his lip trembling. 'It's coming from the Old Hall. Please come!'

I follow him, running so fast the floorboards squeak in pain. I turn the cast-iron handle of the Old Hall. The tall lancet windows show grey-black clouds, like night has fallen early. All the light is coming from within the room itself. A shaking orange light that makes shadows dance along the walls.

Because the floor is etched with lines of fire. Patterns

and whorls, loops and lines, of urgent low flame, like a maze of meaningful cracks has appeared in the flagstones, and the burning mines beneath can now be seen, fingers of fire reaching up, inside, clawing into the house. Juliet is flapping at the horrible flames with a jacket, panicked, nearly in tears.

'My God. What is this, what is this?' Her voice is hoarse with alarm. 'I only came in here for a short-cut, out of the rain. I hate this room. I never come here normally because of all that, and them, and then' – she points – 'then I found this, found this all here, these people, who did this, why did she do this?'

Desperate, I begin to stamp out the flames. But it is difficult. The lines of fire are small but fierce and persistent, and somehow all the more sinister for that. Like a modest display of a much greater power, designed to frighten and threaten: *See what I can do.* There is a smell of petrol in the air, along with smoke, and maybe something else. A perfume?

'Jamie, help me, help your granny.'

He does nothing. He has gone around the maze of little flames and is staring rapt from the other side of the Hall at this flickering display. This smoky light that makes our own shadows lurch around us, palsied, quivering.

Juliet flaps, haplessly, at the flames once more. They are beginning to die of their own accord. Their job done, perhaps. Then she whispers to me, 'She did this. Nina did this.'

Jamie is standing there, smiling and amazed. He predicted this. He told me in the Drawing Room. *There will be lights in the Old Hall.*

No, this is absurd. It is some joke.

Walking around the lines of licking flame, I place a

comforting arm over his shoulder. Then I look at the fiery pattern from his perspective. And now I realize maybe why he is amazed, or scared, or shocked. The dancing lines of yellow fire are not haphazardly arranged. They spell out a burning word.

MUMMY.

82 Days Before Christmas

Evening

David stood at the window, sipping from his tumbler of Macallan, listening to the undergrads laughing on their way home from university, through the ghosts of evening mist. Usually, he liked this time of year, the sense of quickening intellect, under yellowing leaves. But tonight the youth of these students reminded him merely of his advance into middle age, and their happiness emphasized his regret.

Jamie.

Back at his desk, he set down his Scotch, opened his laptop screen and dialled the number, checking the time as he did.

Six o'clock: their regular slot.

His son's face came online.

'Hold the phone up, Jamie. I can't see you.'

'Sorry, Dad. Is that better now?'

'Yes. Yes, that's better.'

David scanned the screen, looking at his son's bedroom. Football posters. Neat bookshelves. A black microscope,

95

hunched like Nosferatu, sitting on a desk. To the right was the window, overlooking the lawns, where you could look down the long slope, all the way to the mines and cliffs. The sky in Cornwall looked brighter than the brooding London clouds here in Bloomsbury.

'Nice evening down there?'

Jamie shrugged, his expression blank. Then he looked away from the screen as if hearing something, in the house.

'Jamie?'

'Sorry. Yes, Daddy. It was really sunny today. Me and Rollo played three and in.'

'Good. That's good.'

'Then we went down to the zawn and played skimming and stuff. It was nice and there was a seal.'

'Ah. I wish I'd been there.'

'Hmm, yeah.'

'I do, Jamie. I really do.'

David stared into his son's expressive eyes and felt the flowering despair. It should be him, the father, skimming stones with his son, not Rollo all the time; it should be him playing football on the lawn, laughing in the cool, mild air of a fine October twilight. But he wasn't there. He was seldom *there*. He was missing far too much of Jamie's childhood. The sensation of this – missing his son's ascent to adulthood – made David feel queasy at the grievous waste. Liquid silver was running into a drain. The boy was growing up and David was missing the last precious years of childhood, as he had missed the years before.

'Are you all right, Daddy?'

'Yes, yes. I was thinking.' He forced a smile. 'So how are things with Rachel? Have you said sorry?'

'Sorry for what, Daddy?'

'For playing that trick, that joke, with the fires, and the lighter fuel.'

David waited, inwardly praying that this time Jamie would confess: that if he casually asked him, like this, the boy would finally yield.

'I didn't do any joke, Daddy. I told you. I didn't! Maybe it was Cassie, or Granny, not me. Maybe it was Rachel, she does funny things, she acts funny sometimes. She can be weird.'

'Jamie – please.'

'Daddy, I didn't do it!'

The boy looked sincere enough. Face eager, pained, truthful; but David was wholly convinced that Jamie had done it. Because Jamie was surely reliving in his turbulent mind an incident from his childhood. When Jamie's sixth birthday had come around, Nina had done this: written Jamie's name in fire on the floor of the Old Hall, as a surprise, like the entire floor was a massive birthday cake and he could make eight hundred wishes. His mother always loved open flames: bonfires, hearth-fires, candles.

David remembered Jamie's cry of delight when the trick was pulled, when his son was ushered, blindfold, into the Old Hall, then the blindfold was whipped away, revealing the flaming words, *Happy Birthday Jamie*, written in fire on flagstone – and then Jamie turned and found all his friends hiding in the darkness, and giggling, and then behind them trestle tables of saffron cakes, and fresh lemonade, and sticks of celery and apple. *That was the best birthday party ever, thank you, Mummy, thank you, Daddy.*

That kind of precious memory would stick with a child. It had stuck with David. The happiness that could never return, the last real happiness they'd known as a family. It was perhaps not surprising Jamie had re-enacted this scene, trying to summon his mother back,

97

by doing a kind of childish fire-magic. Write my name in light and I will reappear.

Yet still the boy wouldn't admit it.

Jamie's face was set firmly in the negative, now. A stubborn, faintly arrogant tilt of the chin. That Kerthen expression.

David sighed.

'OK, we'll talk about it another time.'

Jamie nodded, uncaringly – then offered a tight little frown. 'Can I ask you a question, Dad?'

'Sure. Of course you can. Shoot.'

'Do you love Rachel?'

David had been expecting this question for a while, so he had an answer ready to go.

'Yes. Naturally. That's why I married her. That's why she is here. Or there. In Carnhallow.'

'OK. And, Dad,' Jamie hesitated. 'Do you love Rachel as much as you loved Mummy?'

'No, it's different, Jamie – quite different to that. I will never love someone the way I loved your mother.'

'And do you miss Mummy?'

'Absolutely, Jamie. Every day. We all do. But daddies can get lonely too.'

Jamie nodded, but looked rather melancholy at the same time. David yearned to reach his arm around his son's slender shoulders, give the boy a reassuring hug. But they were at either end of the country. So he reached out by talking.

'Just because Rachel has moved in with us, that doesn't mean anything about the way I loved your mother. It doesn't take anything away from the past.'

'All right, Dad. I understand.' Jamie did a teenagerish sigh, then glanced to the side. 'I'm going to tell Cassie I'll be down soon, she's calling, for supper—'

The boy rested his phone on the desk, so that it was staring at a blank ceiling, a rectangle of pinked whiteness, lit by the setting sun. David could imagine the scene, the view from the house over Zawn Hanna, a dazzle of dying sunlight turning Morvellan black, against the faded gold of the twilit sea.

David checked the clock. He had another file to go through: he had to go back to work shortly. He was too busy even to have a proper phone call with his own child, his grieving son, wrestling with traumas and confusions, and his father's terrible mistakes.

The guilt returned, triumphant. For all his efforts, David was doing what he had once vowed never to do. Reiterating his own father's cruelties.

David's father had deliberately excluded him from their non-existent family life, by sending him to boarding school. Now David's job excluded him from Jamie's life, as he slaved in London, trying to repair the damage his own father had done. The only son was left alone. Again.

It was as if they were destined, as a family, to recycle the same cruelty in every generation. As if Jamie's fate was revenge taken by all those boys sent down the mines. *This is what you made us do, decade after decade, now you Kerthens must suffer the same.*

How had it come to this? It wasn't for lack of paternal love. Sitting here in the calm, orderly silence of his London flat, David recalled his own ferocious happiness when he first held Jamie as a baby: a happiness so great it encompassed a significant element of sadness, within. He remembered a striking phrase his mother had used for parents of newborns, of firstborns, their conflicting sensibilities: *Your heart is cut by a thousand shards of happy glass.*

99

It was painfully true. The happy glass entered your heart when you had a kid and it never went away: needling anxiety, pinpricks of worry and, occasionally, a lancing, inexpressible joy, a happiness so intense you knew that, when you died, this was how you would judge and remember your life: this was what you would think about on your deathbed. Not your career or your accomplishments, not your partners, not sex, not how many cars or wives or holidays or millions you had, but how you had done with your kids. Was I a good father? And were there enough of those diamond-hard, dazzling moments of paternal and filial happiness?

'Daddy.'

Jamie was back.

'Yes. Hi there.'

'Sorry, Cassie wanted something and I had to fetch it.'

'That's fine. But, well, I've got to go myself, soon. Work.'

The boy flinched. Was that a flash of anger, or disgust?

'You're busy?'

'I am. I'm sorry. I am busy, but if I get it all done now, then I promise not to work at the weekend.'

'You said that last weekend, when you came down. But you looked at your phone the whole time.'

David inwardly blushed at the truth of this. Then he remembered his concerns, what he'd wanted to ask, during this phone call. 'Jamie?'

'Yeah?'

'You said something about Rachel. You said Rachel can be weird.'

'Yeah.'

'Why did you say that?'

''Cause, Daddy. 'Cause she can, she can, she asks me things. And she looks for things, in the house.'

David scowled, but tried to hide it. 'Things?'

100

'Things, and stuff. Things that have happened, are happening.'

David calmed himself. He had to do this firmly, but without alarming his son.

'Jamie, she is trying her best to fit. You have to cut her some slack. She's the one who has to adopt our lifestyle, become part of *our* family, and she's trying very hard, getting to know Carnhallow, that's why she asks questions, or maybe seems uneasy. But' – he leaned closer to the screen – 'you do remember our promise, about the past? What we agreed.'

Jamie's eyes widened, though he surely knew what David was talking about.

'C'mon, Jamie. You remember. You have to remember.'

'Yes, Daddy, I know. Don't like talking about it.'

'I know, it's difficult and sad. But I need to stress this again. You mustn't *ever* talk about what happened, that night, anything anyone said, what you saw. You mustn't talk about it, about that night. Agreed? It's like the therapist, exactly the same. Even if someone questions you, if *anyone* questions you, say nothing. Even to Rachel.'

'Nnn.' Jamie shrugged, as if this was nothing at all, or something he was about to ignore.

'Jamie!'

'OK, Daddy, yes!'

Jamie sipped at a can of drink. San Pellegrino. His blue-violet eyes were beautiful, even when seen through a laptop screen. The boy spoke:

'Daddy I have my own question, before you go.'

David smiled, in a fake way, as if everything was made good.

'Of course. Ask anything you like. I know I'm not there much – but I'm always here for you, on the phone, on the screen, always, always.'

'OK, Dad.'

A long pause. Jamie looked nervous.

The light was beginning to fade.

'Jamie? What was your question?'

The boy sighed. And shrugged. He seemed to be wrestling with some dilemma. Finally, he spoke: 'Daddy, is Mummy still alive?'

David gazed, wordless, at his son. He hoped he was mishearing.

But Jamie was now looking directly at his father. Expecting an answer.

Groping for words, David did his best. 'Jamie, mate, she's dead. Your mummy is dead. You know that.'

Jamie was unmoved. The boy shook his head. 'But, Daddy, aren't we meant to see things some people don't see? Because we're fire people? Aren't we meant to be more special, the Kerthens? Because of the legend?'

'No, Jamie. No. That's just a joke, a childish story. Something to amuse people down from London.'

The irony was complex, and bitter. How many times had David told the story to laughing guests, in Carnhallow House? All too many. Because of his Kerthen pride. Because it was another subtle way of parading his lineage, of saying, *This is how noble and ancient we are: we have myths and legends.* Now that vainglory had come back to hurt.

Jamie's eyes were glistening. 'I know it sounds like a story, but it's true, Daddy. True. Sometimes I know she's close again, near me, talking to me, in my sleep, or in the day, in the rooms. It's frightening sometimes. But she is here, she's coming back.'

'Jamie. This is silly. This is nonsense.'

'It's not. I don't think so, Daddy. She is still alive.

102

Everyone says she's dead, but they never found her body, did they? So she must be still here, that's why I can feel her. That's why you made me write to her.'

David closed his eyes, for a second. Quelling his anger. The stupid therapist at Treliske Hospital, with his idiotic questions, his stupid idea of writing letters to a dead mother. What had he done to his son? Letters were disturbing and blurring. Questions were worse.

'Hey.' David sought his son's unhappy gaze. 'Jamie. Mate. Come on. We have to deal with it. Mummy fell down the mine and she isn't coming back. I know it is very sad and confusing, but just because they didn't find the body doesn't mean she can return to life. OK? OK? And the Kerthens aren't special in any creepy or superstitious sense, we're just old. An old family. That's all.'

Jamie was still, evidently, trying not to cry. David gazed on, helpless. *Please let my son be sane.* Why had all this fresh confusion emerged *now*? It came and went, but this was worse than ever. Much worse.

'Jamie. You know I love you. If there's anything you want to tell me, you know you can do that, you can say anything. But Mummy is gone and you have a new stepmother now. We have a new life, a new chance. We have to move on.'

Jamie nodded miserably and reached for his drink. David checked the clock again; if he didn't get to work soon he'd be stuck at the meeting tomorrow. He'd have to deal with this at the weekend, when he went down.

'Jamie, mate, I do have to go. I'm really sorry. But I'll see you guys at the weekend and we can talk then.'

'Mmnnn.'

'Jamie, say goodbye properly.'

But the screen died: Jamie had turned it off first,

103

without saying goodbye. Like a reproach. Like a punishment that David deserved. The bad father. The absent father. Most of all, the lying father.

David picked up his whisky and regarded the depths of tawny liquid, glowing in the glass. Now that he thought about it, now that he focused on the facts, like a good lawyer, Jamie's distance, his odd behaviour, had distinctly returned since the summer. Specifically since Rachel had moved in.

Perhaps it was coincidence? Or maybe it was because she had upset the precious equilibrium he had painstakingly established, in the year following Nina's fall. By asking her questions. *Acting all weird. Looking for things in the house.*

From nowhere, David felt, for the very first time, a flux of fierce resentment at his young wife. He'd given her everything, a new life, a new home, a new family, a new start – all the money in the world – and now, maybe, she was beginning to fuck everything up.

It was possible he had made the most stupid mistake.

What if Rachel continued her prying, like the damn therapists, investigating the accident at the mineshaft? Asking about Jamie's involvement? By inviting her into the house, David realized, now and too late, he had taken a grievous risk, and made a potentially fatal error. Perhaps, after all, Rachel wasn't any kind of replacement for Nina. Beautiful, impulsive, arrogant Nina: willing to do anything for love. No one compared to her.

David stood up, and walked to the windows, sipping his whisky. The laughing students had disappeared. Only one girl remained, standing at a bus stop, checking her phone, which shone an uplight on her fine young cheekbones. She was helplessly beautiful. Yet her beauty made

104

David sad, the feeling of something faraway and forever receding, but never disappearing.

He had once thought that the cure for desire was death itself. But now he wondered. Maybe nothing could extinguish the yearning of human love; maybe it travelled on for ever, through the darkness. Like the light from dead stars.

77 Days Before Christmas

Evening

'You will have blood on your hands. There will be lights in the Old Hall.' The phrases revolve in my mind, like objects of great importance spotlit behind glass. Yet exuding a faint menace, as well.

It is more than three weeks since the flames were found in the Old Hall and we have all reached a halfway satisfying conclusion that Jamie did it, but a penumbra of mystery still surrounds the event, like the circular haze of pain before a migraine. *Why* did he do it? Perhaps it really was a stunt aimed at me, for replacing his lost mother, the lovely Nina Kerthen. Something designed to frighten me. Or was it aimed at someone else entirely?

I look up from my thoughts.

David and I are alone in the Yellow Drawing Room, as the autumn evening dies. He's got a long weekend off, as his company upgrades the office, and he is clearly relaxing.

I am not. I can't stay quiet. One more heave.

'David, about the fire in the Old Hall.'

He flashes me a hard stare. Irritated perhaps. *Oh God, not this subject again.*

'Please. Indulge me, one more time, then I promise I will shut the hell up, for ever.'

He smiles. Sort of. 'Fine. Go ahead.'

'I accept what you say, that he was doing what his mother did, repeating that thing, that lovely trick she played on his birthday.'

'So?'

'I'm still not wholly convinced he did it all by himself. How? How could he have set it all up? He had no time. He was barely back from school.'

'We've discussed this, already, Rachel.' His words are brisk. 'He could have prepared it in the morning, easily. No one goes in the Old Hall, only Nina went there; she was obsessed with the Old Hall, how one day she might restore it.' His lawyerly explanation calms me – even as it annoys me. 'Then when Jamie came back from school, he had time to light them. To do his little ritual, summoning his mother home. It's not difficult: a can of lighter fuel, squirted from a bottle.' David sighs, curtly, 'There's no risk. Nothing can catch fire in the Hall, there's nothing but stone and glass. And he probably intended no one to see it. The flames would have burned out in a few minutes, his magic spell would have been completed, in total secret.'

I shake my head. 'But, to do it so quickly, to write the words on the floor, without being seen, mightn't someone have helped him? Cassie? Juliet?'

'Of course not.' David regards me like a very disappointed teacher looking at an average child who once promised to be bright. 'His granny was the first person to find them. Jamie clearly hadn't considered that might happen, so when Juliet acted so scared he went into denial. He knew he'd done something wrong. And that's why he lied about it then, and ever since.'

'Hmm.'

'You understand that's what happened. You do get this?'

'I suppose so,' I say. 'I suppose that does kind of make sense.'

Reluctantly, I sit back. I also want to mention the incident with the hare, but I still cannot do this. Because doing this implies I do perceive some paranormal and irrational explanation for the events. Therefore I literally cannot speak the words, without labelling myself mad. I also want to mention the letters, but I can't do that either, without revealing that I sneaked into David's study like a burglar.

I have to talk about Jamie in a different way. 'David it's not just the fire that worries me.'

'No?'

'No. It's Jamie's behaviour, when you are away. He spends hours in his room, crouched over computer games, or his smartphone.'

'He's eight. That's what they do.'

'But other times he's roaming the cliffs and beaches, right up Carnhallow Valley, all the way to the moors. You let him wander at will.'

This is the cautious, streetwise urban female in me, daughter of the council estates of south London – *Imagine what could happen in a coffee shop if you left them for a minute.* I do know life in Cornwall is very different. But I genuinely hate it when Jamie roams too far. I fear for him. Because the idea of anything happening to him makes me feel ill.

Putting down his glowing tablet, David slugs his gin

109

and tonic. 'Rachel, naturally – I worry, but I *want* him to be free. After Nina's death it was tempting to wrap him in cotton wool. Yet I have to give him his freedom, have to let him grow up as normal as possible.'

'But all those dangerous paths? And cliffs? David, he's out at all hours, wandering. I know I'm not his real mother, only—'

'He *needs* a mother, Rachel. You got on so well when you met in London. That will return. Give him time.'

Frustrated, I sit back. That's what we are all saying: give it time, give it time. But time seems to be making things *worse*.

The leaded windows are open, to a soft wind that ferries the salted perfume of the ocean. This smell always makes me a little sad. I think this is because we never had seaside holidays when I was young. We were too poor. I am sad for what I missed.

My husband watches me. 'I also want him to know where the Kerthens have lived, over the centuries. All the coves and carns that I loved as a boy.'

He rises and closes the window. Then he returns to his seat and picks up his tablet, courteously ignoring me. But I look right at him. My husband. His handsome, faintly ruthless face illuminated by the glowing screen.

There will be blood on your hands. There will be lights in the Old Hall.

These images. They are so vivid, and so *visual*. Like Jamie can really see things. Like he *has* really seen things.

A rattle of ice makes me jump. David sets his glass, emphatically, on the sidetable. His stare is hard. 'Open your legs,' he says.

I am wearing a shortish patterned dress. And nothing

110

under. That's what he likes me to wear, when he flies home from London. *Nothing underneath*. I only dispense with underwear when Jamie is safely in bed and Cassie has retired. But I do it: for my husband. Because I enjoy the way it hypnotizes him.

'But, sir, I 'ave my chores.'

I gaze back at David, defiant and knowing. He smiles, and frowns, at the same time.

'Then get down on your knees, and clean the floor.'

'I 'spose so, sir, if you must . . .'

This is one of our favourite sexual games. Turning the class differences into role-play. It is silly, but oddly erotic. Adults can play games and tricks, too.

David puts a chair behind the door, so no one can come in. The trick is working. The worries are dispelling. I wonder if he is going to have sex with me on the floor. I want him to do that, hard, without tenderness. We've already done it on the kitchen table, in every corner of the New Hall, under the rowans in Ladies Wood. We may have our problems, but the sex is more compulsive than ever.

The door is secured. David roughly strips the dress up over my shoulders, and then, unexpectedly, pushes me back on to the sofa. His brutality is delicious. He knows instinctively where to bite, where to throttle, where to touch me *like that*. My head is thrown back. I am gazing, mouth open, beyond his shoulder; the last moths of summer flutter helplessly at the leaded window; I see them dancing, or dying, then I gasp as I come. Yet he pushes harder, unfulfilled.

Raking my nails, I scratch his muscled back; I breathe deep, and quick. He is forcing me into another orgasm. Then a third, minutes later, and then he comes himself, biting my neck. Animalistic.

No one else does this to me. No one else has ever done this to me. Not like this.

When I go to bed that night, I hug David's muscular body to my face as he sleeps; I inhale his scent. He doesn't even stir as I squeeze him; he never snores. He is a heavy sleeper. Though sometimes he talks in his dreams about Nina, as if she is here, in bed with us.

And when he does that, sometimes I lie awake and I imagine her lying on the other side of David, staring at me in silence.

76 Days Before Christmas

Morning

By the time I wake up David has gone to work – flown to London – and I get a fresh if not entirely convincing sense of confidence. Yes. This is it. This is how it works. We can do this. We are a family unit. This is our life now.

It's my turn to take Jamie to school, Cassie has chores in the house, then she wants to see some of her Thai friends in Penzance. Chivvying my yawning stepson into the car, we set off for Sennen School, driving along the coastal road.

A chilly drizzle is being sieved from an oyster-grey sky. Wind buffets the car as we drive. I search for a radio station, but they are hard to find, way out here. All I get is static, stray voices. Do this, do that. How did my stepson predict the death of the hare? It is inexplicable. I cannot understand.

Out of the silence, Jamie suddenly speaks. 'What's your special animal, Rachel? Do you have a favourite?'

Are we having an actual conversation? It seems so.

113

The way Jamie can go from chatty normality to that strange enchantment is perplexing – but at least, sometimes, I do get chattiness.

I glance his way, in the mirror. 'Oh, I don't know. How about eagles? I like eagles. Eagles and lions.' I change gear. 'What about you?'

I can see him shrugging, not looking my way, staring out of the misted window. 'I like all the animals, I think. All of them. Even insects. I hate it even when insects die.'

'Yes, that's sad. But don't you have any favourite animals? What about leopards? Leopards are cool. And wolves!'

He is silent for a few seconds. Then he finds my eyes, in the mirror, once more. 'You know, we've got history today. We're learning about the mines. We're doing all about the mines this term.'

'OK. That's nice, that's good.'

'Ask me something, ask me something about the mines.'

'I will, but hold on, I've got to make sure I find the right turning, this fog is getting worse.'

Slowing the car, I steer left. We are climbing up into the moors. The little fields and shivering farmsteads. Stone circles are glimpsed, then gone, shrouded in this gathering mist. Everything is obscured, and dank. Then I see, barely a yard away, a small white metal road sign, leaning into greenery: *Penzance 7¾ miles*.

I'm on the right road. I breathe out, with proper relief. Don't want Jamie to be late for school. I want to do all of this right. I want to defeat the sadness and fall pregnant by David. I want to fill sad yet beautiful Carnhallow with new life. Siblings for Jamie.

'Rachel?'

114

'Sorry?'

'You said you were going to ask me a question.'

'Oh gosh, yes. Well. What's the most interesting thing you learned about the mines?'

'That's easy. We learned about the deads.'

'Sorry?'

'Don't you know what they are? The deads?'

My mouth is a little dry.

'Uh. No. Not sure. What are they?'

'They're the rocks that the mine owners didn't want, the rubbish rocks, without any tin. It's a funny word though, isn't it?' He hesitates, then says it again, quietly, from the back of the car. 'The deads.'

His expression is blank, and neutral. He is staring directly at me, via the mirror.

'And do you know who sorted the deads? Do you know that?'

'No, I don't. But I've a feeling you might tell me.'

'The bal maidens sorted the deads. They were girls from all the villages who would work in bare feet in the mines, sorting the stones. They worked when they were eight years old like me, and they had little hammers to hit the rocks and they stood there with their bare feet in the rain.' He shrugs, and looks out of the steamed-up window, absently tracing letters in the moisture. 'Sorting the deads. Sorting the rocks and the deads all through their lives, for ever and ever till they died.'

I can, of course, surmise where all this comes from: I can imagine what has happened. His school would naturally teach the history of the mines: it is the history of Cornwall, the history that all the kids can see around them every day.

But the effect of this teaching on Jamie must be unique: when he thinks about the deads and the mines

115

and the bal maidens, he must think about his lost mother. Who is dead, but haunting him: because she is still down there. Underneath us. Floating like a ghost, suspended in the tunnels, her eyes open and her mouth open and her hair trailing, with her splintered fingernails.

The deads. In the Kerthen mines. The despair enshrouds as thickly as this mist – it feels like we will, very soon, be lost for ever, marooned off Land's End – and then Cornwall does its familiar but still fascinating trick. The fog parts and, abruptly, we are descending to the wider roads and leafy avenues of the Penzance suburbs. Views of sunlit blue sea between big houses. Jamie's school is at the end of the road. Briskly, I pull in. 'All right, Jamie, we're here now.'

I unlock the passenger door, and turn to say goodbye, but he is already out: slamming the door shut, running from the car and disappearing through the school gates.

For a moment I regard the empty car seat in the back. Then I glance at the window where he was writing. The words are still visible, even as they fade.

I saw it. You did it. It's your fault she died.

I feel a tightening in my chest.

I gaze at the words I saw him write. Deliberately and carefully, on my car window.

Jamie is, apparently, trying to tell me something. Or tell himself something. But it is something so bad he cannot say it in words. So he says it cleverly in fading letters, written in fog.

But what does he mean? Who saw what? Who did what? How can her death be anyone's fault?

116

And now, even as I stare at the words, they disappear. The misted window is demisting, in the milder air of the south coast; the words have now gone, as if he never wrote them. But he did.

My knuckles are whitened around the steering wheel as I drive back, far too fast. Answers surge and retreat, like ocean waves. Outside Botallack, the road takes me close to the cliff edge, almost toppling into the Atlantic. On an impulse, I brake, skidding the car on gritty sand.

Opening the window I greedily breathe the damp air, as if I can inhale the truth. I know this cove. I know its name. I now know all these lovely Cornish names. We've passed Zawn Reeth – the red cove; we've passed Nanjizel, the cavern beside the bay. So this is Carn les Boel, the carn of the bleak place.

I know these names because I am a quick learner. I remember these words because I am smart, a survivor. And because I am smart, I think I've worked out what might have happened, that night Nina Kerthen died.

Jamie has been having visual dreams. Jamie talked of that night in the letters, like a witness. And Jamie has told me he *saw*.

There is one obvious conclusion: Jamie was *there* when it happened. He was a witness, present at the actual death. No wonder he is so disturbed.

But this is another thing that David didn't tell me. And this evasion is infinitely worse. Because David didn't tell the police, either.

Lunchtime

Can I wait until the weekend to force the truth of this out of David? No. He might not even tell me, especially if he is somehow implicated in the death. Which leaves only one person I can speak to. One adult who might know the facts, one Kerthen who might be willing to talk.

It's raining very heavily as I park the car. Running to the front door of Juliet's apartment, in the West Wing, I knock.

Juliet Kerthen answers, promptly.

'Hello, Mrs Kerthen.'

'Hello, Mrs Kerthen.'

'Tiny bit of mizzle?' she says, as the rain continues to pummel the gardens into submission. 'Won't you come in and have a cup of tea? Get in the warm and dry.'

I am escorted inside, the door is shut behind me. Her little apartment smells, as ever, like an old person's house, but in a very nice way. Lavender. Pomades. Hand-made pot pourri. Old-fashioned scents.

'I have been listening to the radio,' she says, as I follow her down her little hallway. 'This Hitler chap must be stopped.'

I pause, embarrassed.

She turns, laughing quietly. 'I may be rather less acute than I was, Mrs Kerthen, but I can still tell a joke.'

We step into her cosy yet messy kitchen. It is always chaotic here, but over the last few months I have begun to understand that Juliet Kerthen is an example of aristocratic squalor: the idea that being truly posh means that you can somehow get away with negligence.

Juliet is making tea. As she opens the brown teapot lid I realize she is pouring spoonfuls of sugar directly into the pot. Not tea. Spoonful after spoonful of sugar. What do I do? I need to point out her error, without offending.

Reaching out a hand, I gently touch her wrinkled wrist with its jangling copper bangles. Juliet does not turn to look at me, instead she looks at the sugar spoon, then she looks at the pot. Without a word she rinses the pot, and starts again.

Her mortification fills the kitchen, like steam. The angle of her shoulders is pained and self-conscious. And now I begin to doubt my reasons for being here. Perhaps I shouldn't ask Juliet my bleak and intrusive questions. The questions with their very frightening implications.

Juliet chatters on, but with a hint of desperation. The weather, the price of wine, anything to cover her mistake. My pity for her is heavy, like something I am dragging behind me.

'I do worry about David working so hard. Like the Japanese thing, where they fall over and expire, from all the toil. Won't you reach for the biscuits? Ginger snaps, I think.'

119

The questions choke in my throat. *Is David lying about his wife's death? Did your grandson witness a murder? Can we have some chocolate biscuits, I don't like ginger snaps.*

Ginger snaps plated, tea safely potted, she guides me into the tiny sitting room, where a bony grey cat snores happily on one chair. Genevieve. The cat opens its eyes, abruptly, as if hoping to see someone else. Nina maybe. The cat sees me, affects a modest but definite hiss – aimed very much at me – and then returns to sleep.

The rain is still lashing Juliet's windows. One of the windows is open, banging in the autumn gales. The wind has an odd, howling quality.

Juliet closes it firmly. 'What a noise, what a noise.' She mutters something inaudible, sits down again. 'You know there is an old Cornish legend about that noise? They say on stormy days you can hear the voices of the drowned, calling out their own names.' She shakes her head. 'Sometimes I do wonder, I do. All those poor boys, down there, all those poor boys in the mines, and the fishermen who drowned. Maybe they never really leave us: the dead. Maybe they are always with us, in some way.'

Our conversation hopscotches. It's like crossing a river on low unsteady rocks; as soon as we alight on a subject that gives Juliet concern, as she feels her mind falter, she leaps on, searching for another, safer topic.

Her one steady reliable subject is Jamie, her beloved grandson.

'Jamie is so bright, quite the smartest little boy, and so striking. I saw him in the nativity play; everyone agreed, so very angelic. Yet with those dark looks, like his father, and those eyes, like his grandfather. Do you think he is happy? I so worry about him. That woman. That woman.'

120

I am not sure what to say. My questions have died inside me, for the moment. Instead I listen.

'He has all those ancestors, but, really, what a curse they are. David worries about this sort of thing far too much. I am a Kerthen! I am a Kerthen! We've been here for a thousand years! Always going on about the rowans. You know, his father was the same, always telling me about the trees. How exciting is a rowan, really? One summer when he was gambling in London I told him I'd get the gardener to chop them all down.'

I smile, and she smiles back.

'He hit me for that, you know. Yes. When he came back. Struck me across the face.'

My smile has gone. I gaze at her. Shocked. Yet she's still chattering away, as if this is some normal thing. 'And that wasn't the first time, dear, though that was the worst. I fear my husband became quite an awful man. He used to say the only good thing about marriage is that it reconciles one to the idea of death. What a thing, what a thing. I suppose I should have married Julian . . . what is his . . . Courted me at Cambridge. But then, such a womanly man. Whereas Richard . . . well, you always knew he was a proper man, for all his faults, just like his son.' She looks at me. 'Of course David is a very different kind of creature. But he does have that same obsession with ancestry, with perpetuating the line. An idée fixe. It is rather tragic, I sometimes think.'

I begin to see my chance. I have to be careful.

'Yet he only had one child with Nina?'

'Yes. Like his father, the irony is piquant. But Nina is so frail. She is so well bred, like a hothouse flower. And all the perfume, the Chanel, the dresses, and those eyes, she was witty of course, and intelligent, but such a frail little thing, and her pregnancy took it out of her I understand, they were in France then, but my dear, don't worry, you are equally as pretty.'

My tea is left undrunk. A word has struck me. That verb. The present tense. *Is*. Not was. I know this is Juliet's failing mind talking, but it still disturbs me. I can't directly ask about David and the 'accident', yet – but I can ask about this.

'Is?'

'Sorry, my dear?'

'You said "is"? Nina *is* so very well bred. Is? Not was?'

The old woman's eyes instantly moisten, and I feel my conscience prickling. She made a silly mistake. And I am vulgar, and clumsy.

'Oh, don't listen to me dear, oh, oh.' This sweet old woman lifts a biscuit to her mouth and I get the sense that she is doing this because if she doesn't she will actually cry, and now I dislike myself. I am stupid. Bumbling. Crude.

Juliet goes into her safe zone, chit-chatting about her grandson again.

'I worry that I haven't seen Jamie happy for a while, he used to be such a happy boy, you know how happy children can be when they are five, or six, you tell them they are going to the funfair and they run around in little circles of happiness. I wish I could have had more. I so hope you will have them, children are so important, they are so special and yet so strange. I think it is because they are closer to God, to the place where we all come from: they are windows into the otherworld. They tremble from the breath of Eternity. We must get more ginger snaps.'

The tea is finished. Juliet seems visibly exhausted, yet

I still need to ask my questions. Because this is probably the moment: when she is tired, off-guard.

I feel awful. But I need the truth.

We exchange a few more pleasantries and she follows me to her door. As she pulls it open, I find the courage. I'm going to come right out with it.

'Juliet . . .'

Her eyes are half closed, her mind elsewhere.

'Yes? Sorry? Mmm?'

'You mentioned Jamie.'

'Yes.'

'Juliet, Jamie told me something this morning. He told me he saw the accident, he told me he was there when his mother died. So I'm a bit confused. Was he there?'

It's a gamble. She may throw me out of her apartment, she may banish me from her company for ever. But she doesn't do any of this. Instead she regards me with a tiny, sweet, saddening smile. And then she says:

'Oh, my dear, there are so many mysteries, so many people in this house. I never know who to believe. But maybe you are right, because you know what they say: The doubting of doubt is the beginning of faith.'

Is this her dementia, or is she saying I'm right? I cannot work it out. She rambles on, 'Anyway, you must come round for tea again, I will ask Cassie to buy some fig rolls. Goodbye, Mrs Kerthen, goodbye. And don't worry about the things you see, we all see things here. We've all seen too much, learned too much, Jamie most of all, he sees it all. Goodbye.'

The door is shut. I walk around the northern exterior of the house. The sea is grey and wild on my left, the black shapes of Morvellan are malignant in the dwindling rain. I am fairly sure Juliet has proved my suspicions.

Jamie was an eyewitness. The worst of my fears are coming true.

And when I reach the East Wing, the great front door, above the oval drive, looks like a gaping mouth, shouting in amazement at me: *Why have you come back?*

73 Days Before Christmas

Late Afternoon

'Can we? Can we please?'

Jamie is adamant. He stares. A black and white boy in his Sennen school uniform, pale skin, black hair. The only colour is the pale pink of his lips, and those wistful blue-and-violet eyes.

'You really want to practise photography, now? Not at the weekend? It's getting cold, Jamie—'

'Yes. No. Please. And I want to photograph the mines. Please?'

Jamie is cheerful on this run home from school: a precious glimpse of the happy boy I first met in London, with David, when we toured the British Museum together. He was fascinated by the preserved animals in the Egyptian Rooms. The mummified cats and snakes and ravens, beaks protruding through discoloured linen; the human organs in jars.

'Any particular mines?'

'Levant, with the man engine,' he says, pointing at a

brown metal road sign, corroded by sea winds: *Levant Mine: 1 mile*

I know of Levant, though I have never been. I know it is one of the biggest of the Kerthen mines. If we have to photograph mines, with all their connotations, this will be better than Morvellan. Anything would be better than Morvellan.

'OK,' I say. 'Why not. Let's do it.'

Swinging the car left, I head for the bedraggled centre of the village. We park. We walk. It is cold, deeply autumnal. Jamie hums a tune. The cliffside chimneys of the Levant mine complex are becoming visible. I can see their dark forefingers of granite on the horizon, framed by the restless sea beyond. I can also see the lattice of winding gear, enormous black metal hoops rusting in the Atlantic weather.

Jamie turns to me. 'Sing that funny song again, Rachel.'

'Really?'

'Yes!'

'All right. Here goes. *I've got pants, I've got pants,*' I wait, getting my timing right. '*I've got pants that are bigger than my aunt's.*'

He bursts into delighted laughter. 'It's funny because it doesn't even rhyme properly. Right?'

'Yep. That's what *makes* it funny. Because it is so stupid.'

'Do it again?'

And so I sing it again – *I've got pants, I've got pants* – and he convulses.

'This is fun.'

Gulls circle above, aimless yet complaining, as we near the cliffs. I'm shivering in the wind, even though I am wearing my thick raincoat.

126

It's been four days since I had that conversation with Juliet. Four days of thinking and confusion, following the revelation; four days of wondering how to take all this to David. I have decided I cannot do this by phone or by email, this discussion could end our marriage.

I am going to confront him, face to face, wife to husband. It is time to cut through the lies. He returns tomorrow evening.

And yet in those intervening days my anger has slowly subsided. Perhaps there *is* a real, innocent explanation behind the mysteries and evasions. Perhaps a logical explanation as to why David might lie, or dissemble, about something so important.

I want this to be the case. I want David to come home and convince me. I don't wish to be the foolish young woman who married in absurd haste, was easily duped by some charming, good-looking bad guy. I still love David. I still want to heal his son, if I can. I still want David and me to have kids. Despite it all.

And, I suppose, I still want to be the Lady of Carnhallow: owner of that mournful yet magnificent house, where the rowans and tamarisks lead down to the milky surf of the murmuring cove. The romance of my journey to that house, from the grotty suburbs of south-east London, utterly seduces me. I can't go back to mediocrity. And London poverty. Taking buses through dismal council estates to a tiny rented flat I can barely afford.

Jamie is holding my hand. I was so lost in thought I hadn't noticed. It makes my heart quicken, a little. This is one of the few times he has done this: voluntarily taken my hand.

But I try not to look at him. I don't want him to be self-conscious about touching me.

'What loses its head in the morning, and gets it back at night?'

'Sorry?'

Jamie chuckles. 'It's a riddle. Can you guess?'

He seems so very young, very suddenly. His face eager and hopeful.

'Oooh, difficult.' I smile. 'Say it again.'

'What loses its head in the morning, and gets it back at night?'

I genuinely do not know. His hand is now swinging mine, like we are playmates. But I can hear the sea's roar of contempt on the wind.

'A pillow! Hah. It's a pillow, Rachel.'

'Ah, very clever.'

My stepson is cheerful. This is good.

'All right Jamie, let's go and take some photos. It's getting dark and it's pretty cold, so we'd better be quick.'

Pressing Jamie's shoulder I steer him up the last slope – before the fierce plunge of the cliffsides, where we stare at Levant mine.

The size of the ruins is astounding; enough, momentarily, to silence us both. Two large, crumbling wheelhouses stand dauntless but empty. Hundreds of concrete columns, further down the cliffs, have the ambience of a roofless, classical temple, but one built for worshipping darker, underground gods. Some of the truly enormous spoilheaps – the acres of the deads, left to rot – are stained yellow, and russet. Poisoned by chemicals, probably.

And all of it stands next to the swaying desolation of the sea.

The vastness is underlined by the loneliness. Although there are rain-speckled tourist signs dotted about, explaining the history, *The UNESCO Listed Cornish Mining Landscape*, we are the only people here – apart from one little girl, in the far distance, half skipping between the ruined columns.

She is in a kind of *Alice in Wonderland* dress, under a purple anorak. I wonder where her parents must be. She is wearing peculiarly small boots, as if her feet are deformed, as if she is being forced to wear something cruelly painful. Yet she is moving very easily. Skipping and jumping.

The girl turns, and looks at me. Now she opens her mouth and points away at something – over there, in the sea. As if she is silently telling me to look in the sea, look, look, *look for answers in the sea*. Then she runs down a path, lost to view.

Unthinking and instinctive, I hug Jamie very close to me. Protecting him: like the girl is a kind of threat. My stepson does not mind my unexpected embrace. He didn't even see the girl; his attention is on the task.

Jamie turns. I let him go. He says he wants to start taking photos. He has taken out his iPhone, of which I faintly but continually disapprove: an eight-year-old with a fancy smartphone. No.

But it makes a good camera. He's already making decent images. He doesn't need that much tuition from me, no one needs that much tuition in photography any more. My profession, photography, was a profession that died. Like Cornish tin-mining.

'Yes, good idea. Start here.' I tap the phone in his hand. 'This is a great place for a shot. You can frame the mines with the sea beyond, it'll be good, it's such an impressive sight.' I glance at the sky, where the sun is a dull disc of nickel behind grey cloud. 'Shame the light is so flat.'

But Jamie is not listening. He is adjusting the phone and snapping. I leave him to it for a while. I want to take my own photos. Lose myself in what was once my vocation.

The tourist signs, neatly arranged in front of the ruins, tell me more than enough of the appalling history. The children who worked here until the 1950s. The arsenic pits that toxified the earth, giving the child workers 'arsenic sores'. The drownings and the injuries, the funerals and the emigration. The men singings hymns as they were sent underground, in their cages. Their voices drowned out by the cold fury of the Atlantic.

Another plaque catches my eye.

The Man Engine.

The man engine was installed in Levant Mine by its owner, Isaac Kerthen, in 1858. The man engine was a kind of automated ladder of platforms, which shifted up and down: the miners had to step on to a platform, which took them up or down a level, then step off; then they repeated the process, as the man engine cycled. Thus they slowly descended or ascended, in total darkness. Although the inherent danger of the man engine was obvious, and many fell down, to death or injury, it was popular with mine-owners because it ensured greater profitability, as the miners got to work quicker.

I can see David's handsome, guilty face even as I read this. *We sat in Carnhallow, eating capons.*
There is more:

In the afternoon of 20 October 1919 an accident occurred, here at Levant. The heavy timbers of the man engine crashed down the shaft, carrying the side platforms with them, and thirty-one men died, decimating the village for ever. Hundreds were mutilated. The man engine was not replaced and the lowest levels of the mine were abandoned.

An engine made of men.

I've lost my desire to photograph this place. The combination of the weather, the girl, the history. I am not inspired today.

Instead, as the last chilly light retreats into dark, I teach Jamie to take different angles, big framed shots of the streamworks, the copper dressing floors, then smaller close-ups – abstracts almost – of damp quartz-granite rocks gleaming with dark tin. The work is repetitive, and pleasing – yet, as the hour passes, Jamie grows moodier. Falling into deep and concerning silence, again. Perhaps it is the thought of the mines, and what they mean, for his mother, for himself, which is affecting him.

'Think we're done for today, Jamie. Shall we go home now?'

He shrugs, saying nothing, an unhappy frown on his face, looking towards me, yet very slightly but intently to my side, once again, as if someone stands next to me. Why does he do that?

Together we begin the short slog back to the car. He doesn't take my hand, he doesn't ask for a song. As we approach the village, he averts his face. The sea air is singing in my ears, it is so cold.

'Jamie?'

He won't look my way.

'Jamie.' I crouch down next to him, putting myself on his level, being a good stepmother. 'Tell me. What's wrong?'

He mutters, his face downcast.

'I'm . . . frightened.'

'Frightened? There's no need to be—'

'But I am, Rache, I'm scared.'

'Scared of what?'

He comes much closer, pressing his face into my woollen sweater, breathing in and out, as if inhaling the scent of fabric conditioner can save him. Then he talks:

'I'm scared! Scared that I can see things. Scared of them. Scared. Please tell me I can't see them, tell me I can't see the future? Tell me I'm not a Kerthen, *tell me. Please.*'

I hug him hard, once more: trying to squeeze the fear out of this little boy.

'Shh. Don't worry. Shush.'

Slowly he lets go of me, but I don't let go of him. I kneel on the damp, dirty concrete of the salt-bitten path – with his cold hand clasped in mine, brushing the hair from his face.

'No one can see the future, Jamie. You can't. No one can. You're slightly lost. Because of your mother. You will get better. It does get better. I promise.'

'No it doesn't. It doesn't.' His words are miserable, his face grey with sadness. Or fear.

'What is it, Jamie? Tell me – what is all this?' I feel real love for him. Burning.

He speaks, though he remains motionless. 'I don't want to see the future 'cause of what I can see.'

'What?'

The wind has chased us from the cliffs, it is all around us now.

'It's frightening. What I can see. It's scary. Don't want it to be true.'

The worst thing is his confessional tone. As if he is making a painful admission.

He goes on. 'Mummy talks to me in the day.'

132

My stepson's face is paler than ever, yet so beautiful, his hair as black as the crow feathers I find in the garden, feathers of the moorland birds, come to shelter from the chilly winds of the carns.

'I can see one thing, one thing in the future which is very bad. Very bad, very bad. Very, very bad.'

'Jamie, listen, this is just daydreams, it's all imagination, because you are sad.'

He looks me directly in the eye, and breathes deep, and then says:

'Rachel, you won't be here at Christmas. Not any more.'

I stare at him. What does he mean? Why does he choose Christmas? 'Sorry, Jamie? What does that mean? Of course I will be here at Christmas.'

Jamie takes another deep, heartfelt breath, then he says, very slowly, as if confessing the most terrible secret, 'You are going to die by Christmas Day.'

I hear a snatch of sea music. Another distant wave detonating on the rocks, the noise of it carried on the wind. I can't deny a grasp of real fear in my throat, in my lungs, everywhere. Christmas. Of all the times he chooses: *Christmas.*

'No. Jamie. Please. Stop this. Please stop this.'

'I wish it wasn't going to happen.' He looks truly anguished. 'I'm sorry, I'm sorry, I'm sorry! But you won't be here, you must be dead by Christmas. Why do I think that?'

'Jamie. Stop.'

Abruptly, he looks away, then looks back. The anguish has gone.

'Rachel. There's nothing we can do I am sorry I am hungry now.'

'Um – uh—'

'Can we go home now?'

I am wholly confounded. This child is surely trying to throw me, to mystify me. To scare me away from Carnhallow. Because I upset him somehow, or unnerve him, or remind him. Or something. But why did he choose Christmas? Can he really sense something? See into me?

No. Of course not.

At a total loss, we continue our walk, to the waiting car. Which looks so innocent and cheerful, like nothing has happened.

Back in the warmth and safety of the vehicle, with Jamie strapped in and acting normal – I find myself accelerating away, too quickly. But no matter how fast I drive, I can still hear that music in my head: the music of the derelict mine. And the gulls crying forlornly from Trewellard Zawn. *You will be dead by Christmas.*

72 Days Before Christmas

Night

David is home. Finally ready to tell me. His plane was late. I've already warned him on the phone that I have a lot of serious questions to ask him. He knows that whatever is on my mind is deeply important, easily a deal-breaker. And now he sits here, in the bright kitchen, its windows dark, and speckled with drizzle.

He always likes to sit in Carnhallow's kitchen. It embodies peace and happiness for him. *Drop scones and clotted cream, and my father away in London.*

Pouring himself a thick finger of Macallan whisky, he looks surprised when I refuse a similar dash of port. It is the only alcohol I usually like: I enjoy the sweetness. But for now I want clarity. This is the moment: our marriage probably hangs in the balance. I cannot trust a man who lies about something as important as a death. Even if it was an accident. If it was an accident.

And I won't mention anything about Jamie, not yet. I need my questions answered, first.

135

David gazes my way, then speaks, his voice terse. As if *he* has had enough of *me*. 'All right then, Rachel. What is it?'

We are sitting on kitchen stools three yards apart. I go for the nerve. 'I know that Jamie was there. When Nina died.'

Only his mouth betrays him. The tiniest grimace.

'How do you *know*?'

'Various ways. I went into your study and read Jamie's letters, the ones you kept, the ones he was writing to Nina, even when you told him not to.'

He looks at me, eyes sparkling with emotion – maybe anger. But his voice is flat. 'Go on.'

'There are other things, little hints, it doesn't matter. The big one is this – he said it, or rather he wrote it, he wrote these words for me to see: *I saw it, you did it, it's your fault she's dead.*'

A scatter of drizzle on the windows. My husband's face is rigid, betraying nothing.

'Anything else?'

'Yes.' I guess this will anger him most of all. I do not care. 'I asked Juliet to confirm it, and she did, basically. She confirmed my suspicions. Jamie was there. He saw the fall. It explains so much.' I cross my arms. 'Tell me I'm wrong, David, tell me I'm right, but tell me. And explain it. Enough of the bloody lies. One more lie and that's it. I'm walking out of the door. And not coming back.'

He stares into the whisky, and I see a passing flash of emotion in his eyes. This is it; our marriage surely depends on whether he is truthful now. Then he looks up at me, once more, and says:

'Yes. It is true. Jamie saw his mother fall. He was there when she died, in Morvellan.'

136

My anger surges into words. 'How? Why? Why didn't you tell me, why didn't you tell the fucking *police?*'

'Wait—'

'You perjured yourself!'

Necking the residue of his Scotch, he pours another inch into his crystal tumbler. It glitters like dirty gold in the bright kitchen light. 'Jamie was an eyewitness. But I lied, we lied, to protect him.'

'I'm sorry? You what?'

'There was an argument, right after Christmas. Nina and I were arguing, as Jamie mentions in those letters – that you *found.*'

'What was the argument about?'

'It doesn't matter.'

'Yes it fucking does.'

'No. It's irrelevant. We were simply bickering, like husband and wife—'

'Tell me!'

'All right. We were bickering about the restoration of the house. She was taking so long, it was so bloody exquisite, thanks to her perfect taste, but each room was taking a year; more. Most of the house is still barely habitable, as you've seen.'

'That's it?'

'Yes, *that's all it was*. But Jamie was always sensitive to our arguments. He didn't like them. And that night it kicked off.'

'How?'

His eyes meet mine. He sips whisky, and dries his lips with a smear of his wrist. 'I am going to tell you. But first, Rachel, I want you to promise not to tell anyone else. Can you do that? It's very important.'

I choose my words with definite care. 'It depends what your answer is.'

137

He frowns. And then shrugs:

'As I said, we were arguing. Repeatedly. You know what Christmas is like, too much booze, too many relatives, too many people in the same rooms. And Jamie is an only child, he always resented that.' David looks abruptly at the door, as if his dead wife is about to walk inside, dropping her coat on a chair.

Then he returns his attention to me. 'Sometimes Jamie and Nina would squabble, too. Sometimes he was cruel to his mother, saying nasty stuff: *Why didn't you give me a brother or a sister?* He knew Nina didn't want any more children. But he had a reason to be peeved: Nina wouldn't even let Jamie have a dog. I *really* wanted him to have a dog, I had a dog when I was a kid, a Lab: it helps so much if you're an only child. But a dog meant hairs on Nina's perfect furniture, hairs on her perfectly restored curtains, from Gainsborough of St James. Therefore: no dogs. And this was yet another Christmas when he didn't get a bloody dog. I think he wrote that to Santa four hundred times. *Please can I have a dog.*'

'You haven't got him a dog since?'

'He says he doesn't want one now. Because, of course, it reminds him of the arguments with his mum. And what happened that night.' David takes another slug of Scotch. I say nothing. Let him fill the silence, let him do the work.

'The cruelty of families,' says David, gazing at the stone hearth of the huge, empty fireplace, once used to cook for a hundred monks. 'The cruelty of families.'

'And?' I don't want any philosophizing.

'It was late at night. We let Jamie stay up, sometimes, especially around Christmas. But this night the arguments went on too long and Jamie came out with some of his worst remarks.' David closes his eyes, as he swallows his liquor, apparently savouring its fieriness.

I am well aware that he is dragging this out like an actor. Like a lawyer in a court, showboating for the jury. And it is working. My adrenaline races. And yet I think I believe him.

At last, he continues. 'Jamie was in a terrible state by the end of this particular argument, and he went crazy, saying he never wanted to see Nina or me again, and she was the worst mummy, and he wished she was dead, then he ran out of the room. Like he says in the letters, if I remember correctly. You know how angry and passionate kids can be, the things they say when they are six. This was bad, though. Very bad.'

I nod, despite myself. I do know this feeling.

'So where did Jamie go? Up to his bedroom?'

'No.' A grimace. 'He ran out of the house, on to the cliffs. Towards Morvellan. Towards the Shaft House. In those days we never bothered to lock it: everyone knew the risks. These days it's locked all the time. I keep one key, there's another in the kitchen, high in the cupboard. Perhaps you *found* it.'

'What happened?'

'It took us a while to realize he was nowhere in the house. Such a ridiculously big house. We were all searching for him. Everywhere. Then outside. Mummy and I were looking in the garden, in Ladies Wood, and Nina was looking for him on the front lawns, the north lawns, and she heard him shout – but Cassie heard him shout first, she heard a cry from the mineheads.'

'How do you know this?'

'Cassie was apparently right at the end of the path, at the end of the front lawn, where the cliffs begin. But she was barefoot. You know what Thais are like.' He

139

breathes out. 'And you can't walk the cliffs barefoot. So she ran back to get boots and told Nina – and then she watched Nina race down Carnhallow towards Morvellan. Of course, Cassie blames herself now. Either way, Nina was first down the path to the mines.'

'God.'

'And that's where Jamie was. In the Shaft House. Stuck on a ledge, like someone who climbed too high up a tree.' David gazes miserably into his Scotch.

The empathy surges inside me; it just does. Poor Jamie.

'I can imagine the rest. You don't have to tell me.'

'No, no I want to tell you.' David stares at the ceiling and sighs, heavily. Sighing with relief at his own confession. 'Nina was in heels, all that is true – in heels and a dress, in the mud and rain, a nice party frock under a coat, it was such a filthy night, late December – and wearing all that she went to rescue Jamie.'

'She fell.'

'She fell down Jerusalem Shaft. Trying to save her son. That's how it happened.'

I have a yearning for that glass of port. I also have questions.

'How do you know this, if no one else was there, if no one else saw?'

His glance is sharp. 'Sorry? No one? *Jamie* was there. He told us, he was sobbing – "she fell, she fell" – already he felt guilty, dragging her down there. That's no doubt why he wrote those words, the words you read – "You did it, it's your fault" – he's blaming himself. You see?'

I scan his face. I want to see.

'But what happened, after that?'

'I got to the Shaft House minutes later. But too late. Cassie helped me carry him back to Carnhallow.'

'Then you went to the police? But you *lied* to them?'

140

'Yes. We did.' His gaze is undaunted. 'Tell me, Rachel, what would *you* have done? Anything different? Think about it. Jamie believed he was responsible for his mother's death. In a certain manner he was, indirectly: telling her he hated her, saying he wanted her dead, then running away and bringing her down to the mineshaft. If he hadn't done that, she wouldn't have died. He was hugely unstable. So I couldn't put him through an inquest. Police questions. His name in the papers. *Son lures mother to death?* Imagine.'

'And Juliet and Cassie agreed? To cover this up.'

'Cover it up? I suppose you could put it like that. But what we said wasn't far from the truth.' My husband's glance has a hint of disdain, or maybe despair. 'Cassie and Mummy love Jamie. They didn't want him to go through any of that, to relive this terrible scene in court. We didn't want him to be the *only witness to his mother's death*, we didn't want him to think about it ever again. We pretended it was a total accident. It was easy to do. She really was drunk, she really did fall, she really did drown. And yes, we came up with a story to protect him, we told everyone else that Nina wandered off alone, down to Morvellan. An accident.' His attention turns to the rainy windows. As if it is too painful to look me in the eye. 'And now you know, Rachel. Is that enough?'

I sit back, calculating. Perhaps this is enough. Or maybe it isn't. David still lied to me, several times, in so many ways. The story is terrible, but the trust is broken, it will take time to rebuild. I won't let men manipulate me again. Not the guy at Goldsmiths or my father, not my husband here. Not Patrick Daly, Philip Slater, not the pale-faced priests at my school – I won't let *any* of that revisit me.

141

And there is still another, nagging question. The only witness to all this, supposedly, was Jamie. Is he entirely reliable? And why is he behaving so oddly, *now*?

'David.'

He is pouring yet more Scotch. 'Uh-huh.'

'You need to know some things. About Jamie.'

I see his eyes glitter, immediately. 'Yes?'

'It's this. He's been acting very strangely, worse than ever. It's not just the words he wrote, on the car window.'

The rain makes an irritable noise at the windows. Like angry scratching. My husband scrutinizes me. 'How, exactly? How is it worse?'

'We were at Levant, this week. Taking photographs. And then suddenly, it was, well – very unsettling. He had a kind of episode.'

David spins his whisky glass on the granite worktop. Thin-lipped. 'And then?'

'He went on about the Kerthen gift, the Kerthen legend. And then he actually said he'd been talking to Nina, that she was back from the dead—' I barely pause, aware that I may sound ridiculous. 'And then, to top it all off, he claimed that I was going to die at Christmas. *Dead by Christmas*. That's what your son Jamie said, two days ago. I would be dead by Christmas!'

David's stare is hard.

I hurry on, acutely discomfited. 'And then he says things to no one, in the house. Like he is talking to his mother. So many things. You already know about the fires, the lights in the Old Hall, how he predicted that. And – and then there was this dream, back in the summer, he predicted that I would run over a hare, and then I did, he predicted that, too – of course, it is all explicable, and yet, and yet, now he predicts I am going to die at Christmas.' I come to a sudden stop. Too late,

I realize I have made that ghastly mistake. Now it is me under scrutiny. David is looking my way, with something like distaste, even revulsion, in his eyes.

I've exposed myself. I said it all wrong. He thinks I am mad. He thinks I believe in this. He think I believe something ghostly is happening. That Jamie can foresee events.

And why shouldn't he think that? Because sometimes I do believe these things.

56 Days Before Christmas

Lunchtime

The sea sang its dutiful verses, Morvellan stood on the cliffs like a dark-robed Methodist priest, sternly lecturing a congregation beneath. And David walked the damp, leaf-strewn path to Juliet's apartment, deep in thought.

'Hello, Mummy.' He could tell, as soon as the door opened, that she was seriously drunk. That was what she did to dispel the memories, and assuage the loneliness.

'Oh, oh, David, how nice to see you. I thought I was joining you for supper tonight, in the kitchen.'

'Yes, you are. But I thought we might talk. Alone, beforehand.'

She was on port wine, probably. His mother often mixed the best vintages with supermarket lemonade.

'Talk, David?'

'About things. Carnhallow. *Rachel.*'

'Carnhallow! Life here used to be so lovely.'

'Mummy?'

She was wandering down the corridor. He realized, too late, that he had set her off, that before he even got

145

a chance to ask any questions, he was going to get one of her more rambling and tipsy soliloquies.

Leading him into the sitting room she sucked at her drink, and stared at some greying photos on the mantelpiece.

'Well. Well, well. Where do I begin. Carnhallow? You know life in Carnhallow wasn't all bad, I did love your father once, before he became so brutish. You Kerthen men are all the same, charming, womanizing, but then, oh . . .'

His mother's expression was dreamy. She was lost in the mazy ballrooms of memory, giddy and dancing, and falling – and with no one to catch her. Not any more.

'Mummy – I—'

It was pointless.

'Did I ever tell you the picnics we used to have? Here. Here. Have a port, Fonseca 2000, I persuaded Cassie to steal it from your cellar. Will you have me taken to jail? You won't throw me down Ding Dong will you, David dear? Mmm? Have a drink. You want to know about life here, darling?'

He took the drink from her quavering hand, even though he didn't want it. He wasn't going to escape this, he was going to have to let her talk it out. His mother's short-term memory was often faulty, but she had tremendous memories of the past, and she liked to speak of them. Because it was all she had left, she was obviously in pain from cancer though she refused any treatment. Because she didn't want her hair to fall out.

David filled with pity for his mother. When she was dead it would be him and Jamie. The last of the Kerthens. And he loved his mother, fiercely. She had protected him from his father's drunken cruelties. So he tolerated her monologues now.

'Oh, the parties we used to have here, David, before

you were born, such parties, summer parties, here, and at Lamorran, Trelissick, Lanihorne Abbey. Always armfuls of flowers, so many flowers, and all the girls from the village, from Zennor and Geevor and Morvah, remember them, making those hollyhock fairies, with the heather under their beds.'

Sitting back, in her cluttered sitting room, he let her words wash over him: these Alzheimery fragments of a shattered lifestyle. Half these memories came from Juliet's parents, and her grandmother and great grandmother – mixed up with recollections of Juliet's own childhood and youth. Yet these chaotic heirlooms were precious: they were much of the reason he was desperate to hang on to Carnhallow. The last memories, the old glory, the Kerthens as they were. The Kerthens of Carnhallow. Somehow he could restore it. Couldn't he?

His mother sipped at her £200-a-bottle port, then dashed it with cheap lemonade, and rambled, lyrically, 'You don't remember, so long before your time, I had you so very late, at forty, much too late for a sibling, we thought I couldn't . . . you know. It was a great joy: you were a great surprise. But I didn't mind being barren, not so much, even if it meant Richard left me. Life was so pretty, I didn't want it to change. I wanted to stay young for ever with the parties and the dancing.' Her smile was giddy, her eyes were closed – dreaming aloud. 'And the breakfasts – the breakfasts were amazing, David. Minted peas in aspic, we had. Bradenham hams, and ptarmigan.'

'Mummy. Darling.'

'And then in the summer, the swimming. My sister and I and all our friends, we were always barefoot, running down the lawns of the allee, straight into the sea.' Another measure of port, a second splash of Lidl lemonade. 'One day we went swimming when we were so hot, we actually dived straight off the big lugger in the bay – and when we swam back to the beach someone had folded our clothes and when we'd got dressed, we rode those old Dartmoor ponies over the dunes, and we went the long way to Carnhallow, through Ladies Wood, it smelt of white clover, I remember, and of wheatstraw, and it was so pretty, that great tide of bluebells, on the green, and then we went into the house and on the elm table there was, oh, everything – plates of lobsters, and dishes of honey, and fresh clotted cream. They gave us milk and brandy drops, saucers of white Carnhallow raspberries. So lovely, so lovely.'

She drank a last gulp of port.

'And that's when I fell in love with your father, David. He'd been away at Oxford and I barely knew him and I was half in love with his cousins but then I saw him, he was very handsome, he came walking down the allee, from Ladies. A young man in a waistcoat and a white shirt stained red with ash bark juice, and he took me into the garden – you don't remember the garden as it was then, old old old, David, so old. The sunlit walls, thick with clove pink, and marjoram, and thyme, and in the middle, in the roundel of grass, there was a wheelbarrow seat, and that's where he sat me down and there's where we kissed. Your father and me, for the first time.'

At last she fell silent. Was it over, this dance of disjointed recollection? 'Mummy, I want to ask you a question.'

She was absent now. Her face was blank. David realized he preferred her animated – if slightly demented.

'Question, darling?'

'Yes. A question. Do you think Jamie and Rachel are at odds? Because I detect a very serious tension. And Rachel is increasingly erratic, making some very strange

148

remarks. And she's hunting, and prying: asking things.' His sigh was exasperated. 'Something has occurred, something is wrong.'

'Life has *occurred*, darling. Jamie already loves Rachel, I can see it. She will be a good replacement. She confuses him, of course he is confused. We are all confused.'

'Sure. But Rachel is acting oddly and I think it is affecting Jamie. The dynamic between them. It's not good, and it's getting worse.'

'Well. What can that be? Tension in Carnhallow, how ghastly. Why don't you ask Nina why there is tension?'

He stiffened. He knew this was probably the dementia, beginning to steal away her mind, and it pained him. 'Mummy?'

'Why don't you ask her? She knows better than anyone, what it's like to move here, in this way, she will understand what Rachel is going through.' She was talking quickly, nervily, yet her eyes were sharp as she fingered the row of pearls around her neck. 'Yes, my darling, ask his mother, or ask your wife, you chose her, and let her do what she wanted, so she will understand better than any, won't she?'

'But, Mama—'

His mother's stare was unnerving. Angry, even.

'Enough of this. Now I must go to sleep. I am exhausted. Must go, must go. There will be people with us tomorrow. We should take them riding in the dog cart if it's a nice day, haven't done that in years, have we, in spring, when the verges are yellow, with all the buttercup? So pretty, so pretty. And the pink, from the cuckooflower—'

The tears were falling again. This time for real.

'Mummy.'

'Don't.'

His darling mother, with all her exquisite, old-fashioned politeness, was snapping at him, fiercely. 'Don't, David. Don't. Please go. I will be better by tomorrow. Leave me alone now. Leave me be with all the people, I don't even know their names. There are people in the house and I don't even know who they are. I see them. I see them. You've invited her in and I have to watch them, at night, in the windows, down at Morvellan. It's utterly unfair.'

David knew this mood: it wouldn't go away quickly. Though this was worse than normal. 'OK, Mummy, I'm going.'

She lifted a hand to wave goodbye. She said nothing.

Quietly he shut the door. Breathing the cool air, he gazed down the valley at the latticed blackness of Ladies Wood, marching onwards to the sea. The autumn berries were bright and red on the rowans, clusters of bloody colour amidst the dark branches.

His mother was, in her own way, entirely right. There were too many ghosts and memories in Carnhallow. The intensity of the past was too much. The last couple of months he'd had the actual urge to move, even though he'd spent his whole life, risked everything, to keep the house: to save it, to maintain it in the family.

Please go. Start a new life. Go.

Yet he couldn't. He could not be the first Kerthen to abandon Carnhallow, the first to quit in one thousand years. He was imprisoned. The past weighed on him like the ocean above the tunnels of Morvellan. And he was another miner among many generations of Kerthens, hewing a life from the bitter rock.

As he walked back to the East Wing, kicking through rusty piles of fallen leaves, he recalled those terrible hours and days. The hunt for Nina's body, the police cars parked around Morvellan.

150

Police frogmen had spent days in rubber suits searching the mines: the Jerusalem Shaft, the Coffin Clista shaft, the great diagonal of the Wethered Cut, all of them interlinked. They'd spent many shifts scubadiving the frigid, dangerous waters, ostensibly hunting for Nina's corpse but, from the off, it seemed an unspoken truth: the search was largely a charade, done for effect.

A week after Nina fell in the water, the Truro detective had sat him down, the grieving husband, and told him the cold and clinical science: the forensic pathology.

Almost all drowned human bodies sink within minutes of death, the policeman explained, because, as water fills the lungs, they become too heavy to float. However, unless these corpses are weighted, or wearing exceptionally heavy clothes, they then float to the surface a few days after death. Gases enter the flesh and bloat the corpse, making the cadavers buoyant. The bodies literally bob up, like obscene bath toys.

But in certain cases that would not happen. Such as, for instance, a body drowned in an ancient, complex, watered mineshaft. That kind of corpse was irretrievable.

So Nina – Nina's cadaver – could, the policeman said, be anywhere. One day, any day, she might resurface, a grisly residue; alternatively, she would never be recovered. David remembered the way the detective had added, as though it was some quip, 'Morvellan would, in fact, be a very good place to dump a murder victim, though of course there is no question of that in your case. Would you more like coffee?'

David had accepted the boiled and tasteless coffee. The aftertaste of that interview remained with him many months later.

Murder.

At the end of the little path, where it turned right for the main door, David paused – caught by the sound of the distant sea singing its mournful song. Like miners hymning their sadness in a Sunday chapel, long ago and far away.

A very good place to dump a murder victim.

39 Days Before Christmas

Evening

I'm talking with David, online. That's the way we mainly connect, these days. That's where we argue.

He snipes at me, from his office, barely hiding his irritation and frustration. I catch myself whingeing, with a horrible hint of a south London snarl, sitting here in the vast, quiet kitchen of Carnhallow. How has my brief and miraculous marriage come to this? A few weeks ago we were happy. Or so I thought. Now we are closing in on Christmas. When I am somehow supposed to die.

Of all the times to choose. *Christmas*. Like Jamie knows me inside out. He knows how to scare me, or unnerve me. How?

And now David and I are at odds. It gets worse.

The irony is that I have some potential and important news to tell him. I think I am pregnant. I am very late: so late, I've lost track. But I've been holding off the test, to make sure it's not a scare. The wounding disappointment of the previous false alarm has made me wary.

The testing kit rests on the kitchen table, I bought it this afternoon; I will do the test tonight.

But even if it is positive, I am not sure how, or when, I am going to give David the joy of this news – not when he is so hostile, when we are arguing so much, when he will barely speak to me. I'm not sure if we will still be married in a year.

He is being hostile right now.

'Rachel, I insist, I am absolutely adamant about this, I don't want Jamie to see a bloody therapist.'

'But why not?'

'Because they do him no good. As you well know. I took him to a therapist after the accident and they messed him up even more. Getting him to write secret letters to his dead mother. It's one reason he thinks she is still alive.'

I flinch. And he sees it. And he pounces.

'Yes. Them. Remember? Those letters you found. When you were snooping around – like some damn detective—'

'I was doing my best for Jamie!'

'Really. Of course. Right.'

'I was!'

He goes to speak, angrily; but I rush on, not giving him time. 'Look, David, this isn't about me. It really is about Jamie. You must see that he needs professional help. Because. You know what he did—'

His chin is tilted forward, with a hint of aggression, even violence. What might this man do to me? For the first time, the playful dominance and submission of our sex life hints at something more dangerous. In my husband.

He leans even closer.

'Really? We know this, do we? What did he do?'

156

I watch those noble cheekbones of his. But I won't let my desire cloud my thoughts, not any more. I might not even tell him if I *am* pregnant. Not yet. I need leverage. He begins to scare me.

'Well, Rachel? Hmm?'

'I was there, I heard him say it.' I struggle not to swear, to lose my temper. 'Jamie is deeply disturbed. He needs professional help.'

David snorts. 'No he bloody doesn't. We've tried that. It doesn't help. And besides, the only witness we have for *much of* this is *you*, my darling Rachel. You. You are the only person who hears him say these things. Are you sure you're hearing him correctly?'

'Yes!'

My righteousness is complicated by sadness. I hate this widening gulf between David and me. I had hoped that my marriage would be an opening up, that it would allow me to reveal all of myself, tell another human everything. Be honest. Be understood. Be forgiven and loved, for what I really am, maybe for the first time. Instead I am reduced to bickering.

The kitchen is silent, the moon glows through the trees outside, as if it is trapped in the branches. A big white screaming mouth in the black. I place a pensive hand on my stomach. Considering the tiny life that possibly stirs inside. A distant astronaut, coming home to earth. A floating sparkle of dust, in the distant black. Yet umbilically linked.

This new child, if I have a child, will be safe, as I was not safe. I will make sure of that.

Quickly I remove my hand. Did David notice that gesture? He is still online, still banging on about child therapists. Why does he hate this idea so much? His vehement opposition is bizarre. As if the shrinks might

157

find out a deeper involvement in Nina's death, something beyond what he has told me.

'Do not take him to a doctor, Rachel. I mean it.'

'Why? What are you scared of? Is there something else you haven't told me? Something you're scared they might find, even now?'

His face tightens with fury. I continue, regardless. 'Is there?'

'No!'

'So what's the issue? You say you've told me everything.'

'I have, Rachel. So do not do it. I order you.'

'You ORDER me?' I feel like screaming Your Son Thinks I Will Be Dead By Christmas. Your Entire Family Is Fucking Crazy.

But that makes me crazy, too. For it is possible I am now part of this family. Umbilically linked.

'David, let's end this conversation. Please. It's only going to get worse.'

He is momentarily muted. Then he offers a tired shrug. I know that tiredness, I feel it too. I am not sleeping properly, haven't been sleeping for a while; vivid dreams disturb me.

David checks his watch, pulling back his white shirtcuff. He is wearing his signet ring with the Kerthen crest, but no wedding ring. This is not unusual. He rarely wears a wedding ring. It's not what people like him 'do', apparently. It is another way he is subtly but clearly posh, in a way I don't even begin to comprehend.

'All right.' He sighs, enormously. 'Look, I guess I'm sorry, it's nearly nine: I've been working for twelve hours straight. Sorry for shouting. It's the strain.' He rubs his eyes. 'I can't even come home this weekend, I've got to work right through.'

158

'Oh that's fine. You stay there. We'll cope with everything on our own. While you cruise around London.'

He winces. And why not? That was a pointless little barb. I'm turning into something I hate: a shrewish woman, nettling my husband. This has to end, one way or another. I need to get Jamie some professional assessment, whatever his father says, and then I can decide my own future: if it is right and safe for me here. And any unborn child. *Dead by Christmas.*

'David, let's talk some other time. When we've both calmed down.'

We end the call. His face gives way to a blank screen. I sit back, and gaze down at my stomach. Imagining a tiny bump. Then I rise and trawl my anxieties through the house, towards the Yellow Drawing Room, where I find Jamie playing a game on his smartphone, cross-legged on the sofa.

Since the outburst at Levant, Jamie has been more conciliatory with me, as if he feels guilty. When I approach the sofa, he flashes me a sad smile, so I sit beside him and give him a little hug. Wanting him to sense the idea, the sweet possibility, of new life inside me. I kiss his forehead. His soft black hair smells of apple shampoo.

'Sorry we argued, Rachel. Sorry about that.'

'Me too.'

I gaze at my stepson. His young eyes are so clear and violet-blue. I can see myself in them. A tiny reflection, brilliantly miniaturized in their icy fire.

'Jamie.'

He yawns. '*Yes?*' He sounds very sleepy. It is way past nine.

'Jamie, I am going to take you to see someone special.'

'Hmm?'

159

'They will sort everything out and everyone will be happy. We'll start very soon. It'll be a secret, between us. You and me.'

He smiles weakly. 'OK.'

'It's nothing terrible, but it's better if we keep it secret. Not tell anyone.'

He nods. Then he says, 'Not even Mummy?'

I stifle my agitation. Nothing I can do or say will ease this tragic confusion. This is, however, further proof that my plan is correct. I cannot continue in this house, continue with this marriage, unless I do what's right by Jamie. He *needs* urgent medical help. Psychiatric help. Whatever David says.

So I chivvy him off to bed, then I return to the kitchen. Where I stare at the pregnancy kit for about ten minutes, like I am trying to make it move with psychokinetic skills. Then I lean forward, pick it up, take it into the nearest downstairs loo.

And now I sit. And wait. And I do not pray.

And then I look down at the little plastic wand that might cast a magic spell on my future.

Two lines.

I am pregnant.

35 Days Before Christmas

Afternoon

'Hello! Rather blowy today.'

Mavis Prisk, the child psychologist, stands in her porch. She is younger than I expected. In smart jeans and a smarter top. Dark hair nicely cut. She is positively glamorous. Barely thirty-five. I am slightly taken aback, and feel shabby in my workaday clothes. Her firm voice sounded middle-aged on the phone – when I urgently arranged this meeting, when I pulled rank and gave her my full name, Mrs David Kerthen of Carnhallow House. From her formal answers and careful phrasing, I had anticipated a headmistressy woman in her fifties. Someone tweedy. Not sexy.

'So this must be the famous Jamie Kerthen.' She smiles and places a protective hand on his shoulder as we climb from the car, and she invites us into the warmth. 'Let's have a cup of tea and then we can all talk.'

The house smells pleasantly of woodsmoke, from a big iron fire. Jamie surveys the place. He looks barely interested, vaguely nervous, and withdrawn. When we step into the white glassy kitchen, Mavis switches on a kettle, and I watch Jamie – as he takes in the spectacular view, over Cape Cornwall. My stepson is studiously gazing out to the ocean, where the partying sea leaps and dances over distinctive black rocks.

'The Brisons,' Mavis says, in an explanatory way, as she pours boiled water. 'The rocks – they're called the Brisons. Locals say they look like Charles de Gaulle having a bath.' She puts the pot of tea and some mugs on a tray. 'Let's go into the study. It's hard to get work done when there's all that' – she gestures at the immensity of blue, oceanic emptiness – 'like a painting that keeps changing. It's actually hard to stop watching.'

The study is indeed quieter. Lined with shelves with apposite titles. *The Handbook of Adolescent Psychology. Asperger's in the Under 10s. Understanding ADHD.* I wonder how this clearly smart, coolly confident woman, this paediatric psychologist with her scientific training, is going to react to my story. My stepson thinks he can predict the future. He has predicted my death. Am I going to mention that last bit? I find it hard to articulate. Because, again, it makes *me* sound delusional. Because a part of me really can't help thinking: *What if? How do you know? How does anyone know for sure?*

To my relief, Mavis Prisk begins with generalities. A smidgen of Cornish gossip. A polite joke. The inevitable mention of the November weather – 'wait till you see January, the stormy seas are wonderful.' Then she skilfully turns to the matter at hand, as if it is a natural evolution in our discussion.

'Jamie, I understand you met with one of my colleagues, Mark Whittaker, at Treliske Hospital, not long after your mother's accident? And he began some therapy with you, asking you to write to your mother?'

Jamie softly blushes. And nods. And says nothing. His face twitches – and a sense of dread enters me. Is this going to be horrid? Cause some inner trauma to emerge – as a violent tantrum?

Mavis nudges, again.

'But you only saw the therapist a few times, is that right?'

Another tiny nod. I am perplexed: I do not comprehend what has happened to this once very confident boy. Why has he regressed into almost total passivity?

I intervene, on Jamie's behalf: 'It was decided that the therapy wasn't helping. The letters, and everything. So it was stopped. But now . . .'

Mavis acknowledges me, with a polite smile. Then turns back to Jamie. 'I know it must be very difficult for you, James. But your stepmother says you are having new issues. She says that you have predicted *things*. That you are actually talking with your dead mother. If possible, I'd like to chat with you about all that.'

Jamie says nothing. His hands are tight fists. He flashes me a hard and angry glare.

'Jamie—' I say. But he ignores my words, as well.

Mavis tries again. 'We're all here to help you, Jamie. Maybe we have some ideas, some techniques, that can help you through all this. No one wants to make you sad or upset.'

Still nothing. His chin is buried in his chest. Virtually autistic. This is painful.

'Jamie?'

Silence.

'Jamie?'

He does not respond.

This is excruciating. Jamie rewards me with me another glare. Mavis, slightly blushing, sips from her

163

tea. Then she glances my way, meaningfully. 'Mrs Kerthen – Rachel? I have an idea. Would you mind, um, stepping out for an hour or so, perhaps take a walk on the cliffs? Then Jamie and I can talk alone.'

I see her logic. Though I resent it, for reasons I can't wholly explain.

Mavis adds, 'This is my job. I assure you I know what I'm doing.'

Perhaps I feel a kind of relief. Jamie's disturbing silence is too painful to witness. Collecting my coat and buttoning it up tight, I give Jamie a hug, to which he does not respond. The boy is locked inside his own emotions. Like the Brisons, black and immobile amidst the roaring seas. Hunched against an impending storm.

'You'll be OK, Jamie. Mavis is here to help.'

His huge eyes regard me. I have no idea what he is thinking. But I guess I have no choice. I've pulled him out of school for this; taken the risk of going behind David's back. I have to leave.

Pushing the door into the gale, I take the walk that Mavis advised. Up the cliffs, to the left.

The wind off the sea is sadistically cold, yet I like it. The sting of the chill has a distracting thrill of its own. I can make out a distant lighthouse perched outrageously on a rock, far to the west, where a shaft of sun spears the writhing waves.

The November wind tousles the grass. Small wintering birds fight the gusts, like tiny fluttering kites, dancing together. Everywhere there are signs, next to the footpaths, overgrown with ferns, warning of Death and Injury in the Mineshafts. I marvel. Even here, on this wind-shattered, uttermost headland, they still mined, wrestling the metal from the chilly rock.

But up here on Carn Gluze there are also weathered

tourist signs for Iron Age tombs: grassed-over tombs and barrows. These ancient remains look like the spoil-heaps from the mines, and the smaller tombs look like capped mineshafts. The chimneys in the fields look like five-thousand-year-old megaliths. The Stone Age and the Victorian, the prehistoric and the industrial, are eroding into each other. The landscape is repeating itself, or maybe cycling around itself, endlessly.

But I will not repeat my history, I will not recycle my past.

I will break free.

Whatever happens to us, to me and Jamie and David, and our baby, I know I cannot go back to London. Back to my childhood world of sticky carpets, and littered parks, and suburban screams. All the menial jobs I did, age sixteen, seventeen, eighteen. To keep my mum and me alive. I escaped all that: I worked and read and educated myself, and I survived. I can't return.

But first I must tell David that I am pregnant, and see if we can be a family. And I shall do this face-to-face. Again. I need to see how he reacts in person, whether it brings him real joy.

This coming weekend. A month before Christmas.

An hour has passed. The wind has dropped, and a low hanging sun gleams through vast black curtains of rain, falling on the distant waves. Soon it will be dark. It's a short walk down to Mavis's house where I buzz the bell, feeling a sudden but ferocious anxiety.

The moment she opens the door, I know I was right: something has happened.

'Come in,' she says, unsmiling. 'Jamie is in the living room, with a computer game.' She coughs. It is an awkward, unmeant cough. 'So we can, ah, talk in the study. Privately.'

165

We move to the study. I don't waste time. 'So what is it? Please tell me. Did Jamie open up? Mention anything about the past?'

Mavis won't meet my gaze. She curls some of her nicely cut hair behind an ear and stares at her bookshelves. And only then at me. 'Well, Rachel . . . First we need to know that children often react strangely to deaths. The death of a parent is consistently rated as one of the most stressful events. Bereaved kids have a threefold increased risk of depression.'

'You think Jamie is depressed?'

'No. Of course he is unhappy. But no, I would not say he is, precisely, depressed. But he is still grieving very badly. And the grieving is going on too long. Something *is* making it worse.'

'What?'

'Ah. I'm not exactly sure. He shows signs of magical thinking. Seeing a causal reaction between his behaviour and events, a link which does not exist. Magical thinking is a not uncommon reaction in a grieving child, but not nearly two years after the death.'

'What else? What about *the predictions*?'

Mavis Prisk's pretty eyes won't face mine.

I persist. 'Did you talk about the predictions, the hare, what he said?'

'Yes, we did. Of course.'

'So?'

A hint of a blush. 'He essentially denies that he said any of this. He says you are . . . ' she frowns, subtly. 'He says you are making it up.'

'But we know that's a lie. He's embarrassed.'

She blinks. 'Of course. Yes. Of course.'

'He set the fires, and said those words.'

'Yes. I know.'

I have to press my point. 'Did he talk about the death of his mother, the accident that night, anything about that?'

'No.'

This is going nowhere. Yet I will not be budged. I have to heal him. Fix this family. Make Carnhallow safe for *my* child. 'What can we do, medically?'

She looks relieved, as if we are moving on to firmer ground. 'I don't have instant solutions, so the best bet is to wait it out, for now. Grief *can* be unusually prolonged. If he gets noticeably worse we could, possibly, consider medication, but obviously that's a choice for the longer term.'

Then she shakes her head, as if she has made a difficult decision, even as we talk.

'Rachel. You should know that Jamie did say something rather troubling.'

'What?'

'He implied, or suggested, or maybe inferred, that the disturbances began . . .'

'Yes.'

Her tone is pretty blunt. 'Well, that they began when you arrived.'

'Sorry?'

She shrugs. 'It's an implication. But he said it.'

'An implication? What exactly are you suggesting?'

'I understand it might be upsetting. But I have to say, I do wonder. It may be that you are upsetting Jamie, causing some of this. I note his new symptoms began when you arrived at Carnhallow.'

I can't help my anger. 'You reckon it's all *my* fault? What a bloody ridiculous thing to say! How dare you, how can you fu—'

Too late, I stop, chiding my vulgar, London self. I

167

know I have crossed the line. My temper has preserved me in the past, but also condemned me.

Mavis Prisk glares at me, flatly. 'I think this is enough, for now. Hmm? Please, I think you had better go.'

'Look, I'm sorry – I flew off—'

'Please go. *Now.*'

Guilty, and frustrated, I collect Jamie from the living room, where he was staring out of the window. At the slopes, the Cape, the simmering sea, turning purple and black, as night cruises in, from the Scillies.

The therapist watches us from her porch, in the gloom of the dusk, as we get in the car, and reverse out of her drive.

When she has disappeared from view, I turn and ask Jamie, trying to be as calm as possible.

'Hey, you. What did you guys talk about? How did that go?'

Jamie says nothing. Naturally.

'I thought she was nice,' I say, hoping my clumsy lies aren't too obvious.

The car rumbles on to smoother tarmac, the sea recedes. We are in the narrow streets of St Just in Penwith, that haunted, handsome old town. The last town of all.

The evening wind kicks at the scarlet plastic Santas strung across the road, making them dance like Cossacks, above the pasty shop. A gap opens up, and I pull out and steer left, heading for the coastal road to Carnhallow.

'There!' shouts Jamie. Very loudly. He is suddenly agitated. 'There. There! That was her face.'

'What?'

'Yes!' He is undoing his seat belt; my stepson is about to get out of the car, even as I drive. 'Yes, Mummy. Mummy. Mummy! There!'

Tingled with panic, I yank the car over, pulling to a very sharp stop, close to whiplashing. Then I slap my hand on the switch, shutting all the locks so he can't jump out.

What is he staring at? Why is he so animated? There isn't much to see. In the wintry twilight, the car windows are black: they reflect the interior, the dashboard light, the car's occupants.

He is looking at us.

Or is he?

Now I notice a little red bus across the road, with interior lights. Right at the back I see a blonde woman. She is turned away, but I can see her profile.

The fear comes in a sudden rush, like frozen needles. Prickling, simultaneously, all over my body. It could be Nina Kerthen. It could. It really *could*.

Yet it surely can't. It's someone that looks like her. Wearing her kind of clothes. That's all. That's what I'm seeing.

Slowly, the bus pulls out, and comes right alongside, and I get a slightly better view. And the anxiety rises in my throat like a sickness, along with an imprisoning panic.

It really is, I think. It's Nina Kerthen. I feel faintly ill.

Nina Kerthen is dead in the depths of Morvellan Mine, and yet here she is, returned – sitting in the back of a humble bus, probably heading down to Penzance. I stare, appalled. My mouth hanging open. The nausea rises. Surely it can't be her. It is but it isn't. It can't be, but it is.

With blithe unconcern, the bus steers away; I mustn't let it escape. I have to know if this is Nina Kerthen: alive. I need the truth. Screeching the car right, then reversing left – making other motorists honk horns at me, furiously – I do a wild and brazen three-point turn, and take the westering road, following the bus.

'Mummy . . . ?'

Jamie is almost crying. His hands cover his eyes. Then he opens his fingers and says:

'What are we doing? Don't follow the bus! It's frightening! Please?'

I have to ignore him, hard as it is. The bus is three cars in front. On these narrow lanes it is impossible to overtake, and get nearer, but it is also impossible for the bus to escape. Hands tight on the wheel, I keep the bus in sight, my mind focused, the sickness thick in my mouth. How can it be her? How can she be alive?

Jamie is still freaking out, and I cannot blame him.

'Rachel! Rachel? What are we doing? Why are you driving the wrong way, why are you driving like this, why are we going after that bus—'

'I just am.'

'You saw the face, you saw what I saw, didn't you – Rachel? – but not the bus, don't chase the bus – no, it's frightening—'

'Jamie, please, I don't want to crash!'

The moorland roads are entirely dark now. Oncoming cars dazzle me with their lights, scarily close. These roads are so narrow. Granite boulders mark sudden curves, where my tyres squeal, where dark trees move. The bus is still there, topping the moors and heading into town. It has an advert for a local Christmas pantomime on the back. *Puss in Boots,* at the Hall for Cornwall. The big cat smiles at me. But we are nearly there now. When we will find out. I feel even more nauseous. What if it *is* her?

'Rachel! I don't want to do this. I'm scared!'

We drive past a supermarket, and the bus pulls over, and stops. Three cars ahead. I strain to see what is happening: people alighting in the cold, in their winter coats, faces orange in the streetlamps, an old lady with

170

a shopping trolley. I lift my head to see Nina, if it is Nina, I am sure it is Nina, still on the bus. The blonde hair. But the bus is too far in front to make out faces, and most of them are facing forward, anyway.

I feel simultaneously terrified, and oddly triumphant.

'Rachel, stop. I'm scared. Don't do this don't do this.'

I've had enough; there is no oncoming traffic. Pressing my foot to the pedal I scoot on to the wrong side of the road, just as the bus begins to pull out – I overtake one, two, three cars – I can sense the other drivers' shock and outrage – *What the hell is she doing!* – but now I am right behind the bus.

'Rachel—'

I can definitely see blonde hair. The bus is trundling down Market Jew Street. Lined with charity shops and cheap hairdressers and a knackered, medieval church. More Christmas lights sway overhead. The next time the bus stops I can stop, climb out, go and see. *I will know.*

And now a man with a road sign steps into my fevered daydream, my frenzy of discovery.

STOP.

Roadworks.

STOP.

'No!'

I am shouting. But I have to stop, or I will kill the man. Yet the bus has slipped through, at the last moment – it is speeding ahead, escaping us. Puss in Boots leers at me as the bus climbs the hilly road, then prepares to turn. And now the smile of the cat has vanished, like the cat in *Alice in Wonderland*. Like it was never there.

'No!' I say. 'No no no no no no!'

I am banging the steering wheel in frustration. I can see Jamie in the mirror, staring at me in shock.

The bus has gone from view. Turned a corner. Another

flow of traffic fills the street, from a side road – and I am still here, stuck behind the man with the STOP sign. The bus could be anywhere by now, I will never catch up. I slap the wheel, again.

Finally – fully five minutes later – the man with the STOP sign turns it around and it says GO and I race down the hill, past the minimarket. I know it is probably forlorn, but I can still try. Veering in front of oncoming traffic, breaking the speed limit, I chase the route the bus took – past a couple of pubs, heading down to the waterside. And yes. *There it is.*

But as I drive close, the disappointment knifes my hopes. The bus has reached its terminus. This is Penzance bus station. And the interior of the bus is dark: it has reached its final stop, and all its passengers have disembarked. The bus driver is locking his door, and walking away, and there is no sign of her.

I will never know now whether that was really Nina Kerthen. I press my face to the steering wheel, and hold my fist to my mouth. I am so close to vomiting. Swallowing the acrid taste of my fears.

34 Days Before Christmas

Lunchtime

Plumstead. Woolwich. Bugsby's Reach. Thamesmead. David had heard of these estuarine non-places of course, these incoherent suburbs straggled along the grey and surging Thames, but he had never seen them. Except perhaps from the Business end of a plane, taking off at City Airport, heading for Ibiza, Paris, Milan, when he looked to the side and idly marvelled at London's sprawl, the glitter of the docklands, the silver oblongs of water, and then the moth-grey-brown of those suburbs. Then a Tanqueray and tonic, thank you.

Now he was here, descended, lost in the backwaters of south-east London, where sofas sat in the pot-holed road for no apparent reason, where the trees snagged plastic shopping bags in their black branches, where the last British natives kept their heads down, and headed for here, this pub, between a tyre garage and an old Georgian mill, the Lord Clyde.

The pub was virtually empty. Just a barwoman in her thirties sporting a black eye, watching the soundless

175

TV on the wall, and two other lunchtime customers: a couple of workmen in hi-viz jackets necking cheap pints of yellow lager. Talking football, with accents not unlike Rachel's. The echo – the reminder – tugged at his conscience. His new wife. The woman he loved.

And now that love had turned to *this*. To this dismal pub. To doubts, and anxieties, and investigations: to a sinister suspicion that had to be confirmed, and maybe used. Because he had to protect his son from his own mistakes.

Who had he really married? Who had he allowed, so hastily, into Carnhallow?

Ray was back from the toilets, zipping himself. Taking his chair. Sipping his Guinness.

David looked at him. Assessing how much he had aged, and therefore how much David had aged, since they last met, maybe five years ago.

Ray was once one of his old friend Edmund's fixers. That was how David had traced him, last week, via friends of friends of Edmund. This man, Ray, an ex-policeman in his early forties, had worked for Edmund for maybe half a decade – doing private investigations, discreet research, edging the right side of the law. Before Edmund had keeled over, aged thirty-seven. Brain haemorrhage. *Could have happened to anyone.*

'He'd have loved this place,' David said.

Ray wiped beer from his lips. 'Edmund? Yeah. He liked lowlife.'

'His boyfriends were always from places like this.'

Ray laughed. 'Too right. Talk about rough trade. Bless his little cottons.' The ex-cop looked uncharacteristically wistful. 'Miss the old bastard. He was funny too.'

David nodded. Forcing himself to be businesslike. He

didn't want to talk too much about Edmund. They didn't need to go there.

'OK, what have you got?'

Ray suppressed a burp, leaned to his side, and grabbed a supermarket carrier bag. He pulled out a slender volume resembling a child's exercise book. As he opened it, David tried not to look at the pages too obviously. Ray's handwriting was small, careful and precise. That was, no doubt, the copper in him. Taking assiduous notes.

Clearing his throat, as if he was in court, Ray explained. 'To be honest, David, your call was a bit of a surprise. Haven't heard from the likes of you in years, and you didn't give me much time. Usually I like to, you know, take these things slowly, build a picture, as it were.' Ray smiled, showing a hint of gold in a tooth-filling, 'But your offer was very generous, so I've been working quick. And hard.'

'And?'

He read from his notes. 'Rachel Daly. Thirty years old. Five foot two. No previous. Irish parents. Mother cleaner, father villain. Born in Woolwich General. Went to St Mary's Primary. Went to Holy Trinity secondary, Catholic comp. Left school early, did basic jobs, cleaning, skivvying, zero hours. Then went to art college: to Goldsmiths. Then escaped.'

'Escaped?'

'Seems like the right word, wouldn't you say? Take a look at this area. Take a look at her CV. Family's typical South London underclass. Knew her kind when I was Job. Tea-leafs, neets, chancers. Vicious semi-criminals.'

'Anything else?'

'When she was a kid her folks lived all over the shop. House in Thamesmead, flat in Charlton, the nasty bit, then a grotty little semi in Abbey Wood, always renting of course. Renting, and then evictions. List of addresses as long as yer arm. Bailiffs in and out the door. Very, very rough.'

David sat back, thinking of his smart, resourceful second wife, who had *made herself from all this*. Admiration surged, despite himself. Rachel had overcome this terrible backstory. It was impressive. That was one of the reasons he'd fallen in love with her.

But then a Christmas carol interrupted his foolish reverie. Tra la la la la. He really had to *stop* thinking this way. He had to remember why he now resented her, too. This woman snooping around Carnhallow. This irrational woman, upsetting his son. This potential disaster. Whom he had married.

'What else?'

Ray looked at his notes. 'Yes. Here's something. They disappear for a while.'

'Sorry?'

'Around Rachel's late teens, the family vanishes. No known address. Dad on his own. Then, a few years later, Rachel enrols at college, Goldsmiths, and by then her mum is living in the country. And, get this: she's living in her own house.'

David sat back. 'But they had no money.'

'Exactly. They disappear, then come back, and they've got enough cash for a little house. Not much, but still, pretty weird. And by that time her dad has gone back to Ireland. He's still there now, Kilkenny. Her mum died a few years later. Lung cancer.'

David took a thoughtful sip of his drink, trying to take away the taste of betrayal. But it was hard. He was betraying Rachel, the woman he loved. But this bad stuff had to be done. Maybe he could find an easy way out. Persuasion, not force. If the worst came true, and the marriage was over, he certainly didn't want to go through a messy divorce. Whatever he did, divorce had to be avoided. Because she could fight it. She could tell the police he had lied about the accident, and if they started investigating . . .

Unthinkable. He needed to be cleverer than that. He was cleverer than that.

'You want another?' Ray was gesturing at David's glass. David waived the opportunity: one G&T was sufficient. He needed his mind at its sharpest.

As Ray ambled to the bar, David gazed around. The workmen had exited into the wintry cold, zipping up those jackets, steeled by three pints of lager for lunch. Yes, that was it. Zip up, move on. Get the job done. Pint.

Ray sat down with another fat glass of Guinness. David leaned nearer. 'Look. I need something now. Something better, stronger.'

'Something you could use for a little bit of blackmail, you mean?'

David said nothing: there was no need. Ray took another slurp of stout and looked at the barwoman with her black eye. 'Someone's been walkin' into doors. Happens a lot round here, their doors must be shite.'

'Ray—'

The man chuckled. 'I do have something else, yeah. Though they're oddly loyal, these people. Thick as thieves. Birds of a feather. All that shit. But there's this one bloke might be able to help. He's the only one willin' to talk about her.'

'And this guy is?'

'Liam Daly – cousin of Rachel's. I've said you'll give him five hundred, if he coughs something nice. He said on the phone he had somethin', maybe.'

'OK. OK.'

179

'Right on time. Here he is.'

The door had swung open; a red-haired man in his early thirties wearing a huge anorak nodded gruffly towards them. He looked mildly hostile. But then, David mused, everyone and everything was mildly hostile round here. Everything was curt, gruff, stunted. Withered by the wind off the estuary.

'Liam, this is David.'

Liam sat down without a word.

'Pint?'

Liam glanced at David, then back at Ray. 'Abrahams. Cider.' A pause. He did not say thank you.

The drink was fetched. Liam unbuttoned his anorak, showing layers of football shirts underneath. A fit man running to fat. Half the pint disappeared in about ten seconds. David felt the frustration rising, and interrupted: 'So Rachel Daly is your cousin?'

Liam glugged more cider, and set the pint-glass on the table. 'Yeah.'

'Go on.'

'Eh. We were close for a while.'

'How close?'

'We went to the same school.'

'And?'

A shrug. More silence. *I'm Dreaming of a White Christmas*. Liam was inert, bordering on defiant. David pressed, 'Liam. I'm not paying you five hundred quid to hear about you snogging by the bike sheds.'

Where the treetops glisten, and children listen.

At last, with a hint of contempt, Liam went on: 'All right, what else can I tell ya? She was a looker, a sparkler. Everyone fancied her, she was funny too, clever. Good for her, getting out of this fucking zoo.' Liam was staring at David, open aggression in his face; but then, David

180

realized, maybe Liam was angry at himself: betraying a friend for money. 'Then somethin' happened. She fell out with her family – dunno why, sure it wasn't her fault. They all stopped speakin'.'

'No idea at all?'

'Nope. Zilch. Her family was a right busload, always in trouble. And her da. Jeezo, what an evil old cunt. Drinking and brawling like a twat. No wonder her sister ran wild.'

'What did the sister do?'

Ray interrupted. 'Rachel's older sister, Sinead, thirty-two. Expelled from her comp for breaking windows. She lives in Glasgow now, she's a nurse. Seems Rachel hasn't communicated with any of her remaining family, dad and sister, since they dispersed.'

David nodded, biting back his irritation. This still wasn't enough. *White Christmas* warbled to its end. Ray apparently sensed his mood; he nudged Liam along.

'Liam, we haven't got all day, can you tell David what you told me. On the phone, this morning. What happened to Rachel. You said you had something that would help us.'

Liam took a long drink, as if he needed the liquor to steady his nerves. Then he gazed flatly at David. 'OK. Not long after her da fucked off, maybe before, dunno, she went mental. Done her nut.'

David felt a quickening: his lawyerly senses alerted. 'You mean Rachel had a breakdown.'

'Yeah.'

'How bad?'

A slight, tantalizing delay. 'Pretty fucking bad. Apparently she was, like, properly off her trolley. They took her to Fraggle Rock. Yeah, she was in some place, locked up, whatyacallit, psycho unit. After that she left,

181

disappeared. Grew up. She got rid of that accent, or most of it. And then she flew away.'

David looked at Liam, then at Ray, then he gazed at the empty glass on his table. He had a kind of prize. Rachel had mental health issues. The worst of his suspicions had been proved horribly correct. And probably this explained it all. Rachel really was making it all up. The woman looking after his son was actively crazy, hallucinating, classically paranoid and persecuted. *I hear voices. They tell me I'm going to die at Christmas.*

He could get his wife sectioned, and taken away, for ever. He had to do this. Before she harmed his son.

David gazed about the pub, feeling the bleakness. Despite this breakthrough, he felt no sense of triumph. If anything, this information made him feel sadder, guiltier. That feisty, funny red-headed girl he'd met at the art gallery eight months ago. That survivor. That girl he'd loved. She was unique. She was the special girl he'd always hoped for.

But she was a girl that had to go.

32 Days Before Christmas

Evening

I am ready. The house is empty. As ever. I am alone, and alone is good, even if it is frightening. Pausing at the top of the stairs, torch in hand, I remind myself why I am here.

When we got home from St Just – and the incident with the bus – Jamie ran straight to his room, wordless. And the first thing I did was check the websites. Check Nina's history. Perhaps she had a sister, close in age. A twin. Half-sister?

No. The gossip columns told me she just had one, much older, brother, who now lives in New York: a banker. And yet I saw Nina, or someone very closely resembling Nina on that bus in St Just.

Or did I?

Since then, the rationalizations have kicked in. Because I need them. Everything else is too confusing, and disturbing. My only choice is to deny it, for now, until I have more evidence, deny it the same way I am denying everything else, like the hare and the fires and

185

the prediction. I have to tell myself it never happened. It was someone who looked like Nina, a little. Or a lot. Until I get more proof.

I didn't see Nina Kerthen. I was upset from the visit with Mavis Prisk. My stepson's unbalanced state has thrown me. My life is affecting me. The hysterical mood of this house, Carnhallow, is infecting us all. Everything that is wrong can be ascribed to misperception and grief. To the perturbing concept of Nina Kerthen, locked in the tunnels, her shredded fingers reaching through the water, towards a light she cannot see.

But there are still deep mysteries here in Carnhallow. And I have to sort them out. Because I am pregnant. I deserve to know what kind of life and house and family my child will be born into.

And David is back in a couple of days. The confrontation looms, like Christmas itself. My special day.

Before then, I will do what I have so far avoided. Investigate Nina. Go down into the basement of Carnhallow, go down into the recent past.

'Come on, Rachel. Do this.' I am talking to myself. *Yes, you are.*

Turning the doorknob, the bleak and neglected stairs yawn below me. I flick an old-fashioned switch on my right – and the damp light feebly illuminates the unpainted steps. I switch the torch on too, in case the antique basement lights give out, which happens often.

Down I go, into that musty and horrible dream of corridors, throwing as many light switches as possible. Past the Gun Room. Past a Game Larder. Past a scuttling noise of mice, or rats, on my left, which speeds the pulse. Then I stall, and peer into the murk.

These corridors go on for ever. Perhaps some of them, somewhere, actually link up with the deeper tunnels under Morvellan. I imagine a map of these tunnels: it would resemble the grey bones of a hand, seen in the dark of an X-ray. A hand that reaches, desperately, beneath the sea.

At the next corner I can smell dust and ancient dirt, yet also a lingering aroma of spice. It is a last dying hint of the life once lived down here in the great kitchens of Carnhallow House.

Here and now, in my mind, the place fills – with real ghosts, with bustle and cheer, from a century back. I can hear the vivid chatter of footmen in livery fetching drinks and ices, then the laughter of pretty housemaids from Pendeen and Hayle, St Erth and Botallack. Sweating cooks in aprons, boys turning spit roasts, someone writing careful menus: *Côtelletes d'Agneau à la Macedoine, Poulets* à *la Langue de Boeuf*. Upstairs I imagine the Kerthens, decorously and contentedly eating the endless food delivered from these basements. The suckling pigs. The golden soufflés. The jugged hare, boiled in its own blood.

Now it is all dead. The romance is over.

My torch-beam, added to the gloomy light from the motionless bulbs, leads me past the Butler's Pantry. I can hear muted squeals. Bats, I imagine, or rodents.

Turning the corner, I come to the Still Room. The door is open. I've never seen that before. What's more: the boxes aren't there. Those large cardboard boxes, with *Nina* written on them. I've seen them here half a dozen times, sitting on the grubby tiles. I've never felt the need to open them before. But now I do – they've gone.

This disturbs me.

Perhaps Cassie moved them, perhaps someone else. Pushing at the next door along, I peer inside. This dismal space is so sooted with dirt it appears to be charred, like there was a minor fire, extinguished by the damp. It is also entirely empty.

The next door is very stiff and requires a serious shunt. Then another. Once I am inside, the room seems bigger, more promising. Shapes of furniture loom. But the light switch doesn't work, so I have to use my torch.

The beam of light glitters on a pile of enormous beaked skulls: turtle skulls, perhaps, for turtle soup. Then a narrow arched window of stone, blinded by bricks, probably a thousand years old, from the monastery that underlies everything.

A venerable chest of drawers dominates the far wall. I have to step over piles of stinking carpet to reach it. I test the first drawer. It is so stiff it takes a proper tug to slide it open. Brisk, determined, I rifle through the contents, burgling the family history.

Everything is in here, everything and nothing: black-edged Victorian letters. Mourning lockets with curls of faded blonde hair. A pair of ancient gloves, some broken chessmen. A box of antique silver buttons with the Kerthen crest.

Nothing.

The next drawer down is slightly more rewarding: ink stands, pen wipers, what look like seventeenth-century mining deeds. With my torch-beam slanting down, I skim-read the papers. The most impressive is a handwritten letter from the Lord Lieutenant of Truro to Lord Falmouth, confirming – I think – the Kerthens' purchase of Wheal Arwenack.

The bottom drawer contains a sheaf of faded photographs of unknown relations. They resemble the framed photos hung along the New Hall. One by one, I examine them. The people are stiff and unsmiling. Standing men and sitting women, posed proudly and formally in front of their mines.

I recognize Morvellan, it is so distinct. There are barefoot bal maidens in headscarves toiling in the background; several are squinting curiously at the distant camera, some are going about their work. A man tugs a tray of rocks with straps over his shoulder, like a beast of burden.

I am sure it would have been horribly noisy: the deafening sound of the mine stamps, crushing the ores, the maidens hammering away at the deads. Yet the ambience of the photo is oppressively muted. Stifled and Victorian.

Everyone in this photo is now quiet. Because they are quietly watching *me*.

Another photo shows Levant mine, and still another, Wheal Chance. All of them with Kerthens in front. *See what we own. This is ours. All of this.*

Something snags. I go back to the first photo.

There is a child in the unnoticed centre of this image of the grand Victorian Kerthens, at the apex of their wealth, stiffly posed in front of Morvellan Mine. A girl in a white dress, with tiny black boots, laced up tight, is sitting on a little chair right next to a vigorously moustached, stern-faced man in his forties, who utterly ignores her.

The resemblance of the girl to Jamie is uncanny. The enormous eyes. The crow-dark hair. But what truly pierces me is the girl's expression. She looks terrified. For no particular reason. Her mouth is half-open, as if she is silently screaming. But perhaps she is trying and failing to smile, in this awful place, with the shrieking stamps behind her, the children with arsenic sores all around.

It is all here. The noble and wicked history of the Kerthens.

Yet I am learning *nothing*. Stepping back from the cabinet, my torch-beam shines at random. On the boxes, with *Nina* written on the side, lodged behind the door. Someone has moved the boxes into this forbidding room. Cassie perhaps. Or Juliet. Maybe it was Jamie – sifting stuff, trying to work out what happened to his mother: why she is still alive, and sitting in a bus, waiting for Christmas, getting ready for the big day. I can hardly blame him for his confusion.

I step up to the enormous cardboard boxes. They are not sealed.

Balancing my torch on the nearest shelf, I open a cardboard flap. The box is full of clothes. Reaching in, I peel away the first dress. It shimmers in my torch-beam, crimson and turquoise, satin and silk, very lovely. Further down in the box there are skirts, scarves, more soft and flimsy dresses. There are perfume bottles here. Chanel. The perfume of a dead woman, the scent of a body my husband so loved to touch.

I have to see what's in the next box. I want to get this done. Urgently, and slightly trembling, I rip the lid open.

As I reach in, a noise freezes me. A human noise, from outside the room.

I wait. Tensed so hard, my thigh muscles hurt. My hands shake.

It is the unmistakable creak of old wooden stairs.

Someone is coming down the steps. They will find me, here, rifling through a dead woman's possessions. A thief caught in the act.

The panic is a metallic taste in my mouth. I think I can hear the sound of someone breathing especially

190

quietly. This makes it all worse. This is someone trying not to be heard.

It cannot be Jamie: he is with Rollo. Cassie is away for the night, staying with friends. Juliet is socializing.

I am alone. And yet, tonight, in the basements of Carnhallow, I am not alone.

The footsteps get nearer, passing down the corridor outside. Then they stop. At the door to this room.

I stare in pulsing fear. Who is trying to frighten me? Who is coming for me? In my mind I see Jamie, I see Nina Kerthen, I see that little girl at the Levant, with her evil little boots, deformed but skipping, pointing at the sea, pointing to the wastes of water, *look look look look look.* The girl that frightened me so much I hugged Jamie close.

'Who is it?' I say, my voice hoarse. 'Who is it? Who's there?'

No one replies. I am trapped. Cornered in this room with the fragrant dresses, and the shouting little girl in the photograph.

'Stop it,' I say. 'Who is this? Nina?'

I am calling out to a dead woman.

The door opens. I shine my torch.

It's Juliet.

She gazes at me, her face snared in my torch-beam. 'Rachel.'

I try to stammer a reply. And fail.

She smiles. 'Thank God. I came back early and I thought we had a ghost. The house is so empty. It's amazing we haven't been burgled! Are you going through Nina's things?'

I am stumped. What do I say? I have no choice. 'Oh God, yes. No. Yes. I'm sorry. But I am.'

She looks at me, then at the boxes. Then at me again.

Her expression is inscrutable in the gloom. 'They're fascinating. You are not alone. I think Jamie goes through them.'

A pause.

'He does?'

She smiles, and puts her hands in the pockets of her old cashmere cardigan. As if this is a normal conversation, over camomile tea or Beefeater gin in the kitchen.

'Oh yes. That's why I asked Cassie to move them in here, make it a little harder to find. It's not good for him. I'd like to throw them all out but David won't let go, won't let go of the memory.'

'But—' I fight to speak. 'But . . .'

'But who can blame Jamie for trying to understand the past? Exactly, dear. All these puzzles. Aren't they the thing? Nina everywhere, everyone's here, no one has really gone. Sometimes I think I can hear the miners, singing, when the wind goes through these basements. They used to have red faces from iron oxide.'

I feel an urge to share, to tell this woman, my only possible ally in Carnhallow, what I saw. Someone very like Nina. On a bus. But I can't. Not yet. Not yet.

'Have you seen all the black dresses? Marvellous, all the little black dresses.' Juliet's smile is indulgent, dreamy. Perhaps she has been on the port already. 'They were the loveliest, I think. Yet so expensive.' She sighs. 'But then, as David always says, death is the price we pay for beauty. Do pick one up, do try it against yourself.'

'Sorry?'

'You are Nina's size. Very similar, apart from the hair. Take up one of her dresses, measure it against yourself, it'll be fun.'

She is definitely drunk. But I don't mind that. It means she might forget this episode.

192

Obediently reaching into a box, I pull out one of the dresses. Shimmering, and black. Then I lay it over myself, like I am casually trying it for size in a store.

'Oh yes!' Juliet laughs, delightedly. 'You are Nina! Surely her. Oh yes.' Her laugh fades. And a quickening sadness takes over. 'Well, I must go, but do carry on. There are books in there as well. Goodnight. Please remember to shut the door tight to stop little Jamie getting in. We have to save Jamie. Jamie is everything. He is the reason for everything.'

And that's it. She turns and leaves, as if we have just met in the Drawing Room and discussed the rose garden. I stand here, stilled, for half a minute, trying to decipher her slurred sentences. But it is hopeless. And there are more boxes. I want to get this search concluded and flee upstairs.

The second box contains lots of documents and files. Figures and quotes. Most of it – all of it? – contracts and letters relating to the restoration of Carnhallow, Nina's great project, which I am trying to complete. In my risible way.

There are letters from fabric companies, upholsterers, interior designers, buyers at auctions, all doing her bidding. Even museums. The torch placed on a shelf, I sift urgently through the papers, as the beam picks out phrases and paragraphs. *A pair of silver gilt Georgian plates. I have found some beautiful gesso mirrors. A pier glass and console table. Two white blanc de chine cripples; two silver flower sprigs from Milan; two large glass Japanese Imari jars: £30,000.*

Thirty thousand pounds.

Deeper in the box is a Moleskine notebook. Nina's neat, angled handwriting is delicate and singular. The notebook conceals a letter. I unfold it and read. She sounds like she is writing to some expert. The letter is unfinished.

I've got a man from Inverie in Scotland to come down and live in a cottage in Zennor, he dyes his own yarns with vegetable dyes to achieve the right colour for the tapestries.

Further down:

The fabric is made and dyed by Richard Humphries; I spoke to the textile dept at the V&A, I've chosen moreen, a woollen material with a silken watermark, very right for the period of the bed and its hangings. Dyed to a misty blue green, just ethereal . . .

This tells me nothing, except that Nina knew what she was doing. And that she never sent this carefully written letter. I do not know why. But, as with that photograph in the gossip magazine, I have the strange sensation that I am now in possession of a clue.

Folding the letter, I replace it in the notebook, and slip the notebook in the pocket of my jeans.

The last box is books, as promised by Juliet. Lots and lots of books. Memoirs, history, novels. Many of the books are in French, too – Colette, Balzac, Simone Weil.

The thinnest book looks especially cherished: it is a hardback edition of Sylvia Plath's *Collected Poems*. Turning it in my hand, I see it is dog-eared and battered, though Nina has repaired the binding – or had it repaired. Clearly a much-loved volume. Weighed loosely on my palm, the book splits, naturally, on one page.

The spine has cracked at this point – this is evidently the poem she liked to read most.

'The Moon and the Yew Tree'.

I don't know much about Sylvia Plath, or about poetry. Novels were my thing, my means of escape when life became unbearable. But the first line of the poem – circled neatly by Nina – is enough to give me the dusty taste of anxiety, once more.

This is the light of the mind

I recall that line very well. It is the epitaph on Nina's tombstone. And I may not know much about Sylvia Plath but I know one thing. She committed suicide.

The questions build and burst, like rainstorms over Cape Cornwall. Like Christmas gales.

Did Nina commit suicide? If she did, that might explain the sense of doom, remorse and secrecy that surrounds her death. That surrounds all of us here, trapped in Carnhallow. But if she did commit suicide, why did she do it? She had everything. Beauty, brains, a son, a husband, a wonderful home. Or so it seemed.

I consider the child I carry, who will inherit half of Carnhollow, but all of this history.

Taking the notebooks upstairs, flicking the lights off, I make for the drawing room. But as soon as I open the door a new sickly fear suffuses me, making the notebooks tremble in my hand.

Chanel. I can smell it. In here. In this room. But this is not a memory of a scent, some trace of something long gone. This is real. This is the perfume of a woman who has just been inside this room, her favourite room, her beautifully restored drawing room: and only this moment departed.

It's Nina's perfume. No one else wears Chanel. She has been in here. She was here a few minutes ago. I know it. I know it. It can't be. But it is. Nina is quietly and invisibly walking these halls and corridors, like she is waiting for me to leave, at Christmas. So she can take my place.

30 Days Before Christmas

Lunchtime

David is finally coming home tonight. This weekend I will tell him about the pregnancy. But the ideas in my head are driving me to the edge. Literally. I am parked on the pier at St Ives, watching the waves. Helpless.

Placing a protective hand over my stomach – my womb – I consider the child within. The line from which this child descends. Greedy, evil Jago Kerthen. Violent, drunken Richard Kerthen.

And David Kerthen: a liar, deceiver, or worse.

What if I am pregnant by a bad man? A man who has inherited the worst of his ancestors, the worst of the Kerthens? Maybe the idea of this, of my foolish credulity, is what sends me mad: because it is my own fault. I saw what I wanted to see: his charm, his looks, his humour. The beautiful son, the ancient house, the thousand-year dynasty. It was my greedy desire to be part of this that blinded me, and condemned me.

I revelled in the jealousy of Jessica and my other

friends when I first brought David to the bars of Shoreditch. Oh yeah. Hey. My new boyfriend. David Kerthen. Lawyer in Marylebone. Family dates back before the Norman Conquest. Owns a fabulous house in Cornwall. Oh, you think he's handsome? Yes, I suppose he is.

All of this done with a fake, self-deprecating laugh.

And now I am pregnant. How will I tell David? How will he react?

Starting the car, trying to clear my clouded mind, I steer myself through the granite zigzags of the little town, up on to the moorland roads. I am more than happy to get lost in these cold, muddy lanes, these strangely mazy roads through Nancledra, Towednack, Amalebra. Past the meagre churches and holy wells, past the bonsai moorland trees, all shorn to the same angle, writhing in the same ceaseless winds.

Topping the hill, the north coast comes into a view: the distant tumult of the Atlantic. There are no ships today. But the waves plough on, silently and very fast. As if they have some grim but important job to do, further up the coast, perhaps someone they have to drown off Port Isaac.

'Zennor,' I say, as I drive into Zennor.

I am talking to myself. Again.

Parking the car, I step out. I've visited this remote, arty village many times, but still its atmosphere surprises. There is *something* here, something to do with the little pub, the humble granite cottages, and then the church: old, small, thickly walled, with narrow lancet windows cut deep into the granite like grievous wounds.

This well-kept church stands in stark contrast with all the ruined Methodist chapels. These chapels remind me, strangely but distinctly, of the ruined tin mines.

Because they are all monuments to dead industry. The seams of faith have been worked out, the precious metals of devotion and belief have been exhausted.

But the stone workings remain. Suffering in the drizzle, crumbling slowly into the cliffsides and the fields, until at last they are overtaken by green nettles and sea thrift, until their broken sills become nests for gulls and choughs.

One day, I suppose, they will be gone entirely.

Part of me resists this idea: the total erosion of religion. I was a devout Catholic as a girl: the simple Irish faith knocked into me at Catholic primary school was hard to knock away. I'd like to believe in God, still: to have that consolation, to think there is something Beyond, a brother for the lonely, a father for the orphaned, an embracing and eternal Lord, gathering the anguished. And a God for my unborn child.

But I can't. My faith died when I was twenty-one. Just after Christmas. And yet now I have faith in a much darker superstition. I believe my stepson can predict the future, and I know his dead mother walks the house, and I know all this is impossible, and it is shredding me to a frenzy of nerves.

Stepping inside the church, I strive to inhale the calming, familiar churchy scent – of rotting flowers, sweetish incense, and mildewed prayer books. Taking out my cameraphone, I take pictures of the various memorials, the Nancekukes of Emba, the Lerryns of Chytodden, and then Jory Kerthen of Carnhallow, 1290–1340, and William de Kerthen of Kenidjack, *dates obscured*, and Mary Kerthen of Carnhallow, 1390–1442. These people will be the ancestors of my child.

Now I find a humbler grave. William Thomas: *kill'd in Wheal-Chance Tin-Mine in Trewey Downs near this*

Church-Town, by a fall of Ground ye 16th of August 1809, aged 44 years.

That was a Kerthen mine. Wheal Chance. And this man died there. Killed by the Kerthens. Everyone is killed by the Kerthens.

The history is inescapable, even as I escape the church. Halfway down the path I come to the grave I cannot avoid: that particular stone.

Nina Kerthen, died aged 33
This is the light of the mind

A chiselled mermaid arcs across a sculpted half-moon. Juliet has told me the Kerthens are meant to descend from mermaids. She also told me about the stone hedges that surround the little fields of Zennor church. *The oldest human artefacts still being used for their original purpose, anywhere in the world.*

The wind is rising, a sea breeze from the west; cold with little nagging cuts of rain. The time is nearly here. The time when I must tell.

I get in the car and drive back as darkness descends, the early winter gloom, at 3.30 p.m., so horribly quick and clammy: not exactly raining, yet with that dampness that rots into your heart. My face is dimlit by the dashboard glow, staring out at the gloom of the moorland road, watching the headlights smear across the arches of Wheal Owles, yet another ruined Kerthen mine. As I drive I keep the window open to the cold oceanic air: breathing the savoury and freezing wind, breathing it deep, trying to keep calm. David is coming home tonight.

At last I take the final turning. And still my mood is dark, and darkening, now I am heading through the oaks, the rowans, the kerthens. Carnhallow emerges through the darkness of Ladies Wood; the hamstone balustrades, the wide south terraces, the older monastic stones, castellated, shadowed in the silver moonlight.

I don't have time to appreciate the antique beauty. Because I have seen David's Mercedes in the garage. He is already here.

And now I somehow know that something will happen. The rainclouds are too black.

Evening

Why is David back so early? Normally he flies around 4 or 5 p.m., then the drive takes another hour, and he arrives around 6.30 or 7. Today he is back at 4.30.

I drop my keys in the brightness of the kitchen, and there is no sign of him, yet the lights are all on, and I can see someone has used the espresso machine. But he isn't here. No briefcase, no raincoat carelessly thrown over a kitchen chair. No necktie un-noosed, with a sigh of relief, and chucked on to the big oak table. No whisky bottle. No gin bottle. So he came in and swallowed coffee and then went – *where*?

Stepping outside the kitchen, all is dark. A few lamps pierce the gloom, but most of the house is shrouded. I think of the bats downstairs in the basement, hanging upside down. Happy in the cold and the black. Eyes barely open. But smiling.

This house chills me now. Its dampness soaks into my bones, drowning me in the dark. And I have to confront David. Dig out the truth, like the vile black tin at the end of the tunnels. Then confront him with my truth. A new baby. Another Kerthen. To go with all the others in the house. Jamie. David.

Nina.

But where is he?

'David?'

The house is so big it answers me with a trailing echo. *David . . .*

'David? Where are you?'

Standing in the New Hall, with its photos of bal maidens in their tatty shawls, I take out my phone and dial his number. Voicemail.

'David?'

Walking to the foot of the stairs, I can see a sliver of light. Coming perhaps from Jamie's room. Switching on more lights – more light, more light – I ascend the grand staircase and walk the landing to Jamie's door with its blue Chelsea FC pennant hanging from a nail. I can hear low voices inside. Like people exchanging secrets.

Something makes me hesitate. Alarm. Fear. A basic silly dread that I will find Nina Kerthen in here, talking to her son. Calmly existing.

Taking hold of my growing insanity, I knock on the door. 'Jamie. Hello, Jamie, it's Rachel.'

There is no reply. But I can hear whispers now. Beyond the door.

'Jamie, please, can you let me in? Can I come in? I'm trying to find your father.'

Another silence; but then Jamie says, 'Come in.'

Turning the knob, I push the door. And there he is, in his school uniform, sitting on his bed. And in the chair near the bed is his father, dressed in his work suit and tie. Their stance is somehow furtive. They look like

203

two people who have been discussing me. I know it. I know it. Their faces say: *We were talking about you.* David's expression is deliberately blank, yet that alone is suspicious. He's making an effort to look normal, and unconcerned.

What were they deciding, or conspiring? How to get rid of me? Abruptly I feel like the worst kind of intruder: an outsider. Someone who shouldn't be here. But I *should* be here. I am proudly, helplessly, inexorably, carrying David's child. Now I belong in Carnhallow as much as them. Even if I don't want to be here, even if I don't want to be one of them: I am.

'David, what's going on?'

His face comes alive, flickers with contempt. 'Going on? What do you mean?'

'Well, you're home so early, and um, now—'

I am about to say, *You are having secret conversations with your son* – but I restrain myself. 'I was unnerved,' I say. 'I came home and the house was dark yet your car was here and . . . it was a bit odd.'

He frowns. 'Are you sure you feel all right, Rachel?'

'Yes, yes.'

'Really?' He stands, and puts a hand on his son's shoulder. 'OK. Jamie. You do that homework and then we can all have supper, unless Rachel has already had food. And drink.'

He eyes me again. A lawyerly gaze. I stammer, defensively, 'No no. No. I had lunch, took some photos at Zennor and – supper would be nice.'

'Good,' he says. 'Let's go down and talk. Let Jamie do his homework.' He turns to his son. 'Remember what we said, Jamie? Remember that promise? What we agreed?'

Right in front of me, David tilts his head, and raises

204

his eyebrows, significantly, towards Jamie. As if to say, *That thing we agreed about Rachel, remember that, and don't tell her.*

Jamie nods in response, then turns to his school bag, fishing out his homework.

What are the two of them hatching? Now I bristle with anger. I have secrets too. But enough of this. He needs to know. And maybe a bit of me wants to put him on the defensive. *You can't touch me now, I'm carrying your child. I'm as good as Nina.*

Taking my arm, David steers me downstairs to the Yellow Drawing Room, turns on the lamps. Closes the curtains on the black winter lawns outside, shutting us off from the winter-black woods, the narrow lane through the sobbing trees, the great black moors. Then we sit down and he starts asking me questions, about my day, about photography, about Christmas arrangements – the most trivial things. Why this interrogation?

He is drinking now. He has one gin and tonic, then another. And still I wait for the right moment, to tell him my secret. Yet something stalls me. I count the clink-clink-clink of ice cubes. Followed by sliced limes, from the Carnhallow greenhouse, speared from a little Georgian silver bowl. Here is the wealth and elegance of his life in one action. The Kerthen signet ring glints on his little finger.

'Do you feel happy here, Rachel?'

He is five yards away, in the chair so carefully recovered by Nina Kerthen. The psychological distance between us is almost immeasurable. I struggle to answer.

'Yes. Well. Yes. It hasn't been easy, but yes, we're muddling through.'

Another big glug of G&T, draining the glass. He pours

himself a third from the fat bottle of Plymouth gin set on a silver tray, alongside the silver tongs and rocks of ice.

'You don't ever feel strange, or scared of things?'

'Scared of what?'

'Does the thought of Nina in the mine unnerve you?'

I shiver. I hide my shiver.

'No.'

'Her dead body in the tunnels, trapped for ever?'

What is this?

'No. It doesn't. Not really.'

'So the thought of her, trapped, a face in the black water, it doesn't give you bad dreams, or make you think strange things? Make you feel persecuted?'

He is implying I am losing the plot. Again. Has he been talking to people? This doesn't make sense. No one is allowed to talk, not even to my husband. And how dare he investigate me, anyway?

I bridle. My own anger isn't far from the surface. 'No. David. I am fine. Please stop this, stop it now.'

'I will stop. Sure. Once you've calmed down.'

'Calmed down? I am *totally* OK. *Totally* fine.' I hurry on, 'David. We're just having problems, we both know that, but we can get through them. We have to get through them. But only if you answer my questions, too.'

He swallows the rest of his rocky gin and tonic, his handsome face smeared with insobriety. His eyes glittering with a sullen drunkenness. I think of his father: Richard Kerthen, and his boozy cruelty. I *see* the father now, see it in David. Yet I still hope he isn't really like that, because David is the father of my child.

'So you'd say you are doing a good job, as a stepmother? Perhaps you still think your stepson can predict things. Do you think that, hmm?'

I am about to snap back – to defend myself loudly,

tell him about the pregnancy – but his phone rings. Silencing us both. He drags it from his pocket, looks at the screen, scowls in puzzlement. Then he waves an irritated hand my way, as if to say: *This is more important than you.* He goes out into the corridor, closing the door to take the call clandestinely.

I want a joint. I cannot. I am pregnant.

The house sits quietly all around us. Waiting. The silk-upholstered chairs are silent but poised. The yellow damask wallpaper gazes at me, suspiciously, with its meaningful patterns.

Getting up, twitching with nerves, I walk to the curtains and pull at a handful of heavy velvet, gazing out at the dark trees lacing the blue-black sky, and the rain that approaches. Like a hunter, down from the moors. But there is no one out there, no one between the moors and the mines, and the carolling sea. No one is watching. The valley is empty.

The door opens. David has returned. There is something about his expression. This I have never seen before. Black dark anger. He is furious. His left fist is clenched. He comes closer.

'You went to see her?'

'Uh—'

'You went to see her. The child psychologist. The fucking shrink. You went to see her?'

What can I say? 'Yes, but—'

'Mavis Prisk rang me. She was quite surprised to find I didn't know. About your little visit. She explained everything.' He is growling. 'How could you fucking do that? How? After I explicitly told you not to?'

'David—'

'How dare you fucking do that? Do you know what could happen?'

He is standing so close his spit hits my face. I can taste the Plymouth gin in his cold saliva.

'You fucking bitch. You *stupid* fucking slut, you little whore, you stupid little cockney *whore*, you did that, you risked everything, you fucking little *cunt* from *nowhere*.'

The blur of his hands is too fast. The first crack of his fist in my face is a white-out. My mind blanks to light. Then he hits me again, very quickly, sending my face spinning left, blood like splattered ink from my mouth, my lips crushed against my teeth. The third blow is a violent slap, it stings so much it makes me choke with pain. I groan as I fall.

I wonder if he will kill me.

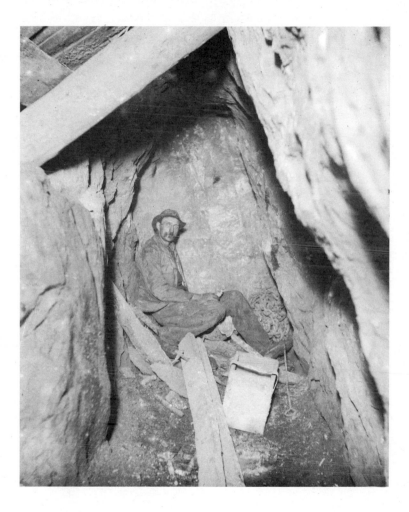

21 Days Before Christmas

Afternoon

'Lovely coffee.'

'Don't thank me, thank Nespresso.'

'Hah, yeah. Should pay more attention to Mum, she loves those ads on telly.'

Kelly looks at me in that innocent way. It strikes me again how young she is. Barely twenty-five, yet apparently in charge of my life. For the moment.

Kelly Smith, fair-haired and freckled, and a little plump in the ill-fitting black uniform of a Police Community Support Officer, has been with me, morning or afternoon, for the last seven days. Sharing cups of tea and coffee, basic suppers. Talking about anything and nothing. Being normal.

It's what I wanted, and now I've got it. Beans on toast, and reality TV. Something regular and simple and unambitious. For months I have been lost amongst the exotic. Beautiful, dead Nina Valéry, handsome, arrogant David Kerthen. Juliet in her dreams. Jamie alone in his room. And in the middle of it all, this house: Carnhallow,

211

baroque in its sadness, tragic in its ruined wealth, still somehow lording it over the rest of West Cornwall.

And then the mines. I look at them endlessly, every day, perhaps more than ever. Because I am desperate now. I *need* to understand, I need to see what the mines are saying, with their upwards–jutting chimneys, giving a forefinger to the heavens. Black gloved fists.

And even as I think of hands, and of fists – it returns. From nowhere, in my mind, I see him again, punching me, his fist slamming in to my face, hard and then harder, his face racked with anger, ugly with violence, like a sexual expression, but horrifying, and the blood spurting bright crimson, blurting from my mouth.

Dizzy and faint, I turn from the kitchen window. I realize I've been staring at the window, blank-faced, mouth half open, like an idiot.

'You OK, Rachel?'

'Yes, sorry, Kelly, yes.'

'Was it a flashback?'

'Yes. Kind of.'

'Well, you can expect that.' She sips more coffee, squints my way. 'But the bruises are going down. You look a whole lot better than you did, when . . . You know . . .'

I know what she is about to say. *When it happened.* When I first went to Treliske Hospital, rushed there by ambulance, following a panicked phone call once I'd heard David leave, slamming the door, when he'd come to his senses and left me bleeding in the corner of the Drawing Room.

When it happened. When the doctor stared at me, pitying, as she patched up my face. When I decided I wanted the police involved. When I first met Kelly Smith,

PCSO. And when I first learned all the language. Book 124D. Domestic Violence Protection Notice. FME statement. Early swabs. *Imminent risk to victim based on DASH, 2009 High Risk Factors.*

'I don't look like a gargoyle any more?'

Kelly smiles, politely.

'Nah, you look a bit dazed, Rachel. But that's not a surprise, izzit? God, is it raining again? My mum's garden will be underwater.'

I touch a finger to my cheekbone, recalling the first time I summoned the courage, and I took up a mirror and looked at myself, the morning after David beat me, seven days ago: my face was vivid with bruises and cuts. At least he only punched me above the neck.

Calming myself, I place a hand on my stomach. My baby is still alive. Still growing inside me. Yet this baby is the child of a man who beat his wife. The father of my child is violent. Whatever I do, wherever I go, I shall be trapped in a room with that thought, for the rest of my life. I will never escape David Kerthen.

Kelly is observing me, her head slightly tilted. Perhaps assessing the way I've placed my protecting hand on my stomach. Let her look. I want this baby to grow, to come soon, to come to her mother. I don't know why I believe this child is a daughter, but I do. Perhaps because I want a daughter. Right now I can't help thinking there are enough men in the world.

Kelly sets down her coffee mug.

'You know, if you hadn't been pregnant we wouldn't have got the exclusion order.'

'Really?'

'Yep. It's pretty unusual. This is your husband's house, he's got no previous history of DV – not on file anyway. And this is where his son lives. Magistrates don't like kicking out parents from family homes, even when they are total and utter bastards.'

She stops. I shake my head.

'Kelly. It's OK.'

'No. I'm sorry. Not my place to judge.'

It's my turn to reassure her.

'Of course you can say it. David's a bastard. How else would you describe him? He did this to me.' I gesture at my face, proving my point. 'He could easily have killed the child inside me. I was lucky.'

She nods. Grimly.

'Well, yeah, that's what I was driving at: what kind of bastard would beat his wife when she's pregnant? You know,' Kelly leans closer, in the humming quietness of the kitchen, with the clinical steel sinks. 'Maybe I shouldn't say this, but I'll bloody well say it. There's a good chance he'll do it again. Don't matter how rich or important he is. They always say they won't, but – I've seen it too many times – a few weeks later, a few months later, there he goes again. On and on. Think of that when the injunction runs out. Three months' time. Think of that, for me?'

I nod, and say nothing.

Kelly picks up her coffee mug, holds it between two warming hands, and gazes about. I see a faint twinkle of wonder in her eyes, probably she is marvelling at the size of the kitchen, as big as some of the many flats I grew up in. Probably as big as her flat, too.

'So you reckon you'll be OK here, on yer own?'

'Yes.'

'I know it's old and big and beautiful, but I reckon it would creep me out. Sorry. Probably shouldn't say that either!' She blushes, sweetly. I shake my head.

'I'm getting used to it.'

214

'Really?'

'Yes.'

And I am. I am getting used to the added darkness, and the intensified silence, since David was thrown out. Sometimes I sit in the Yellow Drawing Room, with all the lights off, listening to the house and the sea. The waves sigh and crash, down at Morvellan, and a few seconds later Carnhallow answers: a cold wind stirs the dust in a moaning basement corridor; a leaded window rattles. As if the sea and the house converse, as if they are conscious of each other, both been here so long. And in between them, Nina walks. Ready to replace me, maybe around Christmas. Everything happens around Christmas.

Coffee drunk, Kelly rises. Apparently my silence has led her to think our conversation is finished, and her duty is done. As she buttons her plain raincoat I have an urge to ask her to stay and keep me company through the endless winter evening, right up to the moment I can creep into my bed and pretend the house is ten times smaller.

Because I am so very alone, tonight. And my sleeping patterns are getting worse. Mostly I lie there. Scratching. Scratching and sometimes sleeping. Last night when I finally slept I dreamed of the hare I killed, I lifted up its dead body, and held it in my hand, its blood dripping down my arm, and then it suddenly came alive, screaming, shrieking, spitting blood in my eyes.

I woke up with my heart pounding anxiously and very painfully. I did not sleep again.

I don't want to be alone in my room, like that, with dreams like that, not tonight.

But Cassie is again out with friends, enjoying her day off. She seeks every chance to leave the house now,

215

looking at me sharply as she leaves. Like I am the guilty party. The bad woman who replaced Nina. Juliet is silent in her apartment. Only Jamie is here. In his room. Barely speaking. He clearly blames me for causing his father's exile, and yet, when we offered him the chance to stay elsewhere, to avoid the upsetting sight of his beaten stepmother, he flatly refused. And wouldn't tell us why.

No, I'm staying.

But he doesn't really talk to me. So I have created the most intense loneliness for myself.

PCSO Kelly Smith is waiting patiently for me to emerge from my daydream. Like she is used to my wandering mind. I rush to reassure. To be normal. No, I'm not mad. Honest.

'Thanks for everything, Kelly. You've been brilliant. I'm not sure I could have got through this week without you.'

'Hey,' she says. 'No worries! I do it for the coffee. That's a joke.'

We walk to the big front door. For a moment it looks like we are going to shake hands. This seems crazy after the week we've been through, so I give her a quick, embarrassed hug, and she looks at me, with curiosity, and maybe pity, and then she touches me very gently on the arm, and says:

'If there's anything, anything at all that bothers you, Rachel, call me.' A pause. 'Even after work? I don't mind! And if you see any sign of him near the house, prowling around, breaking the injunction, call at once, even if it's bloody three in the morning! Promise me you'll do that?'

I nod. And say Yes. Choking back any emotion.

'I will, I will. Thanks, Kelly, thanks so much.'

Keeping myself calm, I watch her walk away, climb

216

in her little car, turn the ignition – then give me a cheery wave through the chilly drizzle. For several minutes I observe the twinned lights of her headlamps dwindling through the woodlands. And then, at the last moment, the very last moment, I want to run out and bang on her window.

Because I also want to confess. Admit my guilt.

I knew from the very beginning – without any nudging from lawyers – that it would be very hard to get a restraining order against David. I googled it all from my hospital bed as soon as I woke, as soon as I felt the stinging pain from my bruises.

My smartphone told me my cause was useless, but I was too angry to give in. Memories of my past had returned in my dreams. So I decided to fight back and to lie. Take revenge.

When the police came in to interview me, and take me home, I told them David knew I was pregnant before he assaulted me. And that he still attacked me, knowing that. Therefore risking the life of our unborn child.

Kelly has told me his reaction was dramatic, in Truro Magistrates Court, when they read out my witness statement, when they told him that my pregnancy was the reason he was exiled from his own home, his beloved Carnhallow. According to Kelly, David actually shouted at the magistrate: *I didn't fucking know, I didn't know she was fucking pregnant.*

But his shouting made his position worse: and so we got the injunction. David Kerthen is not allowed to approach within five miles of Carnhallow for the next three months. David Kerthen is excluded from the valley where his family have lived for a thousand years, amongst the rowans from which the Kerthens took their name.

Because I lied.

I can imagine the pain this causes him, and it doesn't gratify me – but neither does it worry me. Instead, I worry about my lies. If I can lie to the police and to the courts, to get my husband thrown out of his own house, I wonder what else I am capable of doing. To defend my unborn child. To stay here in Carnhallow. This house that I love despite it all, or maybe because of it all. This house that should belong to my daughter and Jamie. The house that is their birthright.

Now I sense the darkness of the house behind me. Waiting to eat us all up. So I stand in the open doorway, gazing out into the fog. My breath makes plumes of white in the freezing dark. Soon it will be Christmas. When things come down the chimney, like a poison gas. And Carnhallow has so many chimneys.

19 Days Before Christmas

Morning

'David, you're a lawyer, how could you have done that, in a court? Lose your temper like some toddler?'

'I don't know. I can't really understand why I did it, snapped so badly. Believe me, I feel guilty. But what can I do about it now?'

David paced to the window of his big hotel room, gazing out over Truro Town Centre. The three spires of Truro Cathedral dominated the skyline of the quaint and pretty little city, spread out before him. They always slightly annoyed him, those towers. Irritated him with their fakery, the ersatz Gothic, pretend-medieval – built in 1900.

Fake fake fake. Like the woman who lied to him, and betrayed him – made him act like a madman, for a few minutes, so he could be thrown out of his Own Fucking House.

The house he'd spent two decades rescuing, when the family was on the brink of bankruptcy, when it was about to be sold.

221

He'd salvaged things by working a hundred hours a week for two decades. Now he was *excluded*. At the very moment when he had the evidence he needed, to eject her from Carnhallow, he'd done the stupidest thing, and got himself banished. Because Rachel lied to the courts.

The anger inside him was ulcerating. He paced from side to side.

'David?'

'Yes. Sorry. I feel like one of those psychotic bears in a shitty zoo.'

'Well, what did you expect?' Alistair's voice was terse. His Scottish accent flavoured with stern disapproval.

'I lost my rag – once. And for that they take away my house?'

'You lost your temper in a courtroom. That's a proximate cause. But the ultimate reason they put an occupation order on is because you beat your wife, David. Your pregnant young wife. You beat her pretty badly. You need to accept that. You need to express proper remorse: the courts will want to see this and be assured of your contrition, and good behaviour, if we are to get the injunction lifted.'

David hung his head. 'I did something terrible, I know. But I really didn't know she was pregnant. She *lied*.'

The Christmas music filtered up from the hotel lobby. Handel. *For unto us a child is given.*

The saddening thought came roaring back. Jamie. His beloved son. He had to save him from all this mess.

'David?'

Sinking wearily on to the oversoft hotel bed, David rested his head in his hands. 'Alistair, I know I'm the villain here. But she provoked me, by going to the psychiatrist.'

'How? Why is that so bad?'

'Al— As I told you. It's very private.'

'And that's it? That's all you can tell me? You keep saying this.'

'Alistair—'

'You're a lawyer, David, a much better paid lawyer than me. You know how difficult it is to assist a client who is so reticent about important details. I'm not sure what further point there is in this conversation.'

'OK, wait. Please. Give me a minute?'

Alistair said he would wait, though he added another modest, contemptuous sigh.

The piped Christmas music percolated up to his hotel room from the lobby. *Hark the Herald Angels Sing.* David thought of all the shoppers in Truro town centre, the Santa in the grotto, the anxious mothers, the overexcitable kids, the phoney commercial silliness of it all, and he felt a pure and piercing sadness. Now he was excluded from his own home, and only allowed access to Jamie when it could be organized outside Carnhallow, the shiny charade of Christmas time seemed unbearably poignant, and seductive.

God and sinners, reconciled.

Was he a sinner? Was he truly evil? He'd done one significantly wicked thing. Beaten his pregnant wife when she had severely provoked him. He'd also done one singular thing, but he wasn't sure that was even wrong.

But deep down maybe he *was* bad, an evil Kerthen, like his dad. Just another one in the line. One of the rich and heartless men in the portraits.

Dark thoughts were crowding him now.

'David?'

'Yes, I'm still here.'

'You need to reassure me you aren't going to break the injunction, and go anywhere in the vicinity of Carnhallow. I know that will be difficult for you, but things will get a whole lot worse if you do. The next exclusion order could be twenty miles and six months. Then it could be a year.'

David tightened his fist around his mobile phone, wanting to strangle it, like an unwanted animal, like her fucking throat. 'But it's my damn home, Alistair. My family's home for one thousand years – I've given my life for Jamie and the house, they've been everything to me.'

'Well now you must be content with your hotel room. I'm sure it's sizeable.'

'Oh, it's fucking beautiful. The breakfast buffet is imperious. They have pink grapefruit juice.'

'You could always rent a flat. For the time being.' Another judgemental sigh. 'And you should be thankful the Family Courts are so secretive. They kept all the names out of the papers, for the sake of Jamie and your wife. To protect their identity, not yours. Nonetheless you benefited.'

'*Benefited?*' David heard himself growling. Actually growling with anger.

'I rather think we're done, aren't we? I'm sure we both have other matters to attend to.'

'Wait – I've got one more question.'

No doubt Alistair was irritatedly shuffling papers, far away in London. But David was paying this guy five hundred pounds an hour. 'Alistair, what if she sues for divorce?'

'What do you mean?'

'Simply that. Now she's pregnant, if she went for a divorce, is it possible she could get the house?'

A deep, long pause.

Jingle Bells, Jingle Bells.

'Difficult to predict, depends on the court and the judge, but . . . You know the precedents as well as me – indeed, better, I imagine.'

'You mean there's at least a chance she would get it. Right? The house? If she got some friendly judge. She could start divorce proceedings now, and on the basis that she is pregnant – and on what I did – she might actually get the house. Carnhallow.'

'It's not entirely impossible, put it that way.'

'Thank you, Alistair.'

'Goodbye.'

He shut the phone off – and stared in cold fury at the window. Trying not to punch through the glass, let the freezing air blast his room. This crazy bitch, this madwoman, she could get it all.

All.

So it had happened. His worst nightmare gathered, like the cold winter rainclouds he could see now through the hotel window, building over steepled Truro, bullying their way from the hills to the west. From Carn Brea, and the cliffs of Portreath.

And beyond that, further west, where the rocks of Penwith began? The rain was probably already falling there, falling on the oaks and rowans of Ladies Wood, pattering on the dank tangled brambles of Carnhallow Valley. Falling on that house, where his son was trapped with a lunatic stepmother – yet stubbornly refusing to leave. Why? It was as if Jamie was growing closer to Rachel, and detaching himself from his own father. He was losing the love of his son, to another.

For the first time in his life, David realized how Nina might have felt.

Evening

'She really believes this?'

'Yes.'

'She really thinks she is going to die at Christmas?'

'Yes.'

'That's distressing. It is also pretty indicative. Schizotypal, maybe.'

Anne Williamson ate an olive. Pensively. And then she discreetly laid a pip on the saucer, and sipped from her large glass of red wine.

Truro's one and only tapas bar was busy; they were tucked in a cramped corner table, in the darkest part of the big and bustling room. This was fine by David. He didn't want to be seen, to be acknowledged. He wanted this done quickly and discreetly. The money was in an envelope in his jacket pocket. Along with all the information.

'In fact, that does sound slightly like a command hallucination. Which is a classic symptom.'

'Yes. She really is crazy, like I said – and she has a

history of it. It's here' – he tapped his breast pocket – 'with a donation. That donation I've been promising your charity, Anne. I know the cuts have taken a chunk of your funding.'

Anne Williamson sat back. He could see the immediate scepticism in her expression, maybe even a hint of contempt.

She was a psychiatrist in her late thirties, she'd known David for years, she'd been to dinner parties at Carnhallow when Nina was alive, with her yacht-building husband. They were now divorced. And David and Anne had slept together during her marriage. So he knew she was no saint.

Her lovemaking, as he recalled, was like her persona: businesslike, and efficient. Here was a woman who liked to get things done. Achieve satisfaction. Two orgasms in an hour. Pull on her jeans.

No love had ever been expressed between them, because they had never been foolish enough for that. Theirs was an exchange of pleasure. Two attractive adults who needed sex. Then a meal. Some intelligent conversation. No strings. Move on.

That was why he'd chosen her. She was smart but not obsessive. More than anything she was deeply pragmatic. He wondered if there was a slight possibility she'd take the money for herself, not mention it to anyone? No. She would do the right thing for the right reasons, albeit in the wrong context. She'd give it all to the Centre at Treliske. She was practical, and cynical – but not venal.

'You don't have to tell people it's from me. Make it anonymous.'

'Yes. I understand.'

The Christmas office-party-goers had filled the bar

with slightly forced laughter. One woman, by the gleaming metal beer pumps – San Miguel, Corona – was wearing gold tinsel on her head. Another had a Santa hat. Leeringly drunk.

He took the envelope out. And put it on the table. And now his lawyer's eyes detected the gleam behind Anne's mild frown.

'You see, Anne, I remembered, when I called you, what I promised, years ago. And I'd like to keep on supporting the Centre, after this – make large and regular donations, over time. I'd hate to see the Centre closed. I know what good work you do with young people in Cornwall. I know they need it.'

Anne sighed. 'We've got a major skunk problem in Penzance right now. The number of mental issues caused by that stuff – it's horrible. And heroin, too.' She gazed at the envelope, distractedly. Still frowning. 'Tourists come down to Cornwall and all they see is the beautiful coast, and the lovely valleys; they don't understand the poverty. But . . . ' She looked away from the envelope. And turned to David. 'Let's go back to your wife. I'm grateful for your generosity, David, but be assured, I will only do this for proper medical reasons.'

'I know.'

'She really believes your son can predict the future?'

He nodded.

Anne pouted, thoughtfully. 'And she hears voices, sees things. And you say she has a history of psychosis? Mental breakdowns?'

'Yes. Yes, yes, yes. All of it. All of it. It's hair-raising. And she's affecting my son, he's told me. They both think they can see his dead mother, see ghosts. Read the notes. So how can she be allowed to look after him, given all that? How can she be allowed to look after my own son? Jamie?'

'I can see why it pains you.'

'So you're agreed?'

Anne was tight-lipped. She looked at her watch. 'I must go.' She looked directly his way, as she stood up, unsmiling. 'I have a date.'

David stood too. Picking up the chunky envelope, he put it in her hand. Without flinching, she took the envelope, put it in her handbag, clasped it shut.

He watched as she disappeared past the girl in the red Santa hat, who was now singing a Christmas pop song. He sat down again. David had a bulbous glass of pricey Tempranillo to finish. A different, drunken woman, with tinsel wrapped around her head, was now kissing some surprised but happy young man, full on the lips.

It was Christmas. That special time was approaching. The time of lawless merriment, when you could do what you liked. The time of misrule.

And David knew what some deep, appalling part of himself wanted to do. What was once a brief, ludicrous fantasy now presented itself as a distant but actual possibility. He had one more chance with the sectioning: using everything that he'd learned – and hope to God that Anne would persuade the second doctor of Rachel's insanity, her psychosis, whatever it was.

And if that didn't work?

Pushing the wine away, he stared glumly at all the cheering and boozing people.

He recalled another phrase his father used to quote, when they drove the coast near Carnhallow, on those few rare days when he talked to his son, when he was at home. It was a line from a poem about West Penwith.

This is a hideous and a wicked country, Sloping to hateful sunsets and the end of time. After saying this, Dad would chortle as if it was some enormous joke, and turn the car and go back to Carnhallow and take the next train to London, and the son was left, alone, in the hideous and wicked country.

And now it felt like things were sloping, once more, to hateful sunsets. And the end of time.

16 Days Before Christmas

Afternoon

Slowly I let out a breath I never even knew I was holding. The house is silent, yet it isn't.

Yet it is: I know these noises are in my head. I have been here before.

The tinsel faintly weighs in my hand. The Christmas tree is naked and green, an innocently sinister presence in the Yellow Drawing Room. I am trying to decorate it, be normal, pretend that we are a regular family. But every few minutes I bite back the fear. And the memories. My husband who beat me. The man who waits behind the door. The man who comes down the chimney.

Draping the golden tinsel over a branch, I bend to the box for another bauble: I want to get this done before it is dark. I want to fight the wintry night outside: when darkness comes across Carnhallow, in two or three hours, I want Carnhallow House to stand proud in its valley, with all its lamps shining. And in the corner of the Drawing Room, I want there to be a great green Christmas tree lavished with decorations, and besieged

233

with boxed and bowed presents, symbolizing happiness and harmony.

I know it is a farce. This family is shattered. But I can try.

Yet even as I loop a golden-yellow bauble over a spiky spruce branch, I hear the brutish voice of my father, downstairs.

It is always him. He will do it again and again. I can predict it, and I am imprisoned in this prediction, and I am going to die at Christmas.

I think maybe a miniature Santa next. Yes. Then another stripy red-and-amber bauble. Then ignore the noises from the basement. They are so frequent now: strange rattlings, doors slamming for no reason, a broken, unhinged window creaking in winter rain – I have chosen to ignore them. Perhaps because I am not sure I am hearing them. Because I have been here before. Locked in madness, locked in a room, not knowing reality from imagination, not knowing hallucination from my hand in front of my face.

I saw Nina. No I didn't. Yes I did. I didn't just see her, I smelled her perfume.

Twining a tiny smiling plastic snowman on the big Christmas tree, I delve into the box for some more tinsel. Nice big bouffant red tinsel. Make the tree positively burlesque. I wonder what sort of Christmas tree Nina installed. No doubt it was elegant. Perhaps I should ask her.

The best explanation I can find, the one that saves me from madness, is that she isn't dead. Nina lives. Perhaps she attempted suicide, but failed, and was saved. I don't know.

But if she isn't dead that means there is some enormous conspiracy, which is almost as crazy as the idea that there is a ghost out there cheerfully riding the buses through the rain-swept streets of St Just. And if she isn't dead then the question is how did she possibly escape from Morvellan shaft? They DNA-tested the gruesome remains. The blood and fingernails left as she struggled to escape, before sinking in the black water.

It is impossible. Everything is impossible.

'Miss Rachel.'

A jump of the heart.

'Cassie?'

'Sorry, Miss Rachel, there people at door. Three people. Want see you.'

'People?'

'Not know. Some people come from Truro. Want speak you.'

She looks anxious. But then she always looks anxious these days, her eyes seeking me out, examining and assessing. Probably she wonders if I am mad, like all the others.

I notice, now, that she is wearing a conspicuous new necklace. A leather thong with a little golden plaque showing the Buddha. I believe I know what it signifies. I've been to Thailand. 'That's nice,' I say. 'Your new necklace.'

'Oh,' she says. 'Yes, I buy online.'

She is blushing. And again, I know why. Cassie is superstitious. And this is an amulet against evil. She now thinks there is evil here, in Carnhallow. And I have an idea that she thinks the evil is *me*.

I look into her eyes. Defiant. 'Please show them in here. And I guess we'll have some tea. On a tray. Thank you.'

Cassie disappears. I wonder who these guests might be; I wonder how I must appear. The bruises have all but gone from my face, but I daren't look in mirrors for fear I will see myself. As I really am. A liar. A madwoman. Falling apart.

Mumbled voices approach: it sounds like a man and two women, talking with Cassie outside the door. The voice of the man is recognizable: it's the Kerthen family GP, Doctor Conner – ostensibly my doctor, though I rarely if ever see him. He is too close to David. I prefer the anonymity of walk-in clinics, overworked obstetricians who barely know my name.

David's doctor steps in, alongside a fair-haired girl, and a tall, smartly dressed woman.

Crossing the room, I extend a hand. The older, taller woman smiles. 'Hello, I'm Anne Williamson. I'm with Treliske. The psychiatric unit. This is Charlotte Kavenna, also from Treliske.' She indicates the young woman. 'A nurse with the psych unit. She's a qualified mental health professional.'

With a shudder of recognition, I realize what is going on: I know because it has happened to me before. Three people. One doctor. A qualified mental health professional. I do not invite them to sit. I realize perfectly well that I am fighting for my life. 'You're here to have me sectioned, aren't you?'

A wince of distaste flashes across Alan Conner's face. He's a decent man, if a bit starchy. I've seen him grovelling to David at social functions. But he is fundamentally OK. And he looks uncomfortable. I can see him looking at me surreptitiously. I wonder if he can see the traces of the bruising, and I wonder if he knows that David did it.

'We're here to do an assessment,' says Anne Williamson, and her voice is crisp. Officious. 'Your husband is concerned—'

'Concerned? *He's concerned?*'

236

Even as I speak, I realize I am shouting. Yelling at these people.

The two doctors gaze at me, startled. Cassie steps into the room with a tray of tea and biscuits and she also stares at me, mouth half-open. The entire house is regarding me with disdain. The crazy woman.

Stupid, Rachel. Stupid. Don't let them see how angry you are, how frightened, how scared you might be of slipping back into psychosis. I have to be an actress now. I have to be Sane Rachel, though my soul is so unstable. To save myself and my unborn baby.

'Please,' I say. 'I was a bit shocked. Please have a seat, and some tea. Do your assessment.'

The nurse speaks: 'You know that you can ask to have someone with you, if you like.'

'No,' I say. It takes an effort to be calm. 'I'm fine. Ask your questions.'

Alan Conner looks like he wants to get this over and done as soon as possible. The nurse is surely irrelevant. So Anne Williamson is my real enemy. The bad cop. She's the one with the calculating eyes, already drilling hard and fast into my head. Wanting to open me up, check the machinery, see where I've gone wrong, where my mind is wonky and broken. Put me back in that room in Woolwich General, from which I barely escaped.

'It won't take too long, Mrs Kerthen,' says Alan Conner.

I pour some tea. I smile blandly. Let them do their shtick. I can handle this, I hope, because I've been here before, with psychiatrists.

Cassie is gone. The room gets ready to pounce. It's me and my madness, and three people I do not know, who have the power to drag me away and lock me up.

The first questions are predictable. Stuff about my life, stuff to make sure I know the name of the prime minister. Anne Williamson sips some tea and asks, 'Do you ever think you are on TV? That people are watching?'

She might as well ask: *Are you actually a paranoid schizophrenic?*

'No. I don't think that.'

Her cup chinks in the saucer. She scrapes the saucer along the table, making a deeply irritating jangly noise. Then, from nowhere, 'Do you, Mrs Kerthen, believe that your stepson Jamie can predict the future?'

A pause. A stupid, dangerous pause. My lower lip is trembling. Or maybe it is my eyelid. I look at Alan Conner. It seems as if he is urging me on, nodding – subtly, discreetly – trying to help. But I am checked. Because I *do* wonder if Jamie can sometimes predict the future. I have wondered that, in idle and credulous moments. And the hare, I don't understand the hare. How could he have foreseen that? It cannot be explained. But I can't admit it. Can't can't can't.

'No, of course not. I don't think that.'

'What about the prediction that you are going to die at Christmas? Apparently, you' – Anne Williamson is looking right into me, as she goes on – 'heard Jamie say that, and it shook you. Is that correct?

Don't pause, don't pause, don't pause.

I pause. There is sweat on my upper lip. I daren't rub it off because that would look mad. 'I did. I mean, he did, well. Um. He . . .' I pause again. Oh, the royal fucking pauses. Why don't they handcuff me and take me away? Put me in an armlock. Restrain me. It's happened before. 'He. He. Um. He. We used to sing this song, I've got pants, I've got pants, I've got pants that are bigger than my aunt's.'

Alan Conner has closed his eyes. The nurse – Charlotte

– is blushing. Embarrassed on my behalf. They are going to take me away.

I gulp some hot tea and manage to garble a better answer. 'What I mean is uh is uh is uh we used to have fun together, stepson and stepmum, and say lots of silly things and I think maybe he said things as a joke, obviously a strange joke, but he was badly affected by his mum's death and . . . Well . . . yes, he said something like that, but of course I don't believe it has any, you know, basis in reality.'

Is that enough? Unexpectedly the nurse takes over, and her questioning is softer, but just as dangerous.

'Do you ever think about your husband's late wife? Nina Kerthen?'

I stall for time. 'What do you mean, "think"?'

Anne Williamson intervenes. 'Have you, for instance, ever imagined that she might still be alive? Sensed her presence in Carnhallow, or elsewhere?'

Quickly. Do not blush, do not flinch, do not admit that you saw her on the bus. Yet I want to say: I saw her on the bus. And I sensed her perfume in this room. I did I did I did. I want to say this, sing it out, be honest. YES, I SAW HER.

My mouth trembles on the cusp of speech. I am going to admit it all. Yes, I saw her on the bus, she is alive, I believe in ghosts. She is back. At last I answer, 'No.'

Conner looks to the ceiling, as if to say *Thanks be.*

Anne Williamson sits up even straighter. I get a sense she is running out of ideas. But I am still scared, and still wary, they can still clap me in irons, prick me with witch-hunting needles, open up my seething brain and see all the scuttling insects under the rock and then they will take me into care. For a very long time. I might not get out. I will not be allowed to look after my own baby.

My enemy has picked up her smartphone and she is clicking on it, seeking some notes.

'I've now got to ask you some really personal questions. About your past. And of course you can still ask someone to be here with you, Mrs Kerthen, if you prefer.'

I am sure I've got to say 'No' to this as well. A surge of defiance rises, for the daughter inside me. Protect her by protecting myself. Yes. I have to be strong and sane for her, my baby girl. It isn't only me, not any more.

David has clearly been investigating me and he has discovered my past. But who cares. I've been through worse.

'I'm fine.' I give her a faked but confident stare. 'Yes. Whatever. Ask away.'

'Is it true you were sectioned when you were younger, and spent some time in Woolwich General Hospital, detained against your will?'

No pause this time. No pause at all.

'Yes.'

Conner steps in. 'We know this must be painful, Mrs Kerthen, but—'

'It's fine.' I look at him and I allow myself a quiet smile. I have a trump card here. This is my past. And my past usually wins. 'You see, I was raped.'

They are silenced.

The mental health professionals stare at each other. I guessed they didn't know *this*. No one knows *this*. It is the law that no one ever learns *this*.

'You were, um, raped?' Anne Williamson looks nonplussed, for the first time.

'Shall I tell you what happened, because you won't find it in the records.'

'Please.'

I can see that Williamson wants to intervene, but she can go jump. This is my special story. No one gets to interrupt.

'I was brought up a devout Catholic, you see. I still believed well into my teens. But after the rape – let's say I never believed again.'

Conner gazes at me, bemused, frowning. I go on, deliberately dragging this out, for effect.

'For a few years, we were at a refuge. Me and my mum. My sister was already gone, most of the time, she had a boyfriend. And then someone broke into the last refuge, and he raped me.'

'Who?'

'My father.'

The silence in the room is the sound of my bitter triumph.

'From the age of nine or ten, my dad abused me. He would come into my room. I remember it vividly, even now.' I am looking Anne Williamson in the eye. 'He would be drunk, always drunk. He'd grab me by my pigtails and . . . put himself in my mouth.'

The nurse cannot look at me. She is averting her face. I feel a peculiar sense of vindication.

'This stopped, my dad stopped, when I was twelve and I started fighting back. I was tough, wiry, angry – and I scratched and fought and nearly took out one of his eyes. So he left me alone from then on. But then he started on my mum. Beating her. On and off. For years. Eventually we moved to refuges around South London, but every time he tracked us down, tried to get in and get at us, and we had to move again.' There

241

is a choke of emotion in my throat. 'My education was screwed by the chaos, the violence, the moving. I had to take any old job from the age of sixteen. Help my mum out. But somehow I got some A-levels, working nights, reading all day. Maybe because I was still a fighter. Determined. And then I was twenty-one. I was going to make my own escape, at last, and go to university, to Goldsmiths. I'd done work for a photographer, assisting. It was nothing much, just minimum wage. But I knew I had talent. And I knew I wanted to do that: learn photography, properly.' I pause, letting the idea weigh on them. 'Then one day I came back to the room, in the refuge, to get my bag, and I had no idea he was inside, waiting for Mum. And he decided I would do, instead of Mum. He grabbed me, punched me, used a knife on me, threatened me. And he raped me, for hours.'

Anne Williamson has nothing to say. The nurse is hiding her face.

'Then, yes, months later, I had a breakdown. I didn't tell anyone. Not at first. I felt a kind of shame, I suppose. But I stopped believing in God, and then when I lost that I felt there was nothing to stop me falling through the floor. I started cutting myself.'

The doctors say nothing.

'It was my mum who called the doctors. She found me slicing my arm, hacking at myself with scissors. I fought the doctors, but she was right. I would have killed myself. In effect I would have let *him*, my father, kill me.'

I do believe the nurse is nearly crying. I look at her, then go on, calmly enough. It all works so much better if I am calm.

'I was sectioned. For a few weeks. For my own

protection. I had a brief psychosis. But only for a few weeks. What is the term? Brief schizophreniform disorder. A brief psychosis. But, I ask you, who wouldn't have gone a bit mad, after all that?'

The silence holds. Then I notice Doctor Conner is standing. He steps around the table, and takes my hand and he holds it in his, and he looks me firmly in the eye.

'I'm so sorry to have put you through all this, Rachel. All this absurdity. I'm so very sorry. I think we've asked more than enough questions. I don't think you'll be hearing from us again.'

Anne Williamson says nothing. She looks guilty. The nurse comes across and shakes my hand as well and then dashes another tear from her eye and the three of them walk to the door. As they step outside, Doctor Conner turns and says:

'I hope you will be all right? I understand David is not here at the moment.' He gives me a look that seems to say: *I understand why.* His smile is earnest and sincere. 'If you want anything, please call me.'

And then he is gone. And I am victorious.

And then I turn and look at my completed Christmas tree.

The little fairy at the top of the Christmas tree is staring right at me. I sense that she knows. She knows that I have told the bitter truth, yet also an enormous lie. She is smiling. Everyone is smiling. It is Christmas, after all.

10 Days Before Christmas

Afternoon

The two of them gazed out to sea. Where that boat still drifted, pointlessly; and where the Lizard mine houses stood inert and black, blocking part of the view.

If only they could be demolished. Swept away. Pushed into the sea and forgotten. Part of David yearned to knock down every single mine in all of fucking Cornwall. Fucking blow them up.

But he couldn't. Like the mines of Morvellan, Levant, Consols, and everywhere along the coast, these mines were Grade One listed. A UNESCO World Heritage Site. Untouchable. Protected. Every resident of West Cornwall, in particular the Kerthens, was cursed to look at them, every day.

The only consolation was that it gave him and Jamie something to talk about, and think about, other than the horror unfolding at Carnhallow, when he got his cherished hours with his son. His one free day a week, when he got to be a father. David was taking all his holidays, to be as close as possible to his son.

They'd had lunch in Pizza Express in Truro and ice creams on the wave-swept pier at Mullion Cove, and now, as the day ebbed, they were striding the coast of the Lizard, smuggling country, staring out towards Penzance and Mousehole. Across the chaos and turmoil of the Atlantic. Twenty years ago it was the kind of view he liked to draw, and paint. Not now.

Jamie was talking.

'Tell me more about the mines, Dad. Did we really own them all? How did they make us rich, the mines?'

These questions – about the mines – had become more frequent of late. It made sense, as Jamie began to realize who he was: the son and heir of the mineral lordship of Penwith.

David pondered an answer: something involving but not too emotional. They didn't need emotional. As the pair of them walked the cliffside path, the winter gusts carried tufts of surf, clipped off the manes of the waves below. The grey-white spindrift nestled in the shivering grass, and melted to nothing. As if it had never existed.

Jamie looked up, as David answered, 'We got rich because the earth is rich. You know, I remember a list my grandfather used to recite, of all the minerals that lie under Cornwall. It was like a poem.' David closed his eyes, searching back, a time of happiness. 'How did it go . . . Yes. Yes, this was it: sulphide of bismuth, arborescent native copper, arseniate of iron crystallized in great cubes. Then foot-wide garnet crystals, prisms of iron, haematite iron, hydrous oxide of iron, magnetic iron pyrites, hornblende mixed with slate, axinite in veins, thallite, chlorite, tremolite, plus jasper, schorl, and traces of gold. All of it here, all of it right here, under these rocks.'

He paused. Jamie was looking at him, eyes wide. Sceptical or impressed, David couldn't say. So David went on, 'Fifteen per cent of the world's minerals can be found in Cornwall. It's more diverse, minerally speaking, than any comparable area on earth, with the possible exception of Mount Olympus, in Greece—'

Jamie interrupted, 'But how did we *get* them, Daddy? How did we get all our mines, like uh, Morvellan and Levant, and how did we get the mines up on the moors?'

'Your clever ancestors. They did some clever deals. We always owned Morvellan. But we bought Pendeen from the Bassetts in 1721. Levant we bought soon after. Often we bought mines when the previous owners went bankrupt.'

'What does that mean? Bank . . . ?'

'Means the owners, or the shareholders, the tributers, ran out of money. Mining is expensive and many investors didn't find the ores they were expecting.'

Jamie tilted his head, 'But we did?'

'Oh yes. We certainly did.'

'And how many men died in our mines, Daddy? Teacher said in school that it was really, really bad, and they died too soon.'

Now David hesitated. He was toiling away, doing his best. But the boulders above him were beginning to roll, booming and muffled. 'Well yes, yes, Jamie, it was pretty bloody grim. They used to get diseases. Horrible. Your grandmother can remember seeing miners holding on to lamp-posts in St Just – young men dying of lung disease, unable to walk home—'

'Why didn't they try fishing, or or . . .'

'Fishing wasn't much easier. I sometimes think the Cornish should have stuck to smuggling. And wrecking.'

247

Jamie stood there. Nodding. Absorbing. Wondering. The brightest of children, but surely given too much to think about. 'Is it true there used to be blind men, Dad?'

'What?'

'In the mine tunnels, the tunnels under the sea? Miss Everett said in class that they had blind men down there 'cause they could see better in the dark so if there was an accident the blind miner would um lead the other miners to a safer place.'

'Yes. That's true.'

David remembered when he had first learned this startling fact: the Gothic quality of it had been shocking, even in the context of those great, Satanic undersea mines. Blind men were, once, employed for their blindness, because they were deemed better able to negotiate the utter blackness when explosions snuffed the candles.

'It sounds horrible, Daddy, what they did. So why did we get to send them down the holes and under the sea?'

'Because—'

'Is it because we were bad? 'Cause the Kerthens were bad people?'

'No, that's wrong, it's nothing like that. Really. You mustn't think that.'

He was trying to disguise his fatherly concern. Jamie's mental disturbance was unquestionably worsening, thanks to the proximity of Rachel. David desperately needed to rescue his son from the madness of his step-mother. But he had no idea how to do this. The law conspired against the lawyer.

The breeze was picking up. They were stationary on the clifftop. David leaned to zip his son's raincoat. Jamie pushed his arm away. 'Dad. I'm OK. I can do up my own coat!'

'All right. All right. Sorry.'

David also knew he was being overprotective, trying to compensate for his intensified absence. But the way he missed Jamie was like an illness, he missed him far too much. Missed the daily things. Simply hanging out with his son, eating together, giggling at a shared joke, all of it. Now that David was entirely excluded from family life, he realized that it was the mundane and spontaneous stuff that mattered most of all. A sudden, rhapsodic game of Pooh sticks with Jamie over a stream in Ladies Wood. Cooking up a random barbecue with Jamie and Rollo on the front lawns in the summer.

With the objectivity of an exile, David could see that these stray times with Jamie had been the best moments of his entire life, the moments when he surprised himself with his capacity for happiness, the times when simple parenting was more intensely joyful than anything else he had done, ever.

And now those spontaneous moments were no more. Their meetings were structured. Life was contrived.

Everything was lost. Or close to being lost.

'All right, Jamie?'

'Yes, Dad.'

Jamie smiled. That puzzled yet wistful smile. A barely hidden sadness in the eyes. 'Daddy, are you going to come home soon? It's not the same without you, it's lonely at home.'

'I hope so, Jamie.'

'Why do I have to meet you so far away from the house? I mean I, um, I had a nice time today, but why is it like this?'

'Because I did a very stupid thing. A very, very bad thing. I'm really sorry about it now, but I had to go live somewhere else for a while.'

'I saw Rachel's face. When I came back from staying with Rollo. Something happened with her, Daddy? What happened?'

This question. *This question.* Rollo's parents had very kindly and temporarily taken Jamie in, for a couple of nights, after his assault, but the boy could not be protected entirely from the truth. And besides, Jamie had then said he wanted to stay in Carnhallow, with Rachel. And would not give a reason.

'Well, Jamie, we had a particular kind of an argument, but it was also very different. It was a foolish thing. I was extremely foolish.'

'OK.' Jamie seemed satisfied, though David wasn't sure why.

The boy looked once more out to sea. So did David. It was what you did. Everyone in West Cornwall looked out to sea when conversation lagged: wherever you went you caught the same gesture, people tailing off into silence, then glancing to the west with a kind of longing. It was as if the landscape had shaped the mind. Living on the trembling edge of Europe, close to the western Celtic afterworld. This place where the rocks and grasses reached towards eternity: it taught the people to do the same.

A slight shiver overtook David. The winter twilight was deepening, and the last scars of surf were turning a silvery pink. Jamie was gazing at that unmoving boat. David thought he'd try one more time.

'Jamie, you do know you don't have to stay in Carnhallow?'

The boy didn't even glance at his father; his gaze stayed firmly directed at the waves.

'You don't have to stay with Rachel. You could come and stay with me, at least at weekends. It's your choice.'

Silence.

At last the boy turned, his blue eyes burning. 'Daddy, you know why I won't do that.'

'Do I?'

'Yes!' There was fury in his voice. 'Yes you do! You do. Mummy is there. Mummy is in Carnhallow. So I'm not leaving her. Not. Not ever not ever. You can't make me.'

'But – Jamie – your mummy—'

'Yes she's dead, yes she's in Zennor, yes she's in the shaft, so you say – but, Daddy, I see her! In the house. It's like she's really there, so nearly real, she's there. And Rachel saw her too. She is there!!'

This was close to breakdown, to something awful.

Man and boy stared at each other. Then the father shook his head: deciding to ignore this outburst; he had no idea of what he might do otherwise. The first and most important thing was to get rid of Rachel. Get her out of Carnhallow. Expunge the source of the madness.

Yet David's plan to get Rachel sectioned had failed. If anything, it had made things worse. His own GP was now suspicious, when before he'd been conspicuously loyal. And his GP knew lots of police officers in Truro. They were probably all chatting. About that singular case of Nina Kerthen. *What really happened that day two years ago? We never found the body. Why did the son behave so strangely? Let's look at it all again.* David's life was about to disintegrate entirely.

Jamie seemed to have calmed. The wind was cold. The boy was blowing warm breath between his fingers.

'Come on,' David said, 'Cassie is going to pick you up from my hotel. We'd better get going.'

As they headed for the car, parked by the King of Prussia pub, David turned. That peculiar, unmoving boat had gone. And yet the sea toiled on, uncaring. Maybe the oceans had swallowed the little vessel, when no one was watching. Things could disappear so quickly in these freezing waters.

9 Days Before Christmas

Morning

David slowed in the December mud and stopped his
Mercedes on a muddied track, well away from the
snaking B road that meandered the coast from St Ives.
He didn't want to be seen by anyone, not here. He was
probably within five miles of Carnhallow already,
breaking the terms of his exclusion order.

Again he seethed with anger at the very idea.
Excluded? From his own house, his own son. The impo-
tence boiled inside him, like the sea at Zawn Hanna.
He was powerless. Castrated by the courts.

Picking up his binoculars, David gazed along the shore.
Between the gaunt rocks and wizened trees of the moors,
and the tumbling grey waves, he could make out the
black, dumb shapes of the Morvellan mine houses.
Carnhallow was invisible, tucked in its cosy valley. Its
roof slates no doubt glistening after the latest shower.

The day was now bright, but very sharp. Snow was
expected later, and more snow was forecast for
Christmas. This was a rarity. Usually they got vivid

winter storms, not frost and snow. David hadn't seen Carnhallow asleep in snow for half a decade: he could remember how deliciously handsome the great house looked in snow, how antique and pretty. He remembered snowflakes sprinkled like large crystals of sugar on the red berries of the holly wreath, adorning the front door.

They'd had snowball fights in the garden, that winter: even his mother had joined in. David recalled the scent of snowflakes on his wife's blonde hair when he kissed her; he saw it all. He was staring, now, at a mental postcard of his own past happiness, the husband hugging the wife, the parents hugging the laughing son. Everyone happy in the snow.

David resisted the prickles of emotion; he used the binoculars again. He had to plan. But what in actuality was he going to do?

If it came to it, he would have to be clever – and careful. He already knew that his second wife was troubled by the idea of Christmas, so that would be a good time to take advantage of her unbalanced state. Christmas was also the perfect time to isolate her, in Carnhallow – David's mother sometimes went to stay with ancient friends over Christmas, the Penmarricks at Lanihorne, the Smithwicks in Falmouth, for a week of goose-fat roast potatoes and sloe gin.

He could encourage her to take up another invitation. He might even be able to entice Cassie away: she was unhappy at Carnhallow, now David had been excluded. David was paterfamilias, the milord, and his absence offended her patriarchal Thai sensibilities. And David paid her wages.

Extract Cassie and Juliet, and Rachel would then be almost perfectly vulnerable. Pregnant and vulnerable. Spinning out of control.

But, if it came to it, what would he actually *do*? How far would he go? To save Jamie?

He scanned the brooding green fields, with their knuckly outcrops of granite, and the very obvious roads that gouged their way through the green-grey fields, heading west. No. He couldn't drive to Carnhallow. That would be too conspicuous. On these lonely moorland roads a car could be seen for many miles.

But if he walked along the cliffs, using the long-distance coastal footpath, no one would see him. It would be easy to keep out of vision. Once he reached Morvellan, he could break into Carnhallow with ease. There were so many ways to gain access. So many basements and tunnels, coalholes and forgotten drains. He'd maybe do it at night, when the rowans and oaks looked like black coral in a midnight blue sea.

He also knew he had to test the route, see how long it would take, the best way of getting close without being seen. And Christmas was fast approaching. So whatever preparations were required, they had to be made now.

Locking his car, slipping arms into his stiff Barbour rain jacket, David buttoned himself against the cold sea wind, and followed the cracked wooden sign saying *Coastal Footpath*. Crows and ravens bickered in the furze on either side.

He was quickly up to his ankles in mud, a slough that was tainted with reeking cow slurry. Taking his phone from his buttoned pocket, he made a note.

Good boots.

Head-torch.

He would definitely need a head-torch, because he would definitely need to do this in the depth of darkness. Christmas Eve perhaps, or the following night.

255

That's when Rachel would be most scared, most maddened, easily tipped into mistakes.

The walk from here to Carnhallow was very rugged: right along the teetering clifftops. He could see the brown houses of Zennor half a mile to his left, and the handsome, weathered church. And its graves. Onwards he trudged, down one cliff, then up on to another headland, then repeating the process, carefully past the Gurnard's Head, past holiday cottages shuttered and padlocked for the winter, then old miners' cottages – tumbledown ruins, wreathed in brambles, like rusty barbed wire.

Newer, glassier houses stood on the higher clifftops. Lights from Christmas trees behind windows showed they were occupied. Though he couldn't actually see anyone on this raw, unpleasant day; the weather was close to tears, cold and damp, and sad.

David was getting near. The trees grew taller, the landscape perceptibly softened, and then he saw the black shapes of Morvellan Mine. This was the spot. As soon as David passed the next copse of oaks he would see the path that led up to Carnhallow, and then the house itself: dreaming in its scoop of valley, protected by its hoop of woods.

This was the most dangerous point from David's perspective. Rachel liked to linger in the kitchen, to gaze down at the mines. If she did that today – or on Christmas Eve, when he returned – she would see him.

David shoved his hands in his pockets, away from the cold. Thinking it all through. If he walked ten more yards he'd be in full view.

How was he going to do it, come Christmas? Breaking into the house was easy enough. But then? Whatever he did, he needed her gone, for ever. And there was no easy solution. David wondered, idly, what Jago Kerthen would have done. Acted without pity, no doubt. Preserved the family at all costs.

Lost in speculation, David looked along the cliffs. And now the panic needled him. He had foolishly wandered close to the mine houses, where he was visible from all sides. And a hundred yards away he could see Cassie, walking the clifftop path, returning towards the house.

She was staring pensively down at the ground, as she approached. It was the only reason she hadn't seen David already. This was potentially a disaster. She was going to stumble upon him breaking the injunction. His plans would be scuppered before he'd even started. And there was nowhere for him to go. If he ran, he'd surely be seen. He couldn't rely on Cassie to stay quiet, and break the law. The injunction would be extended. He'd end up back in court. He had seconds to hide.

The mine. Morvellan Shaft House. He kept that second key for the Shaft House with him all the time. A sign of his ownership. As the mineral lord of West Penwith.

Desperate and clumsy, David juggled for the key. He had seconds to do it, before Cassie found him. Ten seconds, five. Four. He could sense her nearness, as he stuck the key in the rusty padlock, and turned.

Cassie was thirty yards away. Three seconds, two. She must see him now. Two seconds, one. But the chains fell open, and David pushed the door, slipped inside, and shut the door behind him.

Saved.

The mine greeted him like an old friend. It was all as he remembered. Strangely quiet, sheltered from the ceaseless wind, but utterly cold. Roofless, like a ruined church tower: a grim and primitive temple of oddly fine proportions, solidly built. And there was that great big void: the pit that descended a mile.

257

David's heart was beating fast: he felt like a frightened kid. This place, where she died. This place of hurt and suffering, shouts and horror, of men going down into the pits of Hell to work, a mile under the sea, with only the tiny fires of their candles.

Cautiously moving closer to the shaft, David took a brief look down into the blackness. It was too dark to see anything, too deep. A place out of which you could not climb. The perfect place to dump a murder victim.

Picking up a random stone, a quartzite chunk of the deads, David tossed it down the shaft. He used to do this as a boy, to see how long it fell, before the splash. It was somehow irresistible. Everyone did it.

He counted the seconds of silence. The splash, when it came, was strangely muffled. More like a thump, than a splash. As if the stone had bounced on something, then skipped into the water.

Fumbling in the cold, David reached in his pocket; he didn't have a proper torch, but he had the torch in his phone. Switching it on, he went as close as he dared to the very edge of the pit. The sensation was deeply unnerving. These stone slabs were so dangerously slippery. It would be so easy to skid, and topple in. And if he fell he would die too. But he had to see what had muffled the splash.

Crouching, then squatting, David peered over the edge, and held out his phone. Giving him enough light to see the black surface of the water, thirty feet down.

At once, he was sliced to the core with cold horror. Because, quite visible, floating face-down in the ink-black water, was a body.

It was a little bloated, distended by some process of decomposition. Resisting the urge to reel away, David stared. The red dress had been bleached, shredded. It

258

was pinkish-grey, and half dissolved. But the blonde hair, that haloed the head like silvery seaweed, was very distinctive.

It was his first wife.

Nina Kerthen, née Valéry, had returned. Suspended this way, she looked exactly as if she were swimming in the sea off Collioure, snorkelling, hunting for sea urchins with Jamie.

He gazed, rapt, yet aghast, mesmerized by this gruesome spectacle. He couldn't, at first, compute the coincidence: for the first time in a year he had visited Morvellan and this very same moment he had seen the body?

But it made entire sense. Nina might have been floating here for months, unseen. The detectives and pathologists always said there was a chance she would return, one day, it was all a question of those mysterious undersea tides and currents. No one ever came to desolate Shaft House, scene of that Christmas tragedy.

No one would have noticed Nina's corpse, until now. She could have been suspended down there since the summer. Floating on the waters in that dissolving dress, unheralded and unmourned. An astronaut in the black, spinning in darkness.

Now the sadness surged. Grief, and anger, and steely regret. This thing, this pitiful spectacle, was his first wife. The woman he had loved so much, the woman for whom he had taken the most dangerous risks.

And the gruesome sight of her gave him resolve: he had sacrificed almost everything for Nina, Jamie, Carnhallow, the Kerthens. He had taken the greatest of chances to keep it all together, to keep it going. If Rachel threatened to destroy all that, he would do whatever was required.

David placed a hand on the wet slabs, preparing to

leave. But as he did a gurgle from the waters below made him pause.

The body was moving. Some shift in the current, or some underground gas, was flipping the corpse. With a saddening gush the body turned over. Now he was staring at the remains of a face, dead yet partly preserved, expressive yet seriously defleshed. He could see the grin of half a skull, teeth exposed, as she smiled at him.

Was this horror truly Nina? It was impossible to tell, the decomposition was severe. It had to be Nina, yet the effects of two years in the freezing water were so distressing that she was unrecognizable.

The urge to escape was too much. Cassie must surely have gone by now. Creaking the door open, David stole out into the cold, and ran for the woods. Running away from what he had seen. The seabirds laughing at him as he fled.

Eight Days Before Christmas

Morning

I am having a solitary breakfast of toast and Marmite, my childhood comfort food, when Jamie comes into the kitchen. He is already dressed: jeans and Chelsea football shirt. He looks thin, and pale, but his beautiful eyes are as bright as ever. As sad as ever.

'Hey, you. Toast or boiled egg?'

Jamie looks my way and tries to smile. His hair is tousled from sleep. 'Um. Boiled egg and soldiers?'

'Coming right up.'

My stepson pulls a stool and sits at the counter and stares at the windows, and the soft grey sky beyond. We are all lost in a fog of melancholy and anxiety.

'Daddy is seeing me again today.'

'I know, Jamie.'

It's the third day in a row David has asked to see Jamie. I have acceded. We're into the Christmas holidays, and even though I fiercely resent David I will not keep a father from his son. Not at Christmas.

But when Jamie comes back from these now-daily

visits, when he steps out of Cassie's car, he doesn't tell me anything. What he did with David, where they went, what they might have discussed. Generally, when he is in Carnhallow, Jamie goes to his room and shuts the door, communing with the silence.

At least he is here now, in my presence, in the kitchen. Dipping a soldier in his egg, exploding the yolk so it drips like golden blood, he munches, dutifully, silently. Then he stops, slants a glance in my direction – and he rises, and crosses the kitchen to his advent calendar, tacked to the wall. He does this every morning, counting the dates.

'Eight more days till Christmas', he says. Then he shrugs, neither happy nor unhappy. 'That's not long.'

'I know. It's exciting.'

I suppress my anxiety. Eight Days. Just eight days until Christmas.

'It's a penguin. In the picture.'

'Is it? That's nice.'

'Have you heard about how the fathers take care of the baby penguins? I read that once at school. About the penguins, waiting in the snow. It was sad. But the mummy penguins always come back.'

I stare at him. There's a memory here. I can't remember what.

Penguins.

Returning to the kitchen table, he finishes his breakfast toast and I get the sense he is expecting something to happen very soon. But we are all expecting and waiting, and asking. *What is going to happen to us? What will happen at Christmas? How have we ended up in this terrible place?*

I want to scream these questions, but no one will answer. Jamie's grandmother sometimes refuses to pick up the phone these days. She is my only friend, and yet it seems like she is also avoiding me. Like I am becoming absolutely nothing. Totally unwanted.

I know I shouldn't think this, yet I feel it – deep in my mind. I feel it when Jamie finishes his egg and soldiers and I put him in a coat and install him in the car, and Cassie turns the wheel and heads up Carnhallow Valley to the moors. As the car trundles away I sense that Cassie must be staring in her mirror at me. Watching me recede from view. *See, there's your stepmother, disappearing. Soon she will be gone. Christmas is coming.*

NO.

I must shake off this depression. So I busy myself with chores, I rinse the dishes and neaten the kitchen and check the fridge for butter and milk, then I lock myself in my own car and drive through Botallack and Zennor, and over the last moortop hill, where I descend into St Ives, and the big Tesco superstore on the outskirts of town. The store that looks down to Carbis Bay and the lighthouse. Virginia Woolf's lighthouse. The novelist who committed suicide.

The lighthouse is invisible today: a chilly sea fog obscures the view.

Shopping. What could be more ordinary and sensible and regular than shopping, at Christmas? Even though we don't need much.

I am only doing this to distract myself, to get out of the house. My family doesn't talk to me. No one knows me any more, even if they knew me once. So why is everyone looking? Patrolling the festive aisles, pretending to be interested in the *finest* Christmas puddings and the *luxury* mince pies, all I can hear is the piped carols aimed at me. Personally.

Twelve drummers drumming.

Drumming on my head. Bang bang BANG. Eight days left.

A little girl is watching me. She is with her mother. They are lingering in the fruit and veg aisle and the mother is examining tomatoes and standing right beside her, her little girl is gazing over at me with great curiosity. A look of entrancement.

The girl is in a white dress with black leggings, under a pink anorak. She is smiling, her eyes locked on mine as if I am something new yet bizarre, something unwelcome but amusing. Embarrassed, I turn away, pretending to be interested in walnuts and dates and Christmas cheese selections, but I can feel her eyes burning into my spine.

I turn. The girl is still there, she hasn't moved a millimetre and she is staring, rapt, without blinking. Her mother has disappeared.

The tension claws at my skin. Maybe I should help the child, help find her mother, but the idea of doing that is horrific. I am paralysed. And this fucking song bangs out its stupid tune. *Twelve drummers drumming,* just eight days left, just eight till you die, *just get out get out get out. Drum drum drum, bang bang bang!*

The girl is walking towards me and now I realize she is wearing little black boots. Boots which are cripplingly too small for her. And I am seized with dread.

I have no idea why. I look left and right, seeking help, hoping for someone to save me from an eight-year-old girl with tight black boots, but I know that she wants to hurt me.

BANG BANG BANG DRUM DRUM DRUM

I can hear the steppy tick-tock of her tiny feet on the polished supermarket floor. And I know that if the child touches me with one of her pointing fingers she will kill me, I will bleed, I will hurt. My mouth will cough blood like that spitting hare in my hands.

Ten lords a-leaping. Nine ladies dancing.

I am in Tesco supermarket on the edge of St Ives, and there are adverts for special Belgian Christmas chocolates everywhere, and now the child runs to me, she is running right at me, coming for me, and I am cornered, I cower against a wall, crouching down, knowing that when her cold finger touches my skin I will scream and collapse and—

'Stop! Stop stop stop!'

My own shout snaps me open, turns me inside out, and dumps me in grey reality.

Half the store has turned to look. Trolleys are paused, faces are tilted, shoppers are horrified. Look at the mad woman, *look* at her CROUCHING by the readymade canapés.

Gentle Christmas muzak fills the startled silence. And the little girl has run past me. I can see her, over there, down at the distant tills, leaping into the arms of her mother.

This is worse. This is, in its own way, even more ominous. Dumping my trolley by the stacks of brandy butter, I seek the exit. A supermarket manager regards me placidly as I run out of the shop into the drizzly cold air and jump in my Mini. *The mad woman at the supermarket. Did you see her?*

I race the tormenting miles to the house. The moors are grey, the sea is grey, the sky is grey: only the cliffs provide colour, where the green-blue breakers of the sea shatter into silver lacework on the rocks, then retreat in stunned and seething confusion.

Arriving at Carnhallow, I run inside, slamming the door behind me. I lean back on the wall, trying to regain myself. Taking long, long breaths. Gulping chilly quiet air. Inhaling the stillness. Calm, Rachel. Calm.

I must survive. I must be better. I cannot let them win. They are coming for me and I need to outwit them. My Christmas is close, the time of year I fear most of all, and they are making it worse.

But I will not be defeated. Not now, not here, not after all this. I have a good enough brain. I am going to work out the puzzle of what happened to Nina Kerthen and why. I need to find an answer before Christmas Day, when, it seems, all our presents will arrive at once.

Closing as many doors as I can, sealing off the damp black corridors that stretch into disused basements and saddening bedrooms, I walk the hallway, past the prints of Wheal Chance and the Kerthen Count House, and make for the silent, lonely warmth of the Yellow Drawing Room, where the Christmas tree fairy is still grinning at me. Her wand twinkles.

Hello, Rachel.

The noticeable warmth, compared to the rest of the house, is welcome: it shows me I am not entirely losing my way. Because the reduced heating is a logical and coherent choice I have recently made. To lower costs. As I am in charge. Frugal Rachel is running Carnhallow.

Why did we heat so much of Carnhallow, anyway, wasting David's money? Pumping useless warmth into unused sculleries and spidery attics? It was nuts. Now most of the great and ancient house has returned to its ancestral and deserted chilliness, a cold that sharpens day by day as the promised December snowfall approaches.

They say the snowfall might be heavy. Weather announcers are positively relishing the prospect: people love bad weather, the same way they love a murder mystery. Yet here in Carnhallow the murder mystery is real. It is my life. A mystery I need to unravel. And quickly.

The loneliness surrounds me, it hurts me in the heart, the chest, like a species of cancer. Something growing and nasty. A loneliness I thought I had left behind. The girl who cowered in the bedroom. But at least it aids my concentration.

Reaching for my files on the coffee table, I pick up that gossip magazine article of Nina and David and baby Jamie. When I first saw that particular photo of the three of them, months ago, I thought that it held a clue. Some hint as to why Nina might be dead but still alive, some reason why her son seems able to see things in the future.

And I still sense some concealed truth in the photo. The perfect family. *Too* perfect. But how?

I am – or I was – a photographer; this is a photo. I should be good at this. What am I missing here?

The barely seen child reaches a hand for the mother. For elegant Nina. David stands beside them, tall, manly and protective. It is practically a Nativity scene. Christmas in a photo.

The radio is playing 'I Believe in Father Christmas'. Stung by a sudden memory, I look up, eyes misting. My mother used to sing this wistful, lovely, chiming song: I see her swaying, a glass of cheap Chardonnay in her hand, on our rancid Christmas family dinners. I can remember it all, I am too good at remembering. I see cans of lager on the table. Cheap turkey roll cooked in the microwave. Stilton that my dad probably shoplifted.

The day unfolds. My dad getting drunk at 11 a.m.

My sister itching to escape. The horrid stuff on the shower curtains. Mummy asleep. My dad looking at me. I go upstairs, but I cannot get away. Later his fingers slip inside me, his dirty fingers. His whisky breath on my trembling, bare and frightened skin. Happy Christmas, Rachel.

They said there'll be snow at Christmas
They said there'll be peace on earth . . .

Too much, too much. Wiping a couple of stupid tears from my eyes I focus on the photo. Puzzling, thinking, deciphering. But nothing occurs to me, nothing solid or usable. The thoughts slip away.

Exasperated, I slap the photo down, and open Nina's notebook again.

This is maybe more fruitful. I read on, intently, while the silent Drawing Room waits.

As the months advanced – as the initially happy years paraded – Nina Kerthen's note-taking got more chaotic. Her enthusiasm definitely waned over time. In the end she was reduced to taking down snippets of family history, and local folklore: no doubt learned from Juliet.

For trip to Lizard with Jamie. Teach him. History.
Cornwall. Lizard is wrecking and smuggling
country. Origins of Kerthens. Breage, Prussia Cove.
Gunwalloe.

Wrecking lore. If they saw a ship in trouble they
would come down to the coast and wave lights.
Beckoning them in to safety, or so the sailors
thought, but really they were seducing the ships on
to the rocks, so the ships would founder. Break up.

Then some of the wreckers would rush down to the beach and break the skulls of any survivors. So they could steal the rum and tobacco, the sherry and molasses, the gold, brandy, silk foulards.

Why was she writing this? And why was she writing *this:*

Profit and loss. Death and life. I wonder if he ever felt guilt, Jago Kerthen: tristesse for the miners he sent down under the sea, the children he poisoned with arsenic. The villagers he worked from the age of 10 to 30. Juliet says she can remember the scenes in the villages, Four Lanes, Carnkie, St Agnes. On Sundays she says she would walk down the streets of the villages and every cottage would have a window open, and there would be a man sticking his mouth through the gap, désespéré, sucking in air on grey winter Sundays. They were trying to breathe, trying to stay alive one more week, to get them through one more winter. Desperate for cold fresh air to clear their unclearable lungs. And all of them dead within six months? & this is how the Kerthens made their fortune.

The rest of this page, in her notebook, is largely blank. Except for one final sentence. Isolated at the bottom, dated June:

Familles anciennes. *Continuing the line.*

Again I get the sense of a clue, a piece of thread that if pulled might unravel everything, but I have no idea how this might be achieved.

271

After this scribbled entry, the remarks dwindle away. Her writing gets more slipshod, in contrast with the previous neatness. But then, at the very end, she notes one last, piercing image, which reads like a diary entry:

There was a square of light on the flagstones of the Old Hall, this morning, when I came downstairs, and I found a young fox, standing in the middle, trembling, in the light from the leaded windows. I would have once told Jamie.

'I would have once told Jamie.'

That is the last line. Why does it have that contorted phrasing? *I would have once.* Was there some estrangement between them?

And then there is the timing.

August.

The truth slaps me awake, as a whip of cold rain lashes the window, as the Cornish winter tries to get inside the house.

The last entry is August. There are no more notes after that.

Afternoon

Racing out of the Drawing Room, I make straight for the kitchen, down the chilly, shadowed corridors. Faces of venerable Kerthens stare at me as I fly, faces from the photos of mines, the bal maidens in their grimy aprons.

On on on.

In the kitchen cupboards I've got a folder containing all Nina's letters: invoices and receipts, requests and demands for her restorers, upholsterers, the dyers and weavers. She liked stuff in hard copy: liked things written down on paper, not in emails. She wanted records to keep.

I've arranged all of this correspondence by date. Sitting down at the kitchen table, throwing open this second folder, it takes half a minute for me flick through the paperwork, and find what I seek.

The very latest of *these* items also dates to August. August. Which is four months before she died.

This means Nina *stopped* restoring Carnhallow House in August. As I know from her notebook, her interest

273

faded over that spring, and it diffused into a wider curiosity about the Kerthens, Carnhallow, wrecking and mining lore – as summer came along. And then it died completely. But why? The restoration of Carnhallow was, clearly, her passion. She loved it. At first.

And then she didn't love it. And then she stopped. And she began to wonder if the Kerthens were, somehow, evil.

Four months later she had the accident, and drowned. Supposedly.

I am grimly excited now. Maybe I have not been imagining things. Where next?

Jamie's room. The concept stings my conscience; I've never done this before. I so wanted to be a good stepmother. But it is the one place I haven't looked properly. Therefore the one place that might contain the final answers.

The house waits. Looks at me in suspicion. Turning on lights as I go, I climb the chilly stairs. It is already 4 p.m. How did the day die so quickly into dark? And where is everyone? Perhaps Cassie is out shopping, with Jamie, after collecting him from David. Yet they usually return by three, these winter afternoons.

I know Cassie hates taking Jamie to his father: because she hates the extended trip to Truro, that gruelling drive along the winding, slippery, dangerous moorland roads, greasy with frost, then an hour on the windy A30.

Could they have had an accident? Rooted, here, on the grand staircase, I picture her car veering, hit by the raw winter winds, hurtling off the grey-green moors by Stithians. Then I see Jamie locked behind a car window, his mouth opening and closing mutely. The idea of anything happening to him is more distressing, maybe, than something happening to *me*.

Yet this is absurd. Presumably Cassie is waiting some-where, lingering over flat whites in a Truro coffee shop, waiting for David to hand over Jamie. I would have heard if anything had happened. Someone would tell me. They wouldn't completely ignore me, like I don't even exist.

Would they?

The stairs are very dark, and very cold. I should have done this before. Now the freezing winter gloom grips the rooms and corridors. In the deepness of winter, Carnhallow Valley is a cold and lightless pool. A sump of frosty air. And the house is colder than anywhere else. Cold in its bones. Cold in the marrow.

I pace along the corridor, pretending I am not scared. Jamie's room.

My hand hesitates on the doorknob. A hard December wind is soughing, out there, raking through the oaks and rowans. Yet I can hear no cars, no voices, nothing else.

Twisting the handle, pushing the door, I step inside.

The room has an unexpected scent of Pears Soap. His father's soap. I sometimes forget that Jamie is very much his father's boy.

This room is also very tidy. My stepson might be increasingly solitary but Cassie keeps the squalor to a minimum. Schoolbooks are piled carefully on shelves, next to a brace of Harry Potter and C. S. Lewis. A football rocks from side to side in a corner. No it doesn't. It is still.

The bed boasts a big blue Chelsea duvet cover; a picture of some famous footballer I cannot name is tacked neatly to the wall. This could be the room of any eight-year-old boy: it is not obviously the room of Jamie Kerthen, heir to Carnhallow House.

What might I find here? I am looking for something that jars, something that is abnormal. And I don't have to look that hard. It is, surely, the photos. How many eight-year-old boys have photos of their mums in silver frames? Very few, *but Jamie Kerthen does*. The idea is heartbreaking, and it is also agitating. A clue.

Stepping closer to the desk, with its smartphone cable and computer games, I tilt the first image.

This photo was taken in southern France, I suspect: it looks too warm and palmy for Cornwall. Here is a Mediterranean light. Mother and son are standing on a beach. Nina looks young, happy, sunburned – she's in a bikini, but I can see tan lines from the straps of a summer dress. Jamie is next to her, small and vulnerable, in blue checked shorts, yet content to feel his mother's arm draped around his narrow shoulders.

He is sunburned too, and looks about five years old. The two of them, mother and child, are staring at the camera with giddy smiles, I presume David is behind the camera. The wellbeing and contentment is palpable, this is a happy holiday, deftly captured in one image. Later I imagine them having plates of mussels and frites, Jamie playing beach football with local kids. Grilled seafood. Chilled rosé wine. Laughter.

Nina's figure is enviable.

The second photo, angled on the same desk, is newer. I take it up. To me this looks like a photo taken in Carnhallow gardens.

Ladies Wood beyond is red and gold, so this must be a fine day in maybe mid or late October. The bloody clusters of rowan-berries can be seen. It is sunny, but apparently cold: Nina is in a luxurious coat. There is no contact this time, no languid arm draped around Jamie's shoulders. He is in a raincoat, sloping close to his mum, without touching. Jamie looks about six. So this, I deduce, is a photo from the autumn before she died. A couple of months before she died.

If she died.

I look closer.

Her smile is faked. I know a faked smile when I see one. I am a photographer. Few people can convincingly fake a smile – the eyes always give it away – and Nina has failed here. Her mouth curves up but her eyes are cold. And her stance is stiff. And distanced.

Maybe scared?

I drop the photo on the bed: like it is giving me an electric shock. My fingers tingle.

Nina doesn't want to be in this photo. She doesn't want to touch her son. She is pretending. She either dislikes her son. Or she is scared of him.

What happened between them? Why did she stop restoring the house, then start to mistrust, or dislike, her own child, at the same time, the last summer before the accident?

Penguins. Now it comes back to me. Jamie wrote about penguins in those letters. And what else did he write?

I remember that crossed out line.

~~I loved you just as much as daddy, I am sorry~~

The ideas run away with me. Perhaps Jamie showed signs of strangeness or animosity then, too. Rejecting his own mother. Favouring his father. But why would he do that?

I am reaching for the next photo – when I hear it. A noise that paralyses me, sends sharp, anxious pains to my fingertips. It is the weary creak of a door, downstairs. *An internal door.* Where no wind blows. Someone is coming. If it was Cassie, or Jamie, or Juliet, I would have heard cars outside, chatter, the bang of a big door and someone coming in.

And now I hear a voice. Calling up.

'Jamie?'

The voice is young. And it belongs to a woman. It isn't Cassie.

Evening

I have to go down. But I am momentously frightened. Memories assail me, memories of my father downstairs. Shouting my name. *My little Rachel. Where is she? Comin' upstairs for ya.*

The cinema screen of my memories comes alive, flickering with images of me: aged ten or eleven, foetal in my dark bedroom, pretending to be asleep, hoping he won't come in. He always comes in.

You little bitch!

I have to fight this, fight the fear inside, and the fear outside. I grip my hands into defiant fists and take deep cold breaths, then I step through the door of Jamie's room, I talk – I shout out – into the swallowing silence. 'Hello?'

There is no reply.

'Hello?'

The dark windows mock me, the moon looks through the yews and the oaks, mute and inscrutable.

'Hello? Hello?'

Again, no response. I wonder if this woman, downstairs, can tell how scared I am.

All the lights are still on, out here on the landing: yet somehow they do not entirely dispel the dark. Because the house is being invaded by the blackness, and by the cold; the black frigid waters trapped in Morvellan are rising up to engulf us, coming up the shafts, flooding into the basements, then climbing the stairs, creeping and inexorable.

'Who is this?'

I can hear footfalls, not far away. Someone is crossing the hall, downstairs. Heading for the kitchen. Down the long corridor. Or walking towards the Old Hall.

Gathering the last of my bravery, I run to the banisters and look down. There. No. But I hear more movement, very obvious now.

Courage is my only option. Running down the stairs, I strain to see – but, as I do, distracted, not looking where I am going – I catch my foot in the carpets, the stupid rucked carpets, the carpets she laid – and I fall. I slam forward, barking my head against the fine wooden banisters, so pretty and grand. Then I fall further, cracking my knee on the bottom step, turning an ankle. Down to the floor. Down down down, head over feet, tumbling like a stunt artist.

Down. And out.

I yelp in reflex at the pain, turning myself over. That hurt: but I don't care. All I want to know is whether it hurt my daughter? Panting, with the shock of the fall, I reach down and touch the curve of my faintly swollen stomach. I sense nothing, no horrible damage, no bleeding, my baby is apparently OK. But that was a frightening fall. I could have snapped a leg, or a neck. I could have killed myself and my baby.

And now I want to stay still. Lying quiet on the polished floorboards. Pretend I didn't hear or see anything, let her go away. Curl up and hide. Let the shadows leave the great house.

I am sorry for disturbing you.

Carnhallow is silent. I lie here, dazed, on my stupid back, staring at the carved plasterwork of the ceiling. I think I am perhaps concussed. Everything is swimmy.

The house is looking down at me, curious, and derisive. *See, she can't even walk down the steps. She has visions. She sees faces through windows. It's happening all over again. Look at her. Look at her. It's time she did herself in.*

'No!'

I actually talked to the house. I shouted that out. I am talking to the voices. Again.

A pain begins in my ankle, like a prologue. I wonder if I have broken it. As I look up, estimating the agony, the plasterwork on the ceiling melts into patterns, which spin, like a turning kaleidoscope. My vision is blurred. I look to my right, trying to focus, still lying on the floor.

I am staring at Nina Kerthen.

Jamie's dead mother stands at the end of the corridor that leads to the Old Hall, the corridor which always fades into darkness. There is enough light to make out her face.

She gazes at me from the dark, her mouth slightly open, as if she is attempting to speak, but failing. This is surely Nina Kerthen two years older, a little different, but with Nina Kerthen's hair, and her eyes, and her elegant neck. This is the same woman I saw on the bus.

I can hear another Christmas song from the distant radio. I left it on in the Drawing Room.

I turned my face away
And dreamed about you

The music fades and ebbs, my mind ebbs and fades. The lady in the darkness is still there. Not moving. Gazing. Half-smiling. Then at last she moves, forward, coming out of the shadows. Slowly walking towards me. She has one arm extended. I think I see bleeding at the fingertips, her face is pale as fresh snow. She is going to touch me, to touch me, to touch me, with her soft, blooded fingers. Touch my skin, stroke my face.

I close my eyes, filled with horror. She is surely very close, her one hand extended, her fingertips bleeding. This is the test. I count the terrible seconds, my eyes shut very hard.

I could have been someone,
Well so could anyone

I open my eyes.
The woman has gone. The ghost. The woman. Has gone. And now I know. I am hallucinating. There is no other answer. It is happening again.

I *am* seeing things. And hearing things.

And so the confessions cascade, the walls of denial are falling. Surely David was right. He is, he is. I have imagined it all. Everything. This proves it.

I have been piecing together my own lost family: out of madness and memories. Even my little girl is here, too. And why not? After all, as Juliet says: the dead are always with us.

I haul myself on to my elbows. A lot of me hurts, yet my mind is oddly clear. I can see further, now, so

282

much further. A chilling sea mist has thinned away. For the moment.

Crouching, then standing, I test my ankle: not broken, maybe sprained: the pain throbs angrily in the bone. I gaze down that corridor that leads to the Old Hall. I could follow her, but I know I will find nothing. *There is no one else here.* For reasons I can guess, I am seeing the images of dead mothers, and dead children. But why is it happening *now*?

I limp down the antique hallway.

The kitchen greets me with brightness: like a fake smile, too white and cheerful. Slumping into a chair, I rub my ankle. It hurts but my anxiety hurts more. My unborn daughter. And now, as I touch my stomach, protective and frightened, it comes to me. I have to call my sister. I have to know how much I am repeating things.

Sliding my mobile from my pocket I scroll to the number. *Sinead.* I haven't used this number in years. I'm not even certain it will work.

The December winds chuck the last twigs of autumn at the kitchen windows, like the weather is bored with waiting for snow – as I key the digits.

The number rings for eight, nine, ten seconds, until I am sure it will click to voicemail. Then it answers.

'Yes.'

It's her. My sadness dilates, until it reaches my hands, which tremble. My broken family.

'Sinead, it's me, it's Rachel.'

A significant silence. I wonder where she is? Drinking a takeaway coffee in a break, at the hospital? In a car, picking up her kids from the childminder's? I don't know her life any more. At last she answers. 'What do *you* want?'

The coldness kills. I restrain the urge to sob, for me,

for my family, for the past, and say, 'Sinead, I know what you think. I know you hate me.'

Her sigh is curt. 'Rachel, I don't hate you. I just don't want to talk to you.'

'I need your help, Sinead. I think it's happening again.'

Another, briefer silence.

'I heard you got married, some rich guy?'

'Wait – no – wait—'

'Rob told me. Billionaire lawyer or summat. Well done. Happy Christmas. You've got money again. You always liked money.'

'I gave it to Mum! It was for her!'

'Look. I've got to get back to work – I'm on lates – some of us have proper jobs—'

'Sinead, please, please please please, I need your *help*.'

She snorts; but she doesn't put the phone down. 'OK. You've got three minutes. What is it?'

I rush on, before she changes her mind. 'I'm worried that it's happening again, the breakdown, the episodes, everything, but – but I don't know, because I don't know what I was like the first time, because I was in that state. Only you and Mum really know it, really remember.'

'Two minutes.'

'Sinead, please.' I gaze, helpless, at the black kitchen windows. Where has the moon gone? Perhaps it has taken itself to the mines, to look at itself, a white face in black water. 'Please?'

'You were all over the place. Hallucinating. Seeing things. Cracked. By the end you started cutting yourself.'

I close my eyes, clutching the phone in my whitened fingers. 'Yes. I remember the cutting, I don't really remember the visions.'

'Well, you had them all right, Rache. You used to lash out, hear voices.'

'I heard things?'

Her voice is still cold. 'Yep. Commands. Do this do that. Y'know.'

So it is true, I am hearing things again, I have been hearing things all along. Imagining it all.

'But why should it come back now?' The fear inside me is a trapped animal, fighting its way out of my chest. 'The doctors said, they said it was only a temporary thing, a brief schizo episode. A reaction to what happened, what I did. It would never happen again. That's what they said.'

A pause. Winds from the sea, a rattling door.

'Sorry. No idea why it should come back.' Her tone softens. 'Look, Rachel, I'm sorry you're in trouble, I don't hate you. It's all too painful, that's all, and I'm getting on with my life. The boys, my job, y'know. And I have to go.'

'You really can't think of any reason why the . . . ' I can hardly use the words, 'why the madness might return? You're a nurse, you've done mental health training, haven't you?'

I get the sense she is thinking, trying to help, through her resentment.

'Well, mmm, a few months ago.'

'What? What is it? What?'

'Probably nothing.'

'Sinead. Please.'

She exhales, impatiently, 'Well. There's this. I did wonder if the doctors missed a trick.'

'Sorry?'

'With their diagnosis, Rachel. I'm working in obs and gobs.'

'What?'

'Obstetrics, gynaecology. We had a woman in here, about a year ago, with postpartum psychosis. Her behaviour was oddly similar to yours. So I kinda wondered.'

The darkness outside is darker than ever. An iron wind from Morvellan, strafing the gardens.

'If you ever get pregnant again you better watch out, 'cause it can come back. But other than that – I dunno. Look. OK. I really do have to go. I'm seeing Auntie Jenny at Christmas. I'll send her your love if you want.'

'Please do,' I say, struggling for the words. 'Please. Please tell her that. Please tell her I love her, like I love you, give the boys a hug from me, wish them Happy Christ—'

'Bye.'

The call dies in my hands. I drop the phone on the table, considering her words. Could my sister be right? The explanation consoles, yet frightens me. My pregnancy.

Scraping the chair closer to the table, I shift my laptop. Flipping the lid, I brace myself, as I type my fevered and frightened words into a search engine. Pregnancy and Psychosis.

At once the key phrase flashes up:

Postpartum Psychosis.

The logic slots. I never told the doctors about the pregnancy, I was too ashamed about what had happened – and it seemed irrelevant, months had passed. But what if my breakdown was, in part, my own body? Was physiological as well as psychological? That might explain why it returns.

The shame is pointless. I have to know.

I flick to a likely looking website, urgently read the words.

<u>Postpartum psychosis is a dangerous mental illness that affects a woman after she has had a baby.</u>
It can cause delusions and hallucinations and sometimes these are intense or harmful.

It is thought that postpartum psychosis affects around 1 in every 1,000 women who give birth

Yes Yes Yes. No no no. I read on.

Most women with postpartum psychosis will experience psychosis (a 'psychotic episode') and other symptoms very soon after giving birth, usually within the first two weeks, but sometimes it happens several months later.

Psychosis causes people to perceive or interpret things differently from those around them. The two main symptoms are:
Delusions – thoughts or beliefs that are unlikely to be true.
Hallucination usually hearing or seeing things that aren't there; a common hallucination is hearing voices.

Tick tick tick tick tick. But why should it affect me again, now? Here, at last, is the crucial statement.

Mothers who have experienced postpartum psychosis are at significant risk of a second episode. This can happen during or after the next pregnancy.

This is enough. And yet there is more. Chilling and demolishing.

Women with an expectation of postpartum psychosis must be carefully monitored, due to the greatly elevated risk of suicide (5%), and also of infanticide (4%).

I close the laptop lid, and lay a hand on the curve of my pregnant belly, in the silence of Carnhallow kitchen.

The astronaut spins in unsteady space, falling over and over in the darkness; my daughter waits and sleeps, inside me.

Inside her crazy and dangerous mother.

Three days before Christmas

Morning

Doctor Conner sips from his herbal tea, places the cup on the table to his left, and presses his hands together, like he is going to lead us both in prayer. A Christmas tree behind him glitters.

'So, am I mad?'

He shakes his head. 'First—'

'I need to know. Please. Is my psychosis returning? You've asked all your questions, please – this is why I begged you for an appointment, I have to know if I am capable of looking after myself, my unborn baby – and Jamie. I can't let it go a day longer.'

He unclasps his hands, and gestures: Stop. 'Rachel. I have a couple more questions. About your last pregnancy.'

I gaze at him, his amiable face, tilted sympathetically my way; the nice blue-and-white checked shirt, under the lambswool jumper. Then I sigh.

'It's just so difficult.'

'Of course,' he says. 'I'm sure it is.'

I am looking through the big living room windows of this lovely seaside home. The sky is mother-of-pearl grey, tinged with pastels of baby blue, and the first soft flakes of that long-promised snow are falling. There is a lonely dog down there on Maenporth beach, apparently without an owner, barking at the snowflakes like they are frightening things.

He tries again.

'I know how it happened, Rachel . . . You've told me all about that,' he says. 'But afterwards, what happened then?'

Sitting here, I have to force the words, because truth is so much harder than lies. 'It's . . . like this. This is what happened. She was . . . born horribly premature. My baby, my little daughter. Maybe twelve weeks premature, maybe more. They whisked her away, explained she wasn't right, something to do with her legs, her spine. And – and then she died soon after. I never really held her. Never properly held my own baby.' The sobs aren't far away now, as I hit the motherlode of grief. The ore in the rock. 'It's one reason I've been so keen to have kids, to get over that. If. If. If you can. If you ever can. I know I stopped believing the moment they told me my baby was dead. But . . . but it took a while for my breakdown to reveal itself. Which is why, I guess, I never suspected postpartum psychosis.'

The dog is back, on the beach, chasing the snow. Leaping and yapping, almost frenzied. Yet I can't hear anything, the glass muffles the noise. Everything is muted, a hand is clasped over the screaming world. I remember my father's hand over my mouth.

'You see, even as my daughter died, I realized I could take revenge. That's all that I had left.'

Conner's frown is puzzled. 'Not sure I grasp your meaning.'

'I told the police, about the abuse. My dad. I told them about the other rapes. It was time someone was *told*.'

The snow is falling so beautifully and so sadly. Snow on grey sand, snow on a calm steel sea.

'And what happened when you did that?'

'They didn't have any evidence. I'd left it too late. And my little baby, my little girl had been cremated. Of course no eyewitnesses. But my dad ran away, anyway, so my accusation exploded my family. My sister blanked me completely. My Auntie Jenny too. Said I should have stayed quiet, that I'd destroyed the family. My mum felt guilty that she hadn't known, hadn't been there for me, to stop the abuse, all the way back from when I was eight.'

'And yet all of this would be off the record, because of rape law?'

I meet his gaze, admiring his shrewdness; he sees my clever plan.

'Yes, exactly. Rape complainants are anonymous for life. I was protected by my accusation. Even the records of my breakdown – anything that might indicate I was raped, everything was hidden away.'

'And the hospital?'

'I was diagnosed as having an episode. Brief schizophreniform disorder. But this is my point, my sister's point – perhaps they gave me that diagnosis because I didn't tell the doctors in the hospital about the baby—'

'Due to the shame.'

'I couldn't. I told the psychiatrists what they needed, I told them I was abused as a kid, then raped – that was enough. To get help. To get medication. To get anonymity. And to be hospitalized and treated.'

293

Conner's frown returns. He takes another sip of tea. I look bleakly out of the window once more. The dog has disappeared. The world is deserted, the muffling snow has defeated everyone and everything, even the feeble, chilly little waves of Maenporth beach look like they want to give up. To stop. At last.

This is the light of the mind. Elevated risk of suicide and infanticide.

'OK, you know pretty much everything, Doctor Conner. You know why I want to keep my baby, despite everything – it's because I lost one. You know it all. So tell me. Am I mad? Has my psychosis returned?'

He shakes his head. 'It's the most awful story.'

'I don't want sympathy! I want your opinion.'

'Of course.' He waves a hand as if beginning a speech. 'First, let me assure you that psychosis during and because of pregnancy is very rare.'

'But the website – my sister—'

'Google is not your friend, not in this instance. The website is wrong, or at least misleading. It does sound as if you experienced a postpartum psychosis when you were younger, possibly catalysed by the unusual circumstances.' He looks at me, and tries to smile, in reassurance. 'And yes, women who have that kind of psychosis do have a significantly raised chance of experiencing the same problem, *after* a second pregnancy. You will need to see specialists soon: so we can prepare – there are good, safe medications we can prescribe. I will arrange a consultation in the New Year, we can't do much before Christmas, Christmas is too close. Let me look in my diary.'

He picks up his phone, checks a calendar app. I get the abrupt sense this is all fake. A decoy. I have to get out of here. Leave the voices behind.

I force myself to look at Doctor Connor. Waiting. Searching for hope.

'OK,' he glances up. 'The second week of January should be fine.' A pointed stare. 'But to address your question, again. Psychosis *during* a pregnancy is really very rare. That's why it is called *post*partum. I do not buy it in your case. During a pregnancy? Possible, but nope. For one thing, psychotic people seldom refer themselves to doctors, it's almost one of the diagnostic criteria.'

'Then what is happening to me! Did I see a ghost?'

'No.'

'Then who did I see? Nina Kerthen is dead, isn't she?'

He shrugs wearily. 'Yes. She is dead. I saw the DNA results. I was at the inquest. No one could have survived that fall, in that mine, in that cold water. She is dead.'

Somewhere inside I am trying not to shriek. The voices are silent but I am left with my confusion; I sink my face into my upraised palms, lacing my fingers to hide my tears. 'Then what the fuck is happening to me, Doctor? The noises I hear, the woman on the bus, the perfume in the house. Please. Please help me. I'm so alone all the time. I have no one. No one talks to me. Only the house.'

Here it comes. Now at last I am crying. Proper big gasping sobs. I feel ashamed yet I also do not care. I am talking like where I came from. Fucking fucking fucking. And the snow is falling. Because Christmas is here.

Conner gets up, he looks like he is about to hug me: the reflexive response. Instead he puts a firm hand on my shoulder. In turn I look up at him, imploring: like I am six years old, seeking a father who will not molest me.

He finds a tissue, gives it to me, and sits down. 'You said yourself you were concussed when you fell. So you then imagined a figure, you imagined Nina – it was dark, it happens. The mind is predisposed to see human figures where there might be none; it is an evolved response. As for the voices, the bus, that's the stress. You are, to put it bluntly, freaking yourself out. And it's not surprising. Carnhallow House is moody and lonely enough as it is. But the point is: when you are questioned you are entirely lucid. Entirely. You're not mad, Rachel, and this is not a dangerous psychosis.'

'Jamie? The stuff he says?'

A hint of a frown. 'Jamie is a troubled boy. He has not properly recovered from his mother's death. Not yet, anyway.'

'I'm not hearing things, and he is saying this stuff?'

'Yes, very probably. Although it is possible that in your rather febrile state you are embroidering, over-interpreting, feeding off his traumas, hence turning a perfectly ordinary woman on the bus into Nina Kerthen. It is also possible that Jamie is reacting to your anxieties, feeding off you in turn – so there is a negative synergy, an element of *folie à deux*. And now that his father is not present in Carnhallow, he must be even more disorientated—'

He stops. I realize why. He's heard about David and me, and he's revealed that fact, and he is embarrassed.

'You know about the restraining order.'

Conner shakes his head and sighs. 'West Cornwall is a tiny place. I have some lawyer friends in Truro. I couldn't believe it, initially – then I recalled that you had those bruises the last time we met. Despicable. David should be ashamed of himself.'

'Did he ever do anything like that with Nina?'

The doctor looks startled. 'Not that I know of. He was besotted with her, obsessed – I barely saw them then – they lived in London and Paris, mainly, when Jamie was born. Yes they had their rows, towards the end, as anyone does. A bit of ennui, I think – she was bored, stuck down there in Carnhallow. Very bright, very beautiful woman. David's grief was terrible.'

'I'm sure it was.'

There's a bitterness in my speech and I don't bother to hide it. Being bitter is the *sane* reaction. So maybe I am sane.

Finishing my tea I set down my mug. The silence is rewarding. I need to seize on what the doctor has said. I am not mad. This is a window, an opening. I will survive this. There is a way out. We just have to get through Christmas.

'OK, thank you. Thank you so very much.' I glance at my watch. 'I need to get back.'

Saying my goodbyes, I walk to the car, through the thickly falling snow; then I turn the key and drive the miles, through the thickening blizzard.

It is snowing everywhere in West Cornwall: snow is drifting against the Iron Age village of Chysauster, snowing on the moors and churches of Carharrack and Saint Day. It is snowing on the lanes of Chacewater, and Joppa, and Lamorna. It is snowing on Playing Place, snowing on the Roseland, snowing on Gloweth.

And I am tearing up again. As I steer the car for the final mile through Ladies Wood, down the knotted valley, to the beautiful old house, lost in its forests, like that gilded box in a coronet of thorns, I remember when I first came here, and read the history of Carnhallow. Of West Cornwall, of the Kerthens. How I yearned to be a part of it: sitting in the Yellow Drawing Room, watching the summer sun on the lilies, I craved to belong to this injured, yet lovely place. I wanted to be woven into Carnhallow's endless, intricate history. I was ready to be woven into the rowans, I was ready to be rooted: in the Playing Place, where the names Gloweth.

And now it is all gone. The dream is dead. The trees are black and leafless, the snow is tumbling so thick I can barely see the mines on the cliffs, where the tunnels go under the sea.

I park my car next to Cassie's Toyota. Then I go in, and the cold scents of Carnhallow surround me: a jostling of memory and grief. I look along the corridor that leads to the Old Hall, where I thought I saw the ghost of Nina Kerthen. Where in fact I saw nothing. Because I am not mad.

The corridor is dark, but deserted. There is no ghost.

I am exhausted. I can hear Jamie in the kitchen, talking to Cassie. I don't want to greet them. Instead I climb the Grand Stairs and fall wearily into my bed and I fall instantly asleep.

But a dream invades my rest. My father is driving a car and I am in the back. I am ten years old, and it is Christmas and we are going to see Auntie Jenny and he is so drunk the car spins out of control, and he laughs as we hit the child by Carnhallow. I run out. I hug the hare, but they are taking her away, to the sea, to throw her into the sea at Zawn Hanna, and now my hair is tangled in my mouth, by the wind, choking me.

I scream so loud I wake myself up.

Shuddering, tasting the dream in my mouth, I stir from my groggy siesta. Then I reach for a dusty glass of water on my bedside table and gulp. The room is dark, the only light comes from the landing outside. It feels like I have been asleep ten minutes, the sleep was so unrefreshing, but it must have been hours.

And now Jamie comes running into the room. He jumps on to the bed in terror and hugs me tight.

'Rachel, Rachel, Rachel—'

'What is it?'

He is squeezing me so tight it is painful. Pushing him away, softly, I realize he has been crying. His face is pink.

'What is it, Jamie? What's happened? What's wrong?'

'She's come back, she's here – I can see her—'

The cold enters me: that blade made of frost. 'See who?'

'It's Mummy.' He is breathing too quickly, panicking.

Despite the fear that tightens around my own heart, I try to look measured, responsible, sane. I am not mad. I have answered questions. The doctor has told me. 'Jamie, calm down, calm down, shhh—'

'It's her!' He is nearly screaming. 'Yet it wasn't her. She was down at the mines, don't you remember? She was there, it was her. She talked to me, it was her. It smelled like her, like Mummy, like Mummy, like my mummy, it was Mummy yet it wasn't. It was and it wasn't. It is and it isn't.'

'Jamie—'

'She's dead and she isn't. Rachel Rachel Rachel I touched my mummy but I didn't. Rachel I saw my mummy but it isn't her. I hugged her but I didn't. I saw a ghost, Rachel. I hugged a ghost. I've touched a ghost. A ghost a ghost a ghost!'

Afternoon

I had thought I was saved; that the doctor had hauled me from the freezing water. Now I am back in it, grasping in the blackness. Drowning.

Jamie's eyes seek out mine. 'Do you believe me, Rachel? She was there! Down at the mine. With the man engine. I told Daddy and he didn't believe me and I told Cassie and she didn't believe me.'

I have no conception of what to say. Perhaps I should admit I saw her too: tell the child his mother lives, or half lives, in our two deluded minds. But the stuff about the mines confuses further. When was he down there at Morvellan? Why did Cassie let him wander? Everything is confusion: as the stiff winds bully the woodlands outside, as the Christmas weather prepares to dump more snow on this haunted valley.

She really is mad. She's having another baby. Stupid slut.

'Stop,' I say, to myself, to Jamie. To the voices in my head. 'Please, please stop.'

Jamie looks at me, perplexed. 'Rachel?'

'Jamie . . .'

Need to batter my way through this. Shout down the madness. I also have to lie to Jamie. Pretend that I am the sane and stable grown-up, that he can rely on me.

'Jamie, you didn't see *anything*.'

'But, Rachel, I did. It was her but it wasn't. It really was Mummy, I know it, I think. But but. But it was so strange, like a dream? I saw her at the mine, I hugged her. It was windy and cold and she was there, she was, I smelled her, I hugged her, I touched her and she hugged me, she did, she did.'

I can see doubts in his eyes. I can see him questioning his own mind. Oh, I know that feeling.

And the image is stark. Nina Kerthen, pale and slender, beautiful and blonde, in her rich dark coat, coming from the mines, coming for her son. Hugging him close, cold tears in her eyes.

'Where's Cassie?'

Jamie shrugs, unhappily, his voice still tight, and anxious.

'Yellow Drawing Room. Granny and her were talking. Someone came to drive Granny away. Don't know don't know.'

'Juliet is here? I mean Granny?'

'She wanted to see me, see me, before she left, we played a Christmas game, but then she went off and, and and and then I looked out of my window, and it was the right time.'

'And you told her you saw your mummy at the mines. You told Granny?'

He gulps air, nods.

'Yes. Yes I spoke to Granny. Cassie too. She was angry at me. She says ghosts are evil things. She says I shouldn't talk like this. Rachel, why doesn't anyone believe me?'

I can imagine Cassie: scolding the boy. Yet also frightened. Wearing her amulets against evil. I know she has been on the verge of quitting for weeks: the increasingly poisonous atmosphere of Carnhallow makes her unhappy. She has no direct loyalty to me. This might be the clincher, and make her quit. Leaving us isolated and alone.

Suicide.

Or infanticide.

'Rachel?'

'Jamie, I'm gonna – Jamie. Sorry. Look, let's get you some supper, some sausage and mash, hey, how about that?'

He looks at me sorrowfully and sceptically. Those blue-violet eyes pierce me somewhere deep. I think of his mother's eyes, the eyes that stared at me from the corridor that leads to the Old Hall.

No. Yes. No.

I flush with cold at the thought: that chilly, monastic chamber. Something *is* in there. I know it. That's where she was, where she came from the darkness. Something is in the Old Hall.

Yes. Waiting for you.

Grasping Jamie's hand I lead him to the kitchen, where I fry the sausage and pound the mash as Jamie sits at the kitchen counter, reading a football magazine. His beloved Chelsea.

The mash is spooned on to a plate, making a big steaming white dollop. Then I follow with the sausages, straight out of the pan, but I drop one on the floor.

Picking up the sausage, I put it in the pedal bin. There are plenty more sausages, nice and browned. Three should do it. Jamie is still absorbed in his magazine. He barely looks up as I put the plate in front of him. His neck is white and exposed as he bends over the book.

Such a slender neck. Such a pretty child. Those beautiful eyes. The neck is so vulnerable. So white and slender.

Breakable.

'Thanks.'

His voice is now level, his demeanour calmer, after that fierce outburst. Perhaps he is pretending everything is OK. The mention of the mines perplexes. When did he go down there?

Now my mobile phone rings, buzzing and spinning on the granite worktop. Thank God. It occurs to me that it might be David. I find myself wishing it was. I feel a need to talk to my husband. I miss him. And I miss us. I miss what we were and what we had a few weeks back.

And as soon as I think this, my self-hatred surges. This is the voice of the abused child, inside me, forgiving the abuser. David is violent. He beat me. He does not deserve any love.

The phone screen says *Juliet*.

'Hello? Juliet?'

'Rachel. We need to talk.'

She sounds relatively calm. Possibly saner than me.

'Juliet, what is it?'

'Are you in the kitchen? Do you have Jamie there?'

'Yes I do.'

'Is he all right?'

'Um. Fine. Yes.' I don't want to upset Jamie so I walk to the furthest end of the kitchen, by the advent calendar. That way Jamie can't hear me.

The calendar window is open and shows a cheery red Santa on a sleigh. Only three days till Christmas. The snow falls thickly on us all.

'Juliet, he's having supper. He's fine.'

'But he wasn't fine, was he?'

'Sorry?'

The little red Santa in the advent calendar is raising a cup of something. Mead. Or barley wine. His reindeers have big fat red noses, like cherries. Christmas is coming! *The goose is getting fat.*

'Rachel, I am at the Penmarricks' – Lanihorne Abbey. I'm here for Christmas. They collected me earlier. I had to get away, for a few days, you know, I'm sorry, but my health isn't so good of late, all these worries . . . and I need to be nearer a hospital—'

The blackness tightens. Juliet has gone? It's down to me, Cassie and Jamie.

'OK—'

'But, Rachel.' Her voice quivers. Self-conscious and uncertain. 'I have to tell you. I cannot lie, um um. Rachel, before Andrew Penmarrick drove me here I was with Jamie.'

The cold wind knocks at the kitchen door.

'And?'

'It was terrible.' Her voice begins to crack. 'I saw little Jamie, in the kitchen. And my God. My God. I walked in and he was laughing the way he used to, he was happy as I have never seen him since Nina had the accident. It was as if he had actually seen her. And then I asked him why he was laughing, and he got angry with me, angry and frightened, and said, "She is here, she is here already." He was utterly convincing. He believes his mother is back. In Carnhallow.'

'But this is ridiculous—'

'I know. I know. And yet, I believe him, because as he said it I really watched him, very closely. And you know the way he turns his head sometimes and gazes at you rather sadly, when he is *really* telling the truth? It was like that.'

Evening

I can't deny it. I know what she means. I know how Jamie behaves when he is being really truthful. He does exactly what she says.

But this is impossible. I struggle to understand, and to speak.

'So he's seeing a ghost?'

'Yes. I don't know, oh oh.'

'Juliet?'

She is quiet for a moment, then returns. 'What are we going to do? I have no idea. No idea. I would come back but, oh, now it's snowing so heavily, I haven't seen snow like this in many years you know, it happens very rarely. But when it happens, my goodness.' She coughs, deeply, then adds, 'Carnhallow can get entirely snowed in – the roads are so deep and the valley even deeper, you should take care, you should buy food. There are power cuts. Quite immoderate. We had to walk to Zennor one year, we were snowed in for half a week and all we had left were satsumas and walnuts, and eggnog.'

I let her ramble for a moment.

The advent calendar is six inches away. Its windows show penguins and sleighs, Christmas trees and polar bears. Not a single Christian image, which is fitting. Out here in West Penwith, so near to Land's End, this feels very much the pagan Yule. The time of fear and hearth-fires, one last feast to keep out the cold before the monsters prowl.

And maybe I am that monster.

Taking a hold of myself, I intrude on Juliet's fading and tangled memories. She's all I have left. The only source, however unreliable. 'Juliet, please, please – let's get back. Is it possible Nina survived the accident?'

'Ahh. I don't think so.'

'And it was definitely her who fell in the shaft at Morvellan?'

A pause. 'Yes.'

'So that makes a circle, Juliet, a stupid circle. Nina drowned two years ago. Yet you say Jamie is seeing his mother. It's not possible.'

'Rachel, I do not begin to understand. These people here . . .' Her confusion devolves into illogic, I can picture her struggling for words that make sense, sitting by the phone in Lanihorne Abbey. 'Sometimes I think I can sense her, smell her perfume. But of course I'm not right, you shouldn't listen to me. Jamie is the important one. He says he hugged her at the mine.'

'Yes, I know. He told me.'

But I need to know *more*. I am grasping at hope here. If I *did* see Nina on the bus, maybe I am not having a breakdown, not tipping once again into psychosis, maybe Doctor Conner is right, in a way he would not expect.

'Juliet, tell me again what happened the night Nina died. If she's not dead – then something very strange happened, maybe we, maybe I can work it out.'

306

A penguin regards me from a calendar. I wait for my own voices. Silence. Good. Please go away and leave me alone.

Juliet replies, 'But you know it already, the chain of events. So awful, so awful. You know David lied and said Jamie wasn't there, at the accident. When really he *was* there. And you know that David asked us all to stay quiet, for Jamie's sake.'

Turning from the windows of the advent calendar, I look to the windows of the kitchen. Snow is inches deep on the windowsill. Like a shop window faking it.

'So you know all that, so you know as much as me.'

'But you were *the* crucial eyewitness, Juliet. That night, apart from Cassie. It's only you. What really happened?'

'I wanted to tell the truth!' She sounds affronted. 'I did. I truly did. I was in my room. We'd all been drinking, there'd been some Christmas guests, but they'd long gone, it was very late and I was going to sleep, but I was woken – there were voices. Raised voices. Arguing. David and Nina, shouting. Most of it was muffled, but then I heard him scream *How could you say that How could you say it*, screaming, at Nina.' She hesitates: but it is a hesitance born of reluctance, not bewilderment. Juliet clearly knows something, and she is on the cusp of revealing it.

I ask, gently as I can, 'You heard something else, didn't you?' I picture this kind, intelligent old lady at the other end of the line, in a large lordly room, Christmas tree in the background, real candles guttering in the gloom. A log fire in a marble hearth.

Juliet's voice is hung with guilt. 'Nina said something remarkable, something David could not tolerate.'

The pause is enormous. I swear I can hear the icicles forming on the eaves of Carnhallow.

Her answer is sad and quiet. 'I've never told anyone

this, but: I did hear one other thing that night. Nina screamed it so loud you could have heard it at Land's End.'

I hold my breath. The snow falls. On Manaccan and Killivose. On Boskenna and Redruth.

'She shouted, *Why don't you tell him, tell your son our big fucking secret, about his real parents* – And then she laughed as if it was actually some awful joke, some terrible sarcastic joke. But true.'

'Nina implied David wasn't his real dad?'

'Yes.'

'And you didn't tell the police this? Why, Juliet?' There is no answer. The anger boils inside me, like the waves crashing on the cliffs at Levant. I rush on, 'I know why you kept quiet! I know. I know. Because it implicated David? Right? Because it implied he had a motive to kill her?' I am nearly shouting.

Juliet is crying now. Her voice catches in her throat. Dusty and tragic. 'Oh, Rachel. There were so many lies that night, so many. I did what my son told me to do, afterwards, to keep things quiet. To protect Jamie. Shield him from the inquest. Did I do a bad thing?'

I have to restrain myself. 'Yes, I think you did.'

'Ahh.' I can hear the stammer of intaken breaths. 'Oh God. It's awful. I've felt guilty for so long. Perhaps that is why I cannot think straight any more, maybe I imagined so much. Maybe I want her to be alive, because that means David didn't kill her, his own wife, kill Jamie's mother, and she didn't say that terrible thing, and Jamie really is my grandson. I have to believe that, he is all I have. Beautiful Jamie. Oh God. Oh God. Oh God.' She sobs, openly. 'And now the snow.'

Christmas Eve

Morning

We only just make it to the Tesco in St Ives, before it closes for the festivities. I buy everything we need in a frenzy, with Jamie at my side, looking at me, distantly, puzzled yet compliant. We couldn't shop yesterday because it was snowing so heavily, but today there's a break in the weather. The sky is the white of hospital sheets, but the snow has called a Christmas truce.

'Is that it?' Jamie gawps at our trolley as we head for the checkout. 'Rachel. Is that all there is?'

My trolley has one box of crackers. A turkey roll. A few potatoes and Brussels sprouts. A miniature Christmas pudding. Jamie is used to opulent Christmases. Lots of adults laughing, elegant Nina gathering elegant friends. Rumtopf. Single malt whiskies. Galettes and roast geese. And his father paying for it all – generous and charming, dashing and witty. This time it will be me, and Jamie, and Cassie. A small and tragic Christmas. I am used to tragic Christmases. And the sadness that comes after.

'It's not going to be a big dinner, Jamie, just us. But we will have fun, I promise. Lots of presents by the tree.'

'Oh. Oh OK, OK. That's OK.'

His smile is brave. His shoulders look so slender in his favourite red shirt. But all his clothes have a tender and terrible poignancy. His jeans for an eight-year-old, his boyish and innocent blue football tops, his woollen bobble hat for cold winter school runs: no child this small should have experienced so much, should be at the centre of all this.

If only I could think of something reassuring to tell him. Something happy, or cheerful, a joke or diversion. But it is difficult to find a subject that doesn't steer us on to the besieging rocks where we will founder, as a family, the fact of his father's exclusion, my own incipient breakdown, the mystery of his mother's death. And the looming fearfulness of Christmas Day itself.

All around us is danger; even here in the supermarket we are surrounded by Christmas, with all that means – like a boat embayed, like a little skiff approaching the great dark rocks that protect the Cornish headlands: the Manacles, Wolf's Rock, the Main Cages. So many died on this wrecking coast.

'Rachel?'

I shake the daydream away. At least I'm not hearing voices, again. 'Yes?'

'Can I ask you a question?'

'Yes.' I nearly say *please*. I am that desperate for a conversation. Heading for the tills.

'Might it be OK if one day I called you Mummy?'

Jamie's sweet face is turned to mine. To hide my confusion and angst I pluck a tin of beans from a shelf. *He wants me to be his mummy.* This is what I have

310

wanted for ages. But not in these circumstances, amid these Christmas terrors. Maybe I could steal him away, rescue him from all of this. My beautiful stepson. My beloved stepson.

'Um. Yes. Yes. Of course you can,' I say, dropping the beans in the trolley. 'Of course you can call me Mummy if you want to, that's nice, I want us to be a family.'

Want? Want*ed*.

'When Daddy comes back, I can call you Mummy and everything will be OK then, won't it, Rachel? Please?'

I start to speak but he runs on, interrupting. 'It's like Mummy isn't like what she used to be, you know, the mummy down there, or the mines, the mummy in Morvellan? Her face is different now but when I hug her and feel her and smell her I know it is Mummy but how can that be . . . she is dead.' As he tails off, his expression of anguish is unbearable.

'Jamie, darling.' I stoop, and face him, sweep dark hair from his eyes. 'Jamie, you have to be brave. We have to get through Christmas. I'm going to cook this food, some nice turkey and chipolatas, you like chipolatas? And maybe bacon, or a sausage roll, I'll get some nice sausage rolls, and then we'll have a nice little Christmas—'

'Not Daddy? Daddy won't be back on Christmas Day? Won't be with us tomorrow?'

I knew this question was coming. Now I have to deal with it. 'Not to Carnhallow, not for Christmas morning, Jamie – not Carnhallow with you, me and Cassie. No. But in the afternoon, if the weather is OK, Cassie will take you to see him, so you will be with him on Christmas Day, just not at home.'

The pain in his face needs no words. I stand and push the trolley. Have to get out of here, now. The drive here was bad enough: it was all I could do to skid the car along the coastal road, nearly thumping into stone hedges twice, as the wheels whined and slipped. Now the winter light out there is yellowing, and dying.

At the checkout the staff are obviously clock-watching, waiting to knock off at 3 p.m., in their red Santa miniskirts and elf-helper hats, so they can head to the pub. I would love to be going with them: to some happy boozer in pretty St Ives, the Sloop on the harbour perhaps. I am only thirty, young enough to enjoy raucous pubs and Christmas Eve kisses under the mistletoe. But not this year. Instead we must negotiate our painful way along the cliffs to Carnhallow, for a much lonelier scene.

Shunting the trolley into the chilly car park, I start loading our meagre haul into the boot. Seagulls shiver on the fence, knocking their down-curved yellow beaks together; their cackles are stifled, with a hint of panic. And now the snow is tumbling, yet again, threatening to trap us in St Ives.

Why not drive off the cliff?

I force the thought away. Concentrate. This endless and repetitive snowfall was pretty enough three days ago, now it is menacing. *We could be snowed in* – that's what Juliet warned. We might be imprisoned by the drifts and cut off from the grid. I cannot bear to contemplate that other warning implicit in her words: David is, in the end, possibly a murderer.

And if he is a murderer? Could he do such a thing again? He is already excluded from his own house: he is staring at a divorce. I am in the way. We are trapped in Carnhallow.

Kelly Smith, the PCSO, told me, weeks ago: *I've seen it too many times . . . when they do it once, they will do it again.*

I shall call her when we get home. I will, I will, I will.

Or maybe I will not. Slamming the boot and strapping Jamie in the back seat I start the car, working the logic.

'OK?'

'OK, Rachel. OK.'

'Let's go, soldier. This is Team Kerthen, heading for the North Pole.'

Jamie laughs. Faintly.

I am only faintly joking. We need to get home before the roads are impassable.

The dilemma is excruciating. If the police reopen the case and Juliet's suspicions are correct, then David will go to prison. For twenty years or more.

If he is convicted and jailed, David's income ends. We are left with the house, which will have to be sold.

And Jamie will lose a father for twenty years, essentially for ever, when he has already lost a mother. And my baby will grow up without a dad. The conclusion is inescapable: it is better to leave the past where it is: to leave the corpse of Nina floating in the tunnels.

If she is down there.

Flinging dirty snow with my whirring wheels, I pull out of our parking space. The car slides on to the main road, the windscreen wipers are crushing the snowflakes with a special relish.

Turning sharp left, we take the Zennor road. The last of the St Ives suburbs, with their shivering palm trees, quickly yield to the craggy vaults of snowbound moorland, made glitteringly pretty and eerily immobile.

313

All is wrapped in ice and white. The landscape is thwarted, autistic, mute. Icicles hang from granite carns like armouries of glass. The only movement is the sea, which waltzes endlessly, a dance of death. It will never stop. The sea looks hysterical compared to the frozen and motionless earth.

The car tyres skid on the muddy drifts, as more snow falls, turning the mud-stained snow immaculate white, once again. Repeat, repeat, repeat. We are the only people driving the moors, the only people mad enough to be out and about in this freezing-point whiteout.

'Christingle!'

'Sorry?'

From the back seat, Jamie is shouting, and pointing. There is a weathered metal sign saying Zennor Church. And beneath that sign is a temporary placard, which says, *Christingle, Christmas Eve 2 p.m.*

'Can we go? Rachel? Please.'

'Jamie, it's getting dark already, we have to get back, if this snow gets any worse—'

'It was Mummy's favourite! We always went to it. She didn't like Christmas. But she loved the candles. Please please please. Please?'

There is no way I can refuse. *His mother's favourite.* Reluctantly steering the car right, I drive down the silent, snow-paved lane into Zennor. The little pub, the Tinners' Arms, is decked with kiddy-colours of straggled Christmas lights. I can see people drinking inside, enjoying a roaring fire, good cheer, mulled wine, hot punch, dogs snoozing in the warmth. There are more cars parked outside the church, as well, some of them already sporting polar-bear-skins of snow on their roofs. So others are as mad as us, other people have braved this brutal weather.

I slide the car to a stop: almost hitting the churchyard wall. The medieval door of Zennor church is open; a vicar stands there, smiling and benign, greeting arrivers as they shake snow from umbrellas and hats.

Somehow I know what will happen when we scrunch the path to the door: Jamie will pull me left. The gravitational attraction, the black hole of grief, will prove too much. Sure enough, he glances across, and his hand tightens on mine. And now he is tugging me, off the icy, gritted path, towards the softly desolate spot that is his mother's empty grave. The perfectly incised mermaid. The fearful epitaph.

The snowflakes are tumbling on to the churchyard yews, on to the speartips of the cast-iron fence, on to the fine polished granite of his mother's grave, and Jamie kneels directly in front of the tombstone. I cannot bear to watch him kneeling in the icy grit, hugging the gravestone, holding it tight, as if it is his mother, returned. His boyish arms, in his little raincoat, trying to embrace the entire stone, tears rolling down his face as he whispers, 'Happy Christmas, Mummy. I love you, Mummy.'

The crow-dark dusk-light gathers in the west, as the snow falls with exquisite gentility on to his blue Chelsea bobble hat.

'Happy Christmas, Mummy. I'm sorry for making you sad. Happy Christmas. Happy Christmas.'

This is enough. Kneeling down next to him, I try to comfort him. But Jamie's grief is an aquifer, an underground river, unseen until it bursts on to the surface – tidal, swollen, flooding, capable of sweeping everything away.

'Jamie.'

In the corner of my gaze I can see the vicar, observing from the door. A grimace of pity has replaced his beatific

Christmas smile. He surely knows who we are, and what is happening. He knows Jamie Kerthen's tragic story.

'Jamie—' I hug my stepson. 'It's OK. It's OK.'

The tears still come in their dozens. Jamie's cold little shoulders are shaking, from the bitter chill and the agony of grief. The Christmas Eve snow falls on Zennor carn. And yet, this is good, I think. Let it out. Let it come. Let it fall.

For three, four, five minutes I hug my stepson. There is no way I can take his father from him as well. I cannot ring the police.

'Goodbye, Mummy.'

He kisses the gravestone once more, then he wipes the snot from his face with his raincoat sleeve. Snowflakes melt on his long expressive eyelashes. We are quiet, together. Plucking a pebble from the grave he turns it in his hand, as if it is a jewel, and then he stares at me. 'You know, you know Mummy said horrible things?'

'Jamie?'

His words come in a thawing rush. 'They were arguing all the time. I don't know, Rachel, Mummy, they were arguing so much, I don't know why. It must have been important because it made Daddy angry. That night, at Christmas, she said Mummy and Daddy aren't who – who – who you think they are but she said it like she didn't mean it, and then she turned and said – Let me tell you about Mummy, the truth about Mummy – and then I screamed and said No and I said I hated her and I ran to the mine and she tried to reach out to me, to touch me, to say sorry, she slipped.' His face is pink and white with cold. 'So maybe it was something she did or something I did? She said I would understand one day, about Christmas, why it happened.

316

Why she hated it. And—' He looks at me. Desperate. As if he wants to tell me a deeper truth, to go further, but he can't. Not allowed. 'Maybe it was my fault, the things she said in the mine before she fell. Was it my fault?'

I hold his hand. 'Jamie, please. Calm down. Calm down. You know your mummy is in heaven and she loves you, she is looking over you.'

'But if she is in heaven why do you think you are going to die tomorrow, why is she back, taking your place? Who is she?'

I shrug, and look at the ice that rimes the antique and rusting sundial. *The glory of the world quickly passeth.*

His face is red-eyed. 'I don't want you to die tomorrow, Rachel. I don't want you to die, I don't want the other Mummy back any more – she scares me. I don't understand. I don't want you to go, don't leave me alone here with Daddy and a ghost. Don't die at Christmas.'

'I'm not going anywhere. I promise.'

I feel an urgent need to protect the boy, almost as much as the daughter inside me. But I am also trying to stay calm, to work this through. I now know what Nina said: Mummy and Daddy aren't who you think they are. I need to know why she could make such a terrible remark, even as a joke. Who could do that to their own child?

I yearn to know more, clear my clouding mind – but I also want to go home. I must leave this be, for now. Christingle awaits, and Jamie needs it.

Standing up, we brush the grit and snowflakes from our clothes, and pursue the frosted path to the church and the waiting vicar, who takes my hand and wishes me a very Merry Christmas, and as he does, stares

317

me in the face, meaningfully, surely trying to express his sympathy. Then he takes Jamie's hand and says, 'Well hello, little Jamie. It's been a while since we saw you.'

We step inside, taking a pew towards the back. The service begins immediately afterwards, as if God has been waiting for us.

And I am not sure what I am expecting, but the ritual surprises me, and after half an hour it ravishes me. Makes me forget the weather. I need this peace.

I have never been to a Christingle before. I imagine this is a Church of England thing: but I like it. Amidst the horrors, it soothes. Local children carry candles stuck in oranges, and carols are sung as these many candles glitter, like the candles in the felt hats of the miners, climbing down the shafts, bobbing down the tunnels that reach under the sea. And then the vicar stands in the pulpit and talks of the great *prediction*, in the Bible, in Isaiah:

'For unto us a child is born, unto us a son is given: and the government shall be upon his shoulder: and his name shall be called Wonderful, Counsellor. The mighty God.'

And the words are so beautiful they make my eyes tingle, yet again. As if am learning the great truth for the first time. I hold Jamie's hand. One by one the candles are extinguished, until the sacred, scented darkness entirely surrounds us.

For unto us a child is given.

When we emerge, it is near dark. We have about twenty minutes of light remaining. And a new front has been opened: the descending snow is heavier than ever. Pausing by the car door, I touch my stepson's shoulder. 'Jamie. You know. We could go to a hotel.'

His mouth opens. In shock.

I hasten to explain. 'It's just, this snow, it's dangerous.'

'No. No we can't do that. No, Rachel, please. We *have* to go home. We have to go to Carnhallow. Mummy's there. Please. We have to be there. It's Christmas—'

His anguish is rising. And it is decisive. 'OK,' I say gently. 'We'll go home.'

We climb in the car and the car swerves and yaws as it battles the narrow roads, heading west, heading for Carnhallow. Three times I have to stop, back up, reverse, and softly careen into piling drifts, banked against the ancient stone hedges. But somehow we make it to the great gate that leads down to the wood.

The sea is distant, ahead. Like a mighty legion forever advancing, under silver shields. A cold and dark blue dusk surrounds. Once more, the snow has relented, this time with an air of finality: twinkling to tiny spangles of cold and starry dust, then nothing.

End.

There is an air of accomplishment. The weather has concluded its task. Perfected the landscape. Dressed the doomed and lunatic bride. A full moon rises and smiles, complacently, like she is used to this sort of thing. I look up at that moon as I drive, accelerating here, braking there. I imagine that the moon has seen Carnhallow in snow many times before, over the centuries. They are old friends.

'Rachel?'

Too late.

'No—'

The car growls, wildly, on a large patch of black ice – we are speeding up, the brakes will not work.

'Jamie!!'

'Rachel!'

I slam my foot in panic and throttle the car to twenty, thirty, forty miles an hour – and now we slide over the edge of the path and down a frosty slope and Jamie screams.

Christmas Eve

Evening

This is the silence. The silence of the mind, contemplating survival. Shaking my head, I rub snow from my face, then I wonder why I have snow on my face. It is so dark in the car, the dashboard lights have gone out, the engine has died. Jamie?

Urgently I press the little light switch above me, and turn: he is gone. Disappeared. I have lost my stepson. As I lost my baby daughter. These children that never really existed.

'Rachel, I'm here.'

The boy is outside the car, the feeble moonlight illuminates his face: he has opened the passenger door, and made his escape, and a low valley wind is blowing snow into the car. Flakes of crystal and the taste of salt. We are down to the primary sensations. Jamie is standing outside the car, staring in at me.

'Rachel, I had to get out it was frightening.'

'Sorry. God, Jamie. We must have skidded, hit some ice. Are you all right?'

'Yes.'

'I think I must have passed out for a second.'

'Tried to shake you awake.'

'Thank you,' I sigh, as the shock ebbs away. 'I – I'm OK now. But . . .'

Unstrapping my belt I reach for my phone, and turn on its flashlight. A hasty scan shows that my Mini is angled into a ditch, at the side of the path, and that the bumper is shunted into the base of a dark thick tree trunk: which probably stopped the wild skid, yet made me bang my head on the steering wheel, knocking me senseless for a few moments. The car is dented and immovable. The stilled engine steams in the freeze.

The only way in and out of Carnhallow, for a few days, will likely be on foot.

A cold knifing wind, chilled by its journey over snow, slices through that open door. I need to get Jamie straight inside. Perhaps I could call Cassie and forewarn her: but a glance at my phone says I have no signal. We will have to trudge through the woods, right down to the House.

'All right, Captain Kerthen.'

I kick open my own door and step gingerly on to the impacted snow. The mild sprain in my ankle still hurts, from when I fell down the stairs, but I have no other bruises or pains save the ache of whiplash in my neck. And a big fat bruise on my forehead where I nutted the steering wheel.

Holding my phone as a torch, I pace round the car and give Jamie a quick, reassuring hug, though he seems relatively unfazed. Perhaps he sees this as an adventure, something to tell his friends at school. Perhaps not. He is a very brave boy, in his own way.

There is something admirable, deep in his soul. There always was.

Lifting the shopping bags from the boot, we abandon the car and begin the wintry march to Carnhallow. Jamie has his arm linked through mine: we can't hold hands, as I am carrying the shopping in one hand and my phone in the other.

We are two people alone in a noiseless wood that feels as grand as a Bavarian forest tonight, on Christmas Eve. All is regal, and lofty, and sombre. Black trees line the path like mourners. Icicles on wet dark branches sparkle in my flashlight, they are the marvellous fangs of invisible dragons. The fresh young snow beneath our feet has a glow of its own.

We walk, together, stepmother and stepson. And say nothing.

Above us the moon rises, queenly and dismissive; the jewels of the stars are randomly scattered, as if Carnhallow has been looted by angels, and her family diamonds are randomly spilled across the velvet sky.

'It's beautiful, isn't it?' says Jamie, as we slowly walk down the moonlit path.

'Yes.'

Shadows leap on either side, apparently alarmed by our presence.

'But also scary.'

I don't want him to talk this way. 'Soon we'll be back—'

'Do you think she is out here now? In the wood? Mummy loved this wood. Do you think that's her over there?'

I jump at his words. Then chide myself. Rachel. Rachel.

Yes. Rachel. I am waiting.
I ignore the voice. But I heard it. The madness returns.
Daddy don't. Daddy don't.

Jamie is pointing at one withered tree, barely more than a stump; it has two outstretched branches, the twigs like extended fingers, writhing in pain.

'It's a tree, Jamie.'

'No,' he says. 'Over there!'

He's right, I saw *something*. A brief shadow of darkness passing between the black trees, which are ranked so silent, branches weighed down by the snow: like soldiers bowing for the funeral carriage of a passing queen. But what did I see? It was something. Anything. Please let it be anything. Or nothing. Let us get home safely.

It was an owl, perhaps, huge wings casting even bigger shadows from my phone-light.

'No, Jamie, that was the wind, or a bird. We're halfway there now.'

The light of my phone is so meek, it will not stretch more than a few yards. Beyond it, the world is iced, and impenetrable.

'It's like the valley is trying to speak to us, isn't it, Rachel? But it can't. Like one of those people in hospitals you think is dead but isn't.'

'More than halfway there now.'

I am ignoring what he says, even though he is exactly right. Tonight, Christmas Eve, the day before I am meant to die, the world feels like it is immobile but sentient, a patient in a white hospital bed with locked-in syndrome. It thinks and watches, but it cannot move. For the moment.

Desperate to get us indoors.

Onwards we walk. We are nearing the house. Its

windows are square and black, and quiet. The West Wing. The Old Hall.

'Wish Granny was here,' Jamie says, quietly. 'Miss her.'

'Well, when we get to Carnhallow I'm sure Cassie will have something nice for us. Hot and warm.'

My fingers ache in the cold, and there's still no signal. We must trudge on alone. From the faraway cliffs I hear the sea birds, and then the waves, crashing on the rocks beneath the mine stacks.

'Jamie?'

He has detached himself from my arm, and is running towards the great house, towards the doors of Carnhallow. The lights are on.

And Cassie's car has gone.

I catch up, my nose and throat stung by icy breaths. Ransacking my bag with chill-needled fingers, I latch the door. Without hesitation, we both head for the kitchen, both of us wondering – where is Cassie?

The kitchen is welcoming and bright but my hopes are instantly crushed. Cassie has left a note by the kettle, pinned down by a little plastic Santa, a leftover bauble.

Cassie's handwriting is hasty yet legible.

I will skip Cristmas this year but I hope to back New Year. I saw David at Morvellan Mine I think you need to know. Happy Cristmas. I am scared about the thing Jamie see. I am sorry. Byebye.

Replacing the note I look across the kitchen. The shopping bags are sitting on the floor, wet with melting snow that dampens the polished wood. Jamie is taking off his raincoat. What do I tell him? Closing my ears to the voices in my head I step over, and give my beautiful stepson a big, big hug.

'Happy Christmas, Jamie. Happy Christmas.'

Now he is all alone. With me.

Christmas Eve

Evening

Sweetly, sweetly, I breathe in. Staying calm, not hurting anyone. Feeding Jamie milk and biscuits. Then we go into the Yellow Drawing Room and I light a big fire in the magnificent stone hearth. It is a primal act. A fire to keep the marauding predators at bay.

The Christmas tree fairy watches us, calculatingly, from the top of the tree.

We are watching.

Then I turn on the TV and Jamie lies on his stomach, on the big Turkish rug bought by his mother, and he watches *The Muppet Christmas Carol*, a Christmas Eve special. And I sit on the sofa hugging a costly velvet cushion to myself, trying not to think that we are alone in this vast house, so appallingly vulnerable. Him and me. The stepmother with a child that is not hers, a boy who is entirely at the mercy of her faltering mind.

Suicide. And infanticide.

My phone rings. I jump. It's David.

'Rachel. At last. I've been trying for a while. Is Jamie OK?'

I want to cry out; I want to beg him for help; I want to tell him everything. And yet I hate him and despise him, and I fear him. What things he might have done to his first wife. What he might do to me, on Christmas Day, to make that Christmas Wish come true.

'Wait.' I haul myself up and make for the corridor, and the New Hall, where the antique engravings of Kerthen mines line the wall. I may be lost in confusion, but I know that Jamie must not hear this conversation.

'He's fine, David. We're all OK.'

'But the snow—'

'I have noticed. Yes. We've got snow.' I'm not going to tell him about the car. It might give him an excuse to come here. He will be itching for an excuse. 'I don't think you'll be able to see him tomorrow, David. The roads are all blocked. And you can't come here, can you?'

'Well. That's it. I thought you might—'

'Thought I might what?' My voice is raised, I can't help it. 'Thought I might let it go, for Christmas, let you march in here and beat the shit out of me again, really? Really? Because it's Christmas?'

I expect him to yield, and apologize. Instead he is quiet, then curt. 'Look after my son. Are you sane enough for that?'

'Fuck you, David.'

'Look after Jamie, and get Cassie to drop him off with me as soon as this snow has melted—'

'Cassie has gone.'

The hiss of silence. I imagine his angry face, handsome and furious: eyes glittering.

328

'What do you mean, Cassie has gone?'

'What I said. She's gone. For Christmas. Left a note. David, we will be fine. Stop this.'

'Cassie has quit? So you're there all alone? With my boy? Fantastic. Look, Rachel, this is ridiculous, you can't be alone in that house, with my son, over Christmas. You're not capable, not right now. I'll walk to Carnhallow tomorrow. I can walk there. Along the coast. Come to get you.'

The fear fills me. Us, all alone, and then him, arriving along the cliffs. No one to protect us from each other.

'NO. If you dare come here I will call the police.'

'Rachel—'

'No! There is an exclusion order, they will arrest you. Don't be an idiot, David. Don't. Don't do it. Don't.'

This apparently sinks in. He says nothing but he sighs, and this next sigh is concerned, even conciliatory. Is this because he knows I am right? Or is he faking it, lulling me?

'Please, Rachel. I'm only asking that you be careful. Don't let Jamie out of the house. It's dangerous in this snow. And there's something else – Morvellan.'

My turn to react.

'I know. *I know*. Cassie saw you. You were there. You broke the restraining order.'

He is silent, then he speaks:

'I did. OK. I did. What the hell, the point is I left the damn door open, open and unlocked, to the Shaft House. I remembered.'

'What? Why would you do *that*?'

The Muppets are singing a Christmas song on the TV. I can hear it through the door. *O star of wonder, star of night, story of royal beauty bright.* David answers. 'I did, I forgot. I walked away without thinking. The point is, Rachel, it's Christmas! Christmas is the worst time, always was. It's his birthday right after Christmas, and his mother died right after Christmas. For God's sake, you know this.'

'But—'

'Listen to me!! Last year, last Christmas, he tried to get into the mine, but he couldn't find the key. You know where it is. Out of his reach. You have to make sure he's safe.' He pauses, oddly, then he rushes on, 'If he goes to Morvellan he could fall in. Go and lock the door, please. For my son. Please.'

David never pleads or begs. What is he hiding? Something about Morvellan.

'David, I'll keep him indoors—'

'No!'

What is this anger, this desperation?

'Please. I know you loathe me, Rachel. I know this. But lock that damn door. I implore you as a father, not a husband. Do it because you care about Jamie.'

He sounds sincere. For all his lies and manipulations, this is a father talking.

'All right, David, enough. I'll do it.'

'Thank you.'

And yet the anger rises again. 'Don't thank me, you hypocrite. You broke the restraining order. Why? What were you planning? To come and throw me off a cliff, down a shaft, like Nina?'

'Rachel—'

'You can call again tomorrow and wish Jamie a happy Christmas, but don't do anything else. I mean it. If you do it again, if you come within five miles of this fucking house, I will call the police. I will. You know I will. Don't you dare come here.'

The phone call clicks dead. I stand here, heart racing.

Morvellan. I'm not sure what game David is playing with my anxieties, but his own anxiety for Jamie seems clear and truthful enough. I have no alternative. I must go down there, now.

Even as I think this, I realize I've never been to Morvellan. The place where it all happened. Not once have I opened the weathered and padlocked wooden door to that terrible place. The place that might explain everything. The day before I am supposed to die?

I have to go, to protect Jamie. I need to do it for him. Protect the child.

In the Drawing Room my stepson is still engrossed in the movie, the Muppets doing Dickens, the ghost of a Christmas Past. I tell him I am going outside to check on things. He nods without turning, absorbed, his chin cupped in his upturned palms. Apparently calm, as if most of this is in my mind.

Returning to the kitchen, I place the stool under the big cupboard behind the freezer, climb up, open the cupboard door, which is high above childish hands. I can only just about reach for it myself. I scan the rack of keys with their antique, handwritten signs. Scullery. Chinese Bedroom. Engine House.

Here it is. A humble little key, on a hook, under a sign saying *Morvellan Shaft House*. Taking a head-torch from one of the drawers, I swap my trainers for wellington boots, then walk to the kitchen door, and open it to the engulfing cold and dark.

The shadowy path down Carnhallow Valley is ermined with snow. Two or three times I tumble left, leaving handprints in the pillowing drifts. Marking my unsteady path. What a nightmare to do this in heels, in the dark of night, in deepest December, drunk with guilt, trying to rescue your son. Panicking, stumbling. Shouting.

331

Jamie Jamie Jamie. Jamie I am coming!

The rowans drip trickles of chilly water down my neck as I push through their enclosing branches. The tamarisks aim for my eyes. Then the trees shiver, in the Atlantic breeze, as they cede to open space, and wilder air. I am out on the wind-streaked, snow-combed field that leads to the cliff path, and the tiny cove, our private zawn. The snow is thinner here, melted by sea spray. But still very slippery.

I am scared. Don't want to go falling down any mineshafts, in the cold and dark. But I am also determined.

Painstakingly, I make my way along the slender cliff-side path that slithers up and down, with no room for two people to walk side by side. The earth crumbles away to my right, down to the huge and bucking waves. Flickers of salt-water sting my face. An enormous herring gull swoops close and sudden, maybe attracted by the cone-light of my head-torch.

Nearly there. The path divides now, leading leftwards up a steep incline to the Engine House, and rightwards, down an even steeper path, to the Shaft House. I take the second, scrabbly path, crouching, almost sledding through snow and grit on my bottom.

I am here.

David was right. The door is swinging in the wind, inviting me in. The chains of the padlock hang loose. I cannot resist: I have to see where it happened. That drama which rules us, almost two years later.

My head-torch adjusted, I brace myself. I am about to do what I have never done before: step inside Morvellan Shaft House. For a moment I wonder if this is precisely what David intended. That this is some trap. He wants me to fall in.

And yet, I don't care. My curiosity is overwhelming. The door is already open; I cross over.

Inside, it is a little smaller than I expected, and much colder. The fervour of the sea is instantly and spectacularly muffled.

The granite walls are black with damp, mossed to head height. There is no roof. The polygon of hard starred sky is brutally framed above. The arched windows are glassless, like any ruins; the place feels like the tower of an ancient, gutted priory.

Now I look at the one place I don't want to look.

The shaft, the hole, the sea-grave.

It is wider than I expected. Maybe four yards across. David once told me Cornish mineshafts were often no wider than chimneys; but he was referring, perhaps, to the earlier shafts, from the sixteenth or seventeenth centuries. But Morvellan made so much money they poured investment into the mine, right up to the 1880s.

That meant they widened the shaft, I guess, to take all the machinery: the kibbles and man engines, the pumps and cages. The irony is brutal. A narrower shaft would be harder to fall down. If the Kerthens hadn't made so much money, the wife and mother might not have died.

If she died. You know she's come back.

I can also see how very easy it would be to fall here. There is no grille over the yawning hole. No protective wall, or fence. Just flat, damp, slippery concrete, surrounding a big black void. Like the shouting mouth of Hell, waiting to swallow me.

Sliding forward, nervously, then outright crawling on my knees, I stare directly down the shaft.

Nothing.

There is nothing visible. At the top I can make out

sheer curved walls of well-masoned brick. There are a few modest recesses, intended for machinery perhaps, metalwork long since taken for scrap. There is certainly nothing serious to use as a handhold. If you fell down here, you'd fall fast and hard, without hope.

But where is the water? I am surprised: I thought the mine was watered. Then I realize – the sea must be at sea level, which is forty or fifty feet below me, and it must rise and subside with the waves and tides, like a living thing, expanding and contracting. Respiring.

My torch-beam dims to nothing at the distance: a grey-black circle of darkness.

Reaching around in the cold, I seek a pebble or a rock, something to throw. This will do. A chunk of dark rock, veined with a hint of black tin. A piece of the deads. Leaning over, I drop the rock down the shaft and wait. One. Two. *Splash.*

So there is water down there. Again, I imagine Nina's mental terror as she fell into this caging void, banged from wall to wall, severing a vein on some sharp metal or stone, the excruciating pain, the spraying of blood – and then the hard impact in the water. The cold. The frothing. The Drowning.

A few minutes alone in that black water, in this freezing black mine house, and you'd be streaming blood from your fingers as you scraped the wall in desperation, splintering your nails, as the water dragged at you with its icy gravity. I wonder if in the end she yielded, and accepted, drowned peacefully?

No. She felt terror to the end, surely. Such a horrifying way to die, after all. Trying to rescue her son. That's if he really was here. And if it really was him here. And if she really died here. And if she wasn't really murdered.

That's if she was ever here at all.

334

The tunnels stretch deep under the sea and I will never find their end.

The trapped and icy brine stirs, far beneath me. I can hear it shifting. Curious, I look down the pit once more. And my torchlight now returns something very different.

I put a hand to my mouth to stop my own scream.

I am staring at Nina Kerthen – or what remains of her. The black water has ascended, and is displaying Nina's body, like she is raised on a velvet bier.

The fingers are split at the end, one arm is lofted above her head, saluting me; half her face has gone, but it is recognizably a young woman, in a pinkish-red party dress.

Her feet look so sad and bare, like they have come such a long way – she must have kicked off her shoes in her attempt to climb out. And the blonde hair forms a corona, as if her head is streaming silver filaments, or gathering threads of starlight. I wonder how long she has been here, floating sad and unobserved, in the mine.

But one thing strikes me, even from this distance, even with the horrible disfigurement of the face. Is this really Nina Kerthen? Is this really Jamie's mother? The decomposition is so horrible. Her wounds do not help: the blood from her hands, the silvery hair, the nails.

'You used to be able to see the steam from all the miners' breath.'

I swivel, startled. It's Jamie's voice. My first thought is: Nina. Down there. He must not see her. It is far too desolating. But where is he? My torch scans the darkness.

'Jamie?'

Where is he? Did I imagine that?

'Jamie? Don't freak me out? Jamie!'

'I'm here.' He steps out of the darkness. He was right behind the door. He has his own torch, handheld, which he is flashing in my face, blinding me.

'Please, Jamie, I can't see.'

'Sorry, Rachel.' He drops the torch, and flicks a switch, dimming it.

'Jamie. How did you know I was here?'

He shrugs, diffident and embarrassed; face pinched with cold. He steps nearer, almost into the Shaft House, gazing around this awful place.

He must not see in the pit.

'I saw the open cupboard in the kitchen, and the key was gone. No one comes here very much, not any more, not since . . . ' His words stumble to nothing. He looks around. He steps closer.

'No!'

I stand up and push him back, before he can see. Then I physically grab him, pulling him away from the Shaft House door.

He is startled. 'What? What is it? Is there something in there? Is it Mummy? Is she back?'

'No. No, Jamie. She's not there, not there.' Hastily, fumbling in the chill, I rechain the door and close the padlock. 'Jamie, it's too dangerous down here. Your father called to ask me to lock the mine door. That's all. Let's go back. Watch some more TV.'

Jamie looks at me, then at the cold dark brickwork of the minehead, and his eyes fill with sadness as he gazes up at the pointing chimney, accusing the starry sky. This is the death-place.

'I come here sometimes as well, I do, but don't tell Daddy, he told me never ever to come here but sometimes I come here and stand outside and think about Mummy. But I can never get in. Never get in to see if she's really here.' His voice is incoherent with sadness. He is still staring at the chimney. Then he looks out, to the turmoiled sea.

'Jamie, we have to go.' I place a guiding arm firmly around his shoulder. He does not resist. 'Come on, let's go home.'

Together we retrace our steps along the treacherous path, my heart stopping up my throat with tension. Arms linked, we make it on to firmer ground, the gravelled path up the snowy valley. Flakes are drifting, I have snow in my nostrils, clean and pure and fragrant. We are both as silent and stifled as the snow-killed landscape. I have one thought that dominates all others. Nina Kerthen may not be dead. Someone else drowned in the mine. Perhaps that solves it all.

I open the kitchen door and we step inside. Close the door. And Jamie reacts, instantly. Clutching at my arm as he yells:

'Mummy is here. That's her perfume. She's here. You said she's not in the mine so she must be here now.'

Christmas Eve

Night

'Jamie!'

I don't know how to soothe him. His little body is stiff with fear. My own fears are barely confined. The kitchen is so normal with its sparkling red kettle, the grey steel fridge, the cool granite worktops. Yet everything glints, now, with extraordinary potential. Every reflection in metal and glass might be her, moving, entering, opening. Smiling.

I can hear you.

'Rachel?'

I struggle towards logic.

I need to be as normal as possible. So I must do Christmas. I have to perform the rites and rotes of Christmas Eve: they will soothe my stepson. And me.

'Jamie.' I take his clammy hand and sit him at the kitchen table. Then I fetch him a glass of milk. He takes a big brave gulp, as I talk. 'Jamie, there's no one here.'

You are lying.

White milk smears his red lips.

'But that perfume! It's Mummy. Can't you smell it? I want Mummy to stay dead now. It's enough now, isn't it?'

'I can't smell her perfume.'

And I cannot. Not this time. But I can maybe detect another presence. An evil woman, capable of evil things.

'I want Mummy to stay in the mine. Or in the grave at Zennor, wherever she is, I miss her but I don't want her to talk to me any more.'

'Jamie, she isn't talking to you. She can't be.'

But how can I be sure? That face in the darkness, I saw it, coming from the Old Hall. And I have not been inside the Old Hall since. An entire wing of this house scares me; I am returned to being an infant. Frightened of the thing behind the door. Terrified by the voice of my drunken father, at the bottom of the stairs, climbing up to see me.

'She does talk to me. Does.'

'How?'

'She won't let me tell you.' Jamie is blinking rapidly, the deep and painful confusion visible in his eyes. 'I even met her, I did, but it wasn't her, yet it was. It was like a dream, it was my mummy but it wasn't. I met her at the mine. With the man engine.' He stands up, abruptly, and runs to the door, shouting down the hallway, 'Don't need you here, Mummy! Stay away.'

The house answers with a contemptuous silence.

Jamie waits at the door, for his dead mother to respond. I wait for my own voices. The madness he pushed inside me, with his fingers and his whisky breath.

Perhaps David is right and I am in no state to look after a child: perhaps I am deluding myself. Perhaps I ought to give up, call the police, leave Carnhallow, let David take over. But then, he is no better. He is implicated in the death of Nina. Maybe he's not Jamie's father anyway.

The confusion is labyrinthine. Yet again, all the tunnels terminate in a great darkness. I force my mind back to the necessary rituals.

'Jamie, it's Christmas. Let's put some stuff out for Santa.'

The boy, unsurprisingly, looks at me as if I am insane. He sees my gathering madness.

'You know, Jamie. A carrot for Rudolf, a glass of sweet sherry for Santa. Let's put them by the fireplace for when Father Christmas brings the presents.'

This is what my mum used to do. It's one of my only happy memories of Christmas. My mum and my sister and me, we would put out the carrot and then mum would pretend to chomp it like a reindeer and we'd laugh because we knew it was all fake but somehow we wanted to believe at the same time. Because reality was so fucking inferior.

The charm works. In the bottom of the fridge I find a slightly mouldy carrot. In the back of a cupboard: sweet sherry. Jamie's expression softens into a forlorn hopefulness. The white magic of Christmas doing its thing.

Together Jamie and I boldly walk down the hall into the Yellow Drawing Room, where the green tree glitters and the white fairy smiles. Her wand is poised. The TV is still on, broadcasting a church service somewhere in deep and snowy England, people in suits and coats singing hearty carols. *The hopes and fears of all the years are met in thee tonight.*

I realize it must be late, so much time has passed. Is this a Midnight Mass? I gaze out, the curtains are open. Clouds are breaking, and showing a yellowish moon, yet more soft snow is falling, making manic, obsessive patterns beyond the leaded windows. My house looks like a Christmas card. A leering face appears at the window.

341

Cunt.

No. I will not listen. I'm not going to let the voices spirit me off. If I do then I won't return, not this time.

'Come on, Jamie, it's very late now.'

He nods, obedient, trusting. The rest of the house stretches away around us, huge and dark, totally out of scale. We are two people in one of a hundred empty rooms.

'Let's put these out for Santa then get to bed. It's really late and tomorrow it's Christmas, and after Christmas you can see Daddy and everything will be fine again.'

'Yes, Rachel.'

The sherry glass goes on the mantelpiece. Then the carrot, wobbling on its saucer, is placed on the flagstones right in front of the fire.

And now everything goes black. The TV squirts and dies, the lights blink out. An infinite yet barely heard music has stopped abruptly, leaving a pounding silence.

It's a power cut. That's all. But we are immersed in darkness. The house is invaded by night. The only light comes from the starlit snow at the window, and the rigid fear in Jamie's whitened eyes.

'She did it.' He grabs me, hugs me. 'She did this. Please don't let her do it, please don't go, don't die, Mummy, don't leave me here with her.'

Reaching for the sound of his voice I take him and hug his trembling shoulders.

'Shh. Jamie. Shush. It's only a power cut, the snow must have brought down the lines.'

'Scared, Rache. Scared scared scared.'

My heart beats outrageously in my chest. Far too hard. It hurts.

'Don't be scared, don't be. We'll be fine. Let's go to bed now and I bet by the time we get up the power will be back on.'

His body language says *Don't believe you*, and I don't blame him. There are now lots of faces behind him, curious, pressed to the window, lots of whorls and eddies of snow, caught by the moonlight.

'Jamie, I'm back, hello, sweetheart.'

That voice was real?

Help me. I am crumbling. The voice sounded sickeningly real – like it came from behind the Christmas tree, a triangle of black in the black corner, or maybe over the other side, by the TV, another dark shape in the darkness. I have to hide my terror and confusion. I mustn't let Jamie know that I am crumbling, too: falling too far, and much further than him.

Desperate, urgent, I look for my phone. And its torchlight. Another pang of fright seizes me as I realize I left the phone in the kitchen. We will have to go back to the kitchen, in the darkness, past the long corridor that leads to the Old Hall.

'Let's get my phone then go to bed,' I say to Jamie, reaching for him in the cloying dark.

He comes close, buries his head in my stomach, his face downturned. Like he did at Levant, when he predicted my death. That was when it all began, my madness. That was where I had my first hallucination. The little girl with the crippling boots. Like the child in the supermarket. A deformed child, roughly the age my daughter would have been, if she'd lived.

But now it is too late. I have understood too late. *Yes, it's too late now.*

Jamie mumbles, 'Scared, Rachel, scared of the dark, don't want to go out there where Mummy is.'

'Shush. Um um . . .' I am flailing for a solution, some way of getting us through the next twenty-four hours: getting us *both* through, unharmed. I may have to call

343

the police, condemn myself. Yet my mind rebels, ferociously, at the idea. I *won't* let my father win. I can do this. *I just have to get through Christmas.*

'All right, Jamie. I know what. I know what we can do. You can sleep in my room. My and Daddy's room. For tonight.'

He looks up at me, and his eyes sparkle with faint hope. 'Can I?'

'I'll make up the little bed. Yes.'

'And can we have candles? We always had candles on Christmas Eve, because Mummy liked them, that's why she liked Christingle.'

'Yes. Yes of course. Yes.'

The nausea rises inside me and is bitten back. I gaze out at the darkened room, to the windows, where so many black roses bloom. I swear I can smell their scent, it is not unlike Chanel.

'Come on.'

My hand is trembling more than his. Together we fumble our way across the room, linked like miners in a dangerous tunnel, the blind leading the doomed. The dark ungraspable shape of the door is waiting. The blackness has made the house quieter than ever. All the sounds are outside. The freezing wind raking the rowans, the distant sea with its endless anger.

'This way.'

It is even darker in the hallway than in the Drawing Room. I can just make out the white shapes of the old prints, of the old mines, on the wall. The ancient photos of the bal maidens, staring, frowning, into the future. Their dirty miserable faces accusing the Kerthens. *You did it, you did it. It's your fault we died.*

Onwards down the landing. We've got to make it

down the corridor, then we will be safe in the kitchen
– and we can find a light.

'Jamie, I'm home.'

My stepson didn't hear it. Only I heard it.

Jamie clutches my hand tighter. 'I heard something.'

'What?'

Jamie's face is a blurred oval in the black, eyes wide
with amazement. I feel a need to touch his face, to know
that something, someone, is real. 'I heard her. Just then,
Mummy.'

'The kitchen's not far.' I am tugging him so fast he might
fall over. I am so frightened. I cannot look at the corridor.

Jamie tugs me. 'But I heard her! And I know where
is! She's in the Old Hall. She called out to me.'

'Jamie, nothing's in there.'

He is yanking me now: pleading and demanding. He
is a formless shadow in the starlit dark. 'We have to go
there!'

I am choiceless, and panicked. 'All right, Jamie, shh
shhh. We can look tomorrow—'

'No! No, no, it's Christmas Eve. She must be coming
back and she's in the Old Hall, she is she is she is—'

'But wait.' Desperate now. 'Let's get some light first.
It's too dark to see anything. We might fall.'

I have to do this quickly – that's if I can do it at all.
Half-stumbling, knocking into chairs, we flee through
the corridor of shadows and gloom, and we get to the
kitchen. The moon casts her antique light on the glittery
emptiness. But yes, there it is, on the granite worktop:
my phone. When I switch on the app, the cone of
brightness makes deeper shadows in the crowding dark.

'OK. We're good. Now let's go upstairs and—'

'No. You said we could have candles! You said we
could go into the Old Hall! You did.'

345

He runs away from me, and stands in a corner – leaning against the kitchen wall, arm over his face. Trying not to cry. The brave, brave boy.

Every part of my mind burns with pity. The imperative and unignorable tears of a child who has lost a mother. The fear stings, but so does the guilt.

Accepting my allotted role, I stoop, fumble in a kitchen drawer.

'Look. Here we go.'

Two candles and a lighter. He half-turns. I find two saucers, and light the candles. At least this will save my phone battery.

'Let's stick them on these. See.' Tilting the wicks into the lighter flame, I melt the wax, and adhere the candles.

Jamie shifts himself, and eyes me – and comes nearer, his features dancing in the flickering candlelight.

'It's better, isn't it, Rachel? It's what Mummy wants. She loves candles. I want to show her.' He is staring at the yellow flames as they gutter in the noiseless breeze that has no explanation. Unless somewhere in the house a door has been opened.

'There. You have one candle and I'll have the other. Make sure you don't drop it.'

'OK.'

The long dark landing shivers in astonishment at the sight of us, emerging from the kitchen, a stepson and stepmother, each carrying a saucer, and each in charge of a fragile candleflame.

Now we are walking down the hall, turning right. We are actively doing it. Walking along the corridor, crossing the line where the restoration ended, where Nina died, where someone died. The door to the Old Hall looms in front: bewildered by our idiocy.

I can't do it: can't push the door open. I'm too stupidly scared: my father is in there.

Jamie presses the door.

It swings open to a different kind of darkness. That retreats, with a disconsolate whisper, as we enter, with our candles.

We are inside the Old Hall. Where she waits, staring like the woman who floats in her dress in the mine, grinning her fixed and skeletal grin. I wonder if she can see us, in her endless dreams, as her hair drifts on the freezing water.

The darkness is as intense as the cold in here. The tall narrow windows show the perfect circle of the winter moon like a white Japanese mask. Jamie is absolutely still, and staring intensely, his face uplit by the twitching candleflame. He gazes in wonder at something in the corner. I daren't look myself, I cannot face this. Perhaps she is stepping nearer to him: over there, coming nearer, coming for her son.

'Hello, Rachel.'

A hand grabs me, from the darkness behind. It grabs my hair, it twists my hair, forces me down.

I gasp, and fall forward. Did I imagine that? Of course I did. The horrors of my childhood return. I am on my knees, punched from behind, by my own hallucinated fears. I have dropped the candle, its light dies away on the stone floor. Jamie gazes at me, astonished by the sight of his stepmother, terrified, on her knees.

'Rachel, are you all right? Did you see her? You saw her, didn't you?'

'No, no. I was only. It was nothing. It's nothing.'

I pick up the candle. With wobbling, horrified hands. I flick the lighter, reignite the wick, scare the darkness away. The Old Hall is releasing us. She is not here. No

347

one is here. There is no one for miles, the bald moors are snowbound, the cliffs desolate and icy.

I am upstairs.

Jamie holds my hand, and says, 'Let's go upstairs.'

Christmas

'I'm frightened.'

'OK, Jamie, OK.'

David walked to the window of his hotel room, the phone tucked under his chin. He could hear revellers pouring out of Truro pubs down there on the snowy, cobbled roads. Roaring drunk. Christmas Day.

He closed the window, even though his room was overheated: he wanted, he needed, to hear every word his son said.

'So many things happened, Daddy, scary things and the car smashed and I went to the mine and Rachel is—'

'The car smashed? Try and speak calmly, Jamie. Please try and calm down. Are you all right?'

'Yes I am all right only frightened actually Rachel is frightened too I can see it and she is coming back, Mummy is back, like she promised, I can smell her perfume, Daddy, I saw her in the Old Hall, and she's here in the house and—'

351

'Jamie, slow down.'

'I know I know but it's difficult.'

'Where are you now?'

A beer-bottle shattered on a wall outside; the revellers turning into hooligans. Thuggish cheers rose from the streets.

'I'm in my bedroom but I am sleeping in your room, Mummy's room, I mean Rachel's room, tonight, but can you come over tomorrow? I don't think Rachel is OK. Dad?'

His anger rose; David fought to stay sensible, to stay lucid. 'Is she behaving strangely?'

'She talks to people who aren't here. She fell over in the Old Hall like she was pushed.'

'What were you doing there?'

'I thought I heard Mummy's voice. I know there aren't ghosts, Daddy, but I hugged Mummy at Levant and I've seen her everywhere and it isn't her but it is. And now we've got the power cut and it's dark. Everything is cold.'

'All right. I will be there soon. I promise.'

This was it. Any alternatives had been stripped from him. He would have to drive to St Ives, then walk the coastal path through the snow and ice. Through the night. Whatever the risks.

'Jamie, I'm coming over now.'

'Promise?'

As he consoled his son, David searched for the weight of his car key in his pockets. This was the right and only decision: drive and walk and sort this out. And deal with Rachel, once and for all.

'Dad, I've got to go I can hear Rachel coming, she's coming now, she's coming don't want her to hear me talking to you she will be angry. Bye, Dad.'

The call went dead. David didn't have a chance to say goodbye. Perhaps it didn't matter.

He had to hurry. Time was shortening, horribly: his son was fizzling into madness in a house where the only other person was already psychotic. Jamie was in serious danger.

Lacing his boots, bagging a head-torch and gloves, David walked down the muted hotel corridor and out into the snowy hotel car park. Truro's cheery Christmas lights romped and cartwheeled in the icy wind. His own thoughts churned like the snow devils whirring in the empty streets.

The only people in Carnhallow were both teetering on the edge. But were they the only people there?

The evidence mounted. Jamie insisted he could see her, time and again. His own mother now had doubts. The truth was emerging from the sea-mist.

Perhaps the impossible was coming true. Jamie's mother had returned.

Christmas Day

Midnight

Jamie is taking too long. I've made up the little bed in my room, but – checking the clock – it is now past midnight and he has still not come back. I told him to get changed into pyjamas. But that was half an hour ago.

Opening the door a few nervous inches, I call down the landing. His room is near enough for him to hear me.

'Jamie.'

He does not respond. I can see shapes, dark figures, here on the landing. They are in my head. They scamper, like children, playing a game. Tiny feet thumping. Then silence, the sea, the sound of darkness. Then the sad and lonely laugh of one child left behind. *Come back, come back. Don't leave me here.*

There is no safe place anywhere in this whispering house, or in my whispering mind. On the landing, down the landing, I run, ludicrous and hysterical, dressing gown flapping, phone torch aloft, then push at Jamie's door without even knocking.

He's sitting on his bed in pyjamas – and looks up, startled, illuminated by the dying light of his phone. So he was calling or texting someone. His father, is my guess.

They're all coming for you now.

The boy looks exhausted, pale as snow.

'Jamie, come on!'

He flinches. Why am I shouting?

You know why.

'Please. Jamie. Please. Let's go into my room and stay there till dawn. Then . . .'

Then what?

The idea of sitting round the tree opening presents is farcical. And cruel.

'Come now, Jamie. Please!'

With a suspicious glance at me – perhaps a frightened glance – he climbs off the bed, reluctantly takes my hand and we pad back through the darkness, with my phone as the only light in this black-out. Without power and heating, the house is unnervingly cold. My phone is nearly dead: I've used the torch too much.

And of course I cannot recharge it, for there is no power.

Everything is slipping away. All contact with the outside world is dying, the snow is building walls around Carnhallow. So we must build an inner fortress in my bedroom, to keep the bad things away. The bad ideas in my head.

Guiding Jamie urgently to the little bed, I tuck him in, and he lies there with his head flat on the pillow, and his dark hair feathering his white cheek and he looks at me in the shrouding cold, with the light from my torch making shadows of silent animals on the ceiling.

'Are you all right, Rachel?'

'Yes, I'm OK. We need to sleep, and get through till tomorrow.'

His eyes, those eyes he got from his mother, widen in the silence. So very tired, and pink, and violet.

'You're frightening me.'

'I'm sorry,' I say. 'I am really sorry. I'm not myself. But we will be fine.'

Don't tell him what you're going to do to him.

Now I turn the precious torch off, and Jamie says into the darkness, 'Rachel, I did something bad. I'm sorry.'

I reach for his hand. It is small and cold.

'I lied, Rachel. It was me that put all the fire letters in the Old Hall. I wanted to do a spell for Mummy to make her come back, like she promised, because I felt her getting nearer, when I hugged her, at the mines, when we did the photos.'

At least this is one mystery explained, yet still others open up, darkly.

'Jamie, we all lie. Everyone. Me, your father, grown-ups lie too.'

He is not calmed. I can hear his sigh, though I can barely see his face. His voice is fluttering, anxious.

'But she didn't come back, Rachel, and I lied because – because – and I lied other times, I lied at Levant about Christmas, about you, I wanted you to go away at Christmas so Real Mummy could come back, wanted you to go and then I said you were going to die but now, now, now I think it's true, I don't know, oh.'

The anxiety is mixed with yawns. He is desperately tired, even as his hand grasps mine so tight. His words come fast and nervous, scratchy, desperate. It mixes with the noises of the house. The tapping noises, coming nearer.

357

'Mummy said at the mine that Christmas, after Christmas, was really my day, my special day, and she said that one day she knew my mummy would come back and tell me all this and that's why Christmas made her sad and that's why I didn't love her like Daddy, and – and that's why I think she is coming back now and that's why you had to go by then, by Christmas, but it was a secret, a big big big secret. Daddy said I should never tell anyone, what she said, he said I should never even think about it, not anything!'

He stops, exhausted, his eyes shut tight.

I do not begin to understand what he is saying, but I know the agony of the forsaken child. And perhaps I can help him, one last time. Before I am lost. Before it is too late.

'Jamie,' I am whispering. 'I will tell you a secret. I lie too. I lied once, when I was young, a big lie. But I did it for the right reason.'

I'm not even sure if he is awake.

'I said my daddy did something bad to me, and he did but he did it when I was much younger, but it was a good lie anyway. It explained things, it explained why I was pregnant, why I was having such a special baby. And it saved my mummy. A good lie. Sometimes people tell good lies.'

There is no reply: Jamie has fallen into an exhausted sleep. Maybe he did not hear me. But the house did.

For a final moment I look at him. The eyelids flickering as he dreams. I wonder what he is dreaming. This time.

And then, as I think about his dreams, a kind of answer forms. Nina's injuries. Of course. Hair and blood and nails. *Of course*. It all echoes Jamie's dream, from months ago. Hare and blood and hands. Is this, then, what happened in Jamie's mind? Was his apparent prediction a reworking of his mother's death, of the gruesome details from the inquest? I know enough psychology. I've read enough books about depression and the like. I know how the dreaming mind functions. Puns and rhymes and echoes.

But even if it does explain *something*, it is all too late now. The mystery has gone way beyond Jamie. The mystery is in me. I have become the source of the darkness. And of the danger.

I pull myself across the room. Through the murk and away from him. I must keep my distance.

Lying on my own bed, my eyes burning, I stare up into the gloom. I don't regret lying, saying he raped me, made me pregnant: it got rid of him. And anyway, he had abused me, all those other times.

But the pregnancy sent me mad, as this one is sending me mad.

Yes, I am back. Too late now, Rachel.

Above me, his face is painted on the ceiling.

Too late for the truth.

The stats are a poem I must repeat: 5 per cent risk of suicide; 4 per cent risk of infanticide. Pregnancy-related psychoses.

How do I hide from myself? The storm is here in my head, the black waters close over. Because Daddy is in the room again. Daddy is back. Daddy is climbing the stairs. And I can hear the tap tap tap of the miners, underneath us. They are working again: the mine is coming to life. All the secret life, underground, is coming to the surface, and heading up the stairs.

Hello, Rachel, my lil Rose of Tralee

No!

The door opens.

359

No.

I shout, fighting. I am a twelve-year-old girl, fighting off her father – but this time he wins. Maybe he always wins, in the end: maybe this is his revenge, to get inside my head, to make me do things. No matter how hard I close my eyes I can see things. Like the vulnerable neck of my stepson. But I love him. So I have to protect him, hide him away. Hide him in the water, in the darkness. Hide him in the mines with his mother.

No.

Go to the kitchen.

No! I plead with the frigid air. Let me go. Let me not do this. Spare me. Stop this. Let me get through Christmas. Shutting my eyes to the terror of madness, I turn over, pulling the cold damp pillow over my head to fight the noises, and the voices. But my arms itch. Sleep is a ludicrous fantasy. I am lying here on Christmas night, eyes itching and scared, and the snow-mantled cliffs fall down to the waiting sea, trying to shut out the voices. The noises, the silence.

The moors are dead tonight, the crows sleep with their eyes open in the shivering gorse.

Crows can predict the future, too. Did you know that? You know what happens now.

I wonder if Jamie somehow detected my madness, lurking? The fire child foreseeing the danger in me? No. No no no. It's too late.

Here it comes. Here it comes. The black water rising. Tap tap tap. I can hear the hammers of the bal maidens, hammering the deads.

I mustn't let him win. But it is too late. He is winning. Always winning. Stronger than me. Oh yes. Oh yes. *Oh, Daddy.* He is pinning me down. The madness is bigger and older, a dark figure on top of me.

Daddy, stay down there. Daddy, don't come up. Daddy, stay away.

I turn over, my fingernails pressed so hard into my palms I think I can sense hot blood. Like I am cutting myself. And why not? I am good at cutting, I can always cut.

So I have to cut, and chop. I have to slice this open, with a knife.

It is done. I cannot fight this any more, not any longer. Christmas night will never end, so there is only one way to end it. To sing away my fears, like I used to do, when Daddy did what he did, on Christmas Day.

I saw three ships.

If I sing that, I won't care what's going on, won't be aware. I won't feel a thing, won't care how I cut. That's how I dealt with Daddy, that's how I blocked him out *I saw three ships come sailing in. And all the bells on earth shall ring.*

It is my very own special carol. The rosary of the raped.

Now my eyes snap open and they glitter in the dark, because I am ready.

Jamie's breathing is deep and slow, and contented. As if he knows what is going to happen: what I am going to do to him. As if he accepts, and understands – that I do it because I love him. I have to save him from this terrible world. From the ghost of his mother, with her body floating nearer, as the black water rises.

I saw three ships.

Just as long as I keep singing, I shall be fine. I don't need any police, no ambulance, no doctors, no psychologists.

I saw three ships come sailing in, on Christmas Day in the morning.

So I must be about my business. Lightly and gently,

361

I swing my legs from the bed. There is a suppleness in me, now. It is all so much easier than expected. This is going to be much simpler than anyone said. It is as if I can fly.

Crossing to the stairs, I meditate on my task; I must get one of the bigger knives, they will be better. Slish slash, slish slash. Much much better. There's no reason for little Jamie to suffer, not a second longer. I can put him in the grave alongside his mother. He will become a ghost like her. He will be able to return whenever he likes, floating in and out of our lives, he will be released from this torment.

I can see in the dark. It is marvellous. The voices have become lights. They guide me in my quick bare feet to the freezing kitchen, which is as silent as I can remember it. All the appliances have died. They are corpses now. The fridge, the freezer, all dead. Carnhallow house is a mortuary, it is where everything comes to die. It is where everything is moved underground, to the basement and the mine tunnels.

Here's my knife. I draw it from the triangular wooden brick like I am a legendary princess and this is my mythic task. I marvel at its loveliness. Saabaaatieer. It weighs agreeably in my hand. The starlight is enough for me to see the sharpness of the blade, David keeps these knives so sharp, he loves them sharp, that husband of mine, that abuser of women, with a killer for a wife.

Me.

Go upstairs quickly.

If I slip the blade very swiftly across Jamie's white neck, no one will notice; only I will see the blood, staining the snow of the sheets like rosewater on sherbet ice. Saving him from his violent father, saving him from his ghostly mother.

I am singing the song to myself, that happy song, the pretty little carol.

And what was in those ships all three,
On Christmas Day, on Christmas Day.
What was on those ships all three?

A knife. A knife. A knife.
A mother. A mother. A mother.
Back to the bedroom. I grip the knife tighter and tighter. The Christmas tree fairy is smiling, downstairs, beaming with approval, about to snap her wand, and make Jamie go away with a poosh of sparkly Xmas dust. Just like that. On Christmas Day, in the morning.
Let Mummy kiss you.
This is my job now, the one last thing I have to do. In the dark, yellow gloom of the Christmas moonlight I can make out Jamie's sleeping body, in his little day-bed, draped with maternal care, by me, with sheets and blankets.

But I am not his real mother. I am better than a real mother, I am alive. I have two hands, one to hold his hair, the other to strip the blade across his startled, frightened throat, so the blood comes easy and painless. The death will be easy, easy, easy, like Jamie wants to die, wants to see his scarlet blood uncoil like cherry juice, churning into a Stuart silver fingerbowl.

It is Christmas morning, an hour or two before dawn.

I kneel by Jamie's bed. His face is serene and quiet, the white eyelids flickering as he dreams. The sleep of an angel: his beautiful eyes closed, ready and waiting and innocent. The lashes will flutter as I cut, but he will not panic, he will accept his fate.

I am the mother, he is the son, I am allowed to do

363

this, we just aren't related like normal people. The knife is heavy in my hand as I lean closer, not singing my song, trying to work out the best way to kill him.

Four per cent risk of infanticide. One in twenty-five. Not so bad.

I put one hand on Jamie's sleeping head, and I gently stroke the hair, his lovely, soft, glossy hair is caressed by my hand; he is still sleeping and peaceful, I have to lift up the head, and then slip the knife across.

Slide it. Cut it.

Draw it. Like drawing a line, like slicing a line in snow.

I hold it. This moment.

The knife is a millimetre from his innocent skin. In the soft, sad light I can see where the blood pulses in his artery, a tender beating of blood. Start there. Yes.

Put the blade there.

Knife. Child. Voice.

Song. Cold. Dark.

Star. Pain. Air.

Eat. Love. Kill.

Daddy. Daddy. Daddy.

Daddy Daddy Daddy Daddy STOP STOP STOP STOP STOP.

Man engine man engine man engine. He hugged me hugged me hugged me. At the mine with the man engine.

Stop.

I cannot breathe.

Appalled, knife in sweating hand, I stare down in the gloom at my rough, bare knees: what am I doing here, crouched by this bed? I look at my sad white hands, badly scratched, I keep scratching myself, hands clutching a knife.

I am mad. This is madness.

It is all in my head.

Scratches are part of the psychosis. Because I am in a psychosis. And if I know I am in a psychosis, there is hope.

Swaying left and right, kneeling on the cold, bare, polished oak floorboards, I shut my eyes, hard. I know this process, this swinging in and out of rationality, like a wave that crashes, then retreats – revealing the sparkling rocks, only for the surf to come ravaging back.

Pulling myself by my own hair, I drag myself away from Jamie's bed, drag myself into the furthest corner of this dark cold room. The knife falls from my hand as I crawl. I don't care where it falls. In the opposite corner of the bedroom, back against the wall, I hug my knees to my chest and I cry, and I sob, and I rock back and forth, weeping for me, for Jamie, for this, for the sadness of a small girl terrified in her bedroom, terrified of the footfall on the steps, coming to see his trembling Rose of Tralee. For that mother who lay on the bed, crying, as they took her daughter away, the baby she never saw, the premature child.

And then you died, my darling. They told me there was something wrong with you, they told me that you'd died. I believed them. It made it easier.

For unto us a son is given.

How long do I remain here, scratching and rocking, scratching and rocking? I will never sleep again. Yet I fall half asleep. Sitting on my haunches. Inert, unable to move, not letting myself move. In case I look for the knife.

When I stir from my dusty muteness, I open my mouth like a cat. Here I am, here I am. It is still Christmas Day.

There is a faint greying at the edge of the funeral black paper, out there, beyond the frosted windows, so dawn may not be far away.

The knife. On the floor. Do what I say.

I put my hands over my ears and I whisper my song. If I can stay sane enough to make it to daylight, then I will call someone, call the police, call everyone, it doesn't matter any more. I nearly killed Jamie. Let the police lock me up, for ever, I deserve it.

But death is the price we pay for beauty.

'No!' I am talking to no one and to all of them. 'Leave me alone.'

Sing, Rachel, sing the song.

The Virgin Mary and Christ were there,
On Christmas Day in the morning.

Stop. And stop again. I am startled by a brightness; it is like I can see in the dark, like the power is back on.

Virgin.

I gaze around. The bedroom furniture gazes back: gloomy shapes that do not move. Jamie's breathing is the only sound. He doesn't know what I nearly did, what I might still do. Yet I won't do it. Because I can see by the light of the mind: through a window of logic. See answer.

The Virgin Mary. *Say your prayers to the Blessed Holy Virgin, Rachel Daly.*

It's his birthday at Christmas. His special time. When his mummy will come back to claim him. His special day.

I hugged her at the mine with the man engine. I hugged her at Levant. That's where I hugged Mummy. Don't you see, don't you see, don't you see—

I see the light of Christmas morning. I see a woman hugging a boy, I see the light of the Levant.

Grabbing my phone, I turn on its torch. It has a few minutes of power left. It is enough, enough, enough. Jumping up, I run out of the room, past the sleeping boy, downstairs into the Drawing Room where the fairy on the tree is hidden in the dark, but she cannot mock me any more. Only I can see. I am trembling on the edge of a beautiful truth.

Here it is: the magazine, with the photo of David and Jamie and Nina, perfect and elegant in their lovely home. Picking up the magazine, I shine the torch on the image and I realize why it stirred me now, all those months ago. And I try to fight the tremendous choke of emotion, as I do.

It's nothing about the content of the photo: it's the style – the barely seen face of the baby. I recall one particular photographer who used to do that, it was his modest trademark. Desperate and trembling, I flick to the end of the magazine, using my dimming torchlight – and I read the credits, in the tiniest of type: this trivial information of interest to no one but the subject. And me. Photographer, Kerthens, page 27–31: *Philip Slater.*

Philip Slater.

Philip Slater.

I see his face quite vividly. The guy who wanted me to get into Goldsmiths. The freelance lecturer, a friend of the photographer I assisted. He used to come round the studio: flirtatious, manipulative, older – talking of uni. He liked my work, maybe he liked it too much, looking back. But he spoke so smoothly, that day he made his suggestion. *I know a way you can make some money, have a baby, a sperm donation. A rich couple. She is barren. She's trying to find someone to have a baby for them.*

How did Nina know Philip Slater? Maybe she knew someone who knew him? And why do I even care? It doesn't matter – she chose me, Jamie, chose me for you: because I was perfect. I even looked like her, like beautiful Nina Kerthen. And she must have kept it discreet, kept my identity from David, so he never knew. Maybe she never knew the details herself, never knew who I was, to preserve the distance, to insulate them from the truth.

But she chose me.

The snow has stopped falling, I can see the last stars through the window. Dawn is here.

I was poor and pretty, desperate to pay my way into college; I was a girl desperate to get her mother out of the refuge, so she could spend her last years in a decent house; I was a girl who wanted to escape her father, even if it destroyed the family. And why not, when he had destroyed the family years ago? It didn't matter any more: *just give me the money. Save my mother. Let me escape.*

The starlight glimmers. The night is dying, christmas morning is upon us.

You were so premature, born late December, not early March: not what it says on the birth certificate. I remember when the nurses whisked you away – made you disappear, like a magic spell, like you never existed. And it was so easy, too easy: I'd never seen any of the scans, I didn't touch you when you were born, didn't hold you, kiss you, look at you. Nothing. Because I didn't want the bond. And then they told me you were dead, and it made sense, you were born so premature: deformed, they said. And then they gave me the money, anyway, like they felt guilty, too: paying me off, for carrying a baby that died.

Yet my daughter didn't die, because she never even existed. I had a boy, not a girl: they lied to me. We all lie, all the time. Grown-ups lie.

The magazine trembles in my hand. All the lights are trembling. I wonder why I am not crying. Perhaps this is too much for tears.

And all the souls on earth shall sing,
On Christmas Day, on Christmas Day

The answers have come so fast, so brisk and glorious in my manic mind. A fast-spreading crack in thawing ice. That day I first saw you, when I thought I fell in love with David? I didn't, Jamie, I fell in love with *you*. I fell for my own child. And the woman you hugged at Levant mine, when you sensed your mummy: that was *me*. And the face you saw in St Just? That wasn't Nina, that too was *me*: reflected in the car window. I invented the rest, the woman on the bus, in the beginnings of my madness. And the portrait David drew on that summer day, that wasn't Nina, either, that was also me: he made me look like Nina, because he couldn't help it. Because I look like Nina. Because I look like your mother.

Because I am your mother.

And now Nina lies in the mine at Morvellan, and your real mother has come back.

Oh, Jamie. My own child. I have been haunting you, and you have been haunting me. We are the two ghosts in Carnhallow, scaring each other, but now the darkness is dimming to light. And I am trembling with a frightening kind of happiness. I want to wake the world and tell this secret. *Then let us all rejoice again. On Christmas Day, On Christmas Day.* But I know I have to be careful: Christmas isn't over yet, the madness is not over. It won't go away just like that, I have to think this through.

I'm not going to disturb Jamie: he will have to be

told in the gentlest way. I will maybe tell Jamie in the morning. Then I will hug my son, properly, for the first time in my life. But maybe I can call David. I have to call David.

But how?

There is one phone left in the house that might have power. Jamie's. In his room. As I stand, I see that the house is filling with the first and slanted light of Christmas morning. Up the Grand Stairs I go, and there it is. The phone, under the pillow. It is dormant but not dead: I click it into life. The phone has no password. I see he called his father at 11.30 – that was the call I interrupted.

I press redial.

The phone rings: and goes to voicemail.

Where is he? Asleep? Coming here? What?

He's coming for you, he's on the way.

I shout at the voices. The madness is still there. But I have a weapon now.

The truth.

I speak to voicemail. 'David. I know it all. The truth. I know it.' I can't help my triumph. I can't help my exultation. I beat this house. I beat the voices. I worked it out, in the most impossible way. *Unto us a son is given.* 'David. Listen.' I hesitate, deciding how to phrase it: this incredible thing. '*Listen*. I've seen the body. I saw Nina's body in Morvellan. But, David, I know the truth now. She's not Jamie's mother because she couldn't have a baby, could she? And yet you were so proud, you wanted a surrogate, you pretended—'

The voicemail clicks: I've run out of message space. But who cares, I'm going to call him again.

'David—'

'Rachel?'

I look up.

'Rachel?'

It's Jamie.

'Mummy is in the mine. You said on the phone, she's in the mine. She's in Morvellan?'

His bewilderment is palpable. He must have woken, alone and frightened. Perhaps I woke him with my excitement. My shouting.

I sit here on the bed, stunned, muted, gazing at the face of my son – who disappears from the door, running down the landing.

Let him go, I think, *let him run to the bedroom, let him cry, let him be, for the moment. There will be time enough.* But in this moment I am still teetering on the edge of madness. I have to do this calmly, or someone will still get hurt.

What can I do? Call David again, maybe, or call the doctors, sort myself out, take no more risks.

Silence overcomes me. I sit here, emptied and exhausted, staring at the miracle of Christmas, the child in the crib, the son beneath the star. And then a sharp wince of conscience wakes me. Oh God. *Jamie*. What would he do, where would he go, armed with the information I gave him?

Jesus. The mines.

Of course.

I rush to the window that gazes on to the rear garden, that slants down the valley to the mines, and the cliffs, and the sea. The bright light is startling: a blue Christmas day is dawning, and the sharp winter sunlight is intensified by the snow. Those beautiful slopes of pristine snow across which my son is running, down to the great black mines of Morvellan.

Christmas Day

Morning

Boots on bare feet, coat over dressing gown, running along the landing, through the hall, the kitchen. As I race to the kitchen door I look at the high cupboard over the freezer: the cupboard is shut. Jamie doesn't have the key to the Shaft House. At least there's that consolation.

The door is wide open. I run into the cold. The sun is bright in a spangled blue sky and its icy warmth is sharp on my face. I am panting as I tramp down the gardens, into the trees, scrunching the impacted snow.

'Jamie!'

The woods are rustling with ice. Jingling. A crystal world of merriment, the rising sun making the icicles glitter.

'Jamie, stop!'

Tamarisks and rowans, oaks and hazel, ice and snow. The woodlands surrender to open space, now I can see the chimneys of the mineheads above the trees, and the blue-grey ocean heaving beneath.

My eight-year-old son is nowhere in view. He must be over the crest of the clifftops. I am out of the woods, sprinting to the edge.

'Jamie, come back!'

I hear no response, except the crash of waves and the shhhh of surf. The freezing air is a physical pain in my throat and my lungs. Should I even be doing this, pregnant? Of course I should: it was my fault, shouting down the phone, triumphant. And he is *my son*.

On to the paths that hug the cliffs, I see Jamie at the entrance to the Shaft House. He is hammering at the padlock with a rock: my desperate little boy, looking for his dead mother. The image is intensely distressing. Because his mother is *here*. I am alive, and trying to save him, even in my madness.

From this distance I can see the size of the rock, it would easily be chunky enough to snap that padlock – if clattered with sufficient force.

And Jamie is strong for his age. Climbing all the rocks and beaches, roaming on his own. My child of fire.

Black-headed gulls circle ignorantly overhead, the brilliant sea stares beyond us, towards the snowy moors and carns. Our drama is dwarfed by the mightiness of the landscape.

I am close enough to hear him now. A few hundred yards along the cliffs. I can hear him banging at the padlock.

'Stop it, please – Jamie.'

He turns, looks at me as if I am a stranger. He is in his pyjamas, with a coat thrown over them. But he is barefoot. He ran down here barefoot, across the grit and the snow and the ice, through the thorny woods. He returns to his awful and determined task.

Bang, bang, bang.

And then, with a graceful bow, the door swings open as the chain falls to the ground.

The door to Morvellan Shaft House is ajar. Where Nina Kerthen floats. I imagine the winter sun slanting through the glassless windows. Perhaps falling as far as her face. Haloed by black water and silver hair. Forever smiling and forever cold. He will see her and he will fall and I will lose him again.

And now he goes into the Shaft House and I am running down the path.

I hear him scream. He has seen her.

The door yawns in the wind, stirred flakes of snow melt in my mouth.

I stumble as I run, falling to my right, my sprained ankle giving way so that I can barely walk. But for Jamie, for Jamie, I can walk, I can run, I can do anything.

Dragging myself to my feet, I see Jamie coming out of the Shaft House. The gulls and guillemots circle overhead, gazing at us.

'Jamie, it's not her.'

He stares at me.

'Jamie, that's not your mother.'

The sea goes quiet, the sunlight shines, the close-packed snow glitters like vicious diamonds, designed to cut.

'Jamie, *I'm* your mother. It's me.'

The tears are pouring down my face. They will not be stopped, not now.

'I am your mummy, sweetheart. I'm your mother. Jamie darling, it was me all along. You know when you hugged me, at Levant mine, you sensed it then, didn't you?' I can't stop crying. 'It's me. I'm here. I was here all the time, only we didn't know. Your spell with the fire came true. Mummy came back. I'm here.'

Jamie stares at me. I hadn't wanted to tell him like this: it just happened. He frowns, and his eyes widen, as if he is beginning to recognize me, but then I hear a man shouting. '*Jamie!*'

Jamie stares past me over the edge of the grassy clifftop, down to the shivering little beach, Zawn Hanna. The Murmuring Cove.

Don't move, I think. *Please don't move. Don't be frightened.*

The ledge around the Shaft House is dangerous enough at the height of summer. Today it must be hideously slippery, a skating rink of hard ice over polished granite.

But I need to see what has caught his attention. I clamber up a boulder and look down at the cove.

His father is there. On the sand, in the clear pure air of this cold, glinting Christmas morning.

'Daddy,' Jamie shouts. 'Daddy!'

His father is running towards the bottom of the cliff.

Jamie starts to climb down the cliffs. The seagulls circle above him, searching for fish in the freezing sea.

I call out, 'Stop, please—'

We are both shouting at him. 'Stop, Jamie, stop!'

But he has seen his dead mother. And then been told his mother is alive. He is as frightened and as confused as any child can be.

He falls.

One slender moment he is clambering eagerly down the rocks, a terrible second later he has fallen. He plunges into the sea: a direct descent, twenty feet or so.

The splash he makes is tiny. He is only a small child, despite the grandeur of the emotions surrounding him. The sea swallows him with unconcern.

'Jamie!'

But he is gone already, I can't see him. Or maybe that is him: surfacing, spitting, struggling. He can swim, but no child could fight that grasping cold and those brutal waves, not for a minute. The waves shrug and buck, wondering whether to drown my son, or smash him against the black rocks. Or steal his body away.

My voices are silent. The only voice I can hear now is *save him, save him, save him*. But I have a child inside me. My second child.

'Jamie!' I run to the cliff edge.

But his father is even quicker. The parental reflex. I retrace my steps, my ankle shrieking with pain. I do not care. I do not care if I die, as long as I can save my son. I take the only path. It is snowy but not treacherous. It follows an old stream that once guttered into Zawn Hanna. Stumbling over boulders, I scramble down to the beach, throw off my coat and dive in.

I am your mother. This is what mothers do.

The terror shudders through me as I go deep into the freezing waves, water cold enough to stop a heart, but not my heart, not this love. Through the lash of salt-spray, I can see you, struggling, drowning. Your father is in the water too. Swimming desperately to save you.

I go under. The seawater is too cold. But I mustn't die yet. I have to save you. Yet I cannot. We are all going to drown in this Christmas sea, under that singular blue sky. I am upside down, sideways. I am drowning, gulping, thrashing.

'Mummy!' you shout, surfacing. I realize I am close to you, I can reach out, touch you. I grab a wet hand and haul, a fistful of damp pyjama top; I pull you towards me. You flail, panicking, and push me under. I fight towards the air, fight to gasp the freezing air, to keep us both alive, lifting you up.

I have pulled you from the rocks. Now your father is here, and he has you: stronger than me, he shoulders you and swims, saving you. I watch, battered by the waves, treading water, spitting frigid brine. There is a slippery rock here, jutting granite at the foot of a cliff; it gives me some support, but my arms are weakening, the cold is devouring me. The appetite of the sea is unquenched and it will take me.

I go under. Cold water engulfs me. My nose fills with burning liquid and I swallow half a pint. I surface, retching. I am staring out to sea, somehow turned about. But still here, still alive. Perhaps I can survive, drag myself from rock to rock, along the bottom of the cliff, until my feet touch pebbles and sand. Perhaps not. I am going under.

I feel a hand on my trembling, aching shoulder. It is David, your father. His face is white with the numbing cold, but his movements are strong. He takes my arm, he is taking me, he is saving me. Swimming away from the waves, and the rocks, we start to swim outwards.

His eyes are red from the salt, his face white from the cold. As I gulp saltiness, I sink, and his hand reaches for me.

I am falling too far, inhaling salt water. I make a final effort, gasping water, reaching for David's hand, reaching for the shimmering daylight, but then a vast and conquering wave drags me down, churning me, turning me over, and I feel myself break. I cannot fight this. It is over. It is done. I am spiralling deeper into the blue, and then the black. Yielding to my fate, sinking into darkness. And the thoughts descend as the cold overcomes. What does it matter anyway, Jamie? I am only me. I am struggling to swim yet already letting go. Let the sea dissolve my foolish memories, that non-career, the years of sadness and of shame. Maybe I would only confuse you if I lived. I never really mattered. And you wouldn't understand. Let the sea take me away.

Yet the world is beautiful beautiful beautiful. And I am crying as I die, in the darkening cold. The sadness is sublime. The intricate yielding. I just wish I could tell you how much I love you. I am your mother. I never knew you. But, oh, Jamie, my baby boy: the love.

Summer

Morning

David set down his teacup on the sill, and looked through the leaded windows, at Jamie. The boy was playing in the sunlit gardens with Rollo – his old schoolfriend – throwing a half-deflated ball for the dog to catch.

The boys laughed, loudly, as the puppyish terrier caught the ball, and started shaking it: as a proper terrier should. Believing it, no doubt, to be some kind of rat.

David sighed. 'Look at that. A dog. A pet dog makes him happy. After everything he's seen.'

Oliver nodded. 'Should have got him a dog before.'

'I know, Oliver, I know. But there it is. What can you do?'

David spoke over-firmly. The guilt never left him, for what he'd done. Acting like his father: brutish Richard Kerthen. But crucifying himself with guilt, however justifiable, was not going to help Jamie, or Eliza. So David was determined to see the positive. There was no choice. A year and a half had passed. It was time to look forward, as Rachel was doing.

What had happened had happened. It was all family history now.

If the family endured another century or two – and why should they not, given that they had endured a thousand years, already – the strange story of Nina Kerthen, and of Jamie's real mother, would become just another piece of folklore. Another part of the legend, recounted in the pub. That was what David fervently hoped. Otherwise the remorse threatened to overwhelm him.

Oliver spoke, cautiously. 'Isn't it a bit odd, coming here – to see Jamie?'

'Odd?'

'Now that you don't live here, I mean.'

'No,' David answered, truthfully. 'I didn't fight the divorce for a reason. I realized I could never be happy in Carnhallow. And after what I'd done, I deserved to lose it, anyway.'

Oliver gave David a hard stare. Assessing him. Probably Oliver was thinking how diminished David looked, how much older, quieter, greyer. So be it. It was the price he'd paid, along with giving the house to Rachel. And he'd been happy to pay it, because he also gained: David Kerthen was stripped of his past, but also of his cares. His money provided upkeep, his son and daughter would inherit, but David would never again reside in this house where so many awful things had happened.

He didn't have to live within sight of Morvellan mine, and Zawn Hanna, and the cliffs at the end of the valley. The beach where they had all nearly drowned; where David had saved the life of his son and his son's mother, when it was almost too late. So close to total tragedy. They had come so very close. It could all have been very much worse.

He had lost almost everything. He had been a brutal fool. And he was lucky.

Out in the garden, Jamie, his friend and the dog had all moved on, romping towards the woods. Oliver finished his tea, and said 'One of Rachel's friends – Jessica – she was asking questions over dinner last night.'

'She was?'

'About you and Nina. And the surrogacy. I'm never quite sure what to tell people when they ask. There's still a lot of curiosity.'

'The truth,' David answered, 'Tell them the truth. I was totally in love with Nina. An outright obsession. And she was rhapsodically in love with me, likewise. I could never give her up. She couldn't give me up. But she couldn't have kids.'

'Sure, but—'

'You know what I was like back then. A Kerthen of Carnhallow, the name meant everything.' David gestured at the grandness of the room in which they stood. 'Could I have let the line die, would I have been content to die without issue? It was a terrible choice. I either had to give up Nina, and find a different wife, or I got to keep Nina – but then I'd have to accept I would never have my own kids. And so a thousand years of Kerthens would terminate: with me.'

Oliver frowned. 'But Jessica's point is that most people would adopt. That's what everyone does.'

'Hell with them.' David returned the frown with a shrug. 'I was too proud to adopt; I wanted my own genetic offspring. And Nina wanted to do it: it was originally her idea, even if she went through Edmund and his friend Philip. She made *all* the decisions, she paid people to look for someone desperate, and for someone who resembled her. She made sure neither of us knew the mother's real identity. To keep the distance.'

'Yes, I know the *story*,' Oliver interrupted. 'What

bothers people is all the deceptions, and the conse-
quences. You deceived me, for one. It was a friend of
Edmund's that introduced me to Rachel. Years ago. And
I had no idea!'

'Nor did I, Oliver.'

'But then you deceived everyone else. Telling the world
Jamie was Nina's, telling *Jamie* he was Nina's. Jamie
will spend his life knowing that Nina came to regret it,
felt jealous of you, having a stronger bond, all that—'

David was unfazed. 'All true. But if we hadn't done the
surrogacy, then Jamie wouldn't even exist. Which is quite
an argument. Isn't it? Anyhow' – David checked his watch
– 'I don't live here any more. I've said goodbye to Jamie,
and I want to put some flowers on Mummy's grave before
I get home, and Nina's grave, too. Zennor will be full of
traffic, all the tourists coming for lunch, at the Tinner's.'

Oliver nodded.

David asked, 'Any idea where Rachel might be? Must
thank her. She's not obliged to let me into Carnhallow,
it's not in the settlement.'

'Last seen in the Old Hall, ordering builders around.'

His goodbyes made, David did a brisk search of the
house, stepping aside for workmen wielding planks, and
electricians adjusting stepladders. The Old Hall was
especially busy, a bustle of carpenters and decorators.
This austere space was to be the centre of the Retreat.
Where artists could show the paintings, sculptures,
photographs they had completed during their stay in
the West Wing, which was now entirely separate from
the family rooms.

It was Rachel's idea: she was bringing the house to
life, making it pay for itself, and doing it in a way that
David would never have considered. She was saving the
place, so it might stay in the family for another thousand

years: so that Jamie and his sister would inherit a thriving business, as well as an exquisite home.

Rachel Kerthen was truly a survivor, and David respected her all the more for it. Her rare case of pre-partum psychosis had worsened after that terrible Christmas morning, and she had been hospitalized for several weeks. But now she had made a complete recovery. And as long as she had no more children, she should, the doctors said, be fine.

He found her in the kitchen. She was feeding their daughter, Eliza, crooning a song, and swaying gently, to calm the baby. The sun that streamed through the window made her look, momentarily, like a Renaissance Madonna. Raphael, maybe.

There was a cold and significant distance between them now, but that was only right. The important thing was that there was no distance with his kids. David took Eliza in his arms, and kissed her gently on the forehead – then handed her back to her mother. Their baby was pretty.

'I'd better be going. Thanks for letting me come and see Jamie.'

'It's fine. Jamie likes it.'

She looked at him, her face blank, dispassionate. Then they both fell quiet. And Rachel's attention drifted to the windows, and the view – of the gardens sloping to the cliffs, and then to Morvellan. David followed her gaze: down to the mines. It was hard not to look at them.

But then she turned and gave him a brisk little smile, and the spell was broken. David said goodbye, and walked to the door.

The scent of flowers in the gardens was heady. The bluebells glimmered in Ladies Wood, like a cool flame of blue, licking on green. He felt a momentary surge of sadness, the love and the guilt that would never go away – like shadows and light in the rose gardens. So much had been lost. But then he climbed into his car, and realized: he was looking forward to getting home, to his little cottage in St Ives. It was good for access to Jamie, and no trouble to maintain. And the view from the cottage was pretty, and very paintable: gazing right over Porthmeor Beach. Without a single mine in sight.

Afternoon

My weekend guests have all gone now. Jessica was the last to leave. The builders have likewise departed. David has had time with Jamie. Rollo's mum has picked up her son with an invitation to come over, next week, for supper.

Carnhallow is restored to its rightful occupants: me, my daughter, Cassie. And Jamie. The special silence of the house fills the rooms, as does the sweet smell of new paint. The sea is talking to itself: Carnhallow is talking back. The sunlight catches fire on scarlet rugs, on the raspberry red walls of the kitchen garden. It shines on the white tobacco plants under the windows.

I love this place more with every day: as it grows beautiful again. I only wish Juliet could have lived to see it. We all miss Juliet.

Eliza is settled and happy; my daughter sleeps most afternoons around this time, five or six o'clock. It gives me precious time to sit down at the kitchen table with a cup of tea.

Jamie comes running into the kitchen, tanned, in a T-shirt.

'Rachel, I want to talk to Daddy this evening, is that OK?'

'Of course it is. You can call him anytime you like.'

The further words go unspoken. *Yes: you can see your father every weekend, phone him every evening. But he's never sleeping in my house again.* I don't have to say this, though: we all know it.

Jamie nods. 'Thanks. What time is supper?'

'Whenever Cassie gets back from the shops.' I look at my watch, 'Pretty soon, I should think.'

'OK.' He is lingering in the kitchen doorway, a thoughtful expression on his face. Locks of black hair stray over his violet-blue eyes. As I look at him – my son – I like to imagine him playing, one day, with his sister: in Ladies Wood, on a summer's day like this, years ahead. All the windows of the house will be open, and I will sit here and listen to their laughter, as my little girl romps barefoot through the fernstrewn glades, chasing her big brother. She will have the happy childhood I didn't. Or that is what I hope. But no one can predict the future.

Abruptly, Jamie runs over, and gives me the fiercest hug. Burying his head in my neck. He doesn't say anything. He hugs me, then he turns and runs out of the back door of the kitchen, into the kitchen garden, and on to the lawns beyond, calling out for the dog: we've named him Jago.

Then I sit here, content to do absolutely nothing. Watching Jamie play on the grass, with Jago, and the cat, Genevieve, watching the waves play on the rocks, in the distance.

As I sip my tea, stray thoughts occur. Random

memories. Anecdotes about the mines, Carnhallow, Cornwall.

I remember a story Juliet once told me about the coastal mines. How, on the very darkest and wildest nights, the wives and mothers of the miners would stand on the cliffs, with candles stuck in treacle tins, making a choir of tiny gleaming fires, like a constellation of stars. They did it to guide their husbands up the cliffs from the mines, so they would know where to climb. It must have been an oddly beautiful sight: an expression of love, in light.

And then, as the sun slants over Morvellan, setting fire to the waters, I listen to my daughter sleeping, and my son playing with the dog, and I think about the tunnels. Those tunnels that go under the sea.